Indiscretions

**Center Point
Large Print**

**This Large Print Book carries the
Seal of Approval of N.A.V.H.**

Indiscretions

Elizabeth Adler

Center Point Publishing
Thorndike, Maine

This Center Point Large Print edition
is reprinted in the year 2000 by arrangement with
Bantam Dell Publishing Group, a division of
Random House, Inc.

The characters and situations in this book are entirely
imaginary and bear no relation to any
real person or actual happening.

The text of this Large Print edition is unabridged.
In other aspects, this book may vary from the original
edition. Printed in Thailand. Set
in 16-point Plantin type by Bill Coskrey.

ISBN 1-58547-026-0

Library of Congress Cataloging-in-Publication Data

Scott, Ariana.
    Indiscretions / Elizabeth Adler writing as Ariana Scott.
        p. cm.
    ISBN 1-58547-026-0 (lib. bdg. : alk. paper)
        1. Motion picture industry--Fiction. 2. Large type books. I. Title.

PR6051.D56 I53 2000
823'.914--dc21
                                                            99-089394

LONDON, *24 October*

Venetia Haven hurried across Pont Street, her arms full of autumn flowers from Harrods and her head full of questions.

The flowers were for Lydia Lancaster, who, she knew, would have forgotten to pick up any herself, although a dozen guests were expected for dinner. The endless crystal vases and antique washbowls, jugs, tureens, and cachepots, some of them probably worth a small fortune, were crammed with a wilting display of saddened blooms that dripped petals and pollen on every ledge and table in the house. Lydia seemed to notice them only when they were fresh and bursting with color and scent. As they withered, so did her interest. It wasn't that Lydia Lancaster didn't care. It was simply that she never thought about what was next on her crowded schedule until she was faced with it. Her friends were never quite sure whether they loved her despite her casual absentmindedness, or because of it. It was a part of Lydia's exuberant charm that her total interest in the person she was with at that moment tended to eclipse her good intentions to be more practical about such things as regular meals, walking the dogs, getting her children back to school on time with everything properly labeled, or getting the car serviced. And Venetia adored her.

The questions had lurked unanswered at the back

of Venetia's mind all summer, and now, with the change of seasons and the first really gray October day, they had surfaced with an urgency that demanded answers.

Venetia hovered at the edge of the pedestrian crossing, scarcely noticing the surging evening traffic. Her thick sweep of pale blond hair was tossed by the suddenly wintry wind, and she thrust it impatiently behind her ears. Her tall, slight figure was wrapped in the lavish cream cashmere trench coat that Jenny had sent from Alan Austin's in Beverly Hills and she wore it, British style, with warm caramel ribbed tights and matching easy loafers. With her arms full of bronze and yellow flowers, Venetia looked the perfect image of a well-brought-up English girl. Which she was. "Almost," she added with a sigh. That was one of the questions. Jenny wanted her to go home. "I want you to go to college here, Venetia," she'd announced firmly on the telephone, "I miss you." A fine time to decide that, thought Venetia miserably, after twelve years. London was home now; it was Los Angeles that was the foreign land. It's my life, she thought rebelliously, and my future.

My future? She added the big question mark at the end. What do I have to offer? I'm nineteen years old, educated at the very best English schools, possessor of a brand-new, hard-earned cordon bleu cooking diploma. I'm not the least bit academic. I'm five feet nine inches tall, in good shape, and my friends think I'm pretty. And I'm

Jenny Haven's daughter.

The taxi honked impatiently, waiting for her to cross, jolting Venetia from the quick calculation of her assets, although she wasn't always sure whether the last item on the list was an asset or a liability. Anyway, there didn't seem much to build a solid career on.

Her long legs covered the ground rapidly as she turned into Cadogan Square. There wasn't time to dwell on the question of her future now. They'd be lucky, she thought, glancing at her watch, if Lydia had remembered to pick up some food for their guests.

Lydia had insisted on black tie for tonight's dinner, for two reasons, she'd said laughing. First, the ladies would look so much prettier all dressed up and the ones she'd invited tonight could use all the help they could get; and secondly, the dinner was being given for an important business acquaintance of her husband, an American in London on a quick visit, and she thought she'd let him see that England still upheld its traditions and standards. "I'm 'flying the flag,' " she'd said to Venetia, "and Fitzgerald McBain can thank God he's not here for longer or he'd have to endure the full country-house weekend!" Venetia grinned at the thought. Dinner at the eccentric Lancasters' was hazardous enough; a weekend at their country house had been known to throw new guests into a complete panic.

Zigzagging across the square into the cobbled mews, Venetia turned the key in the door of the rambling white house where she had spent most of her school holidays with her friend Kate Lancaster, becoming through the Lancasters' generosity and all-encompassing kindness a part of their big family. After her final year at Hesketh's Venetia, their "lodger," had stayed on. She was, as Lydia laughingly put it, because Jenny had insisted on paying for Venetia's room and board.

The hall, with its green and white geometric David Hicks carpet and drooping flowers, was ominously silent.

"Oh, my God!" The groan escaped her as she surveyed the drawing room. The Labrador wagged a lazy tail from his uncomfortable position on the brocade sofa in front of the fireless grate. The two Jack Russell's dashed to her side, bouncing on their little terrier legs, glad to see her because they knew she could be relied on to feed them. Last night's coffee tray still sat on the low table by the sofa and dust rested untouched on the surfaces of Chippendale library tables and Georgian mirrors.

Venetia strode across the hall, the dogs at her heels, and peered around the door into the dining room. Nothing! The long mahogany table she had expected to find glittering with the Lancasters' old Waterford, Spode, and silver was naked. The small Art-Deco Cartier clock on the sideboard said six-thirty; guests had been invited for eight-thirty. Nothing had been done and there was no sign of Lydia. Venetia thought of the American coming unsuspectingly for dinner in an English home, fresh from the land of ease and efficiency. A mischievous grin lit her small triangular face and wide gray-blue eyes as she imagined him courteously clutching a drink and trying not to look astonished as the hours ticked by and still no dinner appeared. He'd probably be about fifty, married, with three children whose photographs he would display proudly, and his wife would certainly have dinner ready promptly on the dot of seven every evening. In that case, thought Venetia, turning from the empty room and heading for the kitchen, I'd better help keep Lydia's end up. A girl with a cordon bleu diploma was supposed to be able to throw together a banquet at short notice, wasn't she?

The front door slammed and Kate's light voice called cheerfully, "It's me. Anybody home?"

Venetia shot from the kitchen after the dogs, who yapped joyfully now, jumping at Kate's knees.

"Hello, you darlings." Kate hugged each one in turn. "Hi, Vennie." A quick glance at Venetia's face boded disaster. "What's up? Has Henry ditched you?" Kate's merry, dark eyes met her friend's teasingly. "No, don't tell me," she added, realizing what had happened. "Mummy's not back yet, there are hordes of people coming for dinner, there's no food, and the place is a wreck." She grinned at Venetia. "A typical situation in the Lancaster household! She'll probably show up at eight o'clock and expect to be able to throw it all together in five minutes."

"Not this time. I'm afraid it's you and I to the rescue. We forgot that Mrs. Jones has gone off to

9

Majorca for her hols and Marie-Thérèse obviously decided the whole thing was too much for her and took the day off too."

Kate sighed. Marie-Thérèse was the au pair and notoriously lazy but Lydia could never be persuaded to get rid of her. "Think of the poor girl's mother in France," she always said when presented with each maddening example of Marie-Thérèse's inefficiency. "What would she think if we threw out her daughter and said she was no good?" So Marie-Thérèse stayed and did less and less as the weeks went by.

"There are fresh flowers waiting in the kitchen, the table needs setting, get Shaky off the sofa in the drawing room and tidy it up." Venetia dashed for the door.

"But where are you going?" yelled Kate as Venetia slammed the door behind her.

"Shopping!" If she took the Mini and double-parked, she'd just make Europa Foods on Sloane Street before it closed. The question of Venetia Haven's future was pushed once again to the back of her mind.

PARIS, *24 October*

Paris Haven leaned back from the littered drawing-board and stretched her aching back. She'd been working without a break since before lunch and now it was almost dark. She swept her hands impatiently through her long dark hair and glanced at the serviceable carbon-and-steel Rolex that she always wore on her right wrist because she was left-handed and it got in her way when she was sketching or cutting fabrics. The watch was Jenny's birthday present to her—two birthdays ago, Paris remembered with a shock of surprise. She was twenty-four now and she still hadn't made it! And Jenny hadn't let her forget it. "Keep after it," she always said on the phone. "Push yourself forward, always look good and go where it's good to be seen. You're the one with talent, Paris. I know you'll make it." So much for that!

Paris leapt guiltily from the tall chair in front of the drawing board. She'd invited Amadeo Vitrazzi for drinks at eight, and now it was ten minutes before the hour. Oh, God, she hadn't realized it was so late! She glanced around the one large room, whose skylights let in the glowering gray of an October evening in the city for which she was named. That was another of Jenny's eccentric ideas—naming each of her three daughters so oddly. If they'd all lived in Los Angeles as kids it wouldn't have been so bad, but to live in Paris and be *called* Paris had been a childhood burden she didn't care to remember. It was only when she was sixteen and developing her very own individual sense of style that she had felt she could live up to its promise.

The long attic studio, together with a tiny bathroom and a minuscule kitchen, was both her home and her workroom and it was, as usual, desperately untidy, awash beneath a sea of half-finished and dis-

11

carded sketches and a flurry of fabric samples. But despite its disarray it had—like Paris herself—an offbeat, inviting charm.

Leaving the lamp on over the drawing board she crossed to the living end of her abode and began frantically plumping up the caramel velvet cushions on the antique sleigh bed that she'd bought with Jenny's last birthday money and which served as both bed and sofa in her meagerly furnished atelier. A pair of ancient velvet theater curtains, picked up at auction, and faded from their original bold color, had been cut to form a spread for the bed and act as a room divider, hanging from an ornate brass rail effectively bisecting the living area from her "kitchen" and bathroom. Their apricot glow gave a feeling of intimacy to the living end of the white-walled expanse of the atelier itself. Most of the room was taken up by the drawing board, cutting table, and stacks of industrial shelving that held bolts of fabrics and the patterns for her designs, and their colors glowed as vividly as a Matisse against the deliberately neutral interior of the room.

After a long day at her drawing board when her eyes were dazzled with the colors conjured up from her own palette, Paris found it restful in the evening to settle back into an almost monochrome environment. When I've really "made it," she thought, then I shall have an all-white apartment on the Boulevard St. Germain with only a permitted gleam of chrome and steel, maybe some wonderful modern Lalique and some antique mercury glass, but that will be it! Meanwhile, she thought with a sigh, it'll have to be this.

Oh, my God, she was wasting time, it was now five minutes to eight, she must take a shower and get herself together. Amadeo Vitrazzi was Italian and hopefully he would run true to type and be late. She fled through the velvet curtains, casting off her working gear of jeans and sweatshirt as she went. The tiny bathroom gleamed with white tiles she had laid herself, fitting them into place laboriously one by one with a grout mixture that hadn't been quite sticky enough, so that now she constantly seemed to be replacing one or another of them. Paris had infinite patience when it came to design; she just wasn't so good at the practicalities.

The water was almost hot enough tonight and the shower felt good as she soaped her spare, elegant body, pleased with its long leanness. Thank God she had inherited Jenny's legs, and Jenny's deep blue eyes, but Paris had thick dark lashes and her skin was creamy—like her father's, she supposed.

The bell sounded sharply through the atelier, startling her. Could Amadeo be here already? Oh, no, it was the telephone—God, wouldn't you know it, just as she'd got in the shower. Flinging a towel around herself, she ran dripping across the wooden floorboards to her desk, reaching for the phone. The ringing had stopped. Oh, damn it, who could it have been? Amadeo saying he couldn't make it? Oh, no, please let it not be that. Amadeo was important, she needed him. Or at least she needed his silk—the fabulous, softest, most luxurious silk from his factories near Lake Como. Satin-backed silks and Charmeuse silks and crêpe de Chine and slithers of satin that would feel like molten light on the body of a woman wearing Paris's new designs. If only she could get it at the right price—and on credit. Oh, Amadeo Vitrazzi, she thought clutching the towel around her and still hovering near the phone, you don't know how important you are to me!

Now she was really late. And so nervous! To hell with the phone, she must get dressed. Her wardrobe filled one wall and held everything she'd ever designed, and as she had never yet afforded the luxury of a model to fit them on, they were all her own size. It was a good thing she was the right shape for this business, Paris thought, flinging on a sapphire silk shift. Her fingers fumbled with the buttons and she paused and stared at herself in the mirror—no, not this. It wasn't made from *his* silk, and she didn't want him to think she'd ever use anything else. And not this color; she wanted him to see the color in her new designs, not be distracted by what she was wearing. The full khaki skirt and the black crunch-knit vest top were pulled together with a wide belt and her slender feet pushed into khaki canvas boots that rumpled around her ankles. Paris surveyed the result. Chic but not sexy—exactly right. A glint of yellow and apricot on her eyelids, an expert fluff of coral blusher across the cheeks, a thin guava gloss on her lips, and she was ready. Oh, almost. A quick spray

14

of Cristalle—mmm, it was heaven. One day she'd have her own perfumes just like Chanel. Paris stared at the poster-sized blowup of "Mademoiselle" hanging on the wall, the ancient crumpled face lit by that indomitable smile, the chin uptilted arrogantly, and the wide hat at the exact uncompromising angle—still enticing at over eighty. Her idol. She could be like Chanel, an influence, a force, in the fashion world. She knew it. It was just that no one else seemed to recognize it. *Yet,* Paris added firmly.

Ah, there was the bell. He was here. Taking a deep breath and casting a last glance at herself in the long triple mirror, Paris Haven lifted her chin and glided across to open the door, Jenny Haven's smile lighting her lovely face.

ROME, *24 October*

India Haven arranged the half-dozen small watercolors of Venice along the length of the marble mantelpiece and stood back to examine them. Her gaze was critical and a frown furrowed her normally tranquil forehead. The paintings were her own, the result of three weeks' concentrated work. She had captured the first of the autumn mists spiraling across the magical waterborne city with washes of pale color and deft brushstrokes, and set in the antique frames that India scoured the small junk shops of Rome for, they were charming.

India sighed. That described them perfectly.

15

Charming. But not good enough for a major gallery. Still, Marella's small boutique on the corner of Via Margutta would place them prominently in its window and they would be sold within days. Of course the card stating boldly that these were *Watercolors by India Haven (daughter of Jenny Haven)* brought in the tourists by the droves; the boutique could sell as many as India could paint. Marella Rinaldi was a shrewd businesswoman, and if India were at the shop when a potential customer came in, the paintings and India would be displayed almost as a package deal and a quick fifty percent added to the price. They were bought mostly by Americans, for whom Jenny Haven was a public dream. India never failed to be astonished by how intimately these strangers felt they knew her mother, often recounting anecdotes about Jenny of which she herself was completely unaware. How they had met Jenny's daughter in Rome and bought one of her paintings would be the talking point of many an Illinoian or Texan party for a long time after the holiday was forgotten.

The frown faded from India's brow and her spirits began to rise as she collected the paintings from the mantelpiece, wrapped them in tissue, and slotted each one into a box. They fitted exactly. A lemon ribbon around the gold box, and they were the perfect gift. "Mementos of Italy by India Haven"; she remembered Fabrizio Paroli's words with a grin. "Package them, India. You must always give them the little extra touch that they feel they are getting free, and then you can charge ten percent more." And he was right, it worked every time. People were almost as delighted with the pretty box and its ribbon as they were with the paintings. Yes, she thought as she placed the six boxes in the bottom of her big black Gucci satchel and swung it over her shoulder, she certainly had satisfied customers. And these six would pay the rent for the next two months.

India took a quick glance in the enormous mirror surmounting the fireplace and quickly fished the lipstick from the side pocket of her bag. A flash of scarlet on her generous mouth to match the new Ginocchietti sweater, a quick run of her hands through the spiky curls on top of her head, a smoothing of the pigtail that reached to her shoulder blades at the back, and she was ready. Or was she? Hesitantly she turned and looked more closely at her reflection. Her wide brown eyes stared back at her, the whites clear and bluish with health. Small straight nose and a generous mouth that dazzled into a smile as she looked at herself. Pretty, she thought, and sometimes charming— like the paintings. Not worth much in the major galleries, but in lesser surroundings very popular! Damn it, why didn't Fabrizio fall in love with her? Was it that she was only five feet three? Maybe he really liked tall women. She teetered doubtfully for a moment on her high-heeled black boots. With the spiky upstanding curls and these heels, surely she looked at least five six? It was the bane of her life that she hadn't been born taller like Paris and Vennie. They both had Jenny's long American legs and elegant bodies that adapted themselves to almost any kind of clothes. She always had to be careful. Full bosomed since fourteen, India had been forced to the realization that though most men found her wonderfully attractive she would never have the clothes-horse figure of her sisters.

"Smaller and rounder," Jenny had told her, "that's what you were when you were born. Of course, you're built like your father, not me." Fathers weren't mentioned too often in the Haven household and India had known better than to press the matter. But smaller and rounder—though, thank heavens, never fat—was what she was still. However, she looked good for Fabrizio's press reception; the Ginocchietti was wonderful. Italian designers were the best. Except for her sister Paris, of course, she remembered guiltily, but Paris didn't design for her sort of figure. Italians always seemed to keep the true woman in mind when they produced clothes.

India's high heels clattered on the marble tiles of the floor of the Casa d'Ario and she paused for a moment to admire the curves of the staircase with its grand sweep of polished walnut rail and filigreed iron balusters. The old house where she had the first-floor apartment might be crumbling, but its beauty never failed to amaze her. If she had lots of money she'd pour it into this place, restore it to its former splendor, polish its cool rose-and-cream

18

marble, gild its ironwork, lavish its decaying stone with careful new mortar—and banish Signora Figoli's ancient perambulator from the front hall. Signora Figoli must be at least fifty, but she still kept the baby carriage there—just in case, she had told India with a smile. "You never know, with my husband," she had added with a knowing wink, and India had smiled back in amazement. Signor Figoli was a mild-mannered, unremarkable little man, always quiet and polite. Oh, well, she thought with a grin as she dodged the permanent perambulator and caught the sounds of the six young Figolis apparently at war with each other again, maybe it's those long Italian lunches that cause a population explosion—all those warm afternoon siestas with the shades drawn and a little wine still left in the bottle.

The vast wooden door clicked shut behind her and India peered across the road at her tiny Fiat to see if there were another of those ominous yellow tickets on it. She breathed a sigh of relief; no, today she was lucky. Flinging the Gucci satchel on to the minuscule backseat, she folded herself into her car and edged her way into the turbulent traffic of Rome. With luck she'd be able to drop off the paintings first and still be on time for the reception. She didn't want to be late for that. Today was so important for Fabrizio. His Paroli Studios were launching their own line of furnishings, everything from sumptuous colorful fabrics to sleek lacquered tables, fluffy sensual sofas for lazing to severe linear chairs whose pure lines had earned themselves a place in a museum.

Paroli was famous for the best in modern Italian interior design, deriving its initial influences from Erno Sotsass, and his famous Memphis design group, but Fabrizio cleverly diffused avant-garde concepts into an immediately acceptable and appealing form. India always felt that the Paroli Studios should be locked in a time capsule and buried for earthlings to open in the year 2500 as the pure example of the refinement of modern taste in our era.

Fabrizio's supreme knack was in "humanizing" the strong spatial lines of his designs and the open areas that made his rooms flow, by adding a touch of the old. He'd hang a clouded sixteenth-century Venetian mirror over a stark burgundy lacquer console table so that the mirror's curlicued gilded wood frame was reflected in the dense gloss of the table's laminated wood and the mirror in turn would pick up the rich color of the table. He'd place a single exquisite satinwood box inlaid with delicate tracings of rosewood and holly alongside an astonishing streak of scarlet lamp that soared across a table like a spear. His taste was faultless, his judgment as to each piece's value in a setting was exact, and the occasional quirk of the old contrasting with the very newest was pure genius.

Apart from that he was thirty-seven years old and incredibly handsome in a classical Florentine way, with the thick, blond, curly hair and straight-nosed profile of Michelangelo's *David*. He was also married to a very attractive woman from Milan, heiress to an industrial fortune, with two young children whom he adored. And India had been his lover for almost a year.

The traffic was hell, as usual. Her enormous black plastic watch with the silver stars pointing the hours—bought for a few hundred lire in some tacky souvenir shop in Venice simply because she thought it had enormous style—showed, if you could deduce the gaps between the stars correctly, that it was almost eight o'clock. Impatiently India pulled the car out of the jam of traffic on the Via Cesare Augusto and edging her two nearside wheels onto the pavement she reversed, honking down the one-way street. Immediately it seemed every horn in Rome blasted into a cacophony as car drivers shook their fists threateningly and pedestrians shrank against the stone walls of the narrow thoroughfare shouting insults to India's grinning face. "Screw you all," she shouted back happily in her best American, "I'm late!" India Haven had become a true Italian.

LONDON

Every surface in the pine-paneled kitchen at the rear of the mews house was submerged beneath baking trays and platters. The Cuisinart held freshly made mayonnaise laced with garlic, dripping colanders, leaned perilously over the sink as plump juicy lobster tails defrosted—rapidly, Venetia hoped. Spicy avocado halves with cheese topping waited to be

21

baked to creamy perfection and then crowned with a scoop of "caviar." Venetia prayed that the guest from America would not be too much of a caviar connoisseur. A fluffy rice dish jeweled with morsels of red, green, and yellow peppers waited beside a small mountain of *mange-touts* prepared ready for a quick sautéeing and a crisply fresh green salad in a tall glass bowl awaited its final glistening dressing of superb olive oil from Provence and a fine tarragon-flavored white wine vinegar.

Venetia stood back and surveyed it with satisfaction. The lobster tails had been an inspired touch—there was almost no cooking to be done, just the avocados and the dessert. As a concession to the well-known American fondness for all things chocolate, there was to be chocolate soufflé; the mixture was already prepared and only the egg whites remained to be beaten.

It was exactly eight-fifteen as Venetia pulled off the big blue-and-white-striped butcher's apron and simultaneously the kitchen door crashed open. A hand holding a tall glass of champagne poked from behind it.

"For you," said Lydia's contrite voice. "Am I forgiven?"

Venetia laughed. "If that's the good champagne, I'll forgive you anything."

"Roger's best." Lydia's apologetic face peeked cautiously around the door. "I made him open the sixty-nine." Her quick green glance swept the tables. "And it looks as though no one deserves it more

22

than you do. Oh, Vennie, darling, it's a feast. You're so clever—that cookery course was wonderful."

"Just as a matter of interest, Lydia," said Venetia, sipping the champagne, "what were you proposing to feed your guests tonight?"

Guiltily Lydia dragged a package from behind the door and pulled out an enormous rib-roast of beef. "I thought this would be nice. Americans like beef, don't they? I simply didn't think about the time it takes to cook the damned thing! And speaking of time, we must fly and get ready. Come on, Vennie, leave all this. Go and relax in the bath and make yourself pretty. Roger's got the wines under control and Kate's done the table and flowers. The flowers! Oh, Vennie, what would I do without you for an extra daughter? Thank you *so* much."

Lydia flung her arms around her and Venetia rested her head against Lydia's soft cheek. This was really where she belonged.

Kate had run her bath, adding masses of delicious gardenia bath oil, and Venetia lay back in the warm, scented water sipping her champagne. It seemed as though she had never known any other permanent home, not since she was really small. Not until she met Kate. As a lonely child of twelve in her first term at Hesketh's, Venetia was no novice to the English boarding-school system. Jenny had seen to it that she was first ensconced at the tender age of seven at the ramshackle but prestigious Birch House School in the middle of the Berkshire countryside, and to this day Venetia remembered her first sight of the dormitory with its trim iron-framed beds draped with faded rose cotton bed-spreads, each bunched with a comforting cluster of teddies and soft animals; one had even had an old blanket folded neatly into a square, its worn satin binding thinned by the constant softing of small fingers. She recalled the sinking sensation in her stomach as her eyes had swept along the well-pol-ished but battered floors, to the small two-drawer chest that stood by the side of each girl's bed and which was expected to contain all her possessions. On top of each chest, arranged with military preci-sion, were a hairbrush, a comb, and one framed photograph of a smiling family group.

Venetia had clung desperately to Jenny's hand. After three years in the freedom and pleasure of the Montessori school in Malibu this place seemed like prison.

"Be brave, honey," Jenny had said. "Remember you're here because your father was British and you'll learn how to behave like a lady. I'm not having any child of mine ending up as another L.A. show-business brat. And anyway, it'll be fun, you'll see."

They had been shown by a self-possessed seven-year-old to the one empty bed in "Tenderness" dorm, and Venetia had wondered what had hap-pened to the lucky child who had vacated it.

"All our dorms are named after the special quali-ties the school hopes that we'll strive for," an-nounced their young guide with a wink at Venetia,

24

"—Tenderness, Tranquility, Sympathy, Kindness, and Modesty."

"What happened to her?" Venetia had asked in a small voice, pointing to the empty bed that was now to be hers.

"Oh, Candia. She got mumps and her aunt had to come and take her home. Her family is in Hong Kong and I think her mother wants her to stay there until she's old enough for the big school. All our families live overseas." The girl's high-pitched British voice and long vowels had sounded like a foreign language to Venetia.

"There, you see," Jenny had cried triumphantly, "I told you you wouldn't be the only kid here without a family."

"Did you bring your pony?" the girl, whose name was Lucy Hoggs-Mallett, had asked. "Most of us bring them with us."

"A pony?" Venetia's face had expressed her surprise. She could swim like a fish, having first had lessons at the Crystal Scarborough Swim School in Hollywood when she was only one year old; by a year and a half she'd been safer in the water than on her own two feet on dry land and had waved triumphantly to Jenny watching through the "portholes" where proud parents viewed their water-happy offspring. She had taken her first tennis lesson at the age of five, knew how to hold a tennis racket properly, and had a firm backhand and a keen eye for the ball; she was no mean hitter in the baseball games at school and on the beach. But a pony! There had never been room for a pony at the Malibu beach house. An occasional "pony ride" in the mini-fun fair in Beverly Hills before they had closed it down and put up a hospital and a shopping center was as much as she knew of horses.

"You'll have a pony by the end of the week," Jenny had promised. "What color would you like?" It was as if she were choosing a new dress.

"I don't know." Venetia had been doubtful. She wasn't at all sure she wanted a pony, weren't they rather big and pushy?

"Well, just don't get gray," advised the wise Lucy. "It'll only roll in the mud and it takes ages to get it to look clean. Mine's a bay," she added proudly. "That's the best color."

"A bay it shall be," Jenny had decided, setting out Venetia's brush and comb and the silver-framed eight-by-ten photograph of herself taken by Avedon for *Vogue*.

"No." Venetia's voice had cracked with pent-up emotion as she thrust the picture back at her mother. "We're only allowed one picture and I want this." From the battered Snoopy lunch pail that had accompanied her on her previous happy schooldays she brought forth a blurred snapshot of her last birthday party, taken on the beach in front of the Malibu house. A dozen bedraggled denim-clad kids in party hats and with sticky faces beamed toothily at the photographer, and a group of laughing, casual parents lingered in the background.

"That's my home," she had announced to the self-confident English girl, "and those are my friends."

"Oh, you live at the seaside. How lovely."

The simple generosity of Lucy Hoggs-Mallett's acknowledgement of Venetia's world had been endearing, and Venetia had smiled at her, feeling better. Sensing her opportunity Jenny had disappeared to talk once more to the headmistress and then in a flurry of quick good-byes and kisses she had departed. Apart from holidays Venetia Haven never again lived at home with her mother.

Birch House had been run with a light hand and close to the concepts of the names of its dormitories, and the fifty little girls who inhabited those dorms lived in a world of small wooden desks, and firm schooling during the day, but by three-thirty they were free. Free to ride ponies, to look after the piebald guinea pigs and flop-eared rabbits who, like them, were freed from their cages and allowed to lollop across the broad lawns and rustle around the undergrowth followed by the crashing, clumsy feet and tender hands of their owners. Birch House acres spread down to the banks of the River Thames, and sometimes in summer they were allowed to swim in its greenish waters whose chill was so different from the Hollywood swimming pools Venetia had once known.

In the long summer holidays she went home to Jenny, but the shorter holidays were a problem. Sometimes she would be put on a plane at Heathrow and met in Geneva or Rome or Nice by a limousine, to be swept off to join up with her older

27

sisters in some grand hotel. Then Jenny would arrive and they would all be together. And life was completely different. She and Paris and India would be treated like princesses: gentlemen from movie companies would demand to know their dearest wishes so that they might grant them, hotel managers gave them the run of the place, room service waiters served extra scoops of ice cream, and Jenny's latest boyfriend would do his best with his charm to overcome their resentment. It wasn't until she was almost thirteen and had her first crush on a boy herself that Venetia had understood what Paris had meant when she said, "We mustn't be jealous of Jenny; after all, if she didn't have boyfriends none of us would be here."

Paris had been seventeen then and Venetia and India had felt she must surely know what she was talking about. She seemed so much older, and so worldly wise. "Was that what a Swiss boarding school did for you?" Venetia had wondered enviously, admiring Paris's spare, taut, small-breasted figure and polished black hair. Anything Paris wore looked good, and as she didn't have to wear a school uniform she had acquired a motley wardrobe, mixing Californian throw-away sporty chic with French style and an Italian way with color that turned heads wherever they went. She made her young sister feel lumpy and dowdy, and though Venetia vowed to give up puddings at school the following term, on those cold winter days that followed, Paris and her slender chic seemed light years away and school food was all there was. The pudding satisfied some urge other than just a sweet tooth. It was comforting, Venetia supposed, and it was what she needed until she began to take an interest in the opposite sex, and then puddings and puppy fat fell behind her in a forgotten haze and her bones emerged from her plump sweet face, turning her, too, into a more angular, delicate replica of Jenny Haven.

It hadn't been too bad at half-terms at Birch House, where most of the girls came from military or diplomatic families whose work kept them in far-flung places, but when she had moved on to Hesketh's, life and holidays became a more serious problem.

Her first half-term was spent in the headmistress's house on the grounds, and kindly though Miss Lovelace had been, the long weekend alone had been interminable. Besides, it meant the other girls thought she was a spy with a direct line to authority, and therefore they had excluded her from the usual clubbiness of girls who lived together with their sisterly relationships and best friends. And, of course, they knew about her mother. Conversations would stop short when she entered a room and sidelong glances and whispers followed her when she left, and only afterward would she hear about the midnight feast held in the booter, or the secret daring of Melissa Carr, who'd smuggled two bottles of champagne into the sixth-form block after attending Eton's Fourth of

June celebration, Venetia had been in despair; she had longed to be part of it, and if she wasn't to be part of it, then at least let her go back to Los Angeles—back to Jenny. But her desperate letters were answered with illogical equanimity by Jenny, who would send her another box from Theodore's or Fred Segal's, containing gorgeous Californian clothes that bore no resemblance to what the other girls wore. So Venetia didn't wear them, afraid of either being laughed at or causing jealousy.

Kate Lancaster had rescued her from all this. Coming back early from a weekend out and finding Venetia alone in the rambling building that was home to them both, along with the forty other girls in Stuart House, Kate had felt a pang of pity and guilt. She didn't know which emotion it was that made her throw down her weekend case on the bed and rush down the dorm to where Venetia sat alone on her bed.

"Oh, Vennie," she'd cried, "I've had such a super weekend, masses of food, and the dogs were lovely as usual and Mummy forgot we had these French people coming to stay on Saturday night and we already had eighteen in the house. I had to give up my room and have a sleeping bag on the floor. What a laugh! Mummy gets crazier—she once forgot we had the bishop coming for lunch and we had nothing in the larder. Everything in the freezer was frozen solid and the bishop's weakness is good food. You know what she did? She gave him an enormous gin and fled to the kitchen, quickly made some pastry, and boiled up the only thing in the fridge—the meat we get from the butcher specially for the dogs. She chucked in a few herbs and half a bottle of red wine, slapped the pastry on top, and forty minutes later the bishop was saying he'd never tasted a meat pie as good. He was eating the dog meat!" Kate laughed. "The only trouble was we had to eat it too—and *we knew!*"

Venetia found herself laughing along with Kate. "Did it taste awful?"

"Nothing with that much wine in it could taste awful. And what did you do this weekend?"

Kate lay back on Venetia's bed, regarding her through half-closed eyelids. She's really pretty, she thought, but with a mother like hers, who wouldn't be? She considered her own mother, Lydia. A long, elegantly boned face, a wide smile, clear, direct greenish eyes and a mass of reddish hair. Attractive rather than beautiful, but though she never seemed to give it much thought, she always looked just right. Whether she was in high green Wellington boots and a padded green vest, walking the dogs at Ranleigh's, or adorned in taffeta or chiffon for some dinner, she had a quality of "rightness." And that was exactly what Venetia didn't have. She didn't fit anywhere. Was she American? Or was she English? Kate felt even guiltier—they weren't allowing her to be English, she spent all her time here at school, and alone. Once a year Venetia spent time with her mother in California, or occasionally she met her in Europe—and her two sisters. That was all Kate

31

knew about her.

"Vennie," she had said, sitting up abruptly and hugging her knees, "why don't you come home with me in Long Leave—it's the weekend after next— right after the exams? We'll celebrate."

Venetia had gazed at her, dazzled. She was called Vennie, and she had a friend. Kate had invited her home for the holidays and her whole life had changed.

Venetia was still in the bath—the water was getting cold—when the sound of the doorbell intruded on her memories. She jumped guiltily. Goodness, they were here already and she wasn't even dressed! And what was she going to wear? She dried quickly and ran to the cupboard to check. The guests were all older people tonight. Kate had gone to the theater and that meant Venetia would be the only young person there. Never mind, it would leave her free to take care of things in the kitchen, and with a bit of luck Marie-Thérèse would be back to lend a hand. She didn't want the guest of honor to know she was American, she decided suddenly; she wanted to be very English tonight, a Lancaster, not a Haven. The ruffled pink Laura Ashley was a bit too milkmaidish, though, and the red silk from Georgio's that fitted like a second skin and left one shoulder bare was too Beverly Hills. That left the eccentric creamy knit from Joseph with the gray silk-knit over-vest, or the conservative yellow Belville Sassoon that was an old favorite and in which she always felt comfortable.

Venetia hesitated between the two. Oh, to hell with it, she thought, flinging on the creamy knit, why not be eccentric—after all, she was one of the Lancasters! She streaked a sparkle of fuchsia pink over her eyelids and smudged them with kohl, drifted a glitter of pink and gilt across her high angular cheekbones, and transformed her pretty mouth into a vivid hibiscus-pink petal. For a moment Venetia contemplated spraying a streak of matching pink through her pale hair, feeling an urge just to shock people with sheer exuberant youth where decoration is a total art-form and not merely what you wear. Lydia wouldn't have minded in the least, but perhaps it might upset the American. She decided against it. There was just time to slip into the kitchen and check that Marie-Thérèse had decided to return and might possibly be persuaded to lend a hand. The avocados were placed in the oven and instructions as to their removal in fifteen minutes given, and Venetia was ready.

The drawing room buzzed with polite chatter and the discreet tinkle of ice, high-pitched English feminine laughter and charming public-school stammers voicing gentlemanly compliments. Venetia paused at the door to take in the scene. There was never any stiffness at Lydia's dinners, they went with a swing from the start. Dinner jackets were worn with a comfortable air of belonging, no doubt because most of them were at least twenty years old, and dresses were unadventurous but "right." Venetia felt quite outrageous in the Joseph knit.

One man stood out as though he were from another planet. It wasn't just that his dinner jacket was of superb cut and his was the only shirt with two—very discreet and very small—ruffles down the front; he was at the most only twenty-five years old. And, thought Venetia as their eyes met across the room, he was almost dazzlingly handsome.

"Ah, Vennie darling." Lydia hurried toward her. "Do come and meet Mr. McBain." She turned her warm smile on the young man. "This is Venetia Haven, our 'lodger,' " she announced cheerfully, "and also—luckily for you—our chef tonight. Venetia this is Morgan McBain."

"Oh"—Venetia's smile was tentative—"but I thought . . . weren't you supposed to be older?" she asked, puzzled. Morgan McBain's firm, warm hand held hers.

"Unfortunately my father couldn't make it and sent me to deputize. And I'm very pleased he did."

Admiration shone from his eyes, as blue as her own, and Venetia smiled back at him, her spirits soaring. His hair was straight and very blond, as though bleached from some strong sun, and his skin was tanned to a ruddy glow. He looked, she decided, like the kind of American who sailed and swam surpassingly well, a true outdoorsman.

"You are the chef?" His deep voice was puzzled.

Venetia laughed. "That's right. I hope you'll enjoy your dinner."

"If you cooked it, I'm sure I shall, but promise you'll sit next to me. . . ." He gestured conspiratorially toward the other guests. "I guess I'll need some help here."

Venetia gazed at him demurely, with Jenny Haven's devastating wide blue gaze. "I'll see what I can do," she promised. She headed first for the dining room to change the seating arrangements and then for the kitchen where the baked avocados should be just about ready. Life suddenly felt very good.

PARIS

Amadeo Vitrazzi was only fifteen minutes late. Not bad for an Italian, thought Paris, pouring Scotch for her guest and Campari and soda for herself. She stole a glance at him from under her lashes as she arranged the glasses on the black lacquer Japanese tray. Amadeo was leaning against the massive center support beam of her attic studio, gazing around him with an amused smile on his lips. He was an attractive man, smoothly sun bronzed from a summer at his villa in St. Tropez, smoothly spoken and smoothly dark haired, with sharp greenish eyes that were missing nothing as he examined her combined home and workplace. How old? Paris wondered. It was hard to say; he was slender, but it wasn't the slenderness of youth, more the well-worked-out fitness of a man concerned with his appearance. Maybe forty, maybe forty-five, decided Paris, giving him the benefit of that smile again as she walked toward him with the drinks.

"Scotch with ice and soda, signore."

Amadeo Vitrazzi's glance was appreciative. He enjoyed pretty women and this one was exceptionally pretty . . . not exactly his type, though. He preferred them a little rounder, with lusher curves, more fullness to the bosom, like Gina when he'd married her. Gina had been perfection then, a ripe, almost plump, young Italian girl, but that was twenty-five years ago. Gina was more than plump after five children, and now there was a grandchild on the way. Their first. Amadeo was forty-eight and nervously aware that that was awfully close to fifty. His smile to Paris was intimate as he reached for the glass she offered. It felt good to be with a young woman like this; even if she were a little too lean for his taste, that sexy smiling mouth could do things to a man.

"I like your home, Paris. It has charm." He leaned back against the black wooden beam and glanced again around the room. White walls, black beams, a crisscross of exposed pipes lacquered a startling emerald green. Nothing of any value in the room— except the old sleigh bed. "A nice piece, that." He gestured toward it with his glass.

Paris shrugged. "My sister's choice. She knows about these things. I only know about fashion."

Their eyes met, hers deeply blue, intense, and slightly wary. She licked her lips and Amadeo caught the hint of nervousness. He was surprised. What could Jenny Haven's daughter have to be nervous about?

The black Italian lamp that curved across the

drawing table left the rest of the work area in shade, and automatically his attention was drawn to the sketches that littered its surface.

"Would you like to see my designs now?" Paris's hand lay lightly on his arm and he smiled again into her eyes.

"Why not, *cara?* Let's see what you're up to." His tone was indulgent, and Paris quickly led the way across the bare wooden floor to her table. This was her true world, the place of her hopes and her dreams, of her flights of imagination and inspiration, her fantasies of fashion and concepts of style. And her driving ambition. Paris knew she had talent. She knew her capacity for solid hard work. She believed in herself infinitely. All she needed now was someone else to believe in her as much as she believed in herself.

Amadeo was aware of her light breath on his cheek as together they leaned over the table while she placed the sketches in front of him. They were clever, there was no doubt about it. And original— sometimes too much so. His expert eye calculated the retail possibilities of such a line . . . risky but exciting. "You might get the smart, younger boutiques to take some of these. Those on the Place des Victoires, for instance, or one or two in Les Halles. You should make up samples and take them round, *cara.* I'm sure they'll be pleased to try them."

Paris's deep, dark blue eyes widened in horror. "Oh, but it's a *couture* line. I must do the *whole* collection. Don't you see, Amadeo, it all goes together, the colors, the fabrics, the entire feeling."

Amadeo flung back his head and laughed. "You want to start at the top, then, Paris Haven?"

His eyes mocked her and to her horror Paris felt herself blush. *Merde,* she thought angrily, I haven't blushed in years, why am I now? People have laughed at me before. She turned away moodily.

"Why not?"

Her voice trembled slightly and he could see the delicate curves of her profile. Her full, voluptuous mouth belied the slenderness of her body, giving more than a hint of sexuality to her face. He'd indulge her, he decided, glancing at his watch. He had the time and she was intriguing.

"Why not?" repeated Paris turning to face him. "Where else is there to start?"

This time Amadeo hid the smile. It was obvious that Jenny Haven's daughter had a lot to learn.

"A good attitude, *cara,*" he said, slipping his arm around her shoulders and leading her back toward the luxurious sleigh-bed sofa. "Come and sit here and let us discuss it together. Tell me how I can help."

Paris felt the weight of tension and anxiety lift from her like a cloud dispersed by the wind. He *had* liked the designs, then, he must have done. Why else would he want to know how he could help? She refilled his glass generously with whiskey and topped up her Campari, straight this time with just a thin green sliver of lime floating in its rosy pinkness. She sipped it slowly, enjoying its slightly bitter taste.

"You see, Amadeo," she began, "I know I can be a success. I worked for three years in major couture houses. I did everything. I stitched, I did fittings, I learned how to plan out a pattern, I was taught how to cut by a master, I even provided sketches for three of the last collections. My designs *sold*, Amadeo, they were a success! But of course there was no acknowledgment that they were my designs. I couldn't bear the rigid attitude of the couture houses any longer. I needed to be on my own, to develop my own style. And now I feel that I have."

Amadeo took her hand and held it lightly in his. Her skin was soft, the fingers long and slender, and he stroked the hand lightly. Paris's voice had a passion born of her eagerness. Just watching her mouth as she talked, the cushiony curve of her underlip, stirred his excitement.

"Go on, little one, tell me all," he murmured, bringing her hand to his lips.

Paris scarcely felt his light kiss. She was carried away by her own words, by her own desires. She had Amadeo Vitrazzi here now and he was listening to her, she *must* convince him *now*.

"Youth has its own kind of elegance, Amadeo. It demands clothes with more freedom of expression, pieces that can be flung together and yet look like a whole. That's the concept I based my collection on, and that's why it must all be seen together. It can't be taken from boutique to boutique in a suitcase and shown across a counter. My clothes would look like hell seen like that. They need young, moving bodies inside, they are meant to be lived in. You and I both know that the secrets of good dressmaking are line, fabric, and color. I've used the hard-earned apprenticeship where I learned those elements to design *these* clothes. And I've designed them for tactile effect, using contrasts of fabrics. I need buttery-soft suedes, real linen—the sort that creases—coarse cotton knits that feel crunchy against the skin. And silk, Amadeo. The softest, sexiest, most luxurious fabric in the world. The kind that only you produce, Amadeo."

Amadeo leaned back against the cushions, watching her indulgently. She was so intense, this child, so carried away by her ideas.

"Show me, *cara,* show me what you mean," he suggested soothingly.

Paris leapt to her feet. Her smile was radiant now. "Wait," she called over her shoulder, racing across the room to her desk, "just wait a moment while I get the sketches and samples."

Her long sweep of black hair swung behind her as she whirled across the room. Its texture looked almost as soft and supple as one of his own silks.

"Here, you see." She leaned closer to point out a special color, a change of texture, why this one must be in silk, it was the *only* thing she could possibly use.

Amadeo slid his arm around her shoulders and her hair brushed his face. She smelled of some familiar, vibrant scent, warm but not too heavy. He liked that, it meant that you could smell her skin, too, not just the perfume. And this close her skin looked and smelled wonderful.

Paris looked up from her sketches. "Well, Amadeo, what do you think?"

"Splendid, *cara,* wonderful designs and wonderful colors. You are a gold mine of new ideas."

Paris threw her arms around his neck and hugged him enthusiastically. "Of course I am, Amadeo, it merely took someone of your genius to recognize it! I'm going to make a fortune before too long, Amadeo Vitrazzi." She leaned back a little, her hands resting on his shoulders. "But I need your help."

"My help?" His glance was quizzical as he slid both arms around her. "What can I do to help you, Paris?"

Paris wriggled uncomfortably, realizing her position. His hands were stroking her back and his face was close to hers. Too close. She leaned back farther. "I need credit, Amadeo." She wriggled free and rummaged through the sketches littered on the floor at her feet until she came up with an itemized list. "I need your fabrics, but I also need six months' credit, just until I get started. And I need a good price. Only *your* fabrics will do. They are the best, I can't possibly use anything else."

Amadeo knew his fabrics were the best. He also knew that they were very expensive. He'd be a fool to give her credit; only the major houses were permitted to operate on that, and then never six months. And why should Jenny Haven's daughter

41

need credit anyway? Surely the mother would endorse her own child?

"Surely you must have made a few samples," he stalled, "something to show a buyer? Is there nothing I could see?"

Paris hesitated. "They're not in your fabrics," she agreed finally, "so you mustn't judge them on that basis. Just a minute." She uncurled herself from the sofa and he let go of her hand reluctantly, eyeing her body as she ran to the velvet curtain and pulled it to one side.

"Here, there's this, and this. And this one is my favorite."

The garments she held up for his inspection looked formless and yet complicated. They meant nothing to him, and Paris caught the baffled expression on Amadeo's face behind the polite acknowledgment.

"Oh, I *told* you," she said desperately, "that they should only be seen *on*."

"Then, my dear Paris, please put one on."

Unhesitatingly, Paris slid behind the curtain. Her skirt, top, and boots were off in a flash and she stood for an instant clad only in a pair of mint-green satin French knickers. She felt almost breathless with excitement. He was going to look at her clothes. Amadeo was her first audience and she desperately wanted his approval. Sliding the dress over her shoulders she pushed her feet into a pair of high-heeled shoes. A final smoothing of her skirt, a shake of her head to loosen her hair, and she was ready.

Amadeo stared at her as she posed in front of the silvery sheen of the old apricot velvet curtain. The gray silk slashed in one uncompromising straight line across the widened shoulders, skimming the waist to a narrow zigzagged hem that ended two inches above Paris's elegant knees. Bands and diamonds of soft suede angled the skirt diagonally. Paris swung around slowly for him to see the back, where the silk swooped in a low, bloused V almost to her waist. She was right. It was a wonderful dress. But the admiration in Amadeo's eyes was for the girl. He'd been wrong in thinking she was too lean; there were curves all right, in fact all the curves were in the right places. He rose and walked toward her. He needed to touch her, to feel what she was like. Her nipples jutted beneath the gray silk and her parted lips smiled at him tentatively.

"It's wonderful, *cara,* wonderful," he murmured, taking her hand and drawing her toward him. "You were right, you have the touch."

"Really, Amadeo, you really like it?"

Amadeo leaned forward and kissed her gently on the lips. "I love it, *cara,* and on you it looks beautiful."

Paris gazed into his eyes so close to hers. A tingle of excitement ran through her body. He *loved* her designs. Amadeo's hands were on her naked back and he pulled her closer, kissing her gently on the neck, tiny kisses, light and undemanding, but she could feel the tremor of desire as he pulled her closer.

"Tell me," she whispered, "tell me, Amadeo, how you like this dress . . . it's a sexy dress, isn't it, Amadeo? All my designs are like that, that's why they'll be so successful."

Amadeo slid his hand across her gray silk breast. She was still talking about her designs, about this damned dress, when all he wanted to do was rip it off her. He hadn't felt like this in a long time, not even Olympe had done this to him lately. His erection was hard as a rock and throbbing as if it couldn't wait.

Paris laughed when he pressed himself against her; she felt high on excitement, turned on by the promise of the dazzling future that awaited her now that Amadeo approved her designs and would give her credit. Perhaps he'd do more; she might even persuade him to become her business partner. Amadeo's fingers tempted her nipples through the silk and his mouth came down hard on hers. There was no doubt what Amadeo Vitrazzi wanted in return. Paris leaned back a little to allow the dress to slide from her shoulders, watching with detachment as his dark head sank onto her breast, feeling the first blast of sexual excitement hit her as his tongue found her nipples. And why not? she thought. If this is what he wants in return, then he'll have it—and it'll be the best he's had in a long time. You're not going to forget this, Amadeo. Pulling herself from his embrace she stepped back from him, smiling.

Amadeo tugged off his jacket.

"Wait," commanded Paris.

Amadeo waited eagerly as Paris stepped out of the pale green satin French knickers. My God, look at her, wasn't she the most sexily elegant woman alive, posing there naked but for her high-heeled shoes? My God, if he didn't have her quickly this might turn out to be a disaster instead of a success. . . . What now? She was walking slowly toward him, her hands caressing her own body, hesitating on her nipples, drifting lightly over the dark inviting triangle of hair. Amadeo unfastened his belt.

"Wait." Paris took his hand and placed it there, on the soft springy dark triangle, smiling at him while his fingers curved between her legs.

He couldn't stand it, he had to have her. Amadeo tugged at his zipper once more, hearing Paris's teasing laughter as she leaned closer and began to unbutton his shirt.

"Wait, Amadeo, wait," she murmured in his ear, "let me do it for you."

First the shirt, carefully folded and placed across the chair, then the trousers urged lingeringly down over his erection. She still hadn't touched him, she was going so slowly, taking her time, tantalizing him. Amadeo had never wanted any woman so much in his life. Ah, ah, that was it.

Paris knelt in front of him and slowly, slowly, slid her hands across his belly. "Oh, Amadeo," she breathed admiringly, "Oh, Amadeo . . . now you don't have to wait any longer." Her black silken hair was soft against his thighs as she leaned over him, and her mouth was even softer. Amadeo's fingers knotted in her hair as the long orgasm rushed through him—he couldn't wait, he couldn't hold back any longer.

He lay back drained, but Paris Haven's voice was silkily coaxing while her hands moved across his body. Amadeo opened his eyes and met her dark blue intense gaze.

"Wait, Amadeo, just you wait, that was only the beginning."

His body was nice, she thought, straddling him. He was lean and smooth and tanned, and he was almost ready for her . . . it could have been worse.

Jenny Haven's daughter was selling herself.

ROME

India was lucky again. The space on the corner across from the Paroli Studios was just big enough to squeeze in her tiny red Fiat, or almost. The front stuck out just a little, but not enough to matter. India slammed the door cheerfully and slung the satchel over her shoulder. Bending quickly she checked her face and tidied her hair in the offside mirror. She smoothed her black skirt and pulled down the scarlet sweater that wrapped around her in a luxury of evening softness. She was very pleased with that sweater. Perhaps she should pay only one month's rent when the pictures sold and buy the jacket that went with it! She'd see if Marella could get her a discount.

She wondered for a moment whether it was Fabrizio she wanted to look pretty for, or whether it was because his wife would be there tonight. Marisa had never shown even the smallest scrap of jealousy. In fact, she barely showed any interest in India at all, and somehow it made India feel as though she were too insignificant to threaten Marisa Paroli's security. And Marisa was right; India knew it.

A string quartet seated on futuristic chairs that seemed to be carved from blocks of translucent topaz was playing Vivaldi very delicately in the foyer and already the showroom was crowded. Several hundred smartly shod cosmopolitan feet were treading Fabrizio's pastel carpet, and India eyed it with dismay. Spilled champagne, crushed hors d'oeuvres, and cigarette ash were scattered over its newness. She had begged Fabrizio to put down the black just for today, but he'd said that it would defeat the purpose. "They must see the place and the designs as a whole," he'd told her. "Putting in the black would ruin the effect. They'll go back to their papers and write that Paroli has lost his touch, or they'll go on to the next party and tell each other that it was a fiasco, that the colors were all wrong." Hesitating by the door, India wasn't at all sure that he was right this time. After the first dozen, how many had even noticed the carpet?

There was no gentle hum of conversation; it was a full-throated roar, and as she pushed her way through to the bar set up against the right-hand wall, India kept her ears open for snatches of conversation, eager to pick up any comments. Hardly anyone seemed concerned with Paroli Studios or its wonderful interior; all the snippets of talk she heard were of summers on the Costa Smeralda or plans for skiing in Gstaad from women as glossy as any of Paroli's lacquered tables, or of the state of the lire and the latest Wall Street average from bronzed and handsome men who looked as though they need never worry about either.

Fabrizio Paroli watched her elbowing her way through the crush with the unfazed American assurance that always made him smile.

"Look how pretty our little India looks tonight," he murmured to Marisa.

Marisa looked. Her cool glance assessed India Haven's appearance, deduced the name of the designer and cost of her new outfit, and wondered if Fabrizio had given her a raise. The process took her approximately fifteen seconds and there was no malice in it; it was simply the reaction any Italian woman of her wealth and stature made about every other woman in the room, an automatic placing of the girl into a precise economic and social bracket. The only time Marisa ever failed was with the English. It was almost impossible to tell where they were at because they wore what they bloody well pleased and often it would be Marks and Spencer or something run up by their local dressmaker in some odd though possibly expensive fabric cut so badly that any "line" was lost. Only their jewels gave them away, and the size of those dusty sapphires and emeralds had to be seen to be believed, but then of

48

course they were probably heirlooms from colonial days and most likely were owed to the tax collector.

India Haven was a different matter. Alone, she didn't merit a seat at their table at tonight's dinner after the opening. Yet she couldn't be dismissed altogether. Now, if *Jenny* Haven were with her, then of course tonight would be a different matter. Marisa was only rich and social. Jenny Haven was a star.

"I'm going to introduce her to some people," called Fabrizio, already pushing his way through the crowd toward India, smilingly accepting the compliments of his guests as he made his way toward the bar. He liked India. He liked the way she looked, her wide-boned face with its flashing smile that lifted from her mouth with its wonderfully even teeth to her sparkling brown eyes. Even her curly bronze hair, confined at the back in its fat braid, seemed to vibrate with energy. Two years ago, when India had finally come to terms with the fact that she wasn't destined to be a great painter, she had approached him and begged him to take her on as an apprentice. "You see, I must learn something," she'd cried, "and the only thing I know and like is color and form. Interior design is the only answer."

Fabrizio had been quite brutal with her at first, mistaking her enthusiasm for pushiness, her smart appearance and multilingual facility for rich-girl boredom. "It's not all line and color," he'd snarled moodily, "it's plumbing and cement and shouting at workmen and coaxing craftsmen. It's dealing with rich complaining customers who have everything

49

and want you to give them more—and it must always be *different!* It's bloody hard work, and not for your sort at all." His own fight from his poor childhood in Naples had added venom to his words, and India had shrunk back into her chair. Her big brown eyes had gazed at him, reproachfully innocent of ulterior motives, and instantly he'd regretted his words. Not that they weren't true, but even though little could be poorer than a poor childhood in the tenements of Naples, it was no reason for taking it out on the girl. She couldn't be much more than twenty or so. It had been a difficult morning and he was tired. After a glance at his watch Fabrizio had apologized and said he regretted that he had to leave now for lunch. He'd left her sitting there in stunned silence and then he'd turned suddenly at the door and said, "I don't suppose you'd like to have lunch with me, would you?"

He still remembered her response. Her face had lit with the same smile she was giving him now. "Would I?" She'd laughed. "And how!"

Lunch had been fun. And *he'd* done all the talking. He'd told her all about his childhood in Naples, about how its teeming narrow thoroughfares, its jumbled crushing buildings and thronging humanity had made him yearn for space and clean lines, of the scholarships to school, university, the endless architectural training, the design courses, and the long haul to success. And he'd told her of his marriage to Marisa, which naturally had considerably eased that success.

50

"Oh, but it's truly all because of *you*," she'd breathed admiringly. "Mother always said that money doesn't bring success unless you have the talent."

"And how did your mother get to be so wise?" he'd asked with a wry smile.

"She's Jenny Haven," India had said simply.

"India."

"Fabrizio." Her kisses were warm on his smoothly shaven cheeks.

He smelled of Eau Sauvage and Disque Bleu cigarettes.

"It's a success," she said happily.

Fabrizio shrugged. "I suppose so. You look wonderful in scarlet. Did Jenny give you a break and send money?"

India grinned. "Does it look expensive?"

"It certainly does. You'd better remind me on Monday to give you a raise. Someone's got to keep you in the style to which you obviously would like to be accustomed, and if not your mother, I'd better do what I can to help."

"I'll hold you to that, Fabrizio. But what about this carpet—just look at it."

Her eyes, rounded with dismay, made him laugh. "I have a second one ready to be laid tomorrow. I knew this would be ruined tonight—that's the way it is at parties. I'll tell you what," he said with sudden inspiration. "There may be a few cigarette burns, but the stains should come out with cleaning. It'll be useless for the showroom. Why don't you take it for your apartment?" He knew India's apartment and

51

its crumbling cold marble floors could surely use the luxury of his thick pastel woollen carpet, cigarette burns and all.

"Fabrizio Paroli! Do you really mean it?"

He wished Marisa had looked like that when he'd given her the Bulgari ruby necklace at Christmas. "Of course I do. You may have to cut it and patch it here and there, but it will look good in your place."

"Oh," gasped India, "I do *love* you, Fabrizio."

He was aware of heads turning as her distinctive American-accented Italian rang across the room, and he smiled at her. "And I love you," he said loudly. Let them talk, let them think what they wished. Sometimes he thought he really did love India Haven. She was probably the only truly *nice* female he had ever known in his life. And she was his friend as well as his occasional lover—not so often nowadays as he would have liked, but he was a busy man, and also Marisa was becoming suspicious of his every move. That India was also a little bit in love with him was good too; it stroked his ego to think of her when Marisa was sulking and complaining that he neglected her for the business. If it weren't for the children he would be tempted to fall in love with India, and when she looked as adorable as she did tonight he was very definitely tempted. India was sexy and she was fun. But there were the children and he adored them, too, and he never wanted to lose them. Marisa's family was powerful; he would never stand a chance in a dispute over custody.

"Come on," he said firmly, thrusting a glass of

champagne into her hand. "You should be circulating and chatting up the cream of international society who are here ruining our carpets and pretending to admire the lines of my designs. Tell them a few prices and make them gasp; if it's expensive enough they'll have to have it."

India laughed. It wasn't entirely true, but there was enough of a grain of truth from which to make a pearl. They were almost all of them people who had to be *told* what was good, "The public are like bad Hollywood agents," her mother had said bitterly. "They're basically people of undefined taste who have to be told by others that something is good before they believe it. When they read it in the trades or in the dailies, then they'll claim they always knew it was good and use it as a model for new and aspiring artists. Be like that, they'll say, and then you'll be a star. Copies! That's all they want. And the reassurance of everyone else knowing it's good." And that was the reason for this party, so that it would be printed in the glossies and the dailies and read about from eternal Rome to sunny Beverly Hills, from the palaces of the Middle East to the boulevards of Paris and even, eventually, to the rainwashed streets of London.

India leaned quietly against a pillar of faux-malachite, sipping her champagne, staring somberly at the crowd. If these were your clients, then these were the people you had to deal with. This was the one thing that bothered her about the business. Catering to rich women's whims was definitely not her strong point. But rich women were the ones who bought what you offered. It might be their husbands who were paying, but it was the women who must be wooed. A gusty sigh escaped her. It was, after all, damn it, still a man's world. Rich women wanted to deal with men, they wanted a little extra attention. . . .

"Is it that bad?"

The sound of the voice close to her ear startled India and the champagne slopped from her glass over the sleeve of the man in the dark suit standing next to her.

"Oh, I'm so sorry!" Oh, my God, now she'd probably ruined his suit and lost Paroli an important customer. India mopped futilely at the arm with a tiny cocktail napkin. It was very wet. "Oh, dear," she said. Her apologetic brown eyes lifted from the sleeve and met his equally deep brown ones.

"Snap," said Aldo Montefiore.

India's gaze was puzzled; she was still concentrating on the damage she'd inflicted. Who would have thought one glass of champagne could be so wet!

"Our eyes, I mean. They are the same color."

"Oh. Oh, I see." India gazed at him with new interest. He didn't seem in the least bit bothered about his jacket. He was smiling at her, and he was *quite* attractive. Dark hair, faintly curling after a firm brushing and still wet from the shower. He wore it long on the neck, and slightly shaggy. She liked that. And she liked his brown eyes with the curling lashes. And the smile was gentle, tentative even, as though

54

he wasn't quite sure what her reaction would be. Like her, he wasn't too tall—five eight or nine maybe. In her high-heeled boots and with her new fluffy hair she seemed almost as tall as he; for once she didn't have to gaze upward, and for some silly reason that pleased her. Gazing up at a man always gave him a feeling of mastery and her a feeling of being a child with a father. Here was someone with whom she felt equal. And she definitely liked that smile. Oh, goodness, he was talking and she'd missed what he'd said, she'd been so engrossed in gazing at him.

"It was my fault," he repeated gently. "I shouldn't have startled you like that."

"Not at all, I'm just sorry about your jacket. Oh, dear, look at it, it's still so wet. I tell you what— come with me and I'll get a towel from the kitchen." India grinned at him, the brave scarlet of her lips as glossy as her sparkling eyes. "I can't guarantee it'll be good as new," she announced, leading the way, "but it will be drier."

The kitchen was almost as busy as the showroom: relays of waiters picked up trays of hot hors d'oeuvres and harassed chefs maneuvered, grumbling, about the small area.

"Wait here," cried India, darting through the crush.

Aldo leaned against the wall of the corridor out of the way of passing waiters. He had first spotted her parking the red Fiat on the corner and had followed her along the street to Paroli. If she hadn't turned into the showroom he would have followed her to wherever she was going, but it was his good fortune that they had both apparently been going to the same place. He still didn't know who she was, but she obviously knew Fabrizio pretty well, and she knew her way around the showrooms and offices. She must work here. If so, she probably hadn't been invited to the dinner afterward, and in that case, he decided, remembering the smile, he'd skip the dinner and invite her to dine with him in a restaurant. If he messed up Marisa's seating arrangements, that was just too bad. The girl appeared from the kitchen clutching a towel. He didn't even know her name.

"India Haven," she said, mopping his sleeve. "Take off your jacket and let's see how wet your shirt is."

Aldo waved away the cloth impatiently. "Forget the shirt," he said, "it'll dry. How can you possibly be called India?"

She stared at him in surprise. "Very simply. I was conceived there. In a houseboat called *Moonrise* on Lake Srinagar in Kashmir."

"Why not Moonrise, or Srinagar, or Kashmir?"

"An eccentricity of my mother's. My elder sister is named Paris, my younger sister Venetia—an aesthetic variation of Venice. I always say thank God it wasn't Ganges or Katmandu!"

Aldo threw back his head and laughed. "India Haven, have dinner with me tonight."

Her hesitation was delightful. He could read the thoughts behind her translucent brown eyes. First in-

56

terest, then maybe, then firmness. No, she couldn't.

"But why not?"

"I'm invited to the dinner afterward at Fabrizio's. I can't possibly not go."

"Say no more, Cinderella," cried Aldo triumphantly. "We are both going to the dinner."

"Really?" India's laugh filtered along the corridor. "Then I'll see you there. I must leave now, though. I promised Marisa that I'd check everything was ready before the guests came. Not that there's any real need—her staff is more competent than I am."

"You work for Marisa?"

Aldo's arm felt firm under her elbow as they walked back along the corridor.

"No. For Fabrizio. I must hurry. I'll see you there." India strode off on her high heels along the corridor. "Oh," she said, turning as she reached the door, "but I don't know your name."

"Aldo," he replied, "Aldo Montefiore."

Their gaze locked.

"Montefiore," she murmured, her voice sliding velvety over the syllables, "what a *lovely* name." She turned on her heel and was gone, and for a moment Aldo stood there, still hearing her voice saying his name, and then he quickened his pace and followed her through the crowded room.

He found her again outside in the street gazing at the empty space where her tiny red Fiat had been parked. The sign on the wall clearly stated, NO PARKING.

"I expect it's been towed away," Aldo said sympa-

57

thetically. Her misfortune was his advantage. It meant he could drive her to the villa . . . and take her home afterward.

"Oh, damn it!" Angry tears stung India's eyes. She loved that car. She hated anyone else touching it. God knows what state it would be in; the towing trucks were notoriously "uncareful" with illegally parked automobiles. "Now what shall I do?"

"Let's go." Aldo took her arm again and led her across the street to where his black VW Rabbit waited beneath a prominent no-parking sign.

"I don't believe it!" gasped India.

Aldo shrugged.

"They're doing the left-hand side first tonight," he explained. "They'll be back later for those on the right."

"Just my luck! Still, if it hadn't been me it would have been you, and that would have been worse. Imagine having drink spilled all over you by some careless female at a party and then having your car towed away as well."

"Imagine! There probably would have been nothing for it but to retire to the country, to a life of solitude, far from the pressures of city life."

India laughed as he helped her into the car and closed the door. Yes, she definitely liked Aldo Montefiore.

LONDON

Morgan McBain was enjoying himself. This

58

evening, which he had expected to be at the least boring or, even worse, stiffly British and boring, had turned out to be a winner.

His hostess, on whose right he was sitting, had a witty charm that amused him, and the lovely girl on his left was a complete mystery. More so because he kept having this odd feeling that he must have met her before and just couldn't remember where. Vennie. The lovely Venetia.

"It's such a pretty name—Venetia—and so unusual."

Her soft hibiscus-pink mouth parted in a tantalizingly familiar smile and her enormous gray-blue eyes held a glint of amusement.

"It's my mother's idea of a romantic joke. I'm named after the city where I was conceived, Venice—either in a suite at the Cipriani or in a gondola, she's never been quite sure which."

Morgan's deep laugh rang through the room. "Whichever, the result was worth it. I just hope for their sake you have no brothers."

"Two sisters . . . you're not going to believe this . . . Paris and India."

"And the locations?"

"Oh, India's is the best, we always think—a houseboat on a lake in Kashmir. And Paris was the Ritz. She says it's because of being conceived practically next door to Chanel's atelier that she's destined to be a great couturier."

"And is she?"

Venetia shrugged. "It's difficult, but Paris works

59

hard, and when you have as much talent and dedication as she does, then one day you must succeed. Don't you agree?"

Morgan decided against telling her that it didn't always work that way. "And you, Venetia—what's your talent?"

"Oh, me . . . I've done nothing, just school and then a cooking diploma. I have no talent, really."

"But the food was delicious and everything looked so beautiful. That's a talent, Venetia." He wanted to add that she was also breathtakingly lovely, but it was too soon.

"And what about you, Morgan McBain, where were you conceived?"

Venetia's eyes danced with amusement. She liked being here with Morgan, it was almost as if they were having dinner alone; the rest of the table seemed excluded from their private conversation and Morgan McBain's gaze left her feeling elated. His skin looked so firm and tanned and his shoulders so broad beneath that wonderful dinner jacket. He was the most physical man she had ever met.

"I was conceived and born in a trailer on a drilling site in the flattest, most barren stretch of land in Texas. My father was wildcatting for oil and my mother, who adored him, refused to leave his side when I was on the way, even though conditions were primitive. She died two weeks after I was born. She had worked alongside him, helped him . . . he always says that without her he never would have made it."

"Morgan, I'm so sorry." Venetia was embarrassed

that she had asked.

"It was a long time ago. And she was right, my father did make it. He never married again," he added with a wry grin, "though I've had the most glamorous selection of women who just longed to become my momma!"

"Wait a minute." Venetia didn't know why she hadn't put two and two together before. "Of course—*Fitz* McBain! The richest man in the world. Morgan, I'm terribly impressed!"

"Maybe not quite the richest." Venetia was one of the few girls Morgan had ever met to whom the fact that he was Fitz McBain's son obviously meant little more than her wide-eyed awe of the moment. Like his father, he was used to the sudden magic of the McBain name acting as a magnet for every available attractive woman in sight. Some of the most beautiful women in the international society of both Europe and America had tried their best to get either father or son to the altar. And some were still trying.

"You're not in the least impressed," he said, taking her hand in his and squeezing it, "and rightly so. I'm just the hardworking son of a successful father. We're in more than just oil now. Fitz had an urge for real estate, maybe because of those six years living in the trailer in the middle of nowhere. Anyhow, he bought lusher, greener acres in semitropical islands, in the Caribbean; he had an urge for cities so he acquired bits of Park and Madison in New York and plots in downtown Houston and Dallas; he learned to enjoy wines, so then there was a château with a

61

vineyard in France. . . . You name it, Fitz bought it. And then, because he can't bear things just to sit there not making money, he built hotels or converted the existing buildings into hotels. And when he'd finished those projects he turned his interest to shipping, tankers, freighters. He's been working since he was thirteen years old. I was born when he was only twenty, and now he's forty-four. I'm still wondering what he'll get up to next."

"Does it worry you?"

She was listening intently, obviously deeply interested in what he had to say. It broke down any barriers between them, and Morgan suddenly found himself saying something he'd never admitted to any other woman before.

"Sometimes it does, yes. I'm not always sure that I'm going to be able to live up to his standards, his expectations of me." Morgan was serious now. "It's not always easy being the son of a famous and successful father."

Vennie leaned back in her chair, His words had brought her back to her own dilemma. The questions reared themselves once more in the front of her mind. Her future. What was she going to do? What could she do that could possibly succeed the way Jenny had done? There was just no way to make Jenny proud of her; she had no talents, no achievements, she was just an ordinary girl—with a famous mother.

"I know, Morgan," she said in a small voice that was like a sigh. "I know just what you mean. You see,

62

my mother is Jenny Haven."

Lydia spoke across Morgan, who was sitting between them. "Venetia, I think we'll have coffee in the drawing room and leave the men to their port."

"Of course. I'll get Marie-Thérèse to bring it in to us." Coffee was, thank heavens, the one thing that Marie-Thérèse could be trusted to take care of alone, possibly because she drank gallons of the stuff herself. Venetia smiled her excuses to Morgan and the other male guests, and followed Lydia and the ladies from the room.

Morgan turned to watch her go. She was a slender, almost childlike figure in her layers of non-color knits, stylish with that particularly English nonconformity. And she was lovely. He turned his back to the table, accepting the glass of amber port that Roger Lancaster offered. She was Jenny Haven's daughter. Of course, that had been the resemblance that tantalized him. How odd. He'd always thought his father had been in love with Jenny Haven, although as far as he knew they had met only once. But there was no doubt Jenny Haven had been Fitz McBain's idol in his lonely teenage years.

Morgan sipped his port appreciatively as Roger Lancaster began to outline some of the points he wanted him to make to Fitz when he saw him next.

Venetia chatted easily with Lydia's guests, some of whom were mothers of her own friends, but it was as though she were in limbo, waiting for the dining-room door to open and Morgan McBain to reenter her world. Weren't they taking an awfully long time

63

tonight? She glanced at the original Cartier Santos watch that Jenny had found for her when all she wanted in the world was something as simple and easy as a watch. It reminded her again of Jenny, and Venetia bit her lip worriedly. What was she going to do? She couldn't bear to go back to Beverly Hills. Ah, thank goodness, the dining-room door had opened. She gazed expectantly toward the hall as Roger Lancaster shepherded his guests into the drawing room for coffee.

The sound of the phone shrilled through the house.

"Vennie darling, could you get it?" Lydia looked up from pouring the coffee.

"I'll pick it up in the hall." She sped across the room, making for the hall and the phone. Morgan McBain stood in the doorway and he moved aside to let her pass.

"I want to talk to you," he murmured, catching her hand as she sped by.

He was still holding her hand as she picked up the phone to answer, and Vennie turned her head to smile at him.

"Miss Venetia Haven, please."

"Yes, this is Venetia."

"Hold the line please, Miss Haven, Los Angeles is calling you."

PARIS

Paris's head rested in the crook of his left arm.

Amadeo squinted at the thin gold watch that he wore with the dial turned inward on his left wrist. It was a present from his wife, not entirely to his taste, but he was happy to make the concession of wearing it and pretending his pleasure to please her. Nine forty-five. He was already late. He glanced at the crown of Paris's head where the thick dark hair parted softly in a bluish line. She was a lovely girl. It was refreshing to make love to one like this with such youthful energy and drive, not to say single-minded ambition. As soon as they had finished she had asked him again if he really knew how fabulous his fabrics would look in her designs. Of course he knew. A sack would look elegant in Vitrazzi silk. He could swear that she'd been turned on sexually by her excitement with her designs, her clothes, the fabric. He remembered her nipples beneath the gray silk and ran his hand once again across the perfect curve of her breast. Damn it, it was too late. There was no time for a repeat performance, though he was tempted. Removing his arm from her shoulders Amadeo swung his legs over the side of the sleigh bed.

Paris leaned on her elbow watching him with a puzzled frown as he walked across the room to where his clothes lay neatly folded over a chair. He was getting dressed. Of course, it was almost ten o'clock, he must be hungry. Come to think of it, she was starving herself.

"*Caro*," she called, using his own word of endearment, "there's a marvelous little bistro around the

65

corner on the Rue de Buci, it's dark and it's full of lovers and the food is sublime. . . ."

Full of lovers! Amadeo zipped up his pants firmly and thrust his feet into the glove-soft loafers made specially for him in London. What was all this talk of romantic restaurants and lovers? Didn't she understand it was a thing of the moment, a small pleasure in his busy life? A girl like this could be dangerous to a man's marriage if she were allowed to get too close. She was too intelligent, too clever.

"Sorry, *cara*, but I'm already late. I should have been at Olympe Avallon's an hour ago. Of course I wouldn't have arranged it had I known . . ." His smile was apologetic, but his eyes avoided hers.

Paris stared at him. Olympe Avallon was an ex-Dior model who had struck fame and success some years ago with her dancing, flirting strut on the cat-walk, that had put more sex into clothes than was ever seen naked on the stage of the Folies Bergère. She'd parlayed it into three consecutive rich husbands and had only recently divorced her third. Olympe was a legend among Paris models—she was still, at thirty-five, ravishingly beautiful and looked at least ten years younger than her age. Thanks to the generosity of the settlements of her ex-husbands she was also fabulously wealthy, and she was renowned for her amours. Of course, Paris remembered now. There were those pictures in the magazines of Olympe dressed in St. Laurent—or was it Lagerfeld?—on Amadeo's arm at various social functions. Paris felt suddenly very second rate.

She'd been the hors d'oeuvre to Olympe's main course, the *amuse-gueule* for Amadeo Vitrazzi's appetite. Pushing back her hair she dragged the velvet bedspread around her to cover her nakedness. At least she'd got her six months' credit. It had been worth it, it must have been.

"Of course, Amadeo," she agreed desperately, "it was silly of me to expect you to be free at such short notice. Perhaps later in the week we could discuss our business arrangements."

Amadeo glanced impatiently at his watch once again. Didn't this girl know anything? His eyes met hers and he felt suddenly depressed. He had a daughter this age.

"I'm leaving tomorrow for New York, *cara*," he said briskly. "I won't be back for at least a month. I'll have my accounts department call you. Of course I myself have nothing to say in the matter of credit. These things are always up to the accountants." His smile was dazzling as he walked across and kissed her. "Creative people like you and I know nothing of these things, do we, *cara?* But I'm sure if you give them the proper bank references, et cetera, it might possibly be worked out. *Ciao, cara.* It was lovely." His kiss was light and his step hurried as he strode toward the steel door that Paris had painted black to match the beams. *"Ciao, ciao."* A light wave of the hand and he was gone. Amadeo Vitrazzi *never* mixed business with pleasure.

Paris was frozen in place, her mouth fixed into the thin smile that she had managed as he had said good-bye to her. He'd *promised* her! He'd loved her designs, he had said she had genius, a gold mine of talent. And in return she had given him herself. Her puzzled eyes shifted to the soft gray silk dress crumpled into a small heap on the floor where she had stepped out of it when Amadeo had undressed her. The mint-green satin knickers lay at her feet. Oh, God, she thought, beginning to cry, what have I done? The tears slid unheeded down her face as she remembered her decision, remembered thinking that it wouldn't be so bad, that after all he was attractive. And then, goddamn it, she had even *enjoyed* it! She felt cheapened as she fought the despair, and then rage engulfed her. Rage with Amadeo, with herself, with haute couture and silk manufacturers and Jenny who never gave her any money because she maintained that if you were talented you could make it on your own.

Paris leapt to her feet and ran naked across to the drawing table. *"Merde!"* Her arm swept the table clean of the precious sketches. Another blow sent the lamp on its twisted umbilical cord crashing to the ground. *"Merde* to all that!"

She jumped up and down on the sketches, screaming out her anger. "Bastards!" she yelled, running to the shelves and flinging the meager bolts of fabric to the floor, and then, because that wasn't enough to satisfy her rage, she pulled and tugged until the cloth spilled and unraveled in yards of color around her knees. *"Merde* on all fabric manufacturers," she moaned, dashing across to the gray silk dress. One vicious wrench and it was split from top to bottom. "I hate silk, I hate all goddamn silk. . . ." She kicked at the remnants of the dress and her anger rose to a pitch. The lacquer tray stood where they had left it with the unfinished glasses of whiskey and Campari, and Paris paused for a moment to catch her breath. She took a sip from her glass. It tasted as stale and bitter as she felt, and she flung it to the floor with a grimace of disgust. "Fuck you all," she yelled, as she trailed across the room toward the bathroom. "Oh, fuck everything." With a last surge of rage she kicked the bathroom door, remembering too late that she was barefoot. The stinging blow on her big toe brought her to her senses and she sank to the ground clutching her injured foot as the tears flowed anew.

"Paris Haven, you are a fool. You're such a fool," she moaned. She had thought she was so smart, that she was in control. Maybe if she hadn't let him make love to her he would have given her the credit? The thought struck her with an impact equal to the bathroom door. "Yes," she added bitterly, "you are a fool."

The telephone began to ring and she leaned against the wall watching the black instrument without moving. Whoever it was, she was in no mood to talk. In a few minutes it would stop. She waited and waited. There, that was better.

She must take a shower; perhaps if she cleaned herself, washed Amadeo Vitrazzi from her, she might feel human. Oh, damn, there was the phone again! Why didn't they just go away and leave her alone? She hesitated by the bathroom door. The phone shrilled persistently, endlessly. Goddamn it, what was wrong with them? Paris walked slowly toward the telephone. She wouldn't hurry, and then maybe by the time she reached it whoever it was would have given up and stopped ringing. The sound was so shrill. Her hand hovered over the phone. "Yes?" Her voice was small in the sudden silence of the big attic.

"Mademoiselle Paris Haven?"

"*Qui, c'est* Mademoiselle Haven. *Qui est à l'appareil?*"

"*Ne quittez pas, mademoiselle.* Los Angeles *vous demande.*"

ROME

The villa on the Via Appia Antica was vast and decorated, of course, in Fabrizio's faultless style. But despite its perfection India always felt that it lacked charm. It wasn't Fabrizio's fault; he'd provided the backdrop. What was lacking was the human element, the female touches of memorabilia, family snapshots of laughing children taken at the beach, a special satin pillow that had always pleased, a child's nursery school drawing tacked to the kitchen wall, a bunch of flowers bought for their perfume or their riotous, joyful color, not just because they would tone with the decor. Sometimes, thought India guiltily, one could almost wish for a few sticky fingerprints along the pristine surfaces. It was a showroom. Only this time it was Marisa's showroom, not Fabrizio's. Every objet d'art, every painting, every casually placed book, was expensive, in good taste, and guaranteed to be coveted by her guests.

Only the children's rooms were real, and Fabrizio was responsible for that. Marisa had wanted elaborate murals depicting scenes from fairy stories, knights on white chargers and babes in the woods, but Fabrizio had drawn the line. White walls that the children were not only permitted, but encouraged, to paint on, as often as and whenever they liked. Scarlet tubular bunk beds and matching red-and-white cabinets. Vast cupboards for toys and baskets to catch all the oddments that end up on a nursery floor at the end of the day. Climbing frames, a basketball hoop, roller skates. The children, he'd stated firmly, would be normal kids. None of Marisa's "precious" fantasies of perfection here. And five-year-old Giorgio and six-year-old Fabiola loved it.

"India. You're dreaming again." Marisa's voice was silken and soft. "Are you enjoying yourself? You look a little tired."

India sighed. When Marisa said you looked tired it meant you looked a mess. The dinner had been long and India had been placed at the last of the round tables, the one nearest the door, with three men who discussed the car industry through all seven courses and two women who knew each other well, had many friends in common, and who,

71

recognizing that India merely worked for Fabrizio, had contrived to ignore her for the entire evening. Aldo Montefiore's pleadings had been of no avail; Marisa would not change her seating plan and he'd been forced to accept it. She'd watched Aldo chatting and smiling with a pretty girl sitting on his left, whom she knew was Marisa's cousin, and a dazzling socialite on his right who, India had to admit, was stunning.

Marisa had followed her into the powder room off the flagged hallway because she wanted to know how well India knew Aldo Montefiore. Marisa wanted to drop a word of warning now just in case India got too interested. After all, she didn't want any trouble with Fabrizio's little protégée later, did she?

"How did you meet Aldo, *cara?*" she asked, taking a jeweled compact out of her tiny blue leather bag. Powdering her faultless nose gently she caught India's eyes in the mirror.

India rummaged in her big leather satchel, feeling clumsy—as always—next to Marisa. The invitations had said informal, but there was informal and informal, and the scarlet sweater seemed wrong next to Marisa's sapphire cashmere Krizia sheath. "We met at the reception," she said flatly. "I spilled champagne on him."

"Don't worry about it, my dear." Marisa watched as India glossed red lipstick over her mouth. "Nothing could ruin that suit. I doubt that it could stand another day at the cleaners. Of course the poor boy can't afford little luxuries like good clothes. The family is desperately hard up. Aldo is their only ticket to salvation. Of course he'll have to marry money, and with his looks and title it won't be too difficult. There's *so much* money about." Marisa shrugged her almost overly slender shoulders deprecatingly. "Of course you know who he is, my dear, don't you? The Conte di Montefiore, one of Italy's oldest titles. He has that vast place in Venice that's crumbling into the canal. I think you once painted it and gave it to Fabrizio. And then there's the Palazzo Montefiore on the coast. Magnificent but doomed—unless he suddenly makes a lot of money. He got on so well with my cousin Renata, didn't you think?" Marisa picked up her bag and snapped it shut with a firm click. "We all have our responsibilities," she announced with a final slow smile over her shoulder as she drifted from the room.

India was fuming. Anger burned her cheeks red. How dare Marisa warn her off as though she were some servant girl chasing after the lord of the manor? Nineteenth-century nonsense! She wasn't the least bit interested in Aldo Montefiore anyway. The Conte di Montefiore. Her brown eyes gazed back at her from the mirror and she remembered Aldo's smiling voice as he'd said, "Snap." Well, not *that* interested anyway. But he was attractive, and nice. . . .

India stood up abruptly. She was tired. It was time to go home. She'd find Fabrizio, say good-bye, and leave.

The evening was still young. A pianist lazed over the keys of the white grand piano in the hall, singing Cole Porter. Guests were gathering in groups or lounging on the vast sofas, gossiping. White-gloved waiters were serving coffee and tiny delicious chocolates from silver trays. India searched the room for Fabrizio and found him leaning over the piano, absorbed in Cole Porter's magical lyrics that lost nothing with the passage of time.

"I must leave now, Fabrizio. Thank you for a lovely evening."

"India? So soon?" His warm hands encompassed hers, and she thrilled at the light touch. Odd how Marisa was warning her off Aldo, who was obviously earmarked for the wealthy cousin Renata, and not her own husband.

"I'm tired," she said lamely. "It's been a long day and I must be up early to check that the plumbers showed up at the Mondini apartment."

Fabrizio felt a pang of guilt. Sometimes he thought he worked her too hard. He could easily have sent someone else to oversee the workmen at the penthouse they were redoing, but this was the first time she had been allowed to follow a project through from beginning to end, and if she wanted to learn, then she must understand the basics as well as the gloss. Functional plumbing was as important as the color of the tiles in a bathroom.

"Take care, then, *cara*," he said, bending his head and kissing her tenderly on each cheek. "*Ciao*. I'll see you tomorrow." He watched her walk away from him. "India."

She half turned. "Yes?"

"I'll have the carpet delivered tomorrow after-noon."

Her delighted laugh quite made his evening.

India surveyed the Rolls-Royces, Mercedes, Ferraris, and Porsches parked in the courtyard with re-membered dismay. Of course—she had no car! She hovered uncertainly on the steps while the parking valet waited for her to hand him the key.

"The black VW Rabbit, please."

Aldo smiled at her. "He can't mistake it. It must be the only VW in this pope's ransom of automobiles."

"Oh, but shouldn't you be at the party?" India was pleased despite herself and she smiled back at him.

"I always take home the girl I came with," he replied with a twinkle, "and besides, how would you get home if I didn't drive you?"

She hadn't realized how tired she was until she settled back in her seat, wriggling her toes in the black boots. A glance at Aldo's profile showed him concentrating on the still dense traffic. In the lights of passing cars he looked older, even a little sad. She liked his strong dark features with the prominent cheekbones and slightly battered nose. And the dark eyes so like her own. His hands on the wheel were square and firm with a scatter of dark silken hairs across the back. A tiny shiver of response fluttered along India's spine as her gaze rested on his hands.

Aldo shifted his attention from the traffic for an instant and glanced at the girl beside him. She was staring straight ahead, and her face looked pale under the streetlights. She was heart-touchingly pretty. India Haven had a quality that inspired tenderness in a man, and tenderness was exactly what he had been determined to avoid. But he couldn't, he knew that now.

"It's left here." Her charmingly accented voice broke his reverie and he swung the small car quickly to the left and around the corner, following her instructions and concentrating once more on the traffic.

"Right at the next corner and we're there," said India. "It's this building, right here."

The car purred to a smooth stop. "As smooth as a Rolls," said India with an impish grin.

"I've missed my vocation. I should have been a motor mechanic."

"Really?"

Aldo smiled deprecatingly. "No, not really. But I love this little car, she's become something of a passion with me."

A passion. India wondered about his passion. She changed the subject. "Tell me, Aldo Montefiore, what do you do?"

"I manage the family estates. Not very well yet, but I'm learning. And what do you do?"

"I assist Fabrizio. Not very well yet, but I'm learning."

His laugh was low and appreciative, and like his hands, it sent a little frisson through her. India felt herself relaxing; she was enjoying his company, enjoying the way he looked, the way he was. To hell with Marisa and the cousin, she decided suddenly, she was enjoying herself.

Aldo glanced at the building where India Haven lived. Its stone façade looked forbidding and its vast double doors that would lead, as they all did, to a tiny courtyard were firmly shuttered against the night and intruders. Which were her rooms?

"There"—she pointed them out to him—"On the first floor. Too big, really, for just one person and a bit bare yet, but I'm decorating them slowly in the best Paroli style. I hope we didn't spill too much champagne on the carpet," she added with a grin "—tomorrow it's mine. It will enhance the faded marble grandeur of the Haven residence and add considerably to my warmth and comfort on the forthcoming cold winter nights. You can think of me wriggling my toes in its comforting luxury as the snow falls over Rome in January."

"I'll remember to do that," he replied, wondering if she was going to invite him up for a drink.

"I hear you are a count," India said suddenly. "The Conte di Montefiore."

"And I hear you're Jenny Haven's daughter." Aldo's smile was amiable, relaxed.

India stiffened. So that was it. He knew who she was. Her spirits drooped suddenly. And, I suppose, she thought miserably, he thinks I'm another little rich girl, ripe for the picking. Another cousin Renata. Well, he's mistaken. Jenny may have money, but she's worked for every cent of it. Her millions

77

came from her own endeavors and there's no way she'd be happy to see them expended on saving and restoring Italian palaces. You've got the wrong girl, Count Aldo.

The slam of the door sounded angry, and Aldo's face showed his surprise as he leapt after her.

"Good night," said India stiffly, "and thank you for driving me home. I really appreciated it."

"But, India, I want to see you again. Would you have dinner with me tomorrow night? Please say yes. We could go to the little osteria I know in the hills. You'd love it there—Papa Rizzoli does the cooking. At this time of year they'll have a big fire blazing in the hearth—applewood, it smells like heaven. And there's candlelight and wine from their own vineyards, and it's my favorite place. I would love to show it to you, India."

His voice was persuasive, but India steeled herself against his coaxing.

"I have something else on tomorrow night," she answered vaguely.

"Then the next night, or the next. Just tell me when."

"Call me." India retreated behind the big double doors, closing them with a soft thud behind her. She leaned against them, listening until she heard his footsteps cross the pavement and the slam of the car door. The engine started at first touch and the little car hummed away. Only then did she walk toward the lighted hallway. What would it have been like to go to the osteria with him? It sounded like the perfect romantic setting for an evening with a man you liked, or might fall in love with. The scent of applewood, candlelight flickering on ancient whitewashed stone walls, wine straight from the vineyard . . . and Aldo Montefiore with his firm hands and strong profile. . . .

The particular high shrilling call of the Italian telephone system penetrated her consciousness as she idled her way dreamily up the stairs.

A phone was ringing. Her phone! India leapt the last few stairs two at a time, fumbling with her key in the lock. Slamming the door behind her she rushed across the room, flinging her satchel onto the sofa as she went. Maybe it was Fabrizio. Maybe he'd decided to slip away from his guests and spend a few stolen hours here with her.

"Yes." Her voice had a breathy, expectant quality.

"Signorina India Haven?"

"*Si, Pronto.*"

"A call for you, signorina, from Los Angeles."

❦ 2 ❦

25 October

Jenny Haven was dead. The headlines splashed across the newspaper in bold black print with painful finality. The photograph reproduced below showed a laughing blond woman, no longer as young as she was doing her best to appear, but nevertheless beautiful. The line of the jaw might have

79

been a little less perfect than it used to be, the well-known bosom a little less firm, but the eyes were smiling with Jenny's familiar wide, gray-blue gaze, and the full mouth curved in the enticing smile that contrived to be both demure and provocative at the same time. And neither face nor body owed a single point to Hollywood's finest cosmetic surgical scalpels. Jenny had had a fear of hospitals and doctors and the idea of voluntarily submitting herself to the knife had filled her with such horror that even when the edges of her beauty had begun to blur and it had seemed necessary because of her career to "help things along a little," as her agent had suggested, she had been unable to bring herself to do it. Jenny Haven had been the perfect combination of corn-fed middle America and Hollywood glitz. She was the blond girl-next-door and the unattainable star who lived in a rarified atmosphere of blue skies and perpetual sunshine, limousines and lovers, the woman that young men around the world fantasized about possessing and young girls dreamed of becoming.

Venetia folded the paper carefully so that she wouldn't see that headline every time she glanced at it lying on the empty seat next to her. Especially the caption that ran across the top of the picture: "Jenny, the Golden Girl—Suicide?"

Jenny had been fifty years old and they were still calling her a girl. "It's because that's the way they all remember her," Paris had said. "It's affection, Vennie, they're not being unkind." Paris had understood. And yet she was the only one who had *not* protested that it couldn't be true. Paris had remained silent when Venetia and India had sworn it simply couldn't be right, that Jenny, who loved life, would *never* have committed suicide. The newspapers were hinting that maybe pills and booze had had a lot to do with the twisted wreckage of the silver Mercedes at the bottom of Malibu Canyon—that, and possibly a fading career, and the split-up with the live-in lover of the past two years, Rory Grant, almost half her age and into his first big break as star of a new TV series.

The newspapers had thrown it all up, using everything they could find to add dimension to a story whose headline had rocketed around the wire services of the world. Jenny Haven was dead.

The endless tears slid down Venetia's cheeks. She didn't even bother to try to stop them anymore, letting them fall from her swollen eyes, not caring about her blotched face.

It was India who had been most vehement against the suggestions in the papers. "Suicide!" she'd cried, and her brown eyes had flashed with anger. "If Jenny were committing suicide she'd have done it in the Rolls!" She had been so right that it had struck them as irresistibly funny and the three of them, alone in a VIP waiting room at London's Heathrow Airport, had fallen into fits of hysterical laughter that had been even more painful than the tears.

Venetia glanced across the aisle of the private jet to where India sat with her feet curled beneath her and a book in her hands, pretending to read. Venetia hadn't seen her turn a page in the last half hour. Paris lay full length across three seats behind India, one thin arm flung across her face so that her eyes were hidden. The steward had covered her carefully with a blanket and she seemed to be sleeping, but Venetia doubted it.

Venetia stretched her stiff legs. It was weariness that she felt, not fatigue. Too much was happening in her head, too many thoughts, too many questions. Too much guilt. If only she'd gone home when Jenny asked her . . . Abruptly she made her way toward the powder room at the rear of the plane.

A door stood open on the left and she peered in at the compact, luxurious little room that was almost filled by a low bed covered in a soft dark-brown moleskin rug. Subdued lighting, a large mirror, a console by the bed that controlled the television and movie screens and the music system. Fitz McBain's bedroom. She could lie down here, now, if she wanted. The bed was there for her to rest on. Venetia wondered briefly about the man whose bedroom this was, the rich man who owned a dozen luxury hotels, a château in France, and a penthouse in New York's newest and most prestigious building. The plane is his home, Morgan had said. He spends most of his life in transit, flying from one meeting to the next. His father had two of these planes and they were identical. It was almost, thought Venetia, remembering Morgan's story at dinner last night, as though Fitz McBain still lived in the trailer where he'd had his beginnings. A luxurious airborne trailer, but was there really much difference? Fitz McBain was still living "over the shop."

She wandered through to the tiny bathroom and gazed around. Mirrors, crystal knobs on the faucets, bronze tiles . . . very masculine . . . a bottle of Lagerfeld cologne, creamy towels monogramed McB in scarlet. There were few clues to the man who had, when Morgan telephoned him in Hamburg, instantly put his private plane at the Haven daughters' disposal. That, and any help he could offer, which included the two burly bodyguards sitting, as discreetly as two very large young men could, at the rear of the plane, and when they landed in Los Angeles they would be joined by two more.

Fitz McBain had thought quickly. "I'll have the girls picked up in Rome and Paris and get them to London right away. They'll be all right at Heathrow," he'd told Morgan. "We'll get them out before the story breaks. But there'll be trouble at L.A. International—reporters, TV, you name it. Everyone will be there hoping for the scoop on Jenny Haven's daughters. She's kept them out of the limelight all these years and she wouldn't want to see them involved in any flashpulp disputes when they get off the plane. They'll be distraught and tired. A car with two extra guards will be waiting on the tarmac and I'll arrange for them to be taken directly from the plane to my Bel-Air house. That place is a fortress, no one will disturb them there. Once they are settled, they can decide what they need to do."

It was typical of his father, Morgan had thought, that after the first small silence when he had said that Jenny Haven was dead, he had foreseen not just the need to get all three girls to Los Angeles as soon as possible, but also the need to retain their privacy. Fitz McBain was a man who, despite an outwardly flamboyant life-style, had courted privacy all his life.

Venetia examined her pale, blotched face in the gleaming mirror. She looked terrible, but it didn't matter. She turned out the light—and drifted back into the bedroom. The digital clock by the side of the bed offered the times of day in London, New York, Los Angeles, Rio de Janeiro, Hong Kong, Tokyo and Sydney. All you had to do was press the button. It was ten o'clock in the morning in London, and two o'clock the previous night in California. Did that mean Jenny had been dead less time in L.A.?

Vennie curled up on the soft brown moleskin-covered bed and cried herself to sleep.

The book she had been staring at for the past hour slid to the floor with a small thud, but India scarcely noticed. All she saw were images of Jenny's face. Jenny smiling at her, her blue eyes sparkling with amusement; Jenny talking on the phone, running her left hand through her thick blond hair in that familiar nervous gesture; Jenny looking haughtily into a mirror as she clasped diamonds around her neck and snuggled a vast white fox fur coat

84

around her slender shoulders, preparing for the annual Oscar Award ceremony; Jenny soft and laughing, lying in bed while her three young daughters clambered around her begging for another story; Jenny arrogantly demanding only the best hotel suites because "she'd earned it, damn it"; Jenny wide eyed and breathlessly in love with some new man . . . there was always a new man, no one ever lasted. Poor Jenny.

Maybe, thought India, if my father had lived she might have found lasting happiness instead of just temporary pleasure. Jenny had loved him, she told me so. And he had loved her. It hadn't been the way it was with Paris's father, a passion that needed to run its fast-burning course, nor with Venetia's father. That had been an amusing flirtation with a very correct older man, possessor of a great English hereditary title and vast inherited lands, whom Jenny had delighted in seducing, tempting him into realms of sexuality he hadn't known existed and couldn't resist. India never knew if the story of the gondola was an embellishment of Jenny's to add extra spice to the story, but knowing Jenny she would bet it was true. Jenny would have done it just for the fun of remembering this proper but passionate, trouserless Englishman straddling her in a wildly rocking gondola on the dark canals of Venice—and she would have loved the heightened thrill of sex just barely hidden from discovery. Sex wasn't something that Jenny enjoyed only when she fell in love, however brief that emotion might be, it

85

was a way of life for her. Jenny Haven loved to make love—and there were those who phrased that more crudely—but still India was sure Jenny had loved her father.

A smile flickered across India's face as she remembered Jenny's "father stories," told to them bit by bit over a period of years, garnished with more detail as they grew older, until they had become family legends. Paris's "father story" was passionate, Venetia's was fun, but mine, thought India, was romantic, mine was the vulnerable Jenny in love who, on a houseboat in Kashmir, wrapped in the warmth of her lover's arms, saw the still, cool, star-spangled dawn rise over Lake Srinagar . . . and named her daughter India. But this time when the movie the two were making together was over the romance hadn't faded. They were to have been married after his complicated divorce finally came through, but then he was drowned on location in Singapore. Just one of those needless accidents that change so much. It might have lasted for them, and then perhaps Jenny would still be alive too.

Perhaps that's why she kept me close to her, mused India. Is that the reason I was the one sent to schools in the States instead of Europe? Eastern schools, of course—only the best—in line with Jenny's policy that education was of paramount importance in life. First Miss Porter's in New York, and then Vassar, and always with Jenny constantly in touch. India had never felt neglected or unloved simply because they were separated by several

86

thousand miles. Jenny was always there at the end of the telephone, or a quick plane ride away in emergencies like appendicitis or the knee fractured in a skiing fall. Oh, I loved you, Jenny, thought India numbly, I loved you as a mother, I admired you as a hardworking movie actress, and when I was old enough to understand, I loved you for the woman you were.

It hadn't always been easy being Jenny's daughter, and India had alternately basked in her glory and hidden from it, particularly when it came to dating boys and at art school. Boys, because everyone knew—or thought they knew—the real story of how Jenny Haven had made it, though even India didn't know for sure how much of it was true. But she was nervously aware that the boys speculated how much she might be like her mother. It was a fact that Jenny had run away from her small hometown in North Carolina after winning a talent competition singing and tap-dancing in a local beer hall. With the fifty dollars' winnings in her pocket she'd hopped on the Greyhound bus and headed west to the beckoning bright lights of Hollywood, aged thirteen and looking seventeen, tall, blond, sexy, and innocent. Until she hit town. The legend that she had been seduced by a famous old-time movie director with whom she lived for three years while he "guided her career," asserting all the time that he was nothing more to her than a benevolent old uncle, was one that India suspected was true. Jenny's progress in her teens through the arms of

87

the famous older stars, the casting couch to success . . . how much was exaggeration, how much reality? Jenny herself had always laughed at the stories, and dismissed them casually. But she had never denied them, had she?

Anyway, Jenny's bitterness was not at any sexual exploitation. She'd quite enjoyed that—or most of it; there were some scenes she'd rather have forgotten if she could—but at her ignorance. Jenny Haven was convinced that had she had the education, or the "right" background, or better still a combination of both, she would not have had to claw her way to success but could have stepped calmly into her allotted place in Hollywood's halls of fame simply on her looks and talent alone. But would she have? wondered India. Hollywood is filled with astonishingly beautiful girls, many with talent and many without. And who is to say which will succeed?

It was for all these reasons that Jenny, who had married none of her daughters' fathers, was determined that they should be brought up as ladies, that after their first tender years they should be removed from the potential taint of Hollywood and the label of being Jenny Haven's indiscretions. Her girls would grow up only in the best places, they would be educated at only the most exclusive schools, they would be cultured and learn about art and music and books. Any talents that emerged would be encouraged, the right college would perfect them for the road to success. Because, of course, each of her girls would be successful. How could they fail? They were *her* daughters. Jenny had been willing to spend any sum necessary on their education, she'd bought them extravagant gifts, she'd met them in Europe and they had stayed at the grandest hotels. But once their education was finished she had informed them that they were now ready for "life." They would never have to climb the ladder of success the way Jenny had, ignorant, painfully young and desperate, but nevertheless they would "make it" on their own. Jenny had earned her own millions—and so must they.

India sighed with sad remembrance of the burden of being Jenny Haven's daughter with only a minor talent. She'd deserted Vassar to take an art history course in Venice and had fallen in love with Italy. There had been idyllic days at art school in Florence where she had learned her pretty accomplishment of watercolor painting and had also learned that she wasn't talented enough to succeed on Jenny's level.

India glanced at her sister Paris tossing restlessly on the seat behind her. Jenny's mistake had been in assuming that they would all have inherited her ambition and drive, but only Paris had that. Paris needed success, she burned for it, and India had the uncomfortable feeling that Paris would be prepared to do almost anything to achieve it. And what about Venetia? A young Jenny Haven, with that same intoxicating combination of innocence and sexuality that India wasn't even sure that Venetia herself was aware of—yet.

89

And what about me? India stared blankly out of the window at the banked clouds, graying as the plane flew into the night. What do I want from life? I've drifted along just enjoying myself. I think I'm happy . . . I would be if Fabrizio were free. Wouldn't I? Be realistic, India, she told herself with unaccustomed bitterness. Fabrizio will never leave Marisa no matter what he feels for you, and anyway, what does he feel? It was a question she had avoided often before. There had been no one else since she had met Fabrizio, in fact she hadn't even been interested in anyone, until last night and Aldo Montefiore. She remembered his hands on the wheel of the VW, square, firm hands with dark silky hair, the battered profile silhouetted against the streetlamps, and his amused dark eyes gazing into hers. Jenny would have liked Aldo. Oh, what difference did it make? thought India wearily, the Conte di Montefiore was looking for a rich wife and she was damned if she would go through life always as "the other woman"!

Tears slid down her cheeks and dropped onto the pretty scarlet Ginocchietti sweater that she had worn to the party the previous night. After that first call and the numb half-hour alone when she had been incapable of moving, she had called Fabrizio and he had come to her immediately. And then the phone hadn't stopped ringing with instructions and arrangements. It had all been such a rush, there hadn't been time to think about suitable clothes, so here she was arriving for her mother's funeral dressed in scarlet. Oh, Jenny, Jenny, she mourned

90

silently, you expected so much from me as the daughter of the one man you really loved, but there's nothing remarkable about me and I don't want what you wanted. The only trouble is, I don't know what I do want.

Paris's eyes burned with the tears she couldn't shed. When she closed them she still seemed to hear the phone shrilling through her studio. She could see again the gray silk dress, the satin underwear, the broken glass. She could feel again how she had hoped it might, just *might*, be Amadeo . . . and she hated herself again for thinking of him. Worse. What she'd thought about Jenny; she'd blamed her for allowing herself to seduce Amadeo in exchange for his silks, but no one was to blame but Paris herself. And all the time Jenny must have been lying in Malibu Canyon. Why? Why had she been driving alone along Malibu Canyon at four in the morning? Wearing an evening dress?

She hadn't been out that night, the housekeeper had said. Jenny hadn't been feeling well and had stayed in her room. The TV was still on when the housekeeper went to bed at twelve-thirty—she had noticed the time because Johnny Carson was on. The police said it must have happened about four or five o'clock in the morning, but the accident hadn't been discovered until hours later. Why had no one missed her? Probably, thought Paris bitterly, because Jenny had allowed no one to be that close to her. Nobody had *owned* Jenny, not even the live-in

91

lovers. She was a free spirit and loved and lived where she chose. Maybe she died the same way?

Venetia and India seemed convinced that it was an accident, but was that really the truth? Weren't there reasons that might have driven their mother to suicide? The Hollywood dream had died early in Jenny Haven. She had lived it, she was it. It had earned her millions of dollars but she knew it was all a lie. What had success brought her? No husbands, no loving family life, no man in her middle years who cared for her. The only reality was her children, and she had needed to send them miles away from a way of life she had achieved but no longer believed in.

I'm the one who is most like her, thought Paris, and the one who physically was always the farthest away. The eldest daughter, the one kept secret from the world for years because the scandal could have broken Jenny Haven's career. In those hazy childhood years Jenny had been a dazzlingly beautiful secret visitor who came to see her at the villa in France where Paris lived with her "family." Until India had come along, and then Jenny had just shrugged and said to hell with it, let them accept me as I am or not at all. And the public had accepted her liaisons and indiscretions—and her children—as part of the myth. Jenny Haven could do no wrong.

A fleeting thought of her father crossed Paris's mind. What of him? He must have read the papers, seen on television the reports of Jenny's accident . . . or suicide. What did he feel, and did he still remember? How could he forget? Jenny had been at the peak of her success and beauty when she had met him, and he had been a young avant-garde French movie director just on his way up in the world. It hadn't lasted long, Jenny had told her; it had been one of those white-hot passionate affairs where for three whole months they couldn't bear to be out of each other's sight, and the need for physical contact had been so overwhelming that even on the movie set Jenny would break in the middle of a scene, pretending to need direction just to take his hand and hold it to her lips, just to feel his breath against her cheek, and where there had been no time for sleep because the warm evenings and the soft nights and the gray Parisian dawns were spent making love in that vast suite at the Ritz.

No, her father couldn't have forgotten Jenny Haven, though their passion had died as quickly as it had flowered, and when Jenny had known that she was pregnant she had decided that her child had nothing to do with what she had felt for its father. It was hers and she would bring it up alone.

Paris could see Jenny now as the two of them had walked, arms linked, by Lake Lucerne on a bright Swiss autumn day that had gilded her mother's beautiful hair with lemony gold lights as Jenny told her the story of her father. Paris was eighteen years old and it was the first time she had known his name. The sudden knowledge that her father was an international celebrity, famous not just for his work in films but also his reputation as a maker of "stars" from a succession of nubile and beautiful young girls cast in the same mold of pouting lips and pert breasts, tumbling manes of hair and challenging eyes, a man whose picture she and her friends in school had pinned to their walls as someone to dream over in hazy and erotic teenage sexual fantasies, had shocked her into silence. Jenny had looked at her worriedly.

"Maybe I shouldn't have told you his name," she'd said despondently, "but you're eighteen now, Paris. You've never asked me about him since you were seven, but one day you would have wanted to know who he was and I wanted to be the one to tell you. You were a child of passion, Paris, and he could never have been a father to you. Having to be both parents made me be a better mother, don't you think so?" Her eyes had been wistful. Jenny had always wanted so much love—from her friends, from her lovers, and from her daughters.

Paris tossed restlessly, stretched across the velour plane seats, covering her eyes with a soft brown vicuña blanket. Her father was married now to a girl younger than Vennie, the fifth wife in line of succession of the nubile "stars." Paris had never seen any reason to seek him out and let him know of her existence. And now that Jenny was dead he would never know. It would be her secret forever.

Amadeo Vitrazzi slithered again through her mind, his bronzed body thrust against hers, the gray silk in a heap on the floor. "Oh, Jenny, Jenny," moaned Paris as the tears finally came, "I betrayed you. You didn't bring up your daughters to do what you had to do to gain success." And yet the same need was there, the same tense belief in her own talent, the same burning drive to succeed . . . the same sexuality. "Never again, Jenny," vowed Paris. "I'll use every means fair or unfair to succeed—but never again will I trade myself for success."

The thought came to her suddenly, taking her by surprise. But of course there was no need ever to be in that position again. Jenny's millions belonged to them now. Paris began to cry again.

The plane swooped over the dusty urban sprawl, skimming palm trees and azure swimming pools, hovering like some predatory bird over the traffic-packed freeway as it completed its final approach and touched down with a gentle bounce onto the runway at Los Angeles International Airport. With a final backthrust of powerful engines it slowed to a taxiing speed and rolled smoothly toward the cluster of buildings on the perimeter.

They were home.

Paris gripped the arms of her chair, nervously anticipating the events of the next few days. There would be the inquest. And then the funeral. Afterward they would have to sort out Jenny's affairs, business as well as personal, and as the eldest she would have to take charge.

India smiled wearily at her from the seat in front. The bright sweater emphasized her pallor and fatigue-smudged eyes. Her hair seemed to have lost its natural buoyancy and the curls lay like crushed velvet against her skull, reminding Paris of the way she had looked when they were children.

Unfastening her seat belt she looked with concern at Venetia across the aisle. Her blond hair was rumpled and her eyelids swollen and red. She had washed her face, and without makeup she looked about fifteen years old, and very vulnerable.

"Vennie." Paris slid into the seat next to her, putting a comforting arm around her shoulders. "I know it's not going to be easy, but we'll get through. At least we're all together. Just hold on, darling, we'll soon be home." Even as she said it she realized it was wrong. They weren't going home. They were going to Fitz McBain's house. Venetia's blue, tear-washed eyes met hers despairingly. "It'll be all right, you'll see." Paris hoped her voice sounded more re-assuring than she felt.

She fished hurriedly in the bottom of her bag for the dark glasses—the ultimate piece of Hollywood equipment. For the first time she understood why. At least if no one can see into your eyes you retain a little of your privacy.

None of them had any luggage, just hand baggage with a few necessities thrown in at the last moment, and the formalities of customs and immigration were made easy. It left them totally unprepared for the battery of lights, cameras, and microphones waiting in the hall, the babble of voices calling their names, demanding they "Look this way" and "Could you tell the viewers what you think of Miss Haven's possible suicide?" They shrank back into the doorway, blinded by the lights and bewildered by the sudden commotion—and the shocking questions.

"Barbarians," hissed Paris. *"Quelles sauvages!"*

"We're gonna make a run for it, miss." Their two burly guards were joined by two more who placed themselves between them and the cameras. Grabbing their arms, they ran, followed by the horde of newsmen, down the alleyways and across the sidewalk into a waiting limousine. From behind its darkened windows Paris could still make out the curious faces and flashing cameras as the enormous Mercedes pulled smoothly away from the curb.

"I'm afraid they'll follow us, miss," said the guard apologetically, "and there'll be more near the house. But there's a high wall and it's electronically protected. We'll make sure no one intrudes on your privacy. Mr. McBain was most insistent about that."

"Thank heavens for your Mr. McBain, Vennie," said India shakily. "He was the only one who anticipated something like this—I certainly never thought about it. If we hadn't had our escorts we would have been trapped."

Venetia thought of Morgan McBain. His blond sun-bronzed face and last night's dinner party seemed lost in some distant past. She stared out of the tinted windows at the familiar blur of burger stands, drive-ins, and cheap motels, and the surprising scatter of roadside oil wells that she always thought of as being like giant pecking grasshoppers. The evening that had started out so promisingly had turned into a nightmare with the telephone call. Lydia and Roger Lancaster had wanted to come with her, but somehow it hadn't seemed right to bring such loved substitute parents to her real mother's funeral. She was Jenny Haven's daughter—and this would be the last time they would be together.

The limousine with its silent occupants took the hill at the top of La Cienega Boulevard easily, slid through the light on yellow, and turned west on Sunset past the billboards advertising the latest rock success, the newest movie, and the current stars of Las Vegas. India averted her eyes as they passed the leisured lawns of Beverly Hills, where Jenny had lived. Though they had never spent much time there, it was still a sort of home. She'd had birthday parties there as a kid, she'd come "home" on the yellow school bus clutching her paintings and Jenny had pinned them on her kitchen wall, she'd had kids over to swim. And then, too, there had been the long summer weeks spent out at the beach house at Malibu. She supposed the properties would both have to be sold now.

The guard on duty at the West Gate of Bel-Air waved them through and the big limousine puffed its way up the hillside to the pillared, white-brick mansion that was part of Fitz McBain's private world. A young man waited on the broad front steps. "Good afternoon," he called. "My name is Bob Ronson. Mr. McBain wished me to welcome you to his home. I shall be here to look after things for you, so if there is anything you need, anything at all, you just let me know."

Ronson was one of several young men in Fitz McBain's employ, a combination of secretary, personal assistant, and majordomo, intent on working his way up through the strata of the multilayered McBain companies. The position was one McBain allotted only to the most promising and ambitious. He had no time for yes-men, and while he acknowledged that there were those who by choice and natural limitation would remain forever in the middle reaches of his complex operations, there was no place for mediocrity in his personal entourage.

The white house was peaceful and sunlit and Venetia thought it very European. Faded Isfahan rugs covered the polished boards in the hall, and a single priceless English landscape dreamed immortally on this Californian wall. A fine pair of carved Hepplewhite mirrors reflected bowls of flowers on the matching hall tables, and instinctively Venetia bent her head to the peach-colored roses, breathing in their familiar fragrance.

"How lovely," she murmured, wondering whether Fitz McBain chose scented English roses for all his homes, or whether this was the severely suited young Mr. Ronson's taste.

India's eyes gleamed with a professional curiosity as she gazed around the drawing room that spread across the full width of the house, noting a Dufy depicting the Baie des Anges at Nice, an early Pissarro, and two lilied Monets on the walls. In her opinion, without them this room would have fallen into the category of "luxury interior decorator style," though she did admire the color scheme of cream and butter-yellow with touches of a dark teal blue. "I should introduce Mr. McBain to Fabrizio Paroli," she remarked, sauntering through arched glass doors onto the terrace. A swath of green lawn ended at an azure pool, where a silent youth in white T-shirt and shorts wielded a pole, vacuuming the always flawless depths. It was a Hockney painting come to life.

Ronson led them across to a white-porticoed summerhouse that contained changing rooms and a small but well-equipped gymnasium as well as what he told them was Fitz McBain's favorite room. Venetia knew why instantly. It was a room to relax in; you could curl up on the huge black sofas with a book from one of the shelves that lined the room. Or you could just lie back and listen to music on that wonderful hi-fi, blasting it as loud as you wished over the powerful speakers. "What is Mr. McBain's favorite?" she asked Ronson, running her finger across titles that ranged from Bach to George Benson, Vivaldi to Roxy Music, and Mozart to Motown.

Bob Ronson looked surprised. "Mr. McBain usually plays the music he thinks his guests would like to hear. I don't know what he plays when he is alone."

Venetia wondered about that. Morgan had said that there were many women eager for a place in his father's life. Could Fitz McBain often be alone? It was odd being in the home of a man you merely knew about but didn't even know the appearance of. She couldn't recall having seen pictures of him in the newspapers, but then Morgan had said he was a very private man. He must look a bit like the older men on *Dallas*, she decided, sort of burly and middle aged, a ranch hand in a business suit.

India picked up a cue and potted a red on the snooker table, admiring the Victorian fringed lampshades. "This is a terrific room," she announced. "Let's make it our headquarters while we're here."

"I agree." Paris flopped onto a sofa. "It feels more like home."

"Please treat it as if it were your home," said Ronson. "No one will disturb you here. Now, if you're ready, I'll show you your rooms. I'm sure you'd like to rest."

A burly man from the Bel-Air Patrol was waiting for them in the hall. But for the gun at his hip, he could have been the twin of the guards who had accompanied them earlier. Did they breed them specially for the job? wondered Paris, as the man, serious-faced and respectful, informed them that the patrol was on alert and the house would be completely protected at all times. They would have no need to worry about photographers with telephoto lenses climbing trees to snatch a photograph, nor of TV cameras and gossip writers lurking at the gates. His men would see to that.

"Well, that's a relief," commented India. She understood the ways of paparazzi well enough to know that a brief dip in the swimming pool on a hot day could be snapped and captioned "Haven daughter swims in Hollywood sunshine while inquest decides cause of mother's death." It was not a nice world. And the inquest was to take place the day after to-morrow. Thankfully she followed her sisters to the refuge of her room.

❧ 3 ❧

NEW YORK

Raymunda Ortiz lounged in the center of the king-size bed, wearing a virginal white cotton robe, clicking through the television channels with the re-mote control while keeping one ear open to catch what Fitz was saying on the phone. He was *always* on the phone, always talking business. She could swear that phone grew out of his hand—except, of course, when his hands were better employed making love to her. A glance at her white robe—the finest Swiss cotton, embroidered with girlish flowers and ruffled at the neck and hem—confirmed that it *was* virginal; she didn't want him to think she was some kind of whore in sleazy satin. No, she wanted Fitz to understand that no matter what went on be-tween them in bed, she was a *lady,* the sort of lady who could decorate his table, make his home into a social meeting place for the *best* people—a lady suit-able to be his wife. And it was true, she was a well-brought-up Brazilian girl from a good family, mar-

102

ried at eighteen, widowed at twenty-eight, and at thirty-two looking hard for a second husband. Who better than Fitz McBain?

She glanced at him across the room. Fitz, naked but for a towel wrapped around his middle, leaned casually against the table, the phone propped beneath his chin. His dark hair was still wet from the shower, and little rivulets of water trickled down his muscular back. Raymunda thought she'd like to lick each of those drops from his skin . . . if he'd ever get off the damned phone! Impatiently, she changed the channel to a game show, lowering the sound and listening to Fitz.

"Throw the job open to tender, Morgan," he was saying. "It's the only way. And don't touch those Liberian tankers—they've lost two in the past six months."

He was talking to his son. Morgan was a good-looking young man . . . maybe if things didn't go too well with Fitz she should try him instead? No, at thirty-two she was better off with the father; after all, that's where the power was.

Raymunda glanced again at Fitz's back. The drops of water had trickled down beneath his towel. She'd been waiting here, in the virginal robe, when he came back from wherever he'd been last—Hamburg, she thought he'd said. He'd gone straight into the shower after a brief hello, and then he'd got on the phone to Morgan. He'd never even noticed the robe. She looked at it doubtfully. Maybe it was *too* virginal? She unfastened the buttons to the waist and allowed it to fall open a little, displaying her ample and very pretty bosom to advantage. Her olive skin looked smooth and she ran a finger around her nipple, enjoying the responses of her own body.

The real trouble was knowing how to play it with Fitz. It was difficult sometimes when he was making love to her to remember to use ladylike words, and yet she wasn't sure whether a man from his background understood that even ladies liked to fuck? It was a dilemma and playing a dual role was hard work.

"Fitz," she called impatiently, "I *need* you."

He turned his head and smiled at her.

The trouble was, he really turned her on—she liked his tall, spare, muscular body, hardened from those years spent wildcatting in the backlands of Texas, and she liked his thick brownblack hair and his face with its oddly jutting cheekbones and deeply set, dark blue eyes. And she was turned on, too, by the power of his money—it was breathtaking, that kind of power. When you were with Fitz McBain, you felt that the world was yours and that rich men made their own rules. Power was so exciting.

Raymunda slid back the white robe tantalizingly, posing against the pillows; she wanted him now.

"Fitz," she called again, "come here, I want you." He waved an impatient arm and went on with his conversation.

"Goddamn it!" Raymunda sat up again and

clicked channels furiously.

"Wait!" Fitz slammed down the phone and strode across the room to the bed. "Put the news back on, channel two."

"Channel Two! Damn it, I've been waiting here for you to—"

Fitz grabbed the remote control and pushed the button. Channel Two news showed pictures of Jenny Haven and then switched to the scene outside the coroner's office in Los Angeles. Damn, Raymunda, had turned down the sound.

". . . the autopsy showed," said the reporter, "that while there had been a certain amount of alcohol in her blood, Jenny wasn't drunk, and while there was also some evidence of barbiturates, they would hardly have been sufficient to cause heart failure— though there is always the possibility of an unusual reaction with the alcohol. Perhaps Jenny simply couldn't sleep and had taken herself out to the ocean for some fresh air? But why the evening dress? Was she meeting a lover? No one has come forward to claim that privilege. It was stated in court that Jenny was a good and experienced driver and the night was a clear one with no mist blowing in from the ocean. So—was it a tragic accident that took Jenny Haven from us? Or was it the last deliberate act of a woman, saddened at growing older, parted from the three daughters she barely knew, and unable to face life alone?" The reporter turned to gesture at the courthouse behind him. "The coroner this morning found no option but to record an open verdict on Jenny Haven's death."

The picture switched back to the newscaster. "Well, a sad end for a woman we all must have loved at some time in our lives. . . ."

Fitz switched off the television set and sat on the edge of the bed. Now, he supposed, the newspapers would really go to town on the story. Had she? Or hadn't she? They'd drag up every bit of her past that they could—and heaven knows Jenny had been a very indiscreet woman. Fitz figured that right now there must be quite a few people in Hollywood who were praying that Jenny had never kept a diary, or that her housekeeper for the past twenty years would remain loyal and not be tempted by some enormous bribe from the press to tell all.

And of course those three daughters would be the prime target. He'd caught a glimpse of them on the news, running through the air terminal followed by the press. They were as defenseless and vulnerable as their mother had always seemed to be. Only, beneath that softly beautiful surface Jenny was known to be made of steel, tempered by her years of struggle and ambition. She'd packed a lifetime of rejection and being used into those bruising years between thirteen and nineteen—before she became a star. It was something he and Jenny Haven had in common.

"Fitz"—Raymunda ran her fingernails along his spine—"what shall we do first tonight, Fitz?" He hardly seemed to have heard her. She tried again, sliding her hands around his waist, pressing her naked breasts against his back. "I know what I'd like to do." Bending her head she ran her pointed little tongue along the smooth flesh of his shoulder.

Fitz pushed away her hands and stood up abruptly. "Go get dressed, Raymunda."

"Dressed? But why? I'm here—waiting for you. Don't you like me in this robe?" She knew the virginal act had been a mistake, he liked his sex rougher than that. Raymunda ripped off the embroidered Swiss cotton and sprawled across the bed, stretching her long, muscular legs. He'd always liked her legs, he liked the way she gripped him with those strong muscles when he was on top of her.

"Get dressed. We'll go out later."

Raymunda flounced off the bed, dragging the robe around her shoulders and striding furiously toward the door. He hadn't even noticed her, he'd drawn back the curtains and was just staring out into the night.

Through the window the turrets and towers of Manhattan sparkled with a million lights, a scene that brought Fitz unfailing pleasure—though he was never sure whether it was the magnificence of the city itself, or the reminder that he, a kid from the Texas backlands, had made it all the way to being a prince of this toughest of cities, and his palace was this rooftop eyrie from where he could view his kingdom. Tonight he didn't notice the view.

A faint smile lit his severe, attractive face as he remembered that afternoon when he had fallen in love with Jenny Haven. He was thirteen and he had

107

spent his single hard-earned dollar on a seat at the movies and a bag of popcorn that had soon been discarded, forgotten in the surge of emotion he had felt when Jenny's disarming blue eyes had gazed directly into his, smiling at him from the screen of that little Texan flea-pit movie-house. It was the first time he had ever truly known what it was to want a woman, feeling that thrusting urge in his groin not just for some youthful fantasy about the girl with big tits and sticky red lipstick behind the counter of the soda fountain but for this wonderful blond creature of scented flesh and satin lips—for that's how he knew she would be.

He had grown up because of Jenny Haven. Because of her he had known suddenly that there was more to sex than the hurried mutual gropings for experience and curiosity that were his infrequent lot right then. You "made love" to a woman like Jenny Haven.

He had sat through the movie twice and left the cinema only when it closed, begging one of the studio stills that decorated the glassed display panel in the foyer from the amused cashier. That picture of Jenny in sweater and shorts, perched on a stool, a finger held under her coquettishly tilted chin, had adorned the flimsy walls of his many cheap rooms as he wandered through Texas. He had sent for others, and even after he had met and married Ellen, he had still kept them. He believed it was because of what he learned vicariously from Jenny Haven that he had known how to treat

108

women. "You make me feel sexy and beautiful," Ellen had told him, even when they were desperately poor and living in that shabby trailer in the middle of nowhere.

He had met Jenny once, years later, at a party in Beverly Hills. He had been nervous knowing that she was to be there. What if meeting her destroyed the image that he had built up in his mind? She had changed his life once, for the better; reality could destroy the myth. But it had been just like the first time he had seen her on the screen. True, the surroundings were more luxurious, this time it was the private screening room of a Hollywood producer, and this time Jenny had been seated next to him, and, despite his experience, his sophistication, his power, position, and wealth, the memory of that first boyish sexual urge and her proximity had given him an erection that he prayed he could control. When she had leaned over to whisper conspiratorially in his ear how boring the movie was, the touch of her soft breath on his cheek, the slight pressure of her arm against his, and the faint drift of her perfume had almost destroyed him.

He could have tried to win Jenny Haven. He had more than enough to offer. Women found him attractive, they enjoyed his lovemaking and his hard body, they liked his reputation as the rough backlands guy who had made good, and of course they enjoyed the power of his money. But then Jenny had been in the middle of an affair with the Hollywood producer, the timing hadn't been right, and anyway he had still been afraid of destroying the illusion.

Sadly, he pressed the button that closed the curtains, shutting out New York's glittering starry night.

Tomorrow or the next day they would bury Jenny, and he, Fitz McBain, who had always been in love with her, would see that it was done properly. He turned back to his desk and picked up the phone again.

"At least that's over," said India, curled up on the big black sofa in the summerhouse.

"And at least they didn't say it was suicide." Venetia's voice sounded relieved.

"And now there's the funeral." Paris couldn't bear the silence that followed her words, and she walked across to the hi-fi, putting on an album at random. It was Ciccolini playing Erik Satie, and the cool, isolated notes of the piano floated across the room. She lay back against the cushions, staring at the silvery motes of dust caught in a beam of sunlight from the window. October was warm in Hollywood, thank God—Jenny would have hated to be buried in the cold and the rain.

"None of us has suitable clothes," said India at last. "We can't possibly go to a funeral like this—and how can we go shopping? Imagine what the press would say about that."

Despite the private guards, cameramen still cruised the road outside the house, poking their long lenses through the gates, snapping anyone or anything that left. So far none had penetrated the grounds and their privacy, deterred no doubt by the two German shepherd dogs patrolling the wall. But what kept the press out, kept them in, trapped by Jenny's fame and the public's curiosity.

Paris picked up the phone. "I'll ask Ronson what to do. He seems to know everything."

He answered at once. "Oh, Mr. Ronson. It will be necessary for my sisters and I to have some suitable clothes for the . . . funeral. Obviously, we cannot go out, and I wonder if it would be possible to have a store send round some things on approval? Oh. Oh, I see. But what about the sizes? Really? Yes. Yes, that's very kind. Thank you, Mr. Ronson."

Paris sank back into the cushions. "Apparently we don't have to worry about it," she said in an awed voice. "Mr. McBain called an hour ago with instructions about everything. He's been in touch with Jenny's agent, Bill Kaufmann, and her lawyer, Stanley Reubin, about the funeral arrangements. He even discussed the pallbearers with Bill and has called each one personally to ask if they would accept that honor." Just in case, she thought cynically, they might have wanted to refuse. Mr. McBain was a man who left nothing to chance. "The funeral is to be at St. Columba's in Beverly Hills and he's taken care of the seating arrangements and the ushers. He's even selected a plaque to be erected at Forest Lawn—with our approval, of course, but Ronson says it's perfectly plain—just her name and the dates. McBain has thought of it all. Even our clothes. I. Magnin are sending round a selection of suitable things for us to choose from. Mr. Ronson guessed our sizes, as he didn't want to disturb us. Accurately, I might add."

Their amazed eyes met hers. "Fitz McBain did all that?" asked Venetia.

"He did. He thought of absolutely everything." Paris sighed as she contemplated Fitz McBain's power.

"But why? We don't know him. I only met Morgan once, a few nights ago. . . ."

"Then either it was love at first sight, or Fitz McBain was a Jenny Haven fan." Paris stretched out on the sofa luxuriously. "Either way, it feels very nice to be looked after . . ." She didn't add "for a change" but the words seemed to hang in the air unspoken. In the easy luxury of the McBain compound, Amadeo Vitrazzi and her struggle for success and recognition of her talent seemed very far away.

India began to prowl the floor restlessly.

"Being a princess must feel a lot like this," she said, thinking longingly of Rome's teeming thoroughfares and crowded cafés. "I'll be glad when it's over. I can't bear being trapped in this house."

It, thought Venetia, is the funeral. And it would take place the day after tomorrow. How was she to bear it, when maybe if she had come home when Jenny wanted, she would have still been alive. . . .

"Vennie," said India warningly, "there's no use getting upset all over again. Surely we've cried enough!"

Venetia stood up suddenly and headed for the door.

"Vennie! Where are you going?" India hurried

112

after her.

"To the kitchen," she said with a sigh. "I think we need a cup of tea."

Fitz McBain ignored the flashing red light on his office telephone, indicating that there was another call for him, and instead pressed the buzzer that meant he wasn't to be disturbed. He was watching Channel 2's six o'clock news report.

Paris in stark black silk and broad-brimmed hat took Bill Kaufmann's arm as she stepped from the car, lifting her chin defiantly at the television cameras. Her escort walked her rapidly toward the church door, where she turned to check that her sisters were all right. India, wearing a simple black linen suit and holding tightly to Stanley Reubin's hand, almost ran the length of the path. Venetia hesitated as she emerged from the limousine. She wore a short-sleeved black silk dress with a jaunty bow at the neck, and as she took the arm of Jake Matthews, superstar of the screen for two decades, four times Jenny's costar and possibly onetime lover, her stricken eyes fastened on the camera lens in despair. Then, dropping her gaze, she pulled her hat lower over her brow and, helped by Jake, followed her sisters into the church.

The television news summary switched quickly to the scene of Jenny Haven's flower-garlanded coffin being borne up the steps of the church, and to the watching crowds. The pretty red-haired gossip reporter, who considered herself a bigger star than the

113

faded Jenny Haven—after all, she was on TV every night and that was *now*, not twenty years ago—continued her glib narration.

"Among this crowd are many of the people who found Jenny Haven to be a true friend—the commissary waitresses at the studio who she always remembered at Christmas, the grips and carpenters, the wardrobe people, and the hairdressers, all of whom worked hard to make things go smoothly on the set of her films and whose families she remembered to ask about by name. There are the drivers who picked her up to take her to the studio at five-thirty in the morning, a time when few of us look our best, but who swear that even then she was lovely. Yes, around the studios of our town Jenny was known among these 'little' people as a generous woman. Generous with her time, listening to their problems, and often generous with a loan that was really a gift because she didn't believe in loans.

"There were many facets to Jenny Haven, the glamorous movie star who we all knew on the screen, the accomplished actress who could make us laugh, as she did in *Matchless*, or cry, as she did in her Oscar-winning performance as Maggie in *A Time Gone Forever*. Or the difficult star who demanded the best from everyone, whether it was the performance of her costar or the service at the best hotel, because she *earned* it, damn it. Of course there is a facet to Jenny that we don't know about—Jenny as the mother of the three beautiful daughters you saw here at her funeral today. That was the woman few people knew, and they remain the mystery of Jenny Haven's life."

The cameras again followed the Haven daughters as they left the church and got into their car, and then focused on the hearse that held their mother's coffin.

"Today Hollywood said its farewells to possibly one of the most loved and one of the most envied women of our time."

Fitz switched off the television set, walked across to the table, and poured himself a bourbon. Swirling his glass he stared at it moodily. Who would have thought that the youngest one—Venetia—would look so like Jenny? It was uncanny seeing that familiar wide blue gaze staring at him like that of a stricken doe. The eldest girl, Paris, was a sophisticated beauty, very chic and with some of Jenny's proud, steely quality. India was a curly-haired gamine in her severe suit.

He knocked back his drink and poured another. Well, it was over now. And so, at last, was his long, solitary romance with Jenny Haven.

❦ 4 ❦

Bill Kaufmann's red Porsche was, for once, well under the speed limit as he drove along Pacific Coast Highway toward Malibu. The sun felt hotter than it had any right to at this time of year and, closing the windows, he turned on the air conditioning. He was still sweating. Goddamn it, he

115

wasn't looking forward to this meeting one little bit! Why the hell did Jenny have to do what she did? Accident or not, it was goddamn thoughtless of her to leave it all to him and Stan Reubin. What were they going to say to those girls? She'd pampered them all their lives, doling out the luxuries until they'd left school, and then just left them to get on with it alone. He'd argued with her about that, saying she couldn't just abandon them. "But I haven't abandoned them, Bill," shed replied calmly, "I've provided them with all the assets they need in the world and now I'm giving them their freedom."

She'd been sitting in the makeup chair at Burbank Studios while the girl fussed with blushers and lip-gloss and he'd known it was the wrong time to discuss it, and somehow after that there never seemed to be a right time. "Don't worry, Bill." She'd laughed. "I'll always be around to catch them if they fall." Yeah? Well look at them now, Jenny, they're falling and where the hell are you?

He and Myra had been puzzled when she sent them off to Europe. Almost everyone they knew had grandparents who had fled Europe for a better life in America and Jenny had wanted to reverse the process. Where in the world, he and Myra had asked each other, could you find a better place to raise kids than easy, affluent Beverly Hills? Half the world wished they could be so lucky as to live in Beverly Hills! *And* she had the beach house. Wouldn't those girls have been better off there at weekends than at those fancy schools?

Bill Kaufmann had been a Hollywood agent for twenty-five years, during which time he had, with some justification, earned himself the reputation of being "a killer." He didn't like being stuck with that reputation but privately admitted that there had been times when ruthlessness had meant winning, and Bill Kaufmann was destined to be a winner. As a young man with ambition, and streetwise, beat-up good looks, he had maneuvered himself into the position of confidant and friend to the young Jenny Haven, ultimately undermining her relationship with her manager. He had taken over from there as her manager and agent. That is, until three years ago.

Hell, it had been a relief not to have to go through the same endless scene over and over again . . . why hadn't he got her the part in the Hofmann movie and why, when she'd expected the lead in the multimillion-dollar TV miniseries, had he come back with an offer of the part of the older mistress who gets killed off in the first forty minutes?

Bill lit another cigarette and swung the Porsche smoothly through the gates into Malibu Colony, acknowledging the salute of the guard as he turned reluctantly toward Jenny's beach house and his meeting with her daughters. As he parked the car in front of the high, pink-washed stucco wall that screened the house from the street, he hoped Stan Reubin had this under control, because he sure as hell didn't.

It was Venetia who answered his ring. "Hello,

117

Bill." She kissed the man who had been considered their family friend as long as she could remember. "I'm glad you're here. It feels so strange without Jenny."

"You all right, kitten?" He put his arm around her shoulders as they walked into the spacious room that fronted the ocean. The tide was high today, rippling at the foot of the broad wooden deck where the other two sisters were waiting in the shade of the blue awning.

"I'm okay now. I wasn't sure how I was going to get through it all, but at least the worst is over. Come and sit in the sunshine, it's such a beautiful day."

Bill slid off his jacket and tossed it across the back of a chair, bending to kiss first India and then Paris. "Hi, girls, how're ya doing?"

"I suppose we're all feeling relieved—and that's certainly a whole lot better than what we were feeling before." Paris smiled as she got to her feet. "Can I get you something? A cold beer? Some white wine?"

The beer sounded tempting, but his wife would kill him if he went off his diet—or else the beer would. "Just a Perrier, love—no lime."

He leaned against the deck rail, tapping his fingers nervously. Stan Reubin should be here any minute and then they'd get on with this farce. He lit his fifth cigarette of the morning. He shouldn't have and he wondered again if the relief of smoking it were worth the guilt and anxiety he would feel afterward. Goddamn it, what with diet and exercise, no booze

118

and no cigarettes, self-denial had become a way of life; if it weren't for cocaine and sex, where would Hollywood be?

"There's no surf today." India leaned companionably on the rail next to him, gazing at the ocean as it sloped in glassy waves, tumbling in faint, frothy ripples on the sand. A patch of kelp floated darkly, beyond the waves.

"Remember when you taught me to surf all those years ago? I must have been only about seven." She laughed, remembering herself as a skinny, bucktoothed seven-year-old. "I'll let you into a secret, Bill. You were quite a hero of mine for a long time when I was a kid. I thought you were more handsome than any of Jenny's boyfriends and I liked you a whole lot better. I thought you liked me, too, but I figured seven was a bit young for marriage so I decided I'd be noble and unselfish and allow you to marry Jenny—at least then I would have you around forever. But it didn't work out that way."

Her amused brown eyes gazed at his battered face inquiringly. With his mane of silver hair, deep-set eyes, and misleadingly benign expression, he was still quite an attractive man.

"Just for the record, Bill, did you ever ask her?"

He ground out his cigarette impatiently. "No, India. I didn't. Oh, I was in love with her all right— on and off in the beginning and in between the fights, and there were times when we were tempted to take it farther, but thank God common sense prevailed. Your mother and I managed to remain

119

friends for most of our lives, until . . ."

"Until? What, Bill?"

Stan Reubin's famous, booming courtroom voice sounded from inside the house and Kaufmann turned from India in relief, ignoring her question.

"Ah, here's Stan, at last." Taking her arm he walked back into the sun-filled room. He paused for a minute at the door. "And, India, thanks for the compliment."

She grinned back at him. "You're welcome."

"There you are, Bill." Stan Reubin glanced at him coldly. It was his view that Bill Kaufmann should have been able to manipulate Jenny better than he had. After all, wasn't that what he was there for?

"Come and sit down, girls, and let us get on with this. Not that I have much to say, but after I'm done I'm sure you'll have a million questions."

He leaned against the mantel of the empty fire-place with the three girls lined up on the white sofa in front of him. It brought back a memory of some long-ago Christmas with three excited little girls in party dresses and Mary Janes on the sofa in that same house, waiting for the moment when the presents were to be unwrapped. The memory upset him and Stan didn't like to be upset. Emotion got him nervous. He began to pace the floor.

"You know, it's odd," said Paris, "that although we've never spent much time here, this is the house I always think of as home. Only of course without Jenny it will never be the same—'home' to us always meant wherever Jenny was."

120

Stan cleared his throat—a thing he never did in the courtroom. Better get it over with.

"Before I begin," he said silkily, "I want you to know that both Bill and I have agreed that you can call upon us for any advice you need—at any time. You understand?"

They nodded silently, their eyes fixed on him, waiting.

"Your mother, in the last few years, took her business and her career affairs out of our hands. The movie offers weren't coming as often, and the parts were shrinking. Not as many movies were being made, and those that were called for a new generation of actress—not only younger, but of a different type. It wasn't that your mother wasn't a good actress, but the lead roles required someone more contemporary and Jenny wasn't suitable. There were parts she could have had on television—she could have made that transition easily, according to Bill—and these blockbuster miniseries had plenty of openings, but never the lead. I'm afraid she blamed Bill for that, and when I took his side and tried to convince her to look at her career in a different light, remembering that she was no longer thirty-nine and that the business had changed, she accused us both of being traitors and told us to get out of her life."

Stan paused and mopped his brow with an immaculate white linen handkerchief. "She was backed up in this decision by the man she was then living with—"

"John Fields," responded Venetia automatically.

She had met him once on a visit home and even to her naive eyes he had seemed so transparently maneuvering that she had questioned her mother about him. Jenny had dismissed her questions impatiently, telling her that she was becoming too British in her outlook and it was often easy to misinterpret American enthusiasm for aggression, and that she should know better.

"Right. John Fields. Jenny allowed him to take charge of her affairs, and then, when they split up after a couple of years, it was Rory Grant. He was twenty-four and a struggling young nobody actor and she fell for him, head over heels as they say. She nurtured Rory, she groomed him, she took him to Rodeo Drive and let them dress him until he achieved that carefully casual 'style.' They experimented with his hair until they found the shaggy blond look that those in the know decided was exactly right. She paid for his acting lessons and the dance and workout sessions, she rehearsed him for auditions, and as Jenny could still get *anyone* in this town on the phone, she called them all—heads of studios, producers, directors, and told them of this new, young superstar in the making. Rory Grant got to meet everybody."

Bill lit another cigarette. "She was living out her thwarted ambitions in him," he added, "and the bastard knew it. Not that he was unkind to her," he added hastily, seeing their downcast faces, "nor did he ever make her look foolish. He was a nice enough guy—he had what she needed and she offered him what he needed. They seemed quite happy together. For a while."

"Unfortunately," said Stan, "he wanted to help her in return. He tried to straighten out the mess that John Fields had left her affairs in, and instead of turning to us—or at least getting other professional help as we begged her—she allowed him to do it. Bill and I were on speaking terms with Jenny again, but it wasn't like before, and when we tried to offer advice she thought we were criticizing Grant."

"A year ago"—Bill picked up the story—"Rory was offered the lead in a pilot film for a new TV series, and almost at once things started to go wrong between them. He was working—she wasn't. He left the house at five-thirty every morning and got home at eight o'clock at night. All he wanted to do was have a bite to eat, go over his lines for the next day, and be asleep by nine. Jenny was lonely—it wasn't his fault. She knew only too well what that sort of schedule was like, and by God, it was what she had worked with him to achieve. But having gotten it, it began to turn sour on her. There were rows. He tried to appease her." Bill lit another cigarette from the butt of the first. "Listen, girls, Rory was basically a nice kid. Sure he took what she offered, why not? But he wasn't like Fields—he wasn't an exploiter." Bill shrugged. "The rows became a nightly occurrence, the strain began to tell on his work, and when the TV series was picked up by the network Rory knew he had to do something about it—after all, he had his career to consider now. They split up six months ago."

Paris chose her words carefully. "Are you telling me that there might have been a good reason for Jenny to take her life? Is that it? Was she so upset that he'd left her?"

"Don't you believe it! Jenny was a fighter—I never knew any man to get the better of her. Jenny didn't kill herself for Rory Grant!"

"Is that an opinion," asked Paris bitterly, "or do you have proof?"

"No one has any proof," replied Stan. "Jenny was still a lovely woman. There could have been other men, even marriage if she'd wanted it."

"She never did." India leaned her head against the cushions wearily. "She told me that the only man she would ever have married was my father. I think she still loved him."

"Look, girls." Stan checked his gold Rolex impatiently; time was getting on and he had a golf game at the club at eleven-thirty. "There's no point in going over the whole thing again. Personally, I believe it was an accident and I don't suppose going for a drive at four in the morning was that unusual for someone like Jenny—she turned night into day when she wanted to."

He glanced apprehensively at Venetia, who was staring silently out of the window at the sun shining on the ocean. She wasn't planning anything crazy, was she? "You know how unpredictable Jenny was. . . ." He cleared his throat again nervously, taking a sheaf of papers from his briefcase.

124

"We've got to talk business now, though to be honest there's not much to talk about. I'm sorry to tell you that in the past few years your mother and her new 'business advisers' managed to dissipate a considerable fortune. We believe Fields steered a great deal of it into his own pockets, although we have no concrete evidence of that—by which I mean none that would stand up in court. However, the bulk was lost in bad investments and property deals. How anyone could lose money on property deals in this town amazes me, but Jenny seems to have accomplished it. She paid top dollar for land she was led to believe would increase enormously in value once new highways and developments went in. Somebody misinformed her. Wherever she bought was the wrong direction for the new developments: Silicon Valley, for instance—she owns land fifty miles too far away.

"She picked up expensive 'bargains' in prime lakeside residential property at Mammoth Lake. She must have been the only one who hadn't heard that they'd been having a series of quakes there and that her land was on a major fault line—you can't give away property there. It's the same story, time after time. She speculated on the commodities market, and even experienced men can lose their shirts in a couple of months doing that. Your mother gambled on making big profits and she lost."

Stan lifted his head from the papers. "What can I tell you, girls?" He shrugged. "It's all here for you to look at."

Three pairs of stunned eyes met his and he

125

dropped his gaze hastily back to the documents in his hands.

"It's not true! It *can't* be true!" wailed Paris. She couldn't bear it, she just couldn't bear it . . . she didn't want to hear what she knew he was going to say next.

It was Venetia who said it. "But she worked so hard *all her life,* she *can't* have lost all that money!"

Stan looked at Bill Kaufmann, who avoided his gaze and stared silently out of the window. It was fucking amazing, thought Stan, how fascinating that ocean was today.

"Stan, my mother was a very rich woman," said India, trying hard to be calm and matter-of-fact. "Surely part of her fortune was tied up in secure investments and legitimate property? This house, for instance, must be worth a lot of money now."

"Your mother bought this house twenty years ago for seventy thousand dollars. With the spiraling property values in Los Angeles over the past few years, it's now worth four million."

Paris felt relief sweep through her; of course, there was still the house left—and the one on North Canyon Drive in Beverly Hills. "Thank God," she said. "I thought you were going to tell us it was all gone."

Stan cleared his throat again. "The house was mortgaged by Jenny three years ago, and a second mortgage was taken out last year. I'm sorry, Paris, but in effect this house belongs to the First National and City Bank. It's the same story with the Beverly

126

Hills house."

Tears trembled on Paris's lashes as her future receded even farther down a dark tunnel.

"Perhaps it would be better if you told us exactly what there is left," said India. "Then at least we'll know where we stand."

Stan put down the papers and folded his arms, giving them the benefit of his best courtroom pose of sympathy. "Very well, girls. This is it. The houses and their contents will have to be sold to repay the banks and certain other debts. The rest of Jenny's investments are worthless. What comes to you intact is an insurance policy that she took out when she was seventeen. It must have seemed like a lot of money to Jenny then. . . . The amount is ten thousand dollars."

"Ten thousand!"

India ignored the horrified gasp from Paris. Getting up from the sofa she began to pace the floor—it seemed easier to take things standing up; it was obvious someone had better face up to this squarely, and as Venetia seemed to be stunned into silence and Paris was on the verge of becoming hysterical, it had better be her.

"I see. And what about the cars—the Rolls and"—she remembered too late that the Mercedes had been wrecked—"and the jewelry? Jenny had so many beautiful pieces."

"I'm afraid whatever's left will have to go; she'd borrowed so much, y'know, this past year. And now that she's dead the creditors are nervous—

and impatient."

"If only we'd *known*," said Venetia, suddenly emerging from her trancelike state, "we could have helped her. Why didn't someone tell us? *You*, Bill, you knew!"

"I didn't, kitten! I swear I didn't. I knew she and her boyfriend were speculating on the property market, but who wasn't? I promise you, girls, I had no idea of the extent of it."

"She told no one." Stan Reubin paced the floor as if he were prowling a courtroom looking for loopholes in the defense. "It's in the past, girls, you've got to face it. Jenny left you exactly ten thousand dollars." He paused and faced them, hands behind his back, brows lowered in a benevolent scowl. "However, there's no reason for you to worry about the debts. Money's tight this year, what with the pressure on tax shelters and expenses being so high, but Bill and I have agreed to waive any money owed to us by Jenny's estate. And naturally there will be no charge for my services."

He paced the length of the room and then swiveled on his heel and faced them, smiling. "It's not easy getting your hands on *cash* these days, but if you ever needed a few hundred, we'd see what we could do."

Paris felt certain that no one on earth would ever know what an effort it cost her to keep her voice even when she wanted to kill Stan Reubin.

"Stan, Bill, we appreciate your offer—as old *friends* of our mother. But you see, Jenny gave us everything she felt we would ever need. She decided long ago we must make it on our own, just the way she did. It's what she wanted and we three will abide by her wishes."

She glared coldly at the two men who had called themselves her mother's friends and who, she knew, had made vast sums from Jenny's talent and hard work. "The ten thousand will be more than enough for us."

Paris didn't know whether she sat down or whether her legs gave out from under her. All she knew was that this time she hadn't let Jenny down. She had saved her pride—and her mother's.

"It was what Jenny wanted," agreed India. "It's no different from the way it's been since we left school. We've all managed, one way or another, to earn our own living."

"Absolutely," confirmed Venetia. She was only two years out of school and her smile may have been shaky, but her resolve wasn't.

Stan pushed the documents back into his case and prepared to leave. Shit, you had to admire those girls. They were tough little cookies. They'd sat here in this room expecting to hear that they were millionairesses and they'd taken the blow on the chin. There was true Jenny Haven steel there, all right. Maybe she'd brought them up right after all. Anyway, *he* was off the hook.

"I wonder," said Paris hesitantly, "—do you think it would be possible for each of us to choose something, just *one* thing of Jenny's, to keep? Surely the courts couldn't object to that? I mean, I know it all has to be sold, but if we could just *buy* a memento, something to remind us of her. We would pay for them from our ten thousand."

There was the loophole! Stan grasped at it with relief. There was the way to come out of this as the good guy. He'd been a bit afraid of nasty rumors when the story hit the papers—everyone knew he and Bill had been involved with Jenny for years. He'd be able to "lose" a few bits and pieces of personal items in the inventory of her assets, and after all, it was only right that the girls should want something of their mother's. His wife would be the first to support that point of view—*and* she'd make sure to tell everyone on the Beverly Hills gossip circuit how kind Stan had been to them personally.

"Choose what you want," he said magnanimously. "There'll be no need to pay. I'll see it's squared with the estate."

"But if there are creditors . . . ?"

"Please"—Stan was wearing his most winning courtroom smile—"choose what you want. Let me work out the details."

Venetia walked to the portrait of Jenny that hung to the right of the fireplace. It was Jenny at twenty-eight, slender and supple in a gauzy blue evening dress, diamonds sparkling in her blond hair and the familiar wide blue gaze that was so nearly Venetia's own. All her life Venetia had loved that painting. The artist had seen Jenny as she saw herself, the real woman behind the glossy façade. There was a fleeting undercurrent of self-mockery in the smile, as if even then she was aware of playing the role of the movie star, having her portrait painted, and there was a touch of vulnerability that Jenny rarely let anyone see. It was a tender portrait, and for Venetia, it captured her mother exactly.

She ran a finger across the paint as if wanting to touch Jenny. "This has always meant a lot to me," she said. "I've no idea what it's worth . . . ?"

"Take it, take it," said Stan. "I told you not to worry—it's yours." It wouldn't have been worth that much at auction—though possibly the studios might have paid a decent price . . . still, the kid wanted it, didn't she? He lit an immense Romeo y Julieta, puffing on the cigar and waiting.

"I don't know whether I should ask for this," said India, "because like Vennie, I've no idea what it's worth. I guess it's expensive, but it does mean a lot to me. . . ."

"Yeah? What is it?" asked Bill.

"Do you remember the ring she always wore? The ruby? My father gave it to her in Kashmir when she told him that she was pregnant with me. It was their 'engagement ring.' I never saw her without it." Her sad brown eyes met Stan's. "I would dearly like to keep it, if that's possible?"

"Sure. Sure, it's yours, India." Stan spoke quickly before he could change his mind. That was a bit pricier than he had bargained for. Still, didn't he remember that ruby being flawed?

"And Paris? What about you?" India looked anx-

131

iously at her sister. Paris looked so pale, she was afraid she was going to faint.

"Jenny came to see me a couple of years ago," said Paris, so softly that it was as though she were speaking to herself. "It was winter and the weather was icy and crisp, and the sun shone. Jenny was wrapped in this amazing fur that she'd bought from Fende, a softly sheared mink, dyed to such an odd olive tint. She looked so Parisian in it, and for once we looked like mother and daughter." She turned to look at her sisters. "It would make me happy to have that coat."

"Done," said Stan, glad to get out of this one without it costing *too* much; it would have been embarrassing to have to go back on his word. Picking up his briefcase, he opened the door. "So. If you need any advice, you know where to come."

Paris doubted that they would.

Bill Kaufmann felt pleased with himself. It had been easier than he had thought, no tears, no recriminations—no fuss. "That's everything taken care of, then," he said, following Stan through the courtyard.

"Right, Bill," said India, "everything's taken care of." She held out his jacket. "You forgot this."

Bill slung the jacket over his shoulder and headed for the street.

"Thanks for everything, Bill. Drive carefully now, in that fast car," called India.

Did her tone hold a touch of irony? Surely not. After all he'd done? No one could expect him to do more. Could they?

"Well, then, it's good-bye, I suppose." Stan shifted his cigar from his right hand to his left and offered his firm grip to each girl in turn. "Perhaps Mrs. Reubin and I'll be over in Paris in the spring. She likes to get around—do a bit of shopping there, ya know? Listen, Bill, what's that restaurant you raved about? Lasserre? How'd you rate that one, Paris? Good, huh? Well, you count on joining us for dinner there one evening. Something to look forward to, right? And that goes for you other girls as well, if you're in town. Be quite a family reunion." Clamping the big cigar back in his mouth he headed purposefully toward the gleaming, blue Rolls Camargue parked behind the Porsche.

Bill Kaufmann quickly kissed each girl on the cheek. "Anytime you're back here," he called, making for his car, "let me know. Myra'd love to have you stay . . . she was very fond of Jenny."

He slid behind the wheel, waiting impatiently for Stan to turn the Rolls. Why the fuck didn't he hurry up? Thank God, that was it, he could be off! He shifted from neutral into first, enjoying the growl of the engine as it responded to the pressure of his foot. At least it hadn't come out that he was now Rory Grant's agent and Stan was Rory's lawyer . . . not that there was anything wrong with that. Bill lit another cigarette. It was just show biz!

He pressed the button to lower the window, leaning out ready to wave and smile, but the heavy wooden gate was already closed. Goddamn, they might have waited, after all he'd done for them.

India flung herself onto the sofa, pounding the cushions angrily with her fists. "Bastards!" she screamed. "They're nothing but a pair of *bastards.*"

"India!" cried Vennie, shocked.

"Can *you* think of a better name for those two? Do you have any idea of *how much* they must have made from Jenny all these years? It's a lot more than you or I are left with, I can assure you. They were employed—*paid*—to *look after her!* God, it makes me sick just to think of it. As soon as things became a bit rough they just left her to it. Oh, no, Vennie, there's no doubt about it—they are a pair of *shits!*"

"Well?" asked Paris. "What happens now? Do we sit here and rehash Jenny's last few years and all her problems and blame her for losing all her money?"

"It wasn't her fault," cried Venetia defensively. "She earned all her money and she had every right to do what she wanted with it."

"Did she, Vennie?" Paris's voice was bitter. "Parents have a responsibility toward their children, you know. Even though she wanted us to make it on our own, I think she might have given *us* a thought before she made all those wild investments—especially as we had no fathers to help us." Paris was close to tears, and she clasped her hands together tightly, digging her nails into the soft palms. She thought of Amadeo and how desperately eager she had been to get his financial backing. "Oh, damn it," she shouted, unable to

134

keep back her resentment any longer. "Why, why, *why* didn't she give me the money I needed! I would have been a better risk than the ones she was taking. Don't you see? She frittered it all on those young men, while I struggled . . ."

Tears spilled down her face and she dashed them away angrily as Venetia and India helplessly watched.

"I'm sorry," sobbed Paris. "I didn't mean it, really I didn't." She fished a Kleenex from her pocket and dabbed her eyes. "You're right, Vennie. She'd earned it the hard way and she had the right to do what she wanted with it. She was foolish, that's all—and alone, and vulnerable." And, she added silently, nobody understands that better than I do.

Venetia stared out of the window at the expanse of ocean and the evil yellow haze of smog on the horizon. A typical Hollywood day. Every time she returned to this town she knew again why she could never live here. Hollywood's blue skies and sunshine and laid-back casual life-style was the surface that camouflaged the scheming and striving for its glittering show-business prizes. The city enclosed the vulnerable in its luxurious tentacles with a gripping relentlessness, until they were trapped in its tinsel values. Jenny had fought against it—and sent her girls away from its seductive pressures—but in the end she had conformed; for her, too, God lived in Hollywood.

Venetia longed suddenly for the anonymous, rain-washed freedom of London and the casual give-and-take of the Lancaster household. So, what next?

135

She would be all right; she had her diploma and she'd meant to begin work catering directors' lunches in the City, and doing parties and dinners. Kate Lancaster had told her of a good agency to use. She imagined India would continue doing what she was doing—things seemed all right with her, except for Fabrizio Paroli, of course, but that was part of the game. It was Paris who was going to be most hurt by this situation. She was so completely alone. As far as Vennie knew there was no man in her life, all she had was her ambition, and even with her undoubted talent it was going to be a long, hard struggle to make her name as a designer now that even the hope of her mother coming to her help had gone. There was just ten thousand dollars for the three of them. Ten thousand dollars . . .

"Paris," she said, startling her sisters from their brooding silence, "I want you to have my share of the ten thousand. Maybe it'll help toward putting together your collection."

Paris's dark blue eyes lit with a gleam of hope. But no, she couldn't. "It's sweet of you, Vennie, but I can't let you do that. You'll probably need it yourself one day."

"You can have my share too," said India. "Didn't you say you were a better investment than Jenny's young men? You've got the only talent in this family, Paris, and all of Jenny's ten thousand dollars will go to underwrite the first Paris Lines collection!"

Paris Lines . . . ten thousand . . . it wasn't nearly enough to do it properly—but it was all they had,

136

and it was a hell of a lot more than zero, which was all she had had before. Oh, God, they were marvelous, her sisters. Paris flung her arms around Vennie and then India in an enormous grateful hug. "Only if you're sure?"

"Of course we're sure."

"It's such a responsibility—*all* the family money." Paris looked at them nervously, her silken black hair framing her anxious face. What if she weren't good enough after all? No! She *was* good, she was sure of that. But so many things could go wrong.

"Don't worry, Paris," said India reassuringly, "the money's yours, with no strings attached. If you choose to spend it on riotous living, that's your affair—we don't want to know. No strings, okay?"

"No strings," repeated Paris. She would repay them, she'd be the success she'd always known she could be, and then she'd take care of them both— the way Jenny should have done. "You won't regret it," she promised.

"It's time to go, then." India waved from the deck to the two guards idling on the strip of beach in front of the house, occupying themselves by spinning pebbles across the waves. They waved in reply and headed back toward the house.

"Well," she remarked with a sigh, walking towards the door, "this is it." She turned for a last look at the pretty room. The white sofas were crumpled where they had been sitting and ashtrays and empty glasses littered the tables. The big windows framed only the blue-gray ocean and a cloudless sky. "You'd better say good-bye," she whispered.

Paris and Venetia gave the room a last lingering look. It seemed different now it was no longer theirs, thought Paris, a bit shabbier, a little bit tired—the home of a stranger as a prospective buyer might see it.

"I can't bear to go into Jenny's bedroom," whispered Venetia.

"Nor I." Paris turned away.

"I wonder which Jenny it was," said India, locking the door behind them, "who left Beverly Hills to take that last ride down Malibu Canyon. I'd like to believe it was the indiscreet, sexy Jenny heading for an assignation with some new man."

"No! It was Jenny in a romantic mood, longing for a glimpse of the full moon on the ocean." Venetia was sure of it.

Paris was silent. Or maybe, she thought as they walked away, it was the fading movie star of the slightly blurred beauty whose career was going downhill and for whose mismanaged life there seemed no future—except at the bottom of Malibu Canyon.

5

The young valet at the parking lot on Rodeo who looked as if he should be manning the life-saving station on Zuma Beach flipped Rory Grant his keys and gave him a winning smile. One day he, too, would make it big like that; it could happen, you know, this was Hollywood.

Rory sauntered down the street, checking his appearance in Bijan's window as he passed. He looked good, the all-American—or maybe all-Californian—guy with his hair casually longish, casually "sun streaked" and springy, cut so that he could run his casual hand through it in the engaging gesture known to millions of viewers; faded blue jeans, Nike tennis sneakers, expensive Italian polo shirt from Jerry Magnin, and a Missoni sweater tied by the sleeves and slung casually across his shoulders.

He wasn't sure about the sweater—did enough people know that it was Missoni and was almost *too* expensive? Would he have been better off with the plain blue cashmere or maybe the Armani? What the hell, the sweater had cost enough—more than his dad had earned in a month, more than a lot of people earned in a month. He checked his appearance again in the shop window. . . . You're looking good, Rory, real good, like the superstar you are—almost. That's what he wanted to talk to Bill about.

Bill was waiting at a table in the Café Rodeo. He'd been waiting for twenty minutes and figured that Rory would be exactly half an hour late—that's what they usually were when they reached this point of success; after that it was anybody's guess. They had been known to turn suddenly polite and easygoing, but that was rare.

"How're ya doin', Bill?" Rory acknowledged various greetings from around the room and flung himself into the chair opposite Bill.

"Pretty good." This was going to be a complaint, Bill could see it coming. There was a dissatisfied scowl in Rory's unsmiling greeting.

"Salad," said Rory to the waitress, "avocado, shrimp—tell them to add some alfalfa sprouts and some wheat germ. And Perrier." Ever since Jenny had put him on his diet, whittling down his hundred and sixty-five pounds to a muscular hundred and fifty, Rory had been careful what he ate. It was a pity, thought Bill, that he wasn't as careful with what he took. That perpetual sniff wasn't becoming to television's newest star.

"Ya should cut out the coke, Rory," he advised. "You're fucking up the membranes."

"We're not here to talk about my membranes," snapped Rory, checking the room to see who was with whom. "We're here to talk about money."

So that was it. The salary complaint. "What about it?"

"It's not enough, that's what about it." Rory fiddled with the tiny gold spoon on the chain around his neck. It was his only jewelry. Rory had decided against the Rolex on the basis that everybody had one and those who didn't had a cheap copy. He was still waiting to know what wristwatch would be "in" next, so he could be first.

The girl put the salad in front of him and he gave her his big smile. She thought he surely had great teeth.

"Look, Rory, they've upped your money once, you're getting thirty grand an episode now. That kinda money's not to be sniffed at." Bill smiled at his unintended double entendre and Rory glared back at him, over his salad.

"It's not enough. I'm the star of that show, without me it's down the tubes. All those women—*women*, Bill—on the other shows get more than me."

It was true, he *was* the star of the show, but the show was still new. All the others—*Dynasty*, *Dallas*—they'd been running for years. "They've earned it, Rory, they all paid their dues in the beginning."

"Yeah. Well, I don't intend to wait that long. You can tell 'em from me, Bill, that I don't show up for shooting next season unless I get fifty an episode." He munched on the alfalfa sprouts, wishing he liked the taste more. "I mean it, Bill."

Bill kept the benign smile on his face, but he was boiling. After all he'd done, the kid was gonna fuck it up now, just because he couldn't wait awhile—he'd gotten greedy too early.

"Look, Rory," he said, picking at the sandwich he'd ordered, "all you have to do is lay off for a while, get a couple of good seasons under your belt, and then the company'll expect to be hit for more money—that's the way it is these days. They'll be reasonable when they know the show's a stayer. You'll be up there with *Dynasty* yet."

"Now!" said Rory. "No waiting!"

Bill's temper boiled over. His smile was just as gentle and he kept his voice low and even, so that

141

nobody at the next tables would ever have an inkling that anything was wrong.

"You little prick." He smiled. "You'll do as I tell you. Don't start giving orders to me and thinking you're the star—because you and I know you ain't, not unless I say so."

Rory's brown eyes, set under thick blond eyebrows, met his; his hand, holding a forkful of avocado, halted halfway to his mouth.

"Whadd'ya mean? I'm the guy up there on the screen—there's nothing you can do about that anymore."

"No?"

Rory laid down the fork; he knew a threat when he heard one. "It'll be your word against mine," he said defiantly.

"My word," replied Bill, calling for the check, "and Stan Reubin's. Stan's one of our most respected lawyers, Rory, you know that, don't you? They'd believe whatever he said about Jenny's last night on earth."

Rory stared at him as Bill carefully placed a three-dollar tip on the table. "So get yourself back to work, Rory. I'll see you're taken care of all right. Don't you worry about that."

Bill headed for the door and Rory watched him go. Shit, he thought uneasily, wasn't that whole episode dead and buried along with Jenny? What had Bill meant by that?

"Can I get you anything else, Mr. Grant?" The waitress was smiling at him. She was kinda cute. "I

142

love the Missoni," she said, touching the sleeve of his sweater.

"Thanks," smiled Rory. He'd known the Missoni would be a winner.

⚜ 6 ⚜

Morgan McBain prowled the upper level of Geneva's immaculate air terminal, pausing now and then to stare out of the windows at the still-falling snow. It had been coming down for more than three hours now in an ever-thickening white blanket that had brought all air traffic to a halt, closing off Geneva Airport—and himself—from the rest of the world. His plane from Athens had been the last one to land before the storm really took hold and it was impossible to tell how long it might be before the snow eased off enough for plows to clear the run-ways and his flight to Paris to continue.

Leaning against the gallery rail he surveyed the lines at the check-in counters. Frantic couriers were trying to placate groups of irate would-be skiers who very much wanted to be in their mountain resorts, and certainly didn't want to waste their time and money in any snowbound airport. Pretty girls in shaggy fur moon-boots and brilliant ski jackets crowded the bar, and Morgan was on the receiving end of many a friendly and interested smile as he stepped over the scattered baggage and lines of propped-up skis, on his way to buy his third cup of airport coffee. He felt out of place in his dark-gray business suit—and out of touch.

How long has it been since I went skiing? he wondered, recalling the sheer physical exhilaration of the sport, the easy camaraderie of the skiers, and the cheerful charm of those mountain resorts, ringed into intimacy by their snow-capped peaks. Three, or maybe it was four, years?

Whichever, it was too long!

Finding a spare corner, unlittered with skis, he sipped his coffee, eavesdropping on the chatter of "lethal moguls" and "black runs," of who wore the tightest ski pants and was a rotten skier and why Verbier had the best young crowd, the best skiing, and the best-looking chalet girls. These skiers are *my* age, he thought, shocked by the realization that he had automatically thought of himself as older. I'm twenty-five and, like my father, I spend half my life in transit. It's not just skiing—when did I last take a *real* holiday? I'm so wrapped up in the McBain enterprises that I leave no time for my personal life—a few days here, a few days there, and that's all!

His father's yacht, the 150-foot *Fiesta*, was right now moored in Carlisle Bay in Barbados with a complete crew and no passengers. Fitz was in New York and might manage to get down for a week later in the season, and Morgan had spent five days on the *Fiesta* last year in its usual Mediterranean summer ports, drifting from St. Tropez to Sardinia. And that was it! He only visited the hotel they owned in the Bahamas to check the management, or discuss structural extensions and alterations. He was so committed to becoming indispensable in his father's organization and overcoming his personal hang-up of being "the boss's son" that he never allowed himself time off merely to relax. His days were more often spent on a desert building site in Kuwait or at a refinery in Galveston than lying on a beach—or gliding down a snowy mountain.

If he wasn't careful, decided Morgan, setting down his coffee cup, he would become like his father, too driven by his interests in the McBain Corporation to enjoy the rest of life's pleasures.

He smiled back at the girl in the kingfisher-blue ski jacket and jeans. She had burnished red hair and a turned-up nose with a scatter of freckles, and a very inviting smile.

"You look like a skier," she said, assessing Morgan's blond, broad-shouldered good looks, "but you're not dressed like one."

Morgan grinned. "Learned the trade on the slopes of Vail and the powder at Park City, Utah."

"You don't know what you're missing until you've skied in Switzerland," she countered, "but I'll bet you're a black-run man?"

"Off-piste. I'm the adventurous sort."

"I'll bet you are—adventurous, I mean." She gathered together her skis and her boot bag, surveying him carefully. He wasn't that much older than she, but he gave an impression of maturity, of knowing his place in the world and being totally confident in it. It was an attractive quality and he was an attractive man.

"Sure you don't want to get rid of that business suit and come with me?"

A ripple of sexual attraction threaded between them. She was very cute and he'd bet she skied well too.

"Where are you heading?"

"Verbier. It's where all the Brits go."

All the Brits . . . he wondered if Venetia went to Verbier? Funny, he always thought of Venetia as English and yet she was as American as he. Well, nearly.

"Maybe next time. Thanks for the offer anyway."

"Not at all. Pity, though, it could have been fun." She tucked her burnished red hair behind her ears and hefted the skis onto her shoulder.

Morgan watched as she walked across to join her group of friends. There were a dozen of them and they looked very together. An athletic-looking young man put his arm around the girl's shoulder and drew her into the group. They were very jolly, laughing and excited, anticipating the fun they would have on the slopes and in the après-ski clubs.

Morgan turned back to the bar and ordered a Scotch. He was an experienced enough traveler to know better than to drink when flying, but he suddenly felt left out and lonely. It wasn't that there was any shortage of women in his life. He met them all the time. In whichever city he found himself there were half a dozen pretty girls he could call, and a dozen charming hostesses only too willing to invite him to dinner. He attended balls in Monaco and

146

galas for the opera in New York. He played tennis with actresses in Los Angeles and took finicky Paris models to dinners they ignored, in elegant nouveaux restaurants that all seemed to offer the same menu, and, more often than he cared to remember, he ate lonely meals in air-conditioned hotel suites that could be in Frankfurt or Abu Dhabi in their anonymous similarity.

He'd bet that that bunch of skiers over there would have more fun in the next week than he'd had in the past five years.

Life, decided Morgan, knocking back the Scotch, had become very boring. Except for Venetia Haven. In the three months since he'd met her he'd found himself making deliberate excuses and even detours so that he could spend time in London. He had often been able to manage only one night in the city, and it had meant a hell of an early start the next morning, but she was worth it. He'd take her to dinner in some quiet little restaurant she knew and they'd hold hands in the candlelight and he'd find himself unable to stop just looking at her. He didn't see the resemblance to her famous mother so much, perhaps because Jenny was a bit before his generation; what he saw was a delicately boned, blond girl with eyes that changed their depth of color with her change of expression, lighter and sparkling when she was interested, grayer when she was tired, and deeper with a touch of violet when she was moved by tenderness.

Vennie was a girl determined to establish her in-

147

dependence and yet the same girl whose lips trembled under his when he kissed her . . . and that's all he'd done so far, kiss her. Because if it became anything more, with a girl like Vennie it would be a commitment, one he wasn't sure he wanted to make. He knew that she enjoyed being with *him* and not just with Fitz McBain's son. Vennie never demanded to be taken to the most expensive restaurant or club; she was happy with the neighborhood bistro if that was what he felt like, where the lights were comfortably dim, the wine list surprisingly good, and the food adventurous.

A message in French that all flights were subject to long delays crackled over the speakers and was greeted with derisive laughter and cheers by the skiers. Suddenly Morgan felt even more alone in the midst of the busy airport. Making his way briskly back to the VIP lounge, he closed the door on the crowded scene. A half-dozen men read newspapers or dozed on comfortable sofas in the quiet, green-carpeted room. A few others caught up with paperwork or made conversation over a drink. A steward came forward to offer the latest information on the storm and the anticipated length of the delay. At least another two or three hours. If Mr. McBain preferred, he could arrange a hotel room.

"I'll tell you what I'd like to do," said Morgan, handing him the ticket and boarding pass. "Change my flight to the next one for London, will you, and get me a telephone. I have to make an international call."

The steward plugged in the phone next to him and Morgan picked up the receiver and dialed. He wondered if Venetia enjoyed skiing.

The bitter wind had turned the sleet into stinging droplets of ice that reddened Venetia's cheeks as she battled her way from the car park, laden with her food hampers and baskets. Reaching the shelter of the towering office block she dumped her baskets on the floor of the elevator and shook the melting ice from her hair, drying it with the end of her long woollen scarf. Muzak and warmth enveloped her as she pressed the button for the tenth floor. It had taken two trips to get all her equipment from the car, and she was frozen. The elegant gray Italian boots that she'd bought last week when she'd worked three lunches plus two dinner parties and had felt quite rich were stained from the slush out-side—which, she thought glumly, just went to prove either that she shouldn't buy luxuries she couldn't afford or that she'd have to become more practical!

The elevator jolted to a stop and she picked up her basket again, smiling at the receptionist co-cooned in the taupe and dove-gray carpeted silence of the executive floor of Blakemore and Honeywell, investment counselors and management consul-tants. The sleek-haired brunette nodded indiffer-ently and went back to filing her long red nails. "Kitchen's through there, down the corridor on your left." She offered no help and once again it took Venetia two trips with her load.

After all, thought Venetia inspecting the kitchen, it's my job, not hers. Still, the office staff in these places did rather treat you as though you were the scullery maid and they the young ladies of the big house! The directors for whom she cooked were usually all right—they either noticed her and smiled appreciatively, or they made a point of not noticing her while they consumed their lunch and discussed business. Either way was all right with Venetia—so long as they liked her food and paid her, and best of all, if they asked her, through their secretaries, of course, to cook for their weekly directors' lunches on a regular basis so that she could fill up the sparse pages of her engagement book several weeks ahead and know that she would be sure of some income that month.

Work hadn't been as easy to find as she had expected. Schools seemed to be turning out young ladies with cordon bleu diplomas by the score, and every ad in *The Times* attracted dozens of applicants who were often more experienced than Venetia. Through the Lancasters and her own circle of friends she had managed to pick up a job here and there—catering a christening party or an anniversary dinner, and through an agency she had ventured into the occasional weekend house party, or emergency dinner—usually when the regular cook had walked out at the last minute.

Most times Venetia didn't blame them. The attitude of her temporary employers was to act as if she were some irritating servant who should know where everything in the strange kitchen was kept, and should get on with it—fast, without bothering them! Most of the women had proved demanding and difficult to please. The men saw her in quite a different light, as a more decorative kitchen accessory to be plied with gin and tonic while the wife was taking her bath, then an arm around the shoulders and a pat on the bottom and a suggestion of a rendezvous for "a really good meal . . . get you out of the kitchen, hah hah, then afterward . . ." It appeared to be a hazard of her profession and it annoyed her, though so far she'd managed to keep her suitors at bay, and she'd also managed to be quite polite about it because she needed the money. But it would have felt so satisfying to walk out and leave them to explain to their wives just why their dinner party was ruined.

Unpacking her hampers, she produced a delicate terrine of salmon in aspic which she arranged on a bed of fresh cress, garnishing it with slices of lemon and cucumber. The middle-aged directors she cooked for liked simple food, not too fattening but with good ingredients, and the rack of lamb, which she had covered with a mixture of herbs, fine mustard, and bread crumbs and would cook until just pink, had proved a safe bet. She tried always to keep the pudding light—a lemon sorbet with wafer-thin curls of fresh almond biscuits that she had made that morning, or a fresh fruit salad and an interesting cheeseboard. The wines came from the directors' own cellars, so she had no need to bother about those, and with a cold hors d'oeuvre and pudding she had only the main dish and vegetables to cook. These were shopped for the day before and prepared by her in the Lancasters' kitchen at seven-thirty in the morning. She was usually finished by ten with everything packed into her hampers and ready to go. There'd just be time for a quick bath, and then, in her working outfit of a simple skirt and shirt, not forgetting her striped apron, big enough to wrap around her twice and tie at the front, she'd load the car and be on her way.

After switching on the oven to low she made a pot of coffee. Twelve o'clock. With a bit of luck the women who did the tables and cleared the dishes would be here soon: meanwhile there was just time to tidy herself up.

Venetia hurried down the corridor in search of the ladies' room, finding it without the help of the indifferent receptionist, who was involved in some apparently intriguing phone call. The mirror showed that she wasn't *too* bedraggled—her hair and her boots had dried and hopefully she looked both neat and efficient. Tying back her shining blond hair tightly with a scrap of blue ribbon she searched her bag for a lipstick. Morgan's card was tucked in the flap where she'd placed it that morning. A hapless-looking camel leered at her from a rectangle of desert in Abu Dhabi, and with a smile she reread Morgan's message on the back: *Reliable, efficient, cost effective, rustproof . . . who needs a car anyway? Miss you.*

152

He'd taken to dropping her a card from each new place he went, usually with a hastily scribbled *Wish you were here,* or even *Love and kisses.* In the half-dozen times they'd met since she had returned from California a couple of months ago, she'd found herself liking Morgan McBain more and more. He was so easy to talk to, he listened to her problems, and he asked the right questions—the sort of questions that made her see the answers for herself. And, too, she had to admit that it felt good being on the arm of such an attractive man; she'd noticed the way other girls looked at him. Kate Lancaster thought he was *dazzling!* Morgan exuded that special American confidence of power—she had the feeling that he could take care of any situation, just the way he had that awful night three months ago. Of course, she was infinitely grateful to Morgan and his father for that.

And she liked it when he kissed her. In fact, she liked it a lot, and she thought he did too. Why, then, did he do no more than kiss her? Didn't he find her attractive enough? Maybe there was something about her that turned him off. Venetia gazed anxiously again at her reflection in the wall-high mirrors in the ladies' room that contrived to make even her five-foot-nine-inch slenderness appear squat. She was quite pretty—she knew she was really, but sometimes, inside, she didn't feel very confident of her looks. And Morgan hadn't suggested anything other than kisses. . . .

Oh, my God, look at the time! Stuffing his card

153

back into her bag she hurried back to her kitchen.

"I've done the table, miss," the waitress's cheerful voice greeted her.

"Oh! Oh, right, thanks so-o much. I've made coffee, if you'd like a cup." Venetia pushed the roast into the oven and slammed the door.

"Thanks, miss." The comfortable, middle-aged Cockney woman helped herself to a cup and stared at Venetia intently. "I *know* your face," she said. "You look a lot like someone on the telly."

"Really." Venetia smiled and busied herself with the vegetables.

"I've got it! You look like the film star, the one that got herself killed in Hollywood a few months back—Jenny. Beautiful, she was, too. I used to wish I looked like her when I was a girl. Wait a minute . . . no, you couldn't be, not being here and doing the cooking and all that—I mean, you couldn't be Jenny Haven's daughter . . . but I saw you on the telly!"

Venetia smiled shyly. She had thought that once the funeral was over, the attention of the press would be diverted to the next scandal or romance, but reporters had hovered outside the Lancaster mews house for weeks and she'd found herself surprised by photographers when she was shopping in the supermarket or taking the dogs for a walk. She'd even had requests for interviews and had been offered quite a large sum of money by two different rival newspapers for "the true story," which of course she had ignored. There'd even been a mention in Nigel Dempster's column in the *Mail* with a blurred photograph

154

of her with Morgan, getting into a taxi.

"Well, I never—fancy meeting you here, cooking lunch for *that* lot!" The woman's face lit with sudden understanding. "Then that's what the phone call was! Samantha in reception said that the rich American, McBain, was on the phone—calling from a foreign country he was, too, asking for Venetia Haven. So of course Miss Smarty out there tells him there's no such person works here. Oh, she was all smiles this time. He'll have been calling for you, love. Better go and ask her. I think he said he'd call back because he was sure you were expected." She gulped her coffee and smiled at Venetia, delighted to be the bringer of good news, and she knew it was good by the way the girl's eyes brightened. Really pretty she was, just like her mum.

Morgan? Morgan was calling her *here?* "But how did he know . . . ?" Even as she said it she knew how silly it was; of course Morgan would have called home and they would have given him the number. It must be urgent if he couldn't wait until she got home.

"Thank you, thanks a lot," she said, heading for the door. "Oh—could you just keep an eye on the lamb in the oven for me? I won't be long."

Samantha at reception sipped the pink high-protein milk drink that was her lunch and glanced at Venetia with supercilious boredom.

"For you?" Her voice was faintly scornful; obviously the girl was mistaken. The McBains of this world didn't make urgent telephone calls from

155

Geneva to lunchtime cooks.

"I'm Venetia Haven. Didn't he ask for me?"

Samantha's gaze fastened on Venetia for the first time. My God, of course. She was *that* Haven girl, why hadn't she noticed it right off? The phone rang again, purring quietly in this hushed office, and she answered automatically.

"Blakemore and Honeywell. Oh, yes, Mr. McBain. Yes, you're quite right, Mr. McBain. She's here now, I'll put her on the line." Handing the phone to Venetia she sipped her lunch and pretended not to listen.

"Morgan?" Venetia cradled the phone under her chin, speaking softly. "Yes, yes, of course I'm pleased you called, but why here? Is it urgent? It is? Yes of course I ski. . . . When? Oh, Morgan, it sounds lovely, but I'm not sure I can . . . you're snow-bound—how romantic! Yes, of course I'd like to be with you, but I have to work, Morgan. . . . Oh, well, perhaps I could . . ."

Her laugh rang through the silent offices and Samantha glanced at her enviously.

"All right, then, we'll talk about it when you get here . . . you'll talk me into it?" She laughed again. "Okay. Yes. I'll wait for your call . . . yes . . . me too . . . 'Bye."

Venetia put down the phone and drifted happily back toward the kitchen, followed by Samantha's envious stare.

The Rolls from the Palace Hotel whisked them

through the snowy streets of St. Moritz, up the fir-dotted slope to the sprawling, gabled building that looked, thought Venetia, like a chalet that had just kept on growing. The manager was waiting to greet them personally and to assure them that his staff would see to their every comfort. "There's good snow," he informed them, "and more to come—too much, perhaps. But if we are snowed in, Mademoiselle will find plenty to do at the Palace—you can ice-skate on our own rink, swim in our pool, exercise in our fitness room, play squash, bridge, dance—maybe a little shopping. . . ."

"Forget it," laughed Morgan, "Mademoiselle is going up those mountains and back down again as fast as she can. I have a ten-pound bet that I'll beat her—best of five runs."

"What I didn't tell you," Venetia informed him as they headed for the elevator, "is that I first skied here when I was three years old—I came with my mother, and Jenny was quite an athlete. She was a superb skier, and she saw I had the best tuition. Even if you beat me on speed, Morgan McBain—and I'm not admitting that you will—you'll never top my style."

"You're probably right," he replied with a grin. "My training consisted of a half hour when my father showed me the basic moves. Then he hoisted me into a chair lift to the top of the slope and said, 'Follow me.' I had no choice—if I wanted to go down that mountain I had to follow him. So I went. And I loved it—even though I must have fallen a

157

dozen times. He never helped me up, just waited and called instructions to me on how to do it."

As they followed the manager down the corridor Venetia imagined the little boy scared and alone at the top of the white slopes; it must have looked so steep to him.

"He sounds like a very tough father," she commented.

"He was—and is. But he's still the best. He brought me up with no mother around and he did it the only way he knew how." Morgan smiled wryly. "He was determined no son of his was going to grow up soft—money was for good food and a good education, not for pampering."

Venetia privately thought Fitz McBain sounded like a tough old tyrant, but she kept her opinion to herself.

"Your room, mademoiselle." The manager opened the door with a flourish.

It was spacious and sunny and filled with flowers. Two discreet single beds awaited her choice, and Venetia's eyes met Morgan's inquiringly.

"I'm right next door," he explained. "I'll give you fifteen minutes to get into your gear and we're off, okay?"

"Lunch is being served in the restaurant, sir," suggested the manager, following Morgan to the door.

Venetia laughed as she heard his reply. "Lunch? No time for that—we'll grab a bite later at one of the cafés on the mountain."

When Morgan wanted to do something, he did

it immediately! He'd arrived on one plane in London, talked her into abandoning her quest for work, and scooped her off to Switzerland on the next flight. Vennie eyed the twin beds warily. Of course she'd expected to have her own room—Morgan would never be so presumptuous or so indiscreet as to book them into the same room—and anyway things hadn't got to that point between them. Yet. She sat on the edge of the bed, dragged off her boots and jeans, and climbed into a pair of thermal longjohns, a cotton polo-neck shirt, and her ski suit. She pulled on the shaggy fur boots, clipped her bum bag to her belt, grabbed her goggles, and made for the door. Morgan was outside, hand raised ready to knock. "Beat you," he said triumphantly. "Round one goes to me."

"I thought this competition was on the slopes," complained Venetia.

"It is, it is . . . just you watch out, Miss Venetia Haven," he warned. "You're in for a tough time!"

Venetia hadn't remembered that it felt so wonderful. They'd begun on a red run—just to get their ski legs, Morgan had said, though privately she had thought that he was being kind to her and allowing her to chicken out if she felt the black runs would be too much. And they might have, she admitted, unclipping the bindings and shouldering her skis; her knees were trembling from the unaccustomed strain. But it was stupendous: the snow was perfect, the sky was blue with just a ridge of cloud coming up on the horizon, and the sun was hot. Meanwhile, she was here at the foot of the piste waiting for Morgan, who had taken two falls at the top of the slope and had lagged behind considerably. She'd beaten him by at least three minutes, she calculated as he swerved to a stop next to her.

"Beat me—fair and square." He grinned. "Goddamn, Vennie, I didn't believe you when you said you were good—you're terrific. I can see I'll have my work cut out."

"Of course you will," said Vennie loftily, "and the loser buys mulled wine and a sandwich for the winner, right?"

Morgan sucked in his breath. "You don't know what you're letting yourself in for." He shouldered his skis and put an arm around her, heading for the crowded café terrace overlooking the valley. "You may regret it by the end of the week, Vennie Haven. It's gonna cost you!"

The sun dazzled off the snow in a million glinting prisms as they sat, warmed by its rays and the hot wine, and nourished by the crunchy ham sandwiches, contentedly surveying the scene.

It was just about perfect, thought Morgan. He was in the mountains—which he had always loved—on a glorious day which God had provided, with a girl he was falling in love with. He stole a glance at Vennie's profile as she sipped her wine, gazing out across the valley spread below her like a perfect picture postcard. He loved the soft curve of her cheek, the hint of a dimple at the right side that came and went as she talked, and gave her face a charming asymmetrical touch when she smiled. He loved her wide, open blue gaze, the long curving lashes tipped with gold, he loved the way she'd pulled back her hair into a heavy blond ponytail and the delicate line of her back which even in the bulky ski suit seemed fragile. And yet she wasn't. Venetia was strong—not only physically, but in character. He knew how determined she was to make it on her own in her cooking ventures and he wished he could help; surely there must be some way to make it easier for her? For he had the feeling that Vennie wasn't going to quit for anyone or anything until she had achieved her goal.

"Shall we try again?" asked Vennie, pulling on the soft pink-and-gray angora hat that matched her ski-suit. "I'm game to try the black, if you are."

"You're on."

Clomping companionably back across the wooden terrace in their heavy boots, they picked up their skis from the line propped up on the snow outside the café, clipped them on, and glided off toward the lifts. Holding hands as they drifted slowly up the mountain in the chair lift was, thought Venetia contentedly, sheer heaven.

The snow that had threatened in the line of clouds on the horizon had begun to fall heavily as they descended the mountain for the fifth and final time that afternoon, and by the time they reached the Palace it was whirling into a blizzard.

"Just made it," commented Morgan, sticking their

skis and boots in the ski store, "and I'll bet we have a white-out tomorrow."

Venetia groaned, stretching her already tightening muscles. "Ohh, I'm not sure I care. . . . I can only think of soaking in a hot bath and sleeping for a week."

"I'll allow you the long hot bath," said Morgan, "but then it's time for a drink at the bar, a candlelit dinner for two, and after that . . ." Morgan put his arm around her, pulling her close.

"After that?" she murmured, smiling teasingly at him from under her lashes.

"Oh, a little dancing, a little kissing . . ." Morgan's mouth came down on hers firmly, holding her cold lips with his as she tightened her arms about his neck.

"Here we are, necking in the ski store like two high-school kids," grinned Morgan, "and you're freezing. I've never kissed anyone with such icy lips. Come on, we've got to get you into that hot bath. We'll pick up where we left off later."

It was such a good feeling, thought Vennie, hurrying along beside him, to be looked after. It was so *comfortable* being with Morgan.

Vennie was wearing a long soft shift of violet wool, high necked, wide shouldered, and long sleeved, belted in quilted violet satin. On another girl it might have looked vulgar and obvious, thought Morgan, elegant in his dinner jacket, but on Vennie's tall, slender body it looked wonderful. They made a spectacularly handsome couple in a hotel filled with very handsome

162

people, turning heads as they left the cozy warmth of the fireplace in the bar and made their way to the restaurant.

Revived by her bath and fortified by a champagne cocktail, Vennie felt a new woman. Exhilaration flowed through her veins, but a different sort from that which she'd experienced on the mountain. That was from the thrill and excitement of the sport and the glorious day. This feeling was from the sheer happiness of being young, feeling pretty, and being with Morgan.

The waiter seated them at the candlelit table and Morgan reached his hand across and took hers. "Did I tell you you look lovely by candlelight?" he inquired with a smile. "Maybe even better than on the ski slope—though I have to admit, it's close!"

"And you too," replied Vennie teasingly. "Candlelight turns your eyes the color of good port."

"Huh, back to food and drink again. Was that a hint that you're starving?" Morgan kissed her fingers before he released them.

"Of course. You only let me have a sandwich for lunch," said Vennie, running an expert eye down the lengthy list of appetizers. "Good heavens, what a choice."

Morgan watched in amusement as she considered, one finger running down the list, murmuring comments as she read.

"Morgan? Would it be all right if I had *two* starters and no main dish? These are all so good . . . I simply must have snails, but then I'd love some of that mountain ham."

Morgan sighed in mock regret. "No fondue, then?"

"No fondue," she said firmly.

"Thank God." Morgan grinned in relief. "I would have endured it for you, but no one else. Vennie, you can have three starters if you wish, or four or five."

"Two, thank you," said Venetia.

"You really know exactly what you want, don't you?" Their eyes met across the flickering candle.

"Sometimes," demurred Vennie, "sometimes I do."

They ate surprisingly little for two people who had been so hungry, but it all tasted, as Vennie said, "sublime," and afterward they slow-danced, arms wrapped around each other, her head tucked against his chest where, thought Morgan, it belonged. At midnight, fatigue began to take over, and despite the fact that this was not the moment for it, Venetia yawned.

"Sorry," she said guiltily, "it's just that I'm so tired."

Morgan laughed. "Well, at least it wasn't boredom," he said, taking her hand and escorting her through the hotel to the elevator.

"Have you ever been kissed in an elevator before?" he murmured, as the doors closed and they were alone.

"Never," she whispered happily.

His kiss was different this time, less tender and more demanding. It lasted until the doors slid open again at their floor, revealing them to the amused gaze of a waiting couple.

Blushing, Venetia hurried down the corridor holding on to Morgan's hand; she hadn't expected to see anyone, she'd been so lost in Morgan's kiss.

They paused outside her door and Morgan inserted her key into the lock and pushed open the door. He thought she looked tired; the healthy color of the afternoon had drained from her face, leaving her pale and shadowed and very beautiful. He couldn't bear to leave her.

"Vennie?" Her eyes met his. "May I come in for a good-night kiss? I mean, we don't want to be caught out here in the corridor, do we? The elevator was scandalous enough."

Venetia smiled. "I'd like that."

His arms felt good around her, so good . . . she'd like to sleep in Morgan's embrace, it would feel wonderful. Her lips parted under the force of his kiss and Venetia waited for it to happen—that miraculous surge of physical emotion, the fireworks that would explode within you, the passion that left you helpless and trembling. Wasn't that what you were supposed to feel when you loved someone?

Morgan ran his hands down her slender back, pressing her even closer, drifting light, caressing little kisses over her closed eyelids. God, he wanted her . . . he stopped kissing her for a moment to gaze at her lovely face. She looked so beautiful—and so *tired!*

"I'm a brute," he said, kissing her on the cheek. "You're exhausted. You need to be tucked up in bed to sleep until you awake—like the princess in the fairy tale."

That was it, of course, thought Venetia, as he left her with a final kiss, it was just that she was tired. Kicking off her shoes she sank thankfully onto the bed, thinking of Morgan. But you were supposed to feel *more* than this, weren't you? It wasn't as if Morgan were just any boyfriend, he was special in a lot of ways. When she was with him, she always felt so . . . so *looked after*. She couldn't remember having felt like that since she had left home and Jenny for school in England. Yes, Morgan looked after her. Take now, for instance; she knew he had wanted to make love to her, but he had been so gentle and considerate. But shouldn't passion ignore fatigue? she thought uneasily. Shouldn't the touch of his lips have inflamed her? Jenny had always succumbed to passion—if she hadn't, then the three of them wouldn't be here, after all—but from what Jenny had said it was *that* feeling that swept aside everything else. Passion, for Jenny, had been overwhelming. Then why hadn't *she* been overwhelmed?

Vennie pulled off her dress and slipped on the cream silk men's pajamas that had been Lydia Lancaster's Christmas present to her husband and which Vennie had "borrowed" because they were far sexier looking than all those lacy nighties. She creamed the makeup from her face and, shiny and clean, with her hair brushed, she sat, head in hands, and gazed at her reflection in the mirror. She was in love with Morgan, wasn't she? At least, she would *like* to be in love with him. And she thought Morgan was in love with her—that is, she *hoped* he was; he certainly fancied her. Sighing, she turned away from her own puzzled eyes and climbed into bed. With the lamps off she lay in the dark, remembering the fun they'd had together on the slopes, the companionable ride up the mountain hand in hand in the chair lift, the candlelit dinner, the slow-dancing, the kisses in the elevator . . . she'd been lost in his kisses then, hadn't she? Anyway, she said to herself as she drifted into sleep, there are different kinds of love; not everyone is overwhelmed by outrageous passion . . . True love can be more . . . more *comfortable*.

Morgan couldn't sleep. The room was too hot, he decided, climbing out of bed and padding across to the window and peering out. Snow still swirled into the night. Morgan let the curtain fall with a sigh. There'd be no skiing tomorrow, they'd be snowed in. And who better to be snowed in with than Venetia? No one. He knew it. And he knew it was different this time. He'd been in love before— a couple of times, in fact—and both times he'd thought he couldn't live without them, until after a while he'd suddenly found he could, *and* quite happily. But it wasn't going to be like that this time. It wasn't just that Venetia was lovely, nor that he wanted to make love to her—which he did, leaving her tonight hadn't been easy—but she brought out another side in him, one he hadn't been aware he possessed.

For the first time in his life he wanted to look after

someone, to protect her, to care for her. She was such an odd character, so sturdily independent on the one hand, and so innocent and vulnerable on the other. Morgan felt a pang as he thought of her innocence. God, he was a brute, to try to make love to her like that when she was so tired. And she was such a kid really. He'd better watch himself with her, not rush things, let her take it slowly, the way a man should with a girl like Venetia. Making love with her would be a big commitment, one he'd be happy to make in time. Vennie was adorable—she was beautiful, a good companion, he'd had fun with her today. He'd like to take it slowly with her, enjoy it all. He'd call her from whichever country he was in, he'd write, send her flowers, presents, he'd woo his innocent Vennie until she was ready.

Morgan lay on the bed, his hands behind his head, making plans for Venetia.

The days were drifting by so quickly, the way they do on holiday, each one sliding into the next in a flurry of small activities: ice skating with Morgan on the hotel rink; holding hands on the sleigh rides, tucked away from the frosty nip in the air beneath a warm, furry rug, and drawn by horses whose bells jingled in the Christmas fantasy land of snowy mountains and pine forests; beating Morgan at curling, jumping up and down on the ice in triumph as he handed over the five-pound bet—and then buying him a present, the softest gray cashmere scarf, which she'd wrapped around his neck and delivered with a kiss; the joy of skiing again when the snow finally stopped and the pistes were pounded into shape; the candlelight dinners, the dancing, and Morgan's loving, gentle attention. But why, wondered Venetia, dressing for dinner on their last night, why hadn't he tried to make love to her again? What was wrong? He didn't seem any the less loving. Quite the opposite; he was full of small attentions, and he seemed as happy as she; they were always laughing together about something. Then why, damn it? Wasn't she *attractive* enough?

Venetia scowled at her reflection. She had decided to wear the violet shift again—after all, that had seemed to do the trick the first night. Bending forward she shook her thick blond hair free, tossing it back and running her fingers through it until it looked like a rough mane. She'd really layered on the eyeshadow tonight, changing her usual wide-eyed look into a deeper, sultry gaze; she'd emphasized her cheekbones with a darker blusher, and now she colored her mouth a deep violet-pink, glossing her lower lip the way Paris had said you should for a sexy look. Then just a final spray of Penhaligon's Bluebell scent. There. If that didn't do it, she didn't know what would. She had to admit that she looked terrific—she only hoped Morgan would appreciate it!

Venetia, you're ridiculous, she told herself with a laugh; one minute you're not sure whether you want him to make love to you, then you're not sure if you're feeling the way you should when he begins to make love to you, and next you wonder why he isn't making love to you! She couldn't wait to ask her best friend Kate Lancaster what *she* thought. Picking up her bag she glanced around the room. Clothes were scattered across its length, and grabbing them up quickly she flung them into the bottom of the wardrobe, smoothing down the bedspread and removing her pajamas from the chair— just in case, she thought, eyeing the room with satisfaction, just in case he decides to come back with me tonight.

Morgan was waiting for her at their favorite table in the bar, next to the cheery glow of the fire, drinking whiskey and soda. He noticed the heads turn as she paused at the entrance, smiling as she caught his eye. He'd be willing to bet that she didn't even know that every male in the room had turned to admire her. That was one of the nicest things about Vennie, she was so unaware of her own beauty. Tonight she looked different; she was walking a little more slowly, a little more self-consciously, and her glance was not her usual frank gaze. She looked tempting, damn it! It hadn't been easy resisting his natural impulses all week and now here she was looking as lovely as a wild violet and smelling of summer meadows with that sexy Lolita look. Jesus, what was she trying to do to him—?

Vennie kissed his cheek as he stood to greet her, sliding into the seat next to him in a gale of bluebells.

"I like it," said Morgan, coughing as it engulfed him. "That scent you're wearing, I mean."

Venetia gave him her best sexy glance. "Do you?" she murmured, wishing it were called something like Passion Flower instead of Bluebell.

Morgan stared at her in amazement. What had got into her? "Do you feel all right?" he asked solicitously. "You're not too tired, are you?"

Oh, God, I'm obviously not doing this right, worried Venetia, he thinks I'm *tired* and I thought I was looking *sexy!*

"Of course I'm not tired—I'm not tired *all* the time, you know, Morgan!"

"No. No, of course not. Well, then, how about a drink? Your usual champagne cocktail?"

Venetia sipped her cocktail, wishing she were sophisticated enough to drink martinis or vodka gimlets, or some other exotic drink that she knew would only make her feel sick, but might have made her seem older and more glamorous. *Worldly wise* was the right term, she thought. God, she wished she were more like Paris, she would be able to handle this scene perfectly. Why hadn't Jenny sent *her* to the Swiss school instead of the English one! But Paris can't cook, she told herself defensively—and Paris doesn't need to, she replied, she probably gets taken out to grand restaurants every single night by wonderful, sophisticated men!

"Are you bored?"

"What?" Venetia dropped her pose and took his hand. "Oh, no, of course I'm not, whatever made you think that?"

"Well, you were just sort of staring around and

171

not saying anything, and that's not at all like you."

Venetia grinned. "You're quite right," she agreed, "it's not! Anyway, I'm starving, aren't you? I'm going to have the snails again tonight."

"I thought we might have some caviar to start," said Morgan. "I've ordered a bottle of Dom Pérignon to be put on ice."

"Wonderful, I'll have the snails after."

Morgan laughed. "Come on, then, finish up your drink."

The caviar was delicious, the champagne bliss, and the strawberries and cream the ultimate luxury a snowbound winter landscape could provide. Morgan was Morgan, thought Vennie as they danced the night away in a comprehensive tour of every disco in town, and she was Venetia—they were two people who really liked each other, they enjoyed each other's company. It was probably love. *This* was how it should feel, it should be fun and laughter, holding hands and slow-dancing. Maybe they were too young for all that high passion stuff. Romance was all you needed, romance and laughter.

Morgan was longing to wrap his arms around her, to tell her that he wanted her, that he loved her, but it was too soon. She was such a kid; look at the way she was enjoying herself. He'd spent evenings like this with many other girls, and by this time they'd been wrapped around him, as ready as he was for what was to come; but with Vennie it couldn't be like that, he'd cool it, play the gentle lover until she was ready. That was the way to win her, he was sure.

The entire floor of the atelier was covered in clean white sheets. Paris, barefooted, in black jeans and sweatshirt, knelt in the center pinning silvery ruffles down the long, steel-colored satin skirt the model was wearing. The girl, who was naked from the waist up, shivered slightly, noticing the goosebumps on her bare arm as she raised it to check her watch.

"Paris, it's freezing in here," she complained. "I'm gonna catch pneumonia if you don't hurry up."

Her thick Texan twang rang through the room, and Paris sighed. In her opinion all models should keep their mouths firmly shut before they put their very large feet in them. All Finola had to do today was stand there while she pinned the garments on her, and even then she was twitchy as hell.

"I'll do the jacket next," she told her. "I'm just waiting for Berthe to finish the lapels."

Berthe Mercier, the special fine seamstress, sat at a long table in the corner, painstakingly hand-stitching the long curving lapels of a satin jacket. Another, younger, woman sat beside her, hemming a wide linen skirt.

"It's already half past four," grumbled Finola, "and I'm supposed to be at . . . somewhere else by six."

"Where else?" demanded Paris. "You didn't get here until three and I thought you had the whole day free."

"Yes . . . well, I did. But six is the evening, isn't it?"

Paris finished pinning the line of ruffles on the

thigh-high slit at the back of the skirt. "Okay. What time will you be here tomorrow?" She stood back to examine the effect.

"I'm not sure. I'll call you and let you know."

Paris eyed the model speculatively. Something was up, she felt it. Finola was playing some kind of game—but what?

"Look, Finola," she said, adjusting the ruffle just a touch on the left, "I've created all the evening dresses on *you*. I only need another couple of days and we'll be finished. Now, what time will you be coming?"

Berthe Mercier brought over the satin jacket. "It's finished, mademoiselle."

Paris examined the lapels carefully. "That looks wonderful, Berthe—as usual."

Berthe Mercier had worked for all the best Paris houses since she was fifteen and she was moonlighting now to help pay her daughter's fees at ballet school. The training seemed endless and there were so many extra classes, but still, it was worth it—Naomi would be a star one day. As would Paris Haven; she had the confident touch of a master and her cutting was impeccable.

Finola shrugged the jacket over her thin shoulders, fastening it below the waist with the steel lozenge that was its single button. Its fluid fines skimmed her supple body, touching at exactly the right places. The satin fabric and the exaggerated curve of the lapels were a delicious contrast to the masculinity of the color and the cut, as was the sur-

174

prising flirt of ruffles at the back. Finola inspected her reflection in the big mirror on the wall opposite. The jacket left a great deal of her front exposed and she pulled at it petulantly.

"It looks terrific, Paris," she said, moving around in it experimentally, "but I'm afraid if I move too much my tits'll fall out."

"Finola, if you had any tits they still wouldn't fall out, not the way that jacket's cut."

Despite herself Finola laughed.

"Touché, as they say here," she replied. "And now can I go?"

"Where? To get a boob job?" Didier de Maubert slammed the door behind him, laughing as he caught Finola's glare. "Sorry, sorry, *chérie*, I didn't mean it. I just heard the end of the conversation, that's all."

Didier de Maubert, nattily attired in the white suit that was his uniform summer and winter, was Paris's colleague, assistant, and general dogsbody. Which meant that he took care of the "business end," leaving Paris to get on with creating the line. Didier wrote the checks and kept an eye on their finances; he found contacts for buttons, threads, suedes, and satin and got the best prices. He hounded suppliers, fought with the models, he praised the seamstresses, fixed the coffee, made sure Paris ate dinner every night, and dried her tears when she cried from fatigue and the pressure.

Didier had known Paris since she was seventeen and studying design at art school. He had been twenty-three then and had just started a little ready-to-wear line of summer pants and shirts. The clothes had had a jaunty nautical look that had caught on with the summer holiday-wear trade and he'd found himself suddenly successful in his first venture. Since then "Didi's Designs" had had its ups and downs; some seasons he was successful, others less so, but he had managed to keep his head above water in a fickle business, and the friendship with Paris that had started in a sidewalk café patronized by them both had held firm.

It had, of course, remained only a friendship because Didi was, as the gossip columnists phrased it, "a confirmed bachelor." He told Paris long ago that it was probably because his sexual interests were of the alternative sort that their friendship had lasted. "With a woman as beautiful as you," he'd told her, "any other man would have become your lover before now."

Didi had watched Paris's progress—or lack of it—from the time she emerged from the safe cocoon of art college and the frustrations of the couture houses to try to make it on her own. He'd listened to her worries about money and he'd offered to put in a word for her at any of the big ready-to-wear houses that were always on the lookout for innovative new designers, but she'd been afraid of being swallowed up in that vast, impersonal world, of losing her touch and her individuality by giving it too soon to someone else.

Had Didier ever had sufficient capital to spare

he would have financed Paris's couture line himself, but there had never been enough to capitalize a second business. When Paris had returned from Hollywood with her story and her sisters' ten thousand dollars and her ambitions, Didi had offered to help.

Didi slung onto a rail the plastic-swathed garments he'd just picked up from the specialist outworkers.

"Here's something to cheer you up," he called.

Paris pulled off the plastic covers and examined them.

"Didi, they look wonderful."

The row of long linen skirts—oyster sashed with peach suede, frosty-blue with violet, gray with amber—hung next to toning silk blouses cut like wide-cuffed sweatshirts. Pants in the same heavy linen, cropped at the calf, were to be worn with the oversized suede jackets. Even on the rail the clothes looked young and exuberant, and Paris's spirits began to lift.

"That's the first lot completely finished," she commented. "Thank God. I was beginning to think nothing ever would be."

"I told you it would all work out." Didi grinned, looking at his watch. "Paris, we must check on the accessories, and then we have to make a final decision on the location for the show. We just can't leave it any longer."

They had whittled down the choice of venue for showing the collection to two places—one an uninspired salon in a modern hotel that had the advantage of being close to the nerve center of Paris fashion, and the other an extraordinary old Art Nouveau hotel she'd discovered just behind Les Halles, the old wholesale food market of Paris that had been transformed into a lively area filled with little boutiques, bars, and cafés. The decision would be an important one, as would the final details of the accessories, and Paris was tired of making decisions. Each outfit needed the right shoes, hats, or hair ornaments, special belts, "jeweled" pins, necklaces, bracelets, earrings—many of which she had designed herself and were being made up in tiny ateliers scattered throughout Paris. The overall design plan that Paris had carried in her head from the beginning would begin to emerge as a reality with the addition of each separate detail, and as the time grew nearer her nervousness increased. And now Finola was being difficult too! Flinging on Jenny's Fende fur coat she followed Didi down the stairs and into his white 450 Mercedes, double-parked with a ticket on it at the curb.

"*Merde*," said Didi, cheerfully shoving the ticket to join the others in the glove compartment. Tickets were one of the necessary pains of city living. The alternative of actually finding a parking lot or even searching for a legal space to park never crossed his mind—it would have meant walking in this filthy weather, and Didi would never do that.

Didi was the Frenchest-looking Frenchman Paris knew. He had the long pale face and sad dark eyes of a medieval saint combined with the strong curved nose and underlip of a de Gaulle. But he was attractive, always immaculately turned out in his smart white suits—worn in summer with dark blue T-shirts and in winter with pastel blue or pink shirt and tie. From Didi's stories she knew his love life as intimately as her own—or the lack of it. Who had the time for love affairs? There was only work, and more work. And that's all she wanted. Didi was the only person in the world she'd told about Amadeo Vitrazzi.

"Wait, *chérie,* just wait," he'd told her comfortingly. "When you're a star we'll buy our silks from Derome and you can tell Signor Vitrazzi—when he asks smilingly for your order—that his fabrics are not good enough. Then you'll send him back to Olympe Avallon."

"Where first?" she asked as Didi threaded his way through the ferocious early-evening traffic.

"Hats." He hit his brakes and swerved to the left down a side street. "I said we'd be there before five and we're late."

"Oh, Didi, I hope Jean-Luc has got them right."

The hats were the most important of the accessories, and vital to her "look."

Didi double-parked again while Paris hared up the stairs to Jean-Luc's workroom. He was a young man, discovered by Didi, straight out of design school. His imaginative samples had delighted her, but now she was anxious. After all, this was his first commission; what if he wasn't as

179

good as they thought?

Jean-Luc's young wife answered her urgent ring. She held a baby in her arms and smiled a welcome to Paris.

"Come in, mademoiselle, Jean-Luc is waiting for you. Can I offer you some tea—or a glass of wine?"

Paris made a conscious effort to calm herself as she followed the girl into the shabby room. The baby grinned toothlessly at her from his mother's shoulder and she grinned back, touching his chubby hand with her finger. He was sweet.

"Everything is ready for you, Paris." Jean-Luc shook her hand and took her across to the long work-table that filled one wall. Her hats sat on little stands looking like a row of summer flowers in the winter landscape of this drab room.

Jean-Luc had created a pert, veiled pillbox to be worn tilted over one eye in a thirties cocktail mood, a rakish Spanish hat for the suits, and a wide-brimmed straw, trailing with ribbons, for the romantic day dresses. Paris needn't have worried—they were perfect.

"More than perfect," she added, throwing her arms around him, "they're heaven—and you are a genius, Jean-Luc. These hats will be so successful that I won't be able to afford you next year."

Jean-Luc smiled modestly. "I hope you're right, but I'm happy that you are so pleased with them."

"You must come to the show—all three of you," she said, including the baby in her invitation.

Didi hurried into the drab room, his white suit as

outrageously out of place as her hats.

"Didi, look—aren't they beautiful?" Paris tried on the hats for him.

"Fantastic. Wonderful work, Jean-Luc. I knew you could do it. They are superb, thank God. Come on, Paris, we must be off."

He rushed her back down the stairs, put the hats in their boxes in the back of the car, and drove off to the next showroom for the shoes, and after that the jewelry, and then the hair ornaments.

By eight o'clock they were sitting side by side in Didi's Mercedes, exhausted but happy.

"I've only one complaint," said Paris, stretching, "and that's that the blue sandals weren't as good a match for the fabrics as they might have been. Apart from that, *perfect*. Don't you agree, Didi?"

"Thank God, yes." For novice couturiers, thought Didi, they were doing surprisingly well. "Just one thing left," he said. "The salon for the show. Do we see it before or after a drink?"

A drink sounded about right to Paris. But there was still that most important decision to be made.

"I would like," she said slowly, "a very large, very cold champagne cocktail. With a cherry."

"Wonderful," said Didi, starting the car.

"*After* we've seen the salons."

He sighed. "Somehow I knew you'd say that!"

Paris sipped her breakfast coffee and pondered on her decision. There was no doubt that the Art Nouveau hotel was out of the way, but designers were showing their lines out at the racetrack or in marquees in parks now, and the hotel had exactly the right atmosphere for her clothes. Her designs were influenced by the styles of the glamorous Hollywood musicals of the thirties, and she could just imagine Fred Astaire dancing his way down that wide, curving staircase in the entrance. Didi had fought her on it, saying that she should be in the center where the action was and that they would bank the place with flowers so that it wouldn't matter what the room looked like, and she had almost given in, but they had finally decided that the room was too big anyway for her small show. What if only half the invited guests showed up? They'd rattle around in there. So Art Nouveau it was.

Next time, she told herself, putting down her cup and climbing out of bed, next time I'll take an enormous suite at the Ritz and hold a reception and we'll have the show in one of their grandest salons. I'll recapture the spirit of Chanel. Meanwhile, this was what they could afford. Almost afford!

A glance at the window told her it was raining again. Would this miserable winter never end? And God, was it seven-thirty already? She had so much to do before Finola came at twelve. Everything was going well—and on schedule. It was just so hard doing *everything*, though Didi did as much as he could, and between them they were doing the work of five. But what she really needed was someone to coordinate the accessories and someone else to take care of each section of the show, the sportswear, the day wear, and the cocktail and evening wear. Oh, well—she smiled to herself—this time next year it'll all be different. I shall be a huge success, I'll be in my exquisite apartment rising at nine while my assistants and their minions take care of the boring details. I might even go off to my villa in Marrakesh just to "create." . . . The daydream was a pleasant one and she lingered on it while she showered. It was the only nice thing that happened that day.

By one-thirty Finola still hadn't shown up—nor had she telephoned. Paris fussed with the six evening dresses hanging on the rail, each one tailored to Finola's bony curves.

Paris had insisted on having her, despite the high price she commanded, because Finola had the long-legged, wide-shouldered, tapering body of a thirties star and was perfect for the clothes. There were to be four other models in the show, hired just for the day, and their clothes were normal, made in showroom size; any slight adjustments would be made the day before the show. Four girls weren't really enough, she knew it. It would mean a very rapid change for the models, but she couldn't afford any more—because of Finola. And now the bitch was late.

"Didi, *where is she?*"

"Didn't she say she might have a lunch date?"

"Yes—but she said she'd phone."

Didi dialed Finola's number again, listening to the ring. There was no reply. He strode toward the door.

"Where are you going?" called Paris, following

him.

"To find her. You wait here." He ran down the stairs to his car. And when I do find her, he thought murderously, I'll wring her bloody neck.

Finola emerged from the startling new salon of the young Japanese designer who had swept the board with his outrageous and innovative collection just two years previously and had gone on from success to success. She felt very pleased with herself, she'd played a waiting game with them and now they had offered her an enormous sum to do their show. It just went to prove, she thought, hurrying down the steps, that if you held out for what you wanted, then you'd get it in the end. They *needed* her. Of course it was tough luck on Paris Haven, but hers was a little collection and she could get someone else easily enough, although naturally all the best models were already booked.

Didier grabbed her arm as she came down the steps and hurried her toward his car, waiting at the curb.

"Let go of me," yelled Finola. "What do you think you're doing?"

"Doing? I'm taking you to an appointment that apparently you've forgotten."

Finola stared at him guiltily. "What appointment?"

Didi let go of her arm and put his hands in the pockets of his white jacket. It had begun to rain again and his black hair was plastered wetly against

184

his skull. His dark eyes glittered in his pale face and he looked strangely menacing.

"What are you up to, Finola?"

She stepped backward hastily. "Oh, I remember. I was supposed to phone Paris . . . I was just on my way to do that now."

"And what were you going to tell her? That you couldn't make her show? Is that it, Finola? Mitsoko has offered you star position and more money?"

Finola tossed her head angrily, thrusting back her long blond mane. Goddamn, she was getting wet!

"That's right, mister—and I've accepted his offer. I'm afraid I won't be able to do Paris's show. You can tell her to call the agency and get someone else."

Didier wanted to hit her; the urge sneaked the length of his arm and he thrust his hands deeper into his pockets, trying to control himself. The bitch had used them to stall Mitsoko for more money— and to become star of his show. In a way he couldn't blame her, a model's life was a short one, but, Jesus, he could kill her for what she'd done to Paris!

"Fuck you, Miss Texas," he snarled, turning away.

Finola reddened. "And fuck you too—*faggot*," she screamed, oblivious to the stares of passersby.

"Didi, what am I going to do!" Paris's voice held all the despair of Sarah Bernhardt in *L'Aiglon*, and Berthe lifted her eyes from the oyster satin blouson jacket across which she was sewing the thinnest strips of diamanté.

Didier shifted miserably from foot to foot. "We'll

185

call the agency and get someone else."

"There *is* no one else! Everyone, absolutely every single model in Paris, is already booked for the entire two weeks of the collections. My God, Didi, only the dregs are left—showroom models, that's all!"

Berthe listened with interest. So fancy Miss Finola had left them in the lurch, had she? Berthe wasn't surprised; she'd wondered how such a new and struggling enterprise had managed to secure one of the top models, but had imagined that she must be a good friend doing Paris a favor. In her opinion they were better off without her, though of course she *was* a good model and God knows they needed one. Of the four people in this room—herself, Paris, Didier, and the other fine seamstress, Madame Lescort, Berthe was the most experienced and the most professional. There were several things she considered they were doing wrong, but she was only here in her capacity as a needlewoman and no one had asked for her opinion. Still, she wondered what they would do now.

Paris slumped onto the old sleigh-bed and began to cry. "Oh, it's too much, Didi, it's just too much. What can I do?"

Didi perched next to her, feeling helpless. For once in his life he didn't know what to do.

"It'll be all right, Paris, it'll all work out, you'll see. Finola's not indispensable."

"She is, you know she is—for these two weeks, anyway."

186

Didi knew she was right.

"I'll get you some coffee," he suggested, "or a brandy?"

Paris turned her head into the cushions and sobbed.

Berthe could stand it no longer. Putting down the delicate garment she had been sewing she walked toward them. "Excuse me, mademoiselle, m'sieur . . ."

Didier stood up. He was unfailingly polite to the workpeople. "Yes, Berthe."

"I heard what happened with that American model, m'sieur, and I must tell you I'm not surprised. I'm very sorry, m'sieur, mademoiselle."

"Thank you, Berthe, that's very kind of you."

"If you'll permit, m'sieur, a suggestion, I've worked in salons since I was a girl—almost forty years. I have experience, I've seen hundreds of shows—good ones and bad ones—and I've seen all the battles that led up to them. I have an idea, m'sieur. I think we could save your show."

Paris's skeptical glance met Didi's and they both turned to stare at Berthe.

"Sit down, Berthe." Didier took her arm and steered her into a chair. "Now. Tell us. What is this idea?"

☜ 8 ☞

The red Ferrari was parked prominently outside Paroli's showrooms, its wet paintwork gleaming in

187

the light from the windows. Two young men leaned casually against the masterpiece of luxurious machinery, oblivious to the chilling rain drifting along the slick cobbled street, waiting, cameras tucked protectively beneath battered trenchcoats, for Fabrizio Paroli to emerge. Rumor had it that he was more than a little involved with the Haven daughter and twice they'd caught them leaving the showrooms together, and each time he'd driven her to her apartment and each time he'd merely dropped her off there. However, the rumor was a good story and the paparazzi were eager hounds on the scent of illicit romance, ready to do all they could to fan its flames. It wouldn't take much—two people caught in the glare of an unexpected flashbulb could look startled, and startled could be interpreted as "guilty"—if the caption held the right innuendo.

Fabrizio turned up his coat collar protectively as he emerged from Paroli's staff entrance in the alley at the back of the showrooms and mingled inconspicuously with his home-going employees. Head down, he hurried through the alley, cutting along a darkened back street to where the taxi waited on the corner.

India pushed open the door and he stepped inside, shaking the rain from his hair. His cold lips met hers as the taxi set off into the anonymous night.

It was odd, thought India, as Fabrizio's kiss of greeting became more passionate and his hands slid under her fox jacket, how the sudden interest of the paparazzi since Jenny's death had stimulated

188

Fabrizio's romantic interest in her. He seemed to want her all the time, wherever they were, in the office, in the car—even here in the taxi he couldn't wait. His hands were beneath her shirt, caressing her breasts, and India sighed with pleasure. Fabrizio lifted his mouth from hers. His eyes gleamed in the darkness as he took her hand and placed it on his erection. She could feel the heat of his body through the fine tweed of his pants as she caressed him automatically.

"Stop, stop, *carina,*" he murmured, grasping her arm again.

India stole a glance at the taxi driver, whose attention, thankfully, was on the dark rain-wet road in front of him as they made their way out of Rome into the countryside. Fabrizio buried his head inside the soft fox jacket, taking her nipple in his mouth with tiny bites until she cried out.

"Sshh," murmured Fabrizio.

India suddenly remembered the story of Jenny making love to her Englishman in the gondola in Venice—a taxi wasn't quite as romantic as a gondola, but the concept was the same. She began to giggle. Fabrizio, raised his head from his endeavors irritably.

"But why are you laughing, India? What have I done?"

"Nothing . . . you've done nothing—it's just funny, that's all." She threw back her head and laughed, and Fabrizio moved away, straightening his jacket and smoothing back his hair.

"I don't see anything funny," he said, annoyed. No woman had ever laughed at him when he was making love.

His macho instincts—and his erection—were so obviously deflated that India found it even funnier.

"Stop laughing!" commanded Fabrizio. "What's the matter with you tonight?"

"Oh, I don't know." She gasped between giggles. "It's just something I thought about."

"*I* was thinking about *you*," said Fabrizio coldly, "and I supposed you were thinking of me at such a time."

"I was, truly I was . . . it's—well, I just thought of something my mother told me and I realized I'm more like her than I thought."

"Ah, your mother." Fabrizio was filled with genuine Italian sympathy for a lost mother. "Poor little India. You will see, the pain will fade in a while. Sometimes laughter comes from sad memories."

India pulled her fur jacket over her breasts. It was bloody cold making love in cabs. She began to laugh again.

"Really, India, that's enough. You're becoming quite hysterical."

"I'm sorry, Fabrizio, I didn't mean it. It just happened." She tidied her appearance and peered out of the windows. All she could see was a dark country road. "It's very dark out there," she remarked.

"The countryside usually is," retorted Fabrizio.

India sighed. Obviously she'd hurt his finest feelings. To laugh when an Italian was making love to

190

you—even one as sophisticated as Fabrizio—was the wrong thing to do. She'd probably insulted his manhood, when all she'd been thinking of was her own reactions. Something else he'd said was true, though, that he had been thinking of her and at such a moment she should have been thinking of him. She hadn't—and it wasn't the first time. More and more often lately she'd found her thoughts drifting away while Fabrizio was consumed with passion. It really wasn't right to be wondering what was going on elsewhere while a man made love to you in some elaborate hotel bedroom. Was it that the secrecy of the relationship was finally becoming a bore? It wasn't Fabrizio's lovemaking, she could reassure him on that—but something was missing. India took his hand and kissed it and Fabrizio slid an arm around her.

"That's better, *cara*." He snuggled her head onto his shoulder. "You're calmer now."

"Are we almost there?"

"Another half hour. Not long, and then we'll be alone together."

That's the problem, thought India, I miss being with people. Affairs with married men become a lonely business—too lonely. Like this weekend, for instance. Marisa was in Milan visiting her family and wouldn't be back until Monday. Fabrizio had pleaded pressure of work, saying that he must stay in Rome, and had arranged to borrow the country villa of a friend who was abroad. They would have two nights together—only two, because he was nervous that Marisa might surprise him by returning earlier on Sunday. He didn't think she was suspicious yet—she'd laughed at the items in the newspapers and seemed unconcerned—but one never knew.

India snuggled closer to Fabrizio. She enjoyed being with him, she liked him, he was an amusing companion. He was an accomplished lover—and at first she had enjoyed the secrecy. It was easier in the beginning, she remembered; new love affairs bloom in out-of-the-way restaurants, where you were both unlikely to meet anyone you knew. Romance was heightened by assignations in quaint rooms in remote inns, and passion was allowed to take its course in thrilling rendezvous in some secret apartment; you were satisfied with much less in the beginning. But does romance begin to fade simply because it can't be part of the real world?

"What are you thinking, *cara?*" Fabrizio, kissed the end of her cold nose.

"I'm not sure." India stared through the windows into the wet night as the taxi swung through a pair of elaborate iron gates.

The villa sat at the end of a long, straight avenue of poplars, bent and dripping beneath their burden of rain. It looked gloomy and uninviting as they stepped from the taxi, and India huddled under the portico, waiting while Fabrizio settled with the driver and arranged for him to pick them up on Sunday morning.

"The servants were told to expect us," he said,

pressing the bell.

India watched the lights of the taxi disappear down the driveway, leaving them alone in darkness. Fabrizio rang the bell again—and again they waited. The rain on the roof of the portico sounded even louder in the silence.

Fabrizio lifted the heavy iron knocker and rapped at the door. "Damn it, where is everyone?" he demanded. "Hello, anyone home?"

"I sure as hell hope so," murmured India. What if there was really no one here and they were stuck in the middle of nowhere—on a night like this? So much for an illicit romantic weekend!

"Wait here," commanded Fabrizio. "I'll go and find the servants."

"But Fabrizio—what if there are no servants?"

He was already down the steps and heading for the corner of the house. "There are *always* servants."

His voice sounded angry and India hoped he was right. She peered nervously into the darkness. Faint rustlings in the undergrowth and the soughing of the wind in the trees brought back memories of every creepy movie she had ever laughed over—only, now they didn't seem funny. She pressed closer to the door and prayed that Fabrizio wouldn't be long.

Five minutes passed. India hugged her fur jacket around her; it was freezing standing here, there was no escape from that wind. She checked her watch again—another five minutes. Damn it, where was

Fabrizio? Surely he should have found *someone* by now? A branch cracked like a pistol shot, crashing to the ground somewhere in the darkness along the avenue. What was that? Where was Fabrizio?—Where was *everybody?* She couldn't bear to wait here any longer, she'd go and find him. He'd turned right, heading for the back of the house, hadn't he?

Keeping close to the wall, India hurried after him, tripping over ornamental statues and urns in the darkness. Every window was shuttered, so even if there were anyone inside it would have been impossible to catch so much as a gleam of light, but of course the owners were away and all the main rooms would be closed. Fabrizio had been looking for the servants' quarters. An arched gate led around the side of the villa, and India peered through it hesitantly. You're just being silly, she told herself sternly, of course there's no one there, there's absolutely nothing to be afraid of. Lifting her chin she strode through the arch and walked a few steps. If anything, it was even darker here than at the front of the house, and she paused uneasily.

"Fabrizio?" Her voice drifted tentatively on the wind. She listened hard, but there was only the sound of the rain flinging itself against the walls of the villa. "Fabrizio?" She called louder this time and strained her ears for a reply. Something must have happened to him. Oh, God, and she was here all alone without a car, probably miles from the nearest town. Panic gripped her. It was a couple of seconds before she realized that she had heard something, a different sound—yet familiar. A footstep on the gravel. India stood rooted to the spot, straining her ears. Yes, there it was again. Panic stricken, she turned and ran back through the arch—and straight into the man on the other side.

"India! Where the hell have you been?" Fabrizio grasped her by the shoulders. "I've been looking all over for you!"

"Fabrizio. Oh, thank God." Her knees felt weak with relief. "I thought something had happened to you. You were gone so long I got scared."

"What is there to be scared of? If you'd stayed put you wouldn't be this wet. Now we're both soaked!"

"Where are the servants?"

"What servants?" asked Fabrizio bitterly.

"Those servants who are always here—remember?"

"There's no one here. There must have been some misunderstanding about the dates."

"What?" India stared at him disbelievingly. The rain streamed down her face, dripping under her collar. "You can't be serious. Are you telling me that we're here in the middle of *nowhere*—with no car, and no key to this house?"

"That appears to be the situation," replied Fabrizio stiffly.

"Goddamn it." India stamped her foot in fury. "Why the hell didn't we bring my car?"

"You know why—the paparazzi have you staked out—they'd have followed us here! They'd take photos through the bedroom windows! If you thought they were bad in Hollywood, it's no holds barred here, India, and you know it."

"Then why did we come here? I could have met you in a hotel in Switzerland, or France—but no, you had this nice cozy little love-nest only an hour or so away from Rome! Shit!" India's stamping foot kicked out at him, catching him on the shin.

"Aagh!" Fabrizio stepped back, clutching his leg. He glared at her angrily in the darkness. "Violence does not become you, India."

His reply to her kick sounded so stiff and pompous that India laughed. "I thought it was the Neapolitans who were volatile and crazy." She giggled. "But, damn it, you deserved it, Fabrizio."

Turning on his heel he limped back toward the corner of the house.

"Fabrizio, wait! Wait for me!"

She caught up with him under the portico and grabbed his hand. "I'm sorry, forgive me—I didn't mean to hurt you, really, Fabrizio."

"Why were you laughing? You've been laughing secretly all night—it's very annoying, India."

"It's just that this whole situation struck me as being too ridiculous. You should be thankful I'm laughing, Fabrizio, and not crying!"

"It's true, I know." He put his arm around her wet, furry shoulders. "And it's my fault—I should have double-checked all the arrangements, but it's difficult sometimes."

"Well, what do we do now?"

"We break in," announced Fabrizio calmly.

"There's a small window at the back of the house that has been left unshuttered. It probably leads into a pantry near the kitchen. I shall break it with a stone and open the latch so that you can get in."

"Me?" India's eyes were round with astonishment.

"Of course *you*—obviously I am too large for such a window. Come on, I'll show you."

The window was small even for her, and India stared at it doubtfully.

"Isn't there any other way?" she asked in a small voice.

"Not unless you fancy walking six kilometers to the nearest town. Come on, now, India, it's not that difficult. Inside there is warmth and comfort, dry clothes, food and drink." He prayed he was right and that the house hadn't been left unoccupied by the servants for very long. "At least there'll be a telephone," he added.

A phone! The lifeline to civilization.

"Here's a stone," replied India.

The sound of shattering glass was small compared with the roar of the wind that had now reached gale force, and India crouched low, bracing herself against it, as Fabrizio put his hand inside the shattered pane and fiddled with the latch.

"Got it," he said triumphantly, swinging the window outward. "Come on, India—and watch out for fragments of glass."

The window was higher than she had thought; she could only just clutch the sill with her hands.

Fabrizio gave her a leg up and India cautiously pushed her head through the opening, staring into the darkness.

"Go on!" Fabrizio gave her a push.

"I can't see a thing," she called, her voice sounding muffled.

"I know the house," he called back. "I'm pretty sure that this is the butler's pantry. There should be a sink immediately below the window—if you feel down there you should find the taps and then we'll know I'm right. There's no big drop from the window to the floor, so there's no need to be afraid."

India felt forward cautiously; yes, there was the faucet. "You're right," she called, wriggling farther through. If she turned sideways she could just make it.

"I'm in," she called triumphantly. "I'm standing in the sink."

"Good, now I'll tell you what to do. If I'm right, directly opposite you is a door. It leads to a passage. If you turn left and walk all the way to the end you'll come to the door that leads from the kitchens into the side courtyard. If we're in luck the key will be in the lock, because that door is rarely used—there's another one the family uses that leads into the kitchen gardens."

India screamed.

"What is it?" he cried in alarm. "What's happened?"

"Oh, oh, it's all right, it's just a cat. It rubbed against my legs in the dark and scared the hell out

198

of me." The cat puffed at her feet and India bent and picked him up. His warmth felt comforting. "Beautiful puss, you'll stay with me, won't you? You know this house better than I do."

Sitting on the edge of the sink she wriggled to the floor and stood uncertainly, trying to get her bearings.

"I don't suppose you remember where the light switch is?" she called.

"Try next to the door."

Fabrizio's voice sounded fainter and she glared back at the small rectangle of light framed by the window.

"Damn it, puss, what am I doing here?" she whispered as the cat levered itself onto her shoulder, purring happily. "'I could be in some warm, cheery trattoria with warm, cheerful friends drinking warming and cheering red wine and eating my favorite pasta—I didn't have to come all this way to get laid!"

With one hand holding the cat and the other held out in front of her, she made her way cautiously across the room, using the window as a guide. The opposite wall came sooner than she thought, and she banged her hand sharply on the wooden door. He might have told me it was a *very small* room, she grumbled, rubbing her knuckles. She ran her hand down the wall on the right and felt the cold metal plate of the light switch. There it was! Thankfully, India pressed the small button, flooding the room with light, grinning as she heard a faint cheer from

Fabrizio outside.

She glanced at the cat, still clinging to her shoulder. He was as black as the night outside, his fur shiny and gleaming—unlike hers! She stared with horror at her sodden fox jacket. And her new "country tweeds," bought especially for the occasion—nobody had told her that when tweed got wet it drooped!

Sighing, India put down the cat and opened the door. She couldn't see a light switch, but there was sufficient glow from the open pantry door to negotiate the terra-cotta-tiled corridor. The cat skipped ahead of her, waiting while she struggled with the lock and lifted the heavy wooden bar that served as a bolt.

"Got it," she announced triumphantly, flinging open the door.

The cat shot into the night as Fabrizio marched into the house, water dripping from his hair and his coat.

They stared at each other in silence for a minute, and despite herself India began to laugh again. "I'm sorry, Fabrizio, but you look so funny—like someone who fell into a pond."

"You should take a look at yourself," he retorted with a grin. "You look like a drowned poodle. For God's sake, take off that jacket."

Clutching their wet coats they made their way back down the corridor and through a door at the far end.

"Wait here," he called. "I'll turn on the lights."

The hall felt chilly as she waited, and India shivered. What wouldn't she give for a hot bath right now! The room appeared first in a muted glow and then brighter as Fabrizio turned up the dimmers. India glanced up to the frescoed ceiling, where naked nymphs floated on fluffy clouds in a bright blue sky.

"Those nymphs must be freezing," she called. "It feels below zero in here."

"Wait a minute." Fabrizio disappeared through a doorway, emerging a few moments later clutching a bottle of brandy and two glasses. "Come on," he said, "we're going upstairs."

"How about a touch of central heating?" India's teeth were chattering as she followed him up the broad curving staircase that at any other time she would have paused to admire.

"This is your central heating," called Fabrizio, waving the bottle. "Don't worry, you'll soon be warm."

"Here we are." He flung open a door and pressed the switch that turned on the peach-shaded lamps.

It was, thought India, the most perfect cozy cave of a room. The walls were hung with some glowing amber-and-russet Florentine patterned fabric, there were warm coral rugs on the floor, and in the center an immense four-poster bed, curlicued and gilded and draped with soft golden gauze. A small sofa sat comfortably to one side of an old stone fireplace where logs waited in the grate ready to be lit.

"Thank God." She sighed. "I was beginning to

think we'd come to Dracula's castle."

"That would be no place to take a girl like you for a weekend." Fabrizio wrapped his arms around her, pulling her close. She could smell his familiar cologne and she put up her hand to brush back his wet curling hair.

"Poor girl, you're frozen," he murmured in her ear. "We'll light the fire and drink some brandy, and I'll have you warm in no time."

The kindling crackled comfortingly and the well-dried log caught at once, sending out a rosy glow that, while it wasn't yet hot, made them feel warmer just by its flickering presence. India threw her bedraggled fox jacket on the floor to dry and accepted the brandy he offered her.

"Heaven," she murmured, leaning against the mantel, sipping her brandy and toasting her toes over the fire.

"I told you it would be all right." Fabrizio brought her a huge, fluffy towel from the bathroom. "Here, dry your hair," he commanded.

India unbraided her hair, shaking and rubbing it vigorously with the towel until it stood up around her face in a spiky bronze halo. Her face was flushed from the brandy and the flames and, thought Fabrizio, she looked adorable.

"Let's continue where we left off?" he suggested, unbuttoning her checkered country shirt.

"I'd like another drink."

"Later." He slid the damp shirt from her shoulders.

"What about dinner?" India thought longingly of

tagliatelle steaming under a hot fresh tomato sauce flavored with basil.

Fabrizio unzipped her wet tweed skirt, kneeling to pull it down over her hips, tugging it gently past her thighs. India stepped out of her skirt.

"Tights," he groaned, "are the enemy of man."

He slid them off.

"How about a hot bath?" suggested India.

"Good idea," he murmured, burying his face in the softness between her legs.

India laughed.

"I did, didn't I?" she murmured.

"Did what?" His tongue sent ripples of pleasure through her.

"Come all this way just to get laid."

The fire, fueled with fresh logs, cast a flickering glow over their retreat. India sat cross-legged in front of the hearth wearing only a huge cashmere sweater she'd found in a drawer, munching on the slices of Parma ham that Fabrizio was carving from the side they'd discovered on their foray to the kitchen. With a crumbly mountain cheese, some biscuits, and a box of dried figs, it made a delicious dinner for two, washed down with a bottle of Amarone Riserva, filched from the wine cellar.

"Perhaps I'll forgive them after all," decided Fabrizio, cutting another slice of ham.

"Forgive who?" India leaned back, sipping her wine sleepily.

"The Brandinis—for messing up our arrangements."

"Definitely,"—she yawned—"as long as to-morrow we can rent a car—or at least find these elusive servants."

"Consider it done," he said magnanimously. "Come on, you look tired. Let's go to bed."

India climbed into the gilded four-poster, feeling as though she were floating in a golden sea as Fabrizio closed the gauze curtains around them. It was rarely that they managed to spend a night together, and she watched as Fabrizio cast off the toweling robe he was wearing, admiring his muscular tapering body as he slid naked beside her.

"You know, don't you, Fabrizio," she murmured as she lay with his arm around her while the firelight flickered on their curtains, "that this is just a golden never-never land."

There was a shrill buzzing inside her head, and India wished it would go away. It was a familiar sound, like a siren. Why didn't Fabrizio do something about it? She jolted awake as the bedroom door was flung open and the lights switched on.

"Oh, my God," she cried as Fabrizio flung his arms about her protectively.

"Polizia!" barked the man framed in the doorway, a hand on his gun. Two other policemen crowded behind him, and India hastily drew the blanket up beneath her chin.

"Police?" cried Fabrizio. "But what are you doing bursting in on us like this? What's happened?"

"I might ask you the same question, signore."

"I am a friend of the family—they lent me the house for the weekend."

"I see." The policeman's eyes flickered disbelievingly over India. She cowered back, feeling very naked beneath the blanket. "And the signora, too, I suppose?"

"What is all this?" demanded Fabrizio angrily.

"You are both under arrest for breaking and entering this establishment. Do you deny that you broke the window and forced an entrance?"

"No, of course not, but I can explain—"

"You will do your explaining at the police headquarters and I warn you my men are searching the house for the rest of you."

"The rest of us?" India glared at him. "You fool, there are no others. We're spending a peaceful weekend at the house of friends. How dare you burst into my bedroom like this!" Her Italian had a very pronounced American accent when she was angry and the policeman looked at her with new interest.

"A foreigner, I see. . . . Well, I hope you have your passport, signora?"

"Oh, my God," groaned Fabrizio, holding his head in his hands, visualizing the scandal. "This is ridiculous. Can you imagine what the papers will do to us?"

India stared at him in horror. It was only a few hours ago that she had been thinking that she was as indiscreet as her mother. This was getting worse and worse—she didn't want her name spread through the press again, linked, as she knew it would be, to her mother and her mother's indiscretions. She sank back against the pillows, frightened.

"But how did they know we were here?" she whispered to Fabrizio as the men inspected the room, making a note of the food and the wine on the table near the fireplace.

"The alarm, signora." The captain missed nothing. "This whole house is wired—there are pressure pads beneath the carpets in every room. Normally, we would have been here immediately, but with such a storm, the roads were washed out. And now I must ask you to get your clothes and come with me." He ushered his men outside the door. "We will wait outside for the signora to dress."

The door closed behind the policemen. India and Fabrizio, sitting in bed, looked at each other.

"The window . . ." gasped India wildly.

"Don't be ridiculous!" Fabrizio climbed out of bed and pulled on his shirt. "We're in a lot of trouble, India. Oh, not from the charge, obviously it will be sorted out, but from the scandal. We've been caught. I've got to keep Marisa from knowing."

"But how?" India sat on the edge of the bed contemplating the idea of an Italian jail cell and Marisa's wrath and wondering which would be worse.

"I have the feeling," replied Fabrizio, pulling on his pants, "that it's going to cost a great deal of money."

☙ 9 ❧

Rory was upset. Very upset. So upset he was muffing his lines—and as they only gave him a couple to say at a time, it really made him look bad. He sniffed impatiently as the makeup girl repowdered his forehead. Over in a corner the director, Dirk Bonner, was conferring with Shelly James, his female costar. Shelly was nodding her head, eyes downcast, listening intently to what Dirk was saying. Dirk was probably talking about him, putting him down, telling her *she* was the greatest!

Paranoia flared as Rory stomped back onto the location of *Chelsea's Game*—a downtown L.A. jail, the real thing, complete with iron bars and padlocked doors. Unused now and empty, of course, but it still gave him a shudder just being there. Bill had probably got them to shoot here just to back up his threat and keep him in line. Fuck! As if the whole thing were his fault!

"Tell Dirk I'm in my dressing room—whenever he's ready," he said curtly.

As he laid down the neat line of coke, Rory pondered on his problem. He had really lucked out meeting Jenny Haven at that party—at least that's what he'd thought then! She was still lovely, still sexy, and being with her had been a real high in the beginning—before he really got into the coke. Jenny hadn't liked it, and she'd liked it even less when he'd told her she was getting old, that she wasn't moving with the times. Alcohol was the drug of *her* genera-

207

tion—though not Jenny, she was dead straight. *Too* straight! She didn't like his habit and she didn't like his friends. He'd kept it down, kept it quiet, kept her happy, while she burned up her energy in creating him—Rory. Her very own star. Of course, he was a quick learner, and he'd had the basics to begin with, but she'd given him that contemporary macho gloss, she'd gotten rid of his excess pounds, his brown hair, even his moustache in case they thought he was gay.

Then she'd started unloading her problems on him, telling him how she was managing her own business affairs. He'd helped her, given her some good advice, meanwhile just funneling off enough money to finance the coke she was against him taking. So? Where else was he to get the money? He wasn't working yet. And that was another thing— she'd expected to costar with him when he got the television part. Was it his fault that the director wanted someone *young?* She'd started thinking about maybe directing a couple of episodes, but Dirk wasn't letting go of his job to accommodate Jenny Haven—all Dirk needed was Jenny taking the credit for the success of *Chelsea's Game!*

Rory held the paper with the coke to his left nostril and sniffed noisily, then to his right. Jeez, that was better!

Anyway, she shouldn't have let him take so much control—she should have organized her business matters herself, or gotten someone else to do it. Jenny was generous when it came to expensive clothes, dinners for two, and a bottle of champagne, but pocket money was hard to come by; he'd just had to find ways to put a little into his own account. He'd started finding property "bargains" that he told her were so "hot" she'd make a killing; it was easy just to inflate the price and pocket the difference. She'd trusted him completely—after all, the man she was doing everything in her power to help was not going to screw her, was he? Rory grinned at the memory—sure he was, if he needed the money and she wasn't gonna give it to him! It was the same on the stock market. He'd enjoyed playing it at first. He'd made a bit—then lost a chunk. That was her money, not his. When he won, it was his money. He'd tried commodities for bigger wins, lost a lot, pocketed the rest.

He'd left her when she'd realized she was broke. He'd blamed it all on her, told her they were her decisions and he'd only done what she asked. It was true, wasn't it? He'd told her every time he'd got a good tip on the market and she'd said okay. It wasn't his fault that he'd lost more than he'd won—it happened all the time to lots of people. Anyway, it was time to leave, he'd had enough. She acted too old for him, and besides, things were looking good then, he'd just been chosen for the lead in the TV show. He was Chelsea in *Chelsea's Game*.

Everything would have been okay if she hadn't died like that . . . and if it weren't for those bastards Kaufmann and Reubin! They'd blackmailed him! There was no other word for it. Shit! They were good at their jobs, there was no doubt about that, but Kaufmann was taking thirty percent as agent and personal manager, and Reubin had appointed himself his lawyer at a mammoth retainer—the more Rory earned, the bigger the retainer would grow. It's only fair, Rory, Stan had said in that smoothie-lawyer voice of his, only fair, considering the circumstances.

Rory stared at his attractive image in the mirror and reconsidered the circumstances. He didn't like them, nor the possible consequences of them, at all. He was a young man on the threshold of a great career, he had no choice but to be blackmailed by Reubin and Kaufmann.

"Rory?" The assistant director put his head around the door. "Dirk'll be ready in five, okay?"

"Yeah." Rory checked his appearance in the mirror. Goddamn, he was sweating—his forehead needed powdering again. He hoped they wouldn't work late tonight. He had a date with the waitress from the Café Rodeo, the cute one who'd admired his sweater. She was a dancer usually, but she'd had hepatitis and lost her job over at CBS. He planned to take her to Sally Fox's party, it should be a blast. He ought to get some more streaks done in his hair—wasn't it looking a bit dark at the front? Jenny's hairdresser sure was good, though, he'd know what to do.

"Ready, Rory?"

Rory ran his finger along the folded paper that had contained the coke and rubbed it thoughtfully across his gums. He must remember to put the proper inflection on the name in that next shot. . . .

He walked out onto the set, put his arm around Shelly, and waited while continuity checked the shot and Dirk tightened the camera angle. This time he got it in one take.

"Brilliant, Rory, brilliant," called Dirk. "I knew you'd get it this time."

❧ 10 ❧

Venetia knew she shouldn't have come. Lawten Hall was tucked away in the wilds of Wiltshire, in a landscape of frozen fields and stark trees that matched Mrs. Fox-Lawten's personality exactly. When she appeared at the front door and icily instructed her in future to use the servants' entrance, Venetia knew she should have got the message then, and turned around and left her to it. But she had contracted with the agency to cook for a weekend house party of fourteen, and therefore she stayed. And it was three days' work, which would boost her income considerably.

The trouble had started before she had even taken off her coat and Sondra Fox-Lawten had swept into the kitchen to discuss the menus. No mention of a cup of coffee or showing Venetia her room—and it was a good thing she hadn't, because then for sure Venetia wouldn't have stayed. Her room was in the attic, which, when the Fox-Lawtens had renovated the old house, had been omitted

211

from the central heating system. The poky room was furnished in meager junk-shop style, and a single-bar electric fire was its only source of warmth.

The first battle had come over the menus, which they had previously discussed over the phone so that Venetia could do the shopping and precook some of the dishes. Now Mrs. Fox-Lawten had changed her mind—or rather Tony Fox-Lawten had decided he must serve a '64 Haut Brion with the main course at Saturday evening's dinner party—when there would be six extra guests—and so now they weren't to have chicken poached in champagne with white grapes, around which Venetia had built the rest of her menu. They were to have pheasant, which meant that something lighter would have to be substituted for the terrine of wild game she had spent hours preparing at home. And the vegetable would have to be changed. It made a hell of a lot of extra work, and she already had enough on her hands with all those people to serve breakfast, lunch, and dinner—as well as afternoon tea for those who wanted it.

Tony Fox-Lawten had popped in to introduce himself on the Friday evening when he'd returned from the City. "Hear I'm in a spot of bother," he'd said, sticking his head around the door. "Came to apologize." His busy eyes had checked her out and he'd smiled as he crossed the kitchen. "Hello, hello, hello, we don't usually have cooks who look like this." Venetia brushed the hair from her eyes, wishing she'd remembered to tie it back, and folded her arms firmly over her apron. Tony Fox-Lawten was short and tubby with pink cheeks and the bluish chin of a man who had to shave twice a day to keep from looking swarthy.

"It's no bother, Mr. Fox-Lawten," she'd said politely. And then, damn it, she'd told him, "Well, as a matter of fact it was a hell of a nuisance and caused a *lot* more work."

"Sorry, sorry, I'll make it up to you. A bit extra in the pay packet, you'll be all right. How about a drink, eh? Perk you up a bit. You probably need one if Sondra's been keeping her usual pace. Quite a perfectionist, Sondra. How about it, then—gin and tonic?"

It was amazing, thought Venetia, how true to form they all were. Could it be just her rotten luck or were the whole of the English shires peopled with lecherous husbands, freed from the week's City pinstripes and feeling their oats?

Tony Fox-Lawten had taken her refusal in his stride, but he'd adopted the habit of popping into the kitchen, "just to see how she was getting along." Venetia could have managed very well without any Fox-Lawtens hanging around.

Friday had gone fairly smoothly, although the pace was staggering. There had been no time for a meal for herself; she'd had to snatch bits and pieces as she went along. Guests began arriving at three in the afternoon and Venetia had been serving tea from then until six. After that it was drinks at eight o'clock, and dinner at eight-thirty. Which had left her exactly two hours to prepare a meal for fourteen. It was a good thing she'd made the salmon mousse and the summer pudding and brought them with her, or she would have been sunk; and it was a good thing, too, that she'd prepared the turkey pie for Saturday's lunch, because by the time breakfasts were over it was already lunchtime.

The real fight with Sondra Fox-Lawten had come right after Saturday lunch. It had been after midnight when Venetia had gone to bed and she hadn't slept because the room was so cold—she could see her breath floating in the moonlight in front of her. Miserably she'd contemplated getting up and making herself a hot drink but had decided she'd probably wake someone if she did, and she didn't fancy an encounter with Tony Fox-Lawten in her night attire. She'd got up at six-thirty to prepare the pheasants and crisp game chips and to fix breakfast trays to be relayed to the various bedrooms by Mrs. Jones, the daily from the village. After that she tackled lunch. By three-fifteen she had just placed the last dish in the dishwasher and turned on the machine when Mrs. Fox-Lawten came in to see her.

"We shall have tea at five, Venetia," she'd commanded, "and I'd like you to make some nice little canapés to serve with drinks."

"You should have asked me earlier, Mrs. Fox-Lawten," Venetia had said quietly. "I'm afraid there's no time now."

"Of course there's time." Sondra Fox-Lawten raised a well-penciled eyebrow. "You're not doing anything now, are you?"

"Yes," Venetia replied evenly. "Yes, I am doing something. I have been in your kitchen since six-thirty this morning and now I am going to that freezing attic you feel fit to call a bedroom to lie down for exactly one hour and a half until it's time to get tea. After that I will be busy with dinner. I'm sorry, Mrs. Fox-Lawten, but there will be no canapés."

"Well, really!" Sondra's greenish eyes had popped and she had patted her newly set auburn hair agitatedly; no one ever talked to her like that! "I must remind you that you are here to do a job! I'm paying you to cook—not to lie down!"

"I shall cook, Mrs. Fox-Lawten," said Venetia, walking out of the door, leaving Sondra standing there. "Dinner will be on time."

She'd regretted it later. She would probably have been better off making canapés in the kitchen than trying to stay warm in that grim little room.

Tony Fox-Lawten showed up in the kitchen at teatime, just when she was munching on a ham sandwich.

"I see you don't starve yourself, then," he said pointedly. "What's this I hear about a dustup with Sondra?"

"Mr. Fox-Lawten, if I were like my sister India, I would have told Mrs. Fox-Lawten what to do with her canapés and her dinner party. I was at least polite."

"I'll bet you were." He grinned. "You've got better

manners than Sondra. All her family's money comes from butcher shops, and sometimes I think it shows up in the genes!"

Venetia had just decided that maybe Tony Fox-Lawten wasn't all bad when he made his move.

"How about a little drink later, just you and me?" he said, grabbing her hand.

"No, thank you," she said, polite as ever.

"Oh, come on, now."

There was a sound of a footstep on the hall.

"I'll see you later," he called, whisking off in a hurry—no doubt afraid of Sondra's genes, thought Venetia nastily.

And then at seven-thirty, when she was in the throes of preparing dinner, Sondra Fox-Lawten floated into the kitchen in pale blue chiffon and goose-pimples and knocked over the bowl of red-currant puree that was to be served with the pheasant.

"Bloody hell," she screamed, "look at my dress! It cost four hundred last month at Harvey Nichols—how could you be so stupid as to leave the dish on the edge of the table?"

Venetia watched the spreading red-purple patch on the dress, horrified—four hundred pounds! Ruined! But it wasn't her fault, the dress was the floaty sort that caught on everything, she must have flung out her arm and just caught the dish.

"I'm sorry about the dress, Mrs. Fox-Lawten," she said, "but the dish was where it should be. I'm afraid your dress wasn't."

"I shall speak to the agency about this," threatened Sondra Fox-Lawten, stopping herself just in time from saying that she wouldn't pay—that had better wait until later, *after* the girl had cooked the meals. She didn't want to be left stranded, and at least she'd get some value out of her for the ruined dress.

Sondra flounced out of the kitchen and Mrs. Jones, busy with the silverware for the table, commented, "She's a bit difficult, Mrs. Fox-Lawten, but don't you worry yourself, love, it wasn't your fault."

"I know," replied Venetia wearily.

Mrs. Jones disappeared to do her table and Vennie slumped against the fridge, tears stinging her eyes. Damn it, she wanted to make a success of this. Why were there always so many problems? Her vision of an exclusive catering company with herself as its head, supervising all of London's smart parties, began to dwindle.

Tony Fox-Lawten appeared in the doorway, a bottle of gin in one hand and a bottle of tonic in the other.

"Here we go," he said. "I thought you might need a drop of this after I saw Sondra's dress—that puree has gone right through everything, she swears she's stained purple and has to have a bath." He laughed at the idea of a purple Sondra, and despite herself, so did Venetia.

"I'd love a drink," she agreed, "but it really was her own fault, you know. The dish was on the table and she brushed it off with her sleeve."

"Don't worry about it," Tony said, handing her a

drink and omitting to tell her that Sondra had no intention of paying her. "Cheers, then—here's to us."

Venetia's eyes met his over the top of her glass. She could see the pass coming a mile off.

He put down his glass and threaded his fingers through the strings of her blue-striped apron where she had tied them at the front. "Come a little closer," he murmured. "I want to ask you something."

"What?" Venetia hung back as he put an arm on her shoulders, puffing her toward him.

"I'm in London every day, you know. We could see each other there—have dinner perhaps? Maybe at your place?"

"My family wouldn't like it," said Venetia.

"Then somewhere else—you know what I mean. It could be fun—and no Sondra to worry about."

His breath smelled of gin and Venetia averted her face, vainly attempting to prise his hands from her apron strings, as he bore down on her.

Sondra Fox-Lawten stood in the kitchen doorway in her pink satin housecoat observing her husband making advances toward the help.

"You little tart!" Her voice cut shrilly through the quiet kitchen and Tony jumped back from Venetia as though shot.

"Oh, now, Sondra, it's not what it seemed. She just had something in her eye, that's all. The girl didn't mean anything by it."

Sondra was caught in a dilemma. Sod it, she thought, I should have tackled her about it later—I can't tell her to leave now or whatever will I do about dinner? And there's Sunday lunch, and all those breakfasts.

"We'll talk about this later," she said icily, "but I shall make sure to report your behavior to the agency."

Venetia untied her apron. "Call them now, Mrs. Fox-Lawten," she said, walking toward her, "and ask them to send you someone else. I'm leaving."

"But you can't!" gasped Sondra.

An American expression fluttered through Vennie's head. "Wanna bet?" she asked as she brushed past on her way through the door.

❦ 11 ❦

Something was getting on Fitz McBain's nerves. Was it the filthy New York weather? Was it the constant stalling on the petrochemical deal in Latin America? Or was it the capricious antics of Raymunda Ortiz?

Fitz swiveled his gray leather chair, turning from the papers on his desk to the view of Manhattan, almost obliterated today by the rain lashing from a leaden sky. The sight held little charm, and putting his shirt-sleeved arms behind his head he wondered again what to do about that deal. It should have been completed a month ago—licensing agreements had been reached, refineries made available, documents awaited exchange. Everyone they had dealt with had been charming and reassuring—and yet the damned thing still hung fire. It was going to take another trip down to Brazil—his third in two months—another round of reassurances, more lengthy dinners with businessmen and their socially ambitious wives, and at the end, would he have accomplished his purpose and signed the deal? He had to admit that for once he didn't know. What he did know was that he was losing patience with the situation.

He wondered moodily whether it was all worth it—not just this deal but *all* of it, all the wheeling and dealing, the jockeying for position, and beating out the competitors. It had meant everything to him in the beginning, when life was just survival, and then, when survival was taken care of, it had become fun. When, he asked himself, did the fun depart and habit begin?

Perhaps he should give it all up. Retire and hand over to Morgan. And then what? He was forty-four years old and had worked since he was thirteen. What the hell did you do if you didn't work? With a shudder he contemplated a life spent squiring a Raymunda Ortiz from one jet-set party to another. How different might it have been if Morgan's mother had lived? That was always how he thought of Ellen now, as "Morgan's mother." Their love for each other and their youthful romantic passion seemed a long time ago. Maybe they would have had other children and a proper home, not just this selection of desirable properties in various parts of the world for which he paid all the bills, and in which he slept only occasionally. Morgan always said that his plane was his home and Fitz was damned if he wasn't right; he was happier alone in that one room suspended between time changes and continents and surrounded by the clouds than anywhere else on earth.

Enough of that! He'd go to the club and play some squash, get rid of the depression and rev up his energy level a notch or two. Work was the single most important entity in his life. Retirement didn't exist in his vocabulary and the Raymunda Ortizes were a long way down on his priority list.

Fitz pressed the buzzer on his desk and waited for his secretary to answer. Miss Clarke had been with him for ten years. He had always believed in equal opportunity within his companies and she was more than just a secretary, she was his personal assistant with two secretaries of her own; she was part of his life, a keeper of secrets, and he counted her a friend. But he still called her Miss Clarke and she always called him Mr. McBain.

"Hold my calls please, Miss Clarke. I'm going down to the gym to get in a game of squash—I'll be back in forty minutes."

What he needed was a different viewpoint on that Latin American contract, he decided as he changed into a gray track suit in the bathroom that adjoined his office. He'd send Morgan to Brazil; it would be something he'd enjoy, and coming fresh to the situation he'd probably be able to spot what was wrong. One thing was for sure, the Latin

Americans weren't going to tell him. Dealing with them was as baffling as dealing with Japanese—they never liked to say no. A polite agreement and "tomorrow" were meant to make you understand that perhaps they didn't quite agree.

It was exactly the same with Raymunda; she flirted and teased and agreed—and then she'd be aloof and haughty. Raymunda was a beautiful woman, and a sensuous one. He liked being with her—at least when she was behaving reasonably and not like some spoiled teenager—and he enjoyed being in bed with her, very much so, but he had the feeling that Raymunda was playing out the marriage cards. Lately she'd been evasive on the telephone, or aloof over dinner, and had even gone so far as to cancel two dates at the last moment for unspecified reasons.

Why, he wondered, can't she just enjoy it for what it is? I could no more be happy married to Raymunda than she could to me—and she knows it.

Fitz stared out of his fortieth-floor eyrie at the rain. At least he could do something about the weather. The *Fiesta* was lying at anchor in Barbados with a crew ready and anxious for some action. Forget the squash games! The skies there were blue and the sun hot, and didn't he deserve a week off? He'd get Morgan to join him. He could brief him on the Latin American situation and Morgan could fly on from there. Add Raymunda to the package and he'd beaten all three of today's problems. Temporarily anyway, he added, picking up the telephone.

Kate Lancaster sat on Vennie's bed, hugging her friend's old teddy and eating a toasted Marmite sandwich, just the way they had done in the dorm at school.

"There are some tastes acquired in childhood," she announced, taking another bite, "that never leave you. If I were cast away on a desert island I should long for Marmite on soggy toast."

Vennie laughed. "If you were cast away with me I'd make you paw-paw soufflé and coconut pudding. 'Dessert Isle' would be a good name for a restaurant, you know," she added thoughtfully.

"So what about the job at the Café Laurent? Shall you accept their meager offer or hold out for more?"

"I don't know." Wearing a pink leotard, Venetia was dancing energetically to the workout tape on the video. "God, this is killing," she breathed, keeping pace with the tape.

"I don't know why you bother." Kate picked up another bit of toast. "You're in better shape than the girls on the video. I shall wait until I'm fat and forty."

"The idea," gasped Vennie, "is never to be fat and never to look forty! Ohh." She collapsed with a groan onto the floor. "Enough, enough . . ."

Kate leaned over the edge of the bed, surveying her friend as she lay spread eagle on the carpet, gasping. "It seems to me you'll never get the chance to see forty if you keep up this pace. Here, have a Marmite sandwich."

"Thanks." Venetia leaned against the bed, chewing thoughtfully. "Kate, what shall I do?" she asked. "Or rather, do I have any choice?"

Kate Lancaster had glossy brown hair and her mother's green eyes and the face, as her father always said, of a well-fed gamine, slightly plump and very appealing. However, behind that appeal lay the brain of a mathematical wizard. Kate was at Cambridge studying computer sciences, and her nature was analytical and practical.

"Let's examine all the facts, Vennie," she said. "One. You can't go on cooking for those ghastly weekend orgies."

"House parties," corrected Venetia.

"They'd be orgies, all right, if those husbands had their way. Don't interrupt, Vennie. One. No more weekend orgies; two. City lunches are potentially a good business but so far no one has offered you, a full-time job, and occasional work doesn't bring in enough loot."

"Maybe I'm not good enough?" Venetia finished her toast and sank back onto the carpet, her eyes fixed on the athletic, super-fit, smiling Californians leaping their way through aerobic exercises.

"Nonsense—and I said you weren't to interrupt. Now, three. The only other possibility at this point is a full-time job working in a wine bar or a restaurant, and the best of those bets is Laurent's, because they're new and it'll give you a chance to make a name for yourself as a chef. However—and this is a major 'but'—the money they are offering is a pittance because of your youth and inexperience. It's exploitation and they know it—they'd have to pay five times as much for a man with just a couple of years' work behind him, and he wouldn't be nearly as good as you."

"So?" Venetia turned from the video and her eyes met Kate's. "What do I do?"

"I'm damned if I know!"

The phone rang and Kate leapt off the bed to answer it. "That's the trouble with you computer people," Vennie shouted after her, "you lack human response." She turned down the tape, listening to see if she knew who Kate was chatting with on the phone. It must be someone nice, she sounded very up.

"Vennie," called Kate from the hall, "it's for you."

"Who is it?" Venetia unrolled herself lazily from the floor.

"It's Morgan. Hurry up, he's in Barbados."

"Barbados?" Venetia shot to her feet and ran down the hall to Lydia's room, where Kate sat on the edge of her mother's bed, giggling with Morgan McBain.

"Bye, then," she called. "Here's Vennie."

"Morgan, hello. Are you *really* in Barbados? You are? And is the sky really blue and is there still sunshine somewhere in this wet world?" Venetia curled up on the bed and tucked her feet under her comfortably, a smile lighting her face. "Yes . . . I *think* I'm missing you."

Kate watched with interest. There was no doubt

225

in her mind that Morgan was *very* keen on Venetia.

"Morgan, really? You can't mean it? But I can't—I mean it's impossible . . . I might be starting a new job next week. What do you mean, doing what? Cooking, of course—actually, as chef at a new restaurant."

Kate gazed at her anxiously. "What's going on?" she whispered.

Vennie put her hand over the receiver. "He wants me to go to Barbados for a week or two—to stay on his father's yacht. But how can I? I've got to take this job."

"Ohh," groaned Kate, clapping her hand to her head dramatically and falling backward onto the rug, "Venetia Haven, you are so *thick* sometimes, I can't bear it."

Venetia grinned at her doubtfully. "No, no, Morgan, it's just Kate acting silly." She looked at Kate again. "He says you can come too."

Kate groaned louder. "I have exams for the next two weeks, Vennie! But you don't."

"Morgan," said Venetia firmly, "I can't come, it's very tempting, but I can't. I really must take this job. What? Oh, now you *are* joking! You'll check to make sure? Okay. Yes, yes. Right . . . yes, me too. Bye."

"What?" cried Kate. "What now?"

"Morgan said that the chef from the *Fiesta* wants to go back to New York to work, and they have to find someone else. He's pretty sure I could have the job for the entire winter season in the Caribbean." Vennie clapped her hands over her ears at Kate's scream of delight.

"Amazing!" shrieked Kate. "Brilliant! It's option four! Wait a minute, how much will they pay you?"

"Oh, Kate, I don't know," laughed Venetia, "but in any case I don't think that I could accept the job."

"Why ever not? You're good enough."

"It's sort of . . . well, they would really be doing me a favor offering it to me."

"And what else," demanded Kate, "are friends for? I only wish they needed a half-trained computer scientist!"

Venetia laughed. "Then you think I should take the job—that is, if it is offered?"

"Take it," said Kate firmly, "and take a large jar of Marmite with you in case you're shipwrecked on a desert island with Morgan. Give or take a prince or two, Morgan McBain is the catch of the decade, and I think it's you he's after!"

"I'm just a passing fancy," said Venetia, remembering the way Morgan's mouth had felt on hers, the pressure of his strong, slim body as he held her close.

"Don't you believe it," Kate assured her. "He has all the signs of a man in the early throes of love, and you are the object of his secret passion!"

As their eyes met they burst into laughter, rolling on the bed in delight. "Imagine me as the object of anyone's secret passion?" gasped Venetia. "*Me*, a femme fatale!"

Lydia Lancaster wondered what was going on. The two girls were hovering near the phone, pouncing on it every time it rang like lovelorn teenagers—

Which I expect they are, she told herself, picking up the phone and dialing.

"Mummy! Who are you calling?"

Lydia stared at Kate in astonishment. "I'm calling Jennifer Herbert, dear. Why?"

"Ohh, Mummy, *please,* not now—you're always ages with her and we're expecting a call *any minute.* An *important* call," she added, placing her finger on the receiver rest.

"Kate! Really, that's too much—you've cut me off!"

"I'm sorry, Mummy, but *please*—just this once. It's truly important."

Kate stood implacably holding down the phone rest with her finger as Lydia glared at her.

"Who—"

The phone rang and Kate lifted her finger.

"Hello?" said a voice.

Lydia gazed in surprise at the telephone—of course, she was still holding the receiver.

"Hello?" she replied.

"Am I speaking to Mrs. Lancaster?"

The voice was deep and pleasant and totally unknown to her.

"Yes, this is. Lydia Lancaster."

"Good evening, Mrs. Lancaster. This is Fitzgerald McBain."

"Mr. McBain! Good heavens . . . well, how nice." Lydia was surprised. "Of course, we've come to know Morgan very well, he often drops in to see us."

"He told me about that, Mrs. Lancaster, and I'd

like to thank you and your family for your hospitality. It means a lot, when you travel as much as Morgan, to be rescued from the loneliness of hotels and restaurants and taken into someone's home."

"Not at all. And needless to say we were all terribly grateful for your help to Venetia and her sisters."

Lydia glanced at Kate and Venetia's expectant faces as they hovered at her shoulder. So this was the call, was it?

"*Fitz* McBain?" mouthed Kate.

Lydia nodded, listening.

"It's Fitz!" Kate hugged Venetia excitedly. "He's going to offer you the job *personally!*"

"I see. Yes, I'm quite sure she'd be safe with you. And, yes, Morgan is right, she's a splendid cook—and an imaginative one, I'm quite sure you'd be pleased with her. That sounds remarkably generous. Yes, she would have my permission, Mr. McBain, but perhaps you'd better talk to Venetia yourself. Of course, thank you, that sounds wonderful. Good-bye, Mr. McBain."

Lydia handed the receiver to Venetia. "Fitz McBain has called personally to offer you the job on his yacht for the rest of the season—if you want it."

Venetia was smiling as she said, "Hello, Mr. McBain."

"Venetia, I've been hearing about you long distance for some time. It seems that we are now to meet—that is, if you would like the job?" The deep voice had a relaxed, easy accent—American southern that had crossed international barriers somewhere along the way. It was attractive.

"It sounds too good to be true," Venetia replied.

"Don't you believe it. Work is still work, though you may find yourself with time on your hands now and again. I don't manage to get down here as often as I'd like. Morgan suggested I call to overcome any idea you might have that this was a put-up job. You can take my word for it that it's not. Our present chef has been offered a post in New York and he feels it's important to his career to accept. I'm not one to hold any man back from his ambitions, and I've said he can go. So, will you come to us, Venetia?"

"I'd love to—and I promise to do my best. I *am* quite good."

"Morgan tells me you are more than that, and so does Mrs. Lancaster, but we'll see."

"Mr. McBain . . ."

"Yes?"

"I wrote thanking you for all you did for me—us—when my mother died. I just wanted to say thank you again."

"I have your letter, Venetia. I was happy to help. Now"—his voice became brisker—"let us know how soon you can be here and someone in my office will take care of the travel details. Good-bye, Venetia. My regards to your sisters."

Venetia put down the receiver, turning to face Kate and Lydia, both gazing at her expectantly.

"What," she said, beaming, "do you suppose the chef on a luxury yacht is expected to wear?"

Paris's new models fluttered down the runway as vivid as a flock of tropical birds in the briefest little frocks—mere slivers of silk chemise cut dead straight to the hip with the shortest, flirtiest puffball skirts of ruffled tulle in magenta, fuchsia, shocking pink, violet, and sapphire. Paris had dreamed up the dresses yesterday afternoon, inspired by the whip-cord bodies and eager youthful beauty of Berthe's daughter Naomi and her dancer friends.

Berthe's idea had turned out to be a brilliant one; not only had it saved her show, it had added a new physical dimension. Naomi was a dark, slender sprite with Oriental eyes and long legs who would look wonderful in a sack but looked stunning in Paris's clothes. Her friends all had the quality of elegance that ballet imparts through its disciplines, and all were moderately tall, had dark hair, and were almost frighteningly slender. They were more than perfect—they were custom made for Paris's show. These dresses, which she and Berthe had stayed up all night sewing, were meant as a quick, zippy eye-opener to grab her audience right from the start and let them know that this fashion presentation was going to be different, that the world of design had a vital new force on its hands.

Jean-Luc had risen to the occasion, fashioning bunches of fragile silk camellias into tiny, veiled hats worn tilted provocatively over the eyes, in the same hot colors as the dresses and dyed overnight by his poor young wife, who had magenta hands to prove it.

The girls looked fantastic, thought Paris as their long, strong dancers' legs in sheer black tights and the highest-heeled scarlet suede shoes paced the runway challengingly. And a little bit naughty, like a bunch of wild contemporary Carmens absconded from the opera. The look was totally theatrical, totally new, and was one of those spur-of-the-moment inspirations that could be picked up and transformed into a whole new trend, copied internationally—something that could make her name immediately, the way Montana's space-age wide-shouldered suits had, or St. Laurent's tuxedos.

As she watched, Naomi and the other girls dropped their arrogant model-girl attitudes and broke into an improvised samba-strut to the carnival music that Didi was controlling from the tape decks backstage.

God, there was still a crackle on the speakers, Didi hadn't got it right yet! Her eyes searched the chaotic salon for an electrician. How, she wondered, would it ever all be ready by tomorrow? Deliverymen were still trekking in and out bringing the uncomfortable little gilt chairs essential to every Paris show, electricians fiddled endlessly with the footlights, while someone at the back constantly dazzled them with pinspots and flickering strobes. Florists were busily banking the sides of the runway with the enormous creamy lilies that Paris had insisted were in keeping with her thirties mood, though Didi said they reminded him of funerals and were playing havoc with his hay fever. Berthe and her assistants sat at tables in one corner sewing up hems and adjusting sleeves, while backstage the clothes and appropriate accessories were being arranged on racks, each with a girl's name on it, by the dancers who weren't to do the show and who had volunteered to act as dressers. Two makeup girls hovered amid clouds of face powder and glitters of blusher, and the hairdresser and his assistant frantically blow-dried and experimented, trying to capture the exact effect Paris demanded.

The carnival music blasting from the speakers had nothing to do with what was happening on the runway, and the girls hadn't quite got the feel of it.

"Here, like this," Paris called. "I want you to stride onto the stage all together in a burst of color and movement."

She watched approvingly as they got it right the first time, but that music had to be changed. She stuck her head behind the curtains looking for Didi.

"Didi? I don't think that carnival music works. I want something sexy as well as just 'up'—find something a bit rougher, some Stones or Joe Jackson."

Naomi danced back down the runway to some phantom music in her head, capturing exactly what Paris needed.

"That's it, that's it," she called. "Didi, find music to fit that."

Didi was having a rough day. He'd been at the Hôtel de l'Abbaye since six that morning supervising the workmen as they arrived, preventing the electricians from going on strike because Paris said there was no time for a coffee break, quelling the panic when by noon the chairs still hadn't arrived, sneezing his way past the lilies and fighting a losing battle with the crackle on the speakers. He'd had one cup of black coffee and it was now twelve-thirty.

"Why can't you stick with what we've got?" he hissed, glaring at Paris.

"Because we can do *better!* Didier de Maubert, you're not going to let me down *now*, are you?"

Paris's grin was full of elation. She was thriving on sleepless nights and hard work, enjoying the chaos and the action. He'd never seen her like this before, on such a high she was almost flying, and her energy was driving them all before it. Anyone else and he'd have wondered what she was on, but knowing Paris it was pure adrenaline and determination. Still, he was afraid that adrenaline and energy wouldn't be enough to carry her through tomorrow as chief model in place of Finola, as well as supervising things backstage and keeping an eye out front for reactions.

"I'll get changed," said Paris. "The music's 'Avalon'—right, Didi?"

"Right, Paris."

With just slight adjustment by Berthe, Finola's dresses fit Paris perfectly and Didi had to admit as he helped her on with the steel satin jacket that the severe ice-colored dresses looked as good on her as they had on Finola.

"I still think it would be better to let Naomi do this, or else get a girl from the agency," he said.

Paris barely heard him. She slid her feet into the matching pumps, keeping one eye on the girls who were crowding back through the curtains and one on herself in the mirror

"Into the linen skirts and blouses and then the pants and suede jackets," she called, checking her watch and smoothing down her skirt. "You've got exactly ninety seconds. And remember to change the blusher and the lipstick—we don't want magenta with the peach and amber suede. Didi, the music. Let's get going."

"Paris, are you sure you can handle all this? You're needed back here to make sure all the models look exactly as you mean them to, and out front with the press and the buyers."

"Handle it?" Paris stared at him in surprise. "Of course I can handle it—as long as I don't stop to think about it! Come *on*, Didi, we must get through the whole show *once* in sequence to get the timing right and then we can use the rest of the day to iron out the details. We're not leaving tonight until I get one perfect dress rehearsal— just *one*, and then I'll be sure."

"Sure of what?" called Didi over the strains of Bryan Ferry singing "Avalon."

"Of success."

Paris loped down the runway, exaggeratedly elegant in the steel satin, visualizing the contrast it would make with the wedding dress which would follow it at the end of the show, another of the tiny, very short puffball tulle chemises in white with white silk stockings and a long, long veil and train of gold embroidered lace. It would be a sensation, the whole show would be a sensation—she could feel it in her bones.

Didi never wanted to hear *any* of this music again, you could keep Roxy and the Stones and Jerome Kern, and all the rest of it. His head was throbbing. It was after two-thirty. Someone had dashed out at one and brought back sandwiches and milk for the models, and at three they were expecting the six male dancers who, in rented white suits or white tie and tails, would escort the girls on the runway.

To hell with it, they'd have to manage without him for half an hour. He needed a drink. He glanced around the room looking for Paris. She was over in the corner arguing with the electrician about the pink gel he insisted on putting over the lights when she wanted them stark white without even a bit of yellow, never mind pink. Didi left her to it.

The Bar Buenos Aires opposite the hotel offered a comforting old French zinc counter, good Scotch whisky, and a selection of Argentine tangos played over speakers that didn't crackle. Didi could have lived without the tangos but a couple of Scotches later he was feeling much better.

"There you are, Didi!" Paris, in elaborate model's makeup and the green fur coat, appeared at his side. "You're not hitting the bottle are you?" she asked suspiciously. "All I need is to discover that you're a secret alcoholic."

"*Merde!* All I've had is two whiskies and I'm considering the plat du jour. I've been hard at it since the crack of dawn!" Didi controlled his temper. It was just fatigue, he told himself, he was tired, that's all. Who would have thought that Paris would turn out to be such a single-minded slave driver?

Paris ordered a glass of wine. Damn, she thought irritably, is Didi going to crack now, just when I need him the most? Am I going to have to do *all* the work?

"What's the plat du jour?" she asked icily.

"Argentine rice and beans."

Paris began to laugh. "Oh, Didi, here I am—the famous couturier-to-be, on the very eve of her success, eating rice and beans at a *zinc!*"

Didi grinned. "You want rice and beans, then?"

"Of course I do—I'm starving. I just realized I've had nothing to eat today. And you, too, I suppose." She patted his shoulder and leaned forward to kiss him. "I'm sorry, Didi. I didn't mean to be difficult, I just feel so . . . wound up. I've been waiting for this for so long, and now it's here I'm determined that nothing shall go wrong. Am I being very hard on everyone?"

"Not when you put it like that." Didi grinned, wiping the fuchsia lipstick from his cheek. "We're all a bit tired, that's all."

"Tired?" Paris dug into her rice and beans. "I'm not tired. I could go on all night—and if necessary

237

that's exactly what I intend to do."

"Okay, okay. Just allow us lesser mortals to ease up a bit now and then—the odd ten-minute break, a sandwich, a drink . . . you know, the staff of life. . . ."

"Right!" Paris put down her fork and signaled the bartender. "I want to order some champagne," she said as Didi stared at her in surprise.

"Of course, madame."

"A dozen bottles of the best you've got," said Paris grandly, "and trays of hors d'oeuvres—to be sent over the road to the hotel at eight o'clock this evening."

"Twelve bottles of the best . . . you'll ruin us, Paris!" groaned Didi.

"We are already ruined. We've spent our money—and more besides. What difference does a few bottles of champagne make? And it's got to be decent champagne—I'm not going to give my models a headache before the show. Oh, Didi, tomorrow we'll be successful and you won't give twelve bottles of champagne a second thought. That reminds me," she added, sliding off the stool and heading for the door. "Have the drinks arrived for tomorrow?"

"Not yet." Didi paid the bill and followed her. "But they will. I'll call as soon as I get back." You had to admit, she didn't forget a thing.

Paris felt elation zing through her veins as the dancers swung down the catwalk behind Naomi, outrageous in her tiny wedding gown. Six dancers, elegant in white tie and tails, formed her handsome escort, the lighting man had the pinspots perfectly, and at last the crackle had gone from the speakers. The voice of Fred Astaire singing "Night and Day" added romance to the scene as Naomi, smiling demurely, paused at the end of the runway. The lights zapped up suddenly as the music switched to something by the Eurythmics and the other models strode back onto the runway in the brilliant chemises they had worn at the beginning.

God, they looked fabulous—just fabulous. Leaping from her chair where she'd been checking the timing and each outfit to make sure everyone wore the right accessories with the right garment, and that their makeup and hair was as perfect as they could get it, Paris burst into applause.

"Bravo, bravo," she called, "you are all wonderful. I think we've finally got it right. Now, I know you must all be *exhausted*." Groans followed her words. "All right, all right. As soon as you get out of those clothes, champagne will be served."

Cheers and whistles came from the runway and Paris laughed again. She'd forgotten that they were so young and—unlike the professional models—so *un*blasé. They'd worked bloody hard and the champagne was only a small return. After tomorrow, she thought, stretching her aching back, I'll be able to give them all a bonus.

The bottles had been standing in their ice buckets for over an hour since the waiter had delivered them at eight o'clock. The ice had turned to water, but the wine was still cold as Didi eased out the corks and poured.

"The first one's for you," he said, handing Paris a glass. She took his hand, smiling fondly at him.

"I couldn't have done it without you."

"Yes, you could," said Didi, "but thank you anyway." He lifted his glass. "Success, Paris," he said.

"Success," she echoed.

It was almost ten o'clock when Didi dropped Paris off at the atelier, and even then she'd only left under protest.

"I'm not tired, you know," she said, leaning into the car window to kiss him good-bye. "I could have stayed to help clear up and make sure everything is ready for tomorrow."

"No need," said Didi cheerfully. "I'm going back there to check, and anyway, it's all under control."

"Well . . . if you're sure." She kissed Didi again and stepped back onto the curb.

"Didi!" She was back again.

"What now?"

"I've just had a terrible thought. What if there were a fire?"

"My God, Paris, of course there won't be a fire," cried Didi, exasperated. "There's never been a fire at the Hôtel de l'Abbaye in all these years, why would they have one tonight? Anyway, the security guards are there. Nothing can go wrong, I promise you."

"Well, all right then." She looked at him doubt-fully.

"Okay. What is it now?"

"You did remember to send out the invitations, didn't you?"

"Of course I did, you idiot! Go to bed, Paris Haven, and get some sleep, and *stop worrying!*"

"Right, right, I'm going." Paris retreated across the pavement as Didi waved a final farewell and drove off into the night.

It was odd how she didn't feel the least bit tired, she thought, taking the stairs two at a time, espe-cially as she'd been up most of last night sewing those little tulle chemises. God, the girls looked so terrific in them. They'd turned out to be more than just a peppy opener, they were an inspiration.

The atelier looked strange without its shroud of white sheets and clutter of half-finished garments, shoe samples, jewelry, and hats. How much longer, she wondered, shall I live here? Just a few months until I can find something larger—and lighter. I want enormous windows, maybe overlooking the river or a park. With a sigh she flung herself onto the sleigh bed and examined her home. The familiar opaque skylight, the pipes that ran across the ceiling that she'd painted a bright green, the apricot velvet curtains rescued from some sad old theater, the big mirrors on the wall, her drawing table—that was a present from Jenny—her secondhand cutting table, the sleigh bed India had found for her. It was funny, but she'd miss this place. So much had happened while she lived here. Well, she wasn't about to think of that now! She couldn't possibly feel sad tonight. What she felt was lonely, and she didn't like being alone, not with this kind of elation flowing in her veins. She wanted to be with people, to laugh, to dance. What she needed was a party. That was it! She knew she wouldn't be able to sleep tonight anyway. Picking up her phone book she flicked through the pages. Who would be the best bet? Of course, Jules Santini, he was always giving parties—and if he wasn't, then he'd surely know who was.

Olympe Avallon was enjoying Henri's party for several reasons. First, she loved his gray stone minimanor, tucked away off the Bois de Boulogne, filled with the prettiest things and, more often than not, the prettiest people. Second, Henri always served excellent food and Olympe was notoriously hungry at parties. The quality of the wines served depended on the size of the party—better for small numbers—and tonight there was quite a crowd, sixty or seventy. That meant it would be the "house white" from Henri's own vineyard, which wasn't bad, or the red, which was poison. Thirdly, she was looking sensational tonight in her new winter suntan and the white Valentino, just a supple slink of jersey that slid off one golden shoulder tantalizingly and clung to her beautiful buttocks as closely as it dared. Catching a glimpse of herself reflected in the big hall mirrors, Olympe knew she was the best-looking woman there tonight—white in winter was always a knockout, especially with her big gray eyes and tawny blond hair. She looked, she decided, giving herself the benefit of her own generous smile, beautiful, interesting, and expensive. Of course, Barbara Dumont looked pretty good, but everyone knew she'd just had "the big F.L."—not a line on her face and she was at least forty-two. Quickly Olympe checked her own face in the mirror again; no, thank God, at thirty-five she was still all right. Forty was the right time for a facelift and she had a long way to go yet. Still, she wished she were twenty-six again and that her face—and her body—could be flawless forever. Which led to her fourth reason for enjoying the party tonight. There were at least two men here she was currently very interested in, again for different reasons.

Bendor Grünewald was titled—only a papal title, but a very old one, and it *was* "Prince"—and he was very, very rich and currently very interested in her, though she was keeping him guessing. Bendor was well known in all the places where the beautiful people gathered and his reputation as a playboy had lasted for almost thirty years, ever since he emerged from under his German family's thumb as inheritor of the family industrial empire. He was really keen, she could tell. Now he was getting close to fifty and reaching the marriage market. It was time to start a dynasty—every rich man of fifty wants a son.

Then, of course, there was Hugo Reresby, who was just about the sexiest man she'd met in at least a year. You'd never know it to look at him, she thought; Englishmen were so deceptive with their ruddy-cheeked glow of good health and the polite blue eyes of well-brought-up schoolboys. It wasn't until you got them in bed that you knew where they were really at!

Hugo caught her glance and waved hello from across the room. Olympe debated whether she should go over to him, or make him come to her, as he would, of course, eventually. She scanned the room quickly to check if his wife were here. No, not tonight. Good.

She loved this room; the big square tiles of black-and-white marble scattered with party guests in brilliant colors looked like an exotic chess game for giants.

"Olympe!"

She turned as her name was called. It was Henri, looking amazingly "gay" in a caramel silk shirt and leather pants worn tucked into American cowboy boots.

"You don't mean to tell me you're alone?" he asked, kissing her. "Everyone knows there are a dozen men lined up at your door for the pleasure of your company—some of whom I wish would line up at mine!"

Olympe tucked her arm through his, wandering with him across the hall. A rhythmic thudding came from the disco in the cellar below.

"I'm alone," she agreed, "for a while. . . ."

"Say no more." Henri smiled. "Just tell me . . . which one is it, Bendor or Hugo?"

"It all depends on how I feel tonight . . . what my secret desires are," she teased.

"Your secret desires are always for steak and strawberries," replied Henri, leading her toward the dining room and the lavish buffet. "You're a simple girl at heart, Olympe."

"Why does no one see that but you, Henri? I *am* simple, I like nothing more than to eat, to drink wine, to lie in the sun, to dance, and to make love. Behind this exotic façade is a true bourgeoise."

Bendor had spotted her from across the room and appeared at her side.

"Don't destroy my illusions, Olympe," he said. "It's the other woman I'm after, the exotic one, the beauty who lives on fresh air and rose petals."

"Take my word for it," said Henri, "it's steak and *pommes frites*. God knows why she doesn't put on weight. If it were me I'd gain five pounds overnight."

"Now, that girl," said Olympe, pointing to Paris, who was poised just inside the door, wrapped in her green Fende mink, "must eat rose petals. Who is she, Henri?"

"I've no idea." Henri assessed Paris rapidly. "But I *love* that coat!" He drifted off in Paris's direction.

"Olympe," said Bendor pleadingly.

"Well?"

"Will you come out to dinner with me—alone?" Bendor put a possessive finger under her chin. "Steak and *pommes frites* if you like?"

Olympe considered. Her opaque gray eyes met his, speculatively. Bendor leaned closer. She had a

245

mouth that any man would want to kiss, to bite even . . . and if he ever got her alone he would do just that. And then he'd have her walk for him—up and down the room like when she was a model, because everyone knew that Olympe had the sexiest walk ever.

Olympe took a baton of celery from a dish on the table. Her square white teeth crunched it with a crisp firmness that sent chills down his spine.

"Do you know," she said, taking a second bite, "there's just one place in the entire world I'd really like to have dinner tonight."

"Where is it? Tell me," demanded Bendor.

"Oh, it's just a little place." Olympe took a piece of carrot and dipped it in the aioli sauce. "Nothing grand, but the food . . . ah, Beny, it's wonderful."

"Yes, yes?"

"Of course"—she sighed—"it's impossible. . . ."

"*Merde*, Olympe, where is it?" demanded Bendor. "Let's go."

Olympe looked at him doubtfully. "It's called Julie's, Beny. They serve seafood—lobster with fresh garlic mayonnaise, and crab and swordfish steaks, fresh from the sea. The Caribbean Sea . . . off Barbados."

"We'll go," said Bendor, gripping her arm tightly, "—you and me, Olympe. We can go now, tonight."

Olympe burst into laughter. "Oh, Beny, how boring! I *knew* you would say that. Couldn't you see I was just *teasing* you? I'm quite happy here, you know, with the asparagus and the celery—and a

246

strawberry or two." She drifted along the table, picking a morsel here and a morsel there.

"Olympe, *when* will you have dinner with me?"

"Didn't we just have this conversation?" Bendor was very keen, thought Olympe, pleased.

Hugo smiled from across the room and Olympe smiled back, secretly, so that Bendor didn't see.

Over by the door Henri took Paris's cold hand in his.

"Do I know you?" he asked, putting up a finger to stop her as Paris began to explain. "No, no, don't tell me. I'm just glad you came to my party. I'm Henri Sander. And you are?"

"Paris."

"How appropriately named—a stroke of genius on your mother's part? Paris who?"

"Paris Haven. I'm a friend of Jules Santini, I'm supposed to meet him here."

Henri helped her off with her coat, enjoying its softness.

"I haven't seen Jules yet," he said, tossing the coat on the big chest in the hall, "but I must tell you I *adore* your coat."

"It was my mother's," Paris explained automatically, and then wished she hadn't.

Henri noted the initials embroidered on the lining: "JH."

"I see." He smiled. "*That* Paris. Well, your mother was a genius, my dear." He put a friendly arm around her shoulders. "Now, come with me. There are some people I'm sure you'd like to meet."

Paris had meant to avoid Olympe Avallon. She'd spotted her, of course, as soon as she walked in the door. Olympe was so damned gorgeous and flamboyant it was hard not to—no woman had the right to look that good *all* the time. There were always pictures of Olympe in the European magazines. In *Hola* and *Oggi* and *Tatler* you'd find Olympe, sunbathing in the very minimum thong on some yacht in St. Tropez, with no makeup and her hair pulled back, half naked and quite spectacular; or socializing at the racetrack in a chic little St. Laurent and a perfect hat, discreetly made up and well bejeweled; or at some charity ball at the Savoy in London, outclassing the English in their frills, just by sheer elegance. No wonder Amadeo Vitrazzi had run off to keep his appointment with her after their little "episode." Olympe was a woman no man would want to lose.

"Paris," said Henri smoothly, "I'd like you to meet Olympe Avallon and Prince Bendor Grünewald—Beny to you. This is Paris Haven."

Such an interesting face, thought Olympe as she said hello, fantastic cheekbones and that lovely black hair . . . a good body, too, taut and slender.

"Are you a model?" she asked. "If not, then you should be."

"I'm a designer," said Paris stiffly, "although tomorrow I must admit I am also to be a model."

"Oh? For whom?" Why was the girl being so stiff with her? wondered Olympe. Had she said something wrong?

"For my own designs. I'm showing my first collection tomorrow."

"How exciting." And who, wondered Olympe, was going to go to the girl's collection when everyone knew that Mitsoko had changed his day at the last minute because his "stars" had not boded well? His show was the most sought after in Paris; even she'd had trouble getting a ticket.

"But you must be Jenny Haven's daughter," said Bendor. "I feel I *know* your mother. I grew up with her—on the screen, of course."

"Careful, darling," said Henri, "your age is showing. Now, come along with me, Paris. I want you to meet some more people."

Henri shepherded her through to the dining room where his guests nibbled on the food and gossiped about mutual friends and places. What was that little friction he'd felt between Olympe and Paris? Had they met before? It was intriguing . . . perhaps he could even stir it up a little.

"Hugo," he called, "here's someone I'd like you to meet."

Hugo Reresby shook Paris's hand firmly. He had a pleasant, straightforward gaze, thought Paris, and smooth ruddy skin that looked as though he spent a great deal of time outdoors.

"You're Paris Haven," said Hugo. "I've seen your picture in the newspapers."

Paris smiled at him; for once she didn't mind the reference to the publicity and her mother.

"Is that a plus or a minus?" she asked.

"Oh, absolutely a plus." Hugo took her hand. "Will you dance with me, Paris?" He led her down the stairs to the cellar, where the music had changed from the earlier wild boogie to something softer. As Hugo's arms went around her, Paris knew exactly what it was that she was looking for tonight—and Hugo Reresby was just perfect.

Olympe was annoyed. Bendor was being boring and Hugo had disappeared. She'd drifted from room to room with Bendor trailing behind her, begging her to leave with him and go back to his place. As if she would! Olympe never entered into casual affairs on that level. Matters were always very well planned, everything carefully thought out and arranged. That was the way she liked it—nice and secure. It wasn't easy living the life she did on very little money. There was her apartment and her car, clothes were all right, of course, because the designers liked to dress her, but men friends were expected—no, *contracted*—to contribute to her "comfort." It worked quite well, and over the years—since she was twenty—she had amassed quite a nice little capital, because one day there would surely be old age. Naturally, before then she expected to have had a couple more financially successful marriages behind her, but a girl had to be *careful* about these things. The Hugos of her life were purely for pleasure. It was Bendor she might have to marry—if she could push him into it—though she had the sneaking feeling that in the end he'd marry some strong, healthy eighteen-year-old who'd bear his children, while he kept her as a mistress on the side. No deal.

"Henri, have you seen Hugo?"

"Of course, darling. He's downstairs, dancing with Paris Haven . . . where he's been all night." Henri's eyes sparkled wickedly. "Perhaps you should join them," he suggested.

Olympe took a strawberry from a silver dish and bit into it thoughtfully. "Winter strawberries always seem different," she commented, "—so tasteless." So Hugo had found Paris, had he? Or more likely Henri had found Paris for Hugo. Well, maybe he was right, maybe she should just go along downstairs and see. What was that saying? If you can't beat them, join them? She drifted toward the stairs.

"Beny, I'm going to powder my nose," she said exasperatedly, "you cannot come with me."

"Why not?" he murmured, running his hand along her naked arm.

"Bodily functions are meant to be kept private," snapped Olympe, pulling her arm away. "Now, go and get another drink, I'll be back in a few minutes."

Paris was sitting on the pile of cushions in an alcove at the far end of the cellar. Hugo's arms were around her and she was kissing him. She'd been kissing him for about an hour—nothing else, he hadn't touched her, just held her and kissed. And it was heaven; her body, burstingly alive with the day's adrenaline, was responding without being touched.

Hitching up her skirt Olympe sat cross-legged

251

on the cushions in front of them, watching. Candles flickered in the wall sconces that Henri considered exotic lighting for his dungeon disco, and the flickering orange flame highlighted the girl's long black hair. Hugo must have unfastened it, because she hadn't noticed it being that long earlier. One of Hugo's hands was on the girl's back, the other on the nape of her neck. They were enjoying each other, there was no doubt about that—they hadn't even noticed she was watching. Or if they had, they didn't care. It was interesting, thought Olympe, to see Hugo kissing someone else like that . . . she knew exactly how Paris must feel right now. A throb of excitement rippled through her belly as she leaned closer.

Hugo took his mouth away from Paris's tender lips.

"Beautiful," he murmured, "lovely, lovely Paris." He stroked her face tenderly with just the tips of his fingers and Paris sighed happily.

Hugo turned his head and smiled at Olympe. She was sitting, chin propped on her hand, watching them, and she smiled back. He had known she was there, of course.

"Hugo," said Olympe, "I saw your wife in the hall. She was looking for you."

"Really?" Hugo's reply was lazy, uninterested. His right arm was around Paris and his left hand caressed her hair.

Her *silken* hair, thought Olympe. She stretched out a smooth, suntanned arm toward him. A bunch of silver keys glimmered in the candlelight. "Why don't you take these?" she smiled. "There's no one at my apartment. You can take Paris there."

Paris turned her head and looked at Olympe. She was smiling, friendly . . . conspiratorial. Paris glanced at Hugo doubtfully and he smiled back at her.

"I think," said Hugo softly, "that is a very good idea. What do you say, Paris?"

His arm tightened, pulling her fractionally closer. She wanted to kiss him again, she wanted more than kisses.

"Wonderful," she whispered.

Hugo reached out to take the keys from Olympe and their glances met.

"Say thank you to Olympe, Paris," he said. "You don't know how kind she's being to us."

"You remember where the drinks are, Hugo." Olympe uncrossed her legs and stepped back from the cushions. "Give Paris anything she wants." She was smiling as she went back to join Bendor, still waiting patiently in the hall.

Olympe's bed was very, very big—American style. After her narrow sleigh bed Paris felt quite lost lying there alone and naked in the middle of it. She wished Hugo would hurry up, he'd gone to get drinks for them. Champage, he'd said, because this was a celebration. She seemed to be celebrating everything all at once and she'd had so much champagne already today she was floating on the bubbles. It was true, her body felt light as air—probably from the joint she'd shared with Hugo, made from Olympe's neat little stash of the very best grass. At least, Hugo said it was the best and he seemed to know. He knew a lot about Olympe. He knew where she kept her grass, he knew that there was always a bottle of champagne in the refrigerator—just in case; he knew that the blanket on the bed was cashmere. But if, as she suspected, Hugo and Olympe were lovers, then why had Olympe lent him her apartment?

Paris turned on her side, pushed the button on the tape deck, and switched the tape over. It was Richie Havens singing "I'm Not in Love." The melody and his rasping voice seemed to hit some new corner of her soul; she felt wrapped around by the music, absorbed.

There was a clink of glasses as Hugo walked naked into the bedroom carrying a bottle and three crystal champagne flutes. Hugo naked was fantastic, thought Paris dreamily, darker skinned than you would have expected with his fair hair; strong legs; tight, muscular buttocks; and the most delicious "equipment." She stretched luxuriously and smiled at him. Hugo had known exactly what to do with his equipment, and from the look of him he was ready to do it again.

"Why three champagne glasses?" she asked, running her hand along his thigh as he sat next to her on the bed.

Hugo dropped a kiss on top of her dark head.

"Olympe's back," he said casually. "She said she

might come in and share a glass with us."

"Olympe?"

"Well, it *is* her flat, darling," chided Hugo gently. "Paris, your hands are shaking."

A few drops of wine fell onto her breast and he bent his head to lick them up.

"Did I tell you," he whispered, "that you taste wonderful?"

He leaned forward and spilled a little more of the champagne over the dark triangle of hair, smoothing it in with his fingers as Paris sighed with pleasure.

Hugo took a sip of his champagne, still caressing her. "Smooth," he said, "you're so smooth, and slippery and tempting. . . ."

Paris didn't want the champagne, she wanted Hugo, now, inside her, just the way he'd done it before. He'd found her rhythm perfectly; they could have made love together a hundred times before, that's how well they'd known each other instinctively.

It was a pretty scene, thought Olympe, standing in the doorway. The soft lights, her big bed with its massive headboard, painted with cherubs and garlands, the soft, urgent music, and the two beautiful people, naked, soft skinned, peach colored under the lamps. She drifted over to the bed and bent to kiss Hugo. Paris lay as if turned to stone, Hugo's fingers still caressing her as Olympe kissed him.

"Beautiful," murmured Olympe, "you both look so beautiful. I didn't mean to interrupt. I just felt

255

lonely . . . a glass of champagne sounded tempting."

She slipped off her shoes and curled up on the bed at Paris's feet.

"May I?" she asked, taking the glass from her hand. Her eyes met Paris's in a secret smile. "Isn't Hugo the most romantic man you ever met?" she whispered. "He knows just how you feel, just what you want him to do without even telling . . . he's such a good lover. And it always feels so good to be well loved."

Putting down her glass Olympe moved to kiss Hugo on the mouth, lingeringly. Her hands fluttered tentatively across his belly and Paris felt his hand tighten—he was kissing Olympe and caressing her! She watched in fascination as Olympe bent her head over Hugo; she could see her pink tongue busily tasting him. Hugo turned his head and smiled into Paris's eyes.

"I think Olympe should stay, don't you?" he said softly.

Excitement blasted through Paris—the wine, the grass, the adrenaline, the erotic scene, gave her a charge she'd never felt before. She wanted Hugo to do things to her and to Olympe, she wanted to share him with her, to watch what she did, what he did. . . .

Olympe wriggled out of the white shift and lay down next to Paris, running her hand along the length of her body. Paris shuddered and moaned as Olympe's soft fingers circled her nipples and then traveled the length of her body to join with Hugo's, tangling in that triangle of soft, springy black hair. Her eyes were closed in ecstasy and she opened them to look at her new lover. Hugo was on one side of her, Olympe on the other, and she wrapped an arm around each of them as Olympe's mouth closed on hers in a kiss. A kiss she didn't want to end.

Olympe cruised the streets of the Marais *quartier* in her tiny Citroën, searching for the Rue de l'Abbaye, thanking God she'd never succumbed to the temptations of the big car. She was the world's worst driver—a fact acknowledged by the frantic honking of horns as she cut across two lanes of traffic, swooped back around a rotary and then drove maddeningly slowly along the street she'd just traversed. It was three-thirty and she'd been searching for the Hôtel de l'Abbaye for almost an hour—Paris had been right when she had said it was "tucked away behind Les Halles"; it was tucked so far you couldn't find the damn place.

Olympe tapped an impatient, well-gloved finger on the steering wheel, waiting for the traffic lights to change. A clock in the jeweler's window on her right showed three-forty and Paris's show had started at three. If she didn't find the place soon she'd be too late. Damn, and she'd missed the Mitsoko showing for this. Still, she'd promised and Paris was such a darling. A smile flickered across her face as she remembered the previous night. It had been wonderful, Hugo had brought out the best in them. Oh, God, those idiots were honking at her again. Sliding

257

the car into first, Olympe maneuvered cautiously through the lights. This damned hotel must be *somewhere* near here, and she'd better find it quick.

At four o'clock she found it. She spent five minutes trying to squeeze the Citroën into a parking space that was just big enough and finally abandoned the car with the back wheels sticking out into the road. Wrapping her full-length Revillon fox around her to keep out the chill, she sped across the road, ignoring the traffic and the whistles of the workmen on the building site opposite. Thank God, she thought, pushing open the engraved plate-glass doors, I've made it.

The strains of Roxy's "Avalon" mingled with the scents of calla lilies and cigarette smoke in the corridor, and she smiled as she pushed open the door— Paris was even playing her song. The hundred little gilt chairs were sparsely filled with people who looked to her like friends. On the front row a half-dozen girls sat with open notebooks, sipping champagne and gossiping together. Olympe knew every buyer and fashion editor from Rome to New York, and she didn't recognize any of these. She assessed them accurately as assistants to the assistant fashion-editors of magazines and newspapers, maybe even just secretaries enjoying the free show and champagne on tickets passed on to them by indifferent women who had more important things to attend, like Mitsoko's show and the lavish party he would throw afterward—it was at Versailles this time. Olympe wished she'd gone too. There was no doubt that this was a disaster.

The door swung shut behind her and a dark young man in a white suit appeared. His smile was strained as he asked if he could help.

Didi recognized her of course—but what was Olympe Avallon doing here?

"Would you care for some champagne?" he asked as Olympe took a seat near the door, watching the brilliantly lit runway intently. These weren't even models, she realized as Naomi danced across the runway, followed by the other girls, swirling their gauzy capes over oyster-colored gowns. But whoever they were they were terrific—and so were the clothes. Damn, she wished she'd been here for the beginning. Paris swept onto the runway in a steel-gray outfit that was a knockout—stunning! Olympe's professional eye noted the cut, the fit of the jacket, the superb ruffled detail on the slit skirt. And Paris was beautiful, a great model for her own designs.

Flashbulbs popped at the back of the room and Olympe turned quickly to check them out—she hadn't noticed photographers when she came in.

Three young men were being pushed back through the doors by Didi, who was gesticulating angrily. Of course, they were paparazzi from the gossip magazines, here to gloat about the death of Jenny Haven's daughter's fashion show. Olympe shifted uncomfortably on her tiny chair. Oh, dear, she wasn't so sure she wanted to be around for the wake.

Paris stalked from the runway, her cheeks blazing and her mouth tight with anger. The models,

259

changing rapidly into their bright chemises, glanced anxiously at Paris as Naomi glided past in her bridal gown, flanked by her handsome escort. Sliding their feet into their little scarlet high-heeled shoes, they thrust through the curtains after Naomi—all together in a burst of movement and color just as Paris had shown them.

Paris ripped off her jacket and skirt and flung them on the floor. "Dear God," she said over and over, "dear God, what did I do wrong? What happened? Why did no one come?" Throwing on her black sweatshirt and jeans, she tugged frantically at her boots. It was over—finished. She'd lost and she didn't know why!

Olympe slid quietly past Didi at the door.

"Dazzling," she whispered in his ear, "fabulous . . . tell Paris I'll call her later this evening."

Didi watched as she hurried away down the corridor. He didn't know why Olympe Avallon had been there, but she was the only person of any consequence who had come to Paris's show—the rest were the sort who would show up anywhere for a free drink. And could he use a drink! The girls were posing on the runway smiling at their sparse audience and the scatter of applause. It was over. There was just time for a couple of quick Scotches over the road at the Bar Buenos Aires—and then he'd have to face Paris. He had five minutes to think of what he was going to say.

Olympe had meant to call Paris, she really had, but

260

as it turned out there had been so little time. When she got home the flowers were waiting, masses of early jasmine and spring blossoms from the south. And the note from Bendor. He had taken a villa in Barbados and planned to fly out a group of friends that night on a chartered jet. Without her it would be meaningless. Would she come?

It was a good feeling knowing she had so much power over him, thought Olympe, throwing resort wear into her battered Vuitton bag. All she'd done was suggest Julie's—and he'd taken the bait. He'd recognized that the two of them alone was a "no go" area and had arranged this discreet house party as a bribe. And it was fair enough, she thought, zipping up the bag on the few clothes it contained—they were all she'd need, because she could always buy anything else she wanted there. This was her chance to find out if Bendor's intentions toward her were strictly honorable—or not. She hoped they were.

᎒ 13 ᎒

Myra Kaufmann was giving one of her Sunday-morning brunches and she was annoyed because the day had turned cloudy with a chill wind blowing. She hoped the men would be able to get in their tennis game before it rained.

The big round table in the dining room was arranged with platters of roast beef, salami, Jarlsberg cheese and cream cheese, lox, smoked sturgeon, bagels, bialys, and rye bread. Bill was fixing the champagne and orange juice—mimosas he called them—and the urn was perking with good strong coffee. On the sideboard keeping hot were scrambled eggs with lox, and buttermilk pancakes with a giant jug of maple syrup.

Enough cholesterol to kill the lot, she thought, assessing the average age and fitness of her guests. Imagine her, Myra Kaufmann, single-handedly wiping out half the industry with her Sunday brunch—producers, heads of studios, lawyers, fellow agents; no writers or directors, though: Bill couldn't stand "creative" people on Sunday mornings, said he had enough of them all week!

Jessie Reubin came in with Stan—the front door was open to indicate "open house" and the wind was whipping through the hall; she'd have to close it, maybe just leave it open a crack, so people didn't have to ring.

"Hi, Jess, how are you?"

They pecked each other on the cheek. Jessie was a thin woman, very "into" smart clothes. She probably starved poor Stan at home and that's why he always ate so much here. They all did, including Bill. It was probably the one time their wives let them forget the diet and their own forebodings about being left alone and widowed and destined, like horses to pasture, for Palm Springs or Palm Beach.

"I'm great, Myra. Stan's taking me over to Paris next month. We usually go about this time of the year. He likes to eat and I like to shop, it's a mutually satisfying vacation. The others never are. You know, Myra, I like to sit by a pool somewhere in the sun—not my *own* pool, of course—but Stan hates that. He gets all restless and twitchy, says he can't even get a good card game in those resort hotels."

"I know just what you mean," agreed Myra, handing her a mimosa. "I like the Mauna Kea or the Kahala myself. Hawaii's always nice."

Jessie sighed. "Maybe you and I should go and leave those two to fend for themselves for a while. Don't you think it would do them good?"

Myra laughed, imagining Bill trying to cope on his own.

"No chance," she said. "I'd be gone ten days and he'd have gained ten pounds. If I don't watch him like a hawk he'll be sitting in front of the TV set, drinking beer, eating peanuts and popcorn, and smoking two packs. You should watch Stan, too, Jessie, he's gaining. Have you tried the Stillman?"

Stan piled his plate with salami and cheese, adding a little potato salad and a spoonful of hot mustard for good measure, listening to what Bill was saying.

"So I figure that all in all it's best to keep the kid happy—we both know what happens when stars get irritated, the work goes to hell and the studios don't want to know any more. I talked with Myron and he tells me the most they can do is five more per episode—that brings him to thirty-five thousand dollars, Stan, and that's *good* money. I said okay, but what about a few perks—you know, a sweetener, a new car, a trip? Myron said they'd been planning on doing some foreign locations, they've got a good story line for a three-parter, each episode to be shot in a different place—New York, London, and the islands—probably Barbados. He's willing to move the whole thing up and do the location shooting fairly soon—it'll give Rory a break, you see, Stan. Get him away from here, let him play the star somewhere else, where people think stars are really stars." Bill put a mimosa in Stan's free hand.

"Sounds good." Stan finished his salami on rye and headed toward the scrambled eggs and lox. "How soon is soon?"

"Couple of weeks' time for Barbados—while the weather is still good. Then New York and London."

"Good. Keep him happy, Bill. He's been onto me about buying that big place on Benedict Canyon, but I've told him he's not ready for it—yet, he has to wait at least a year to make sure the series is sticking, then he can have whatever he wants. Within reason, of course. And after my fees and your commission, and his taxes . . ."

They were laughing as their wives joined them.

"Come on, you two," said Myra, "you're supposed to mingle with the other guests, not talk business."

"We're mingling, we're mingling," murmured Stan, turning away regretfully from the pancakes and maple syrup. "Did Jessie tell you I'm taking her to Paris next month? She'll cost me a fortune, of course, always does."

"She's worth it, Stan," said Myra loyally; after all,

264

the wives had to stick together in this town, there were enough gorgeous young girls undermining their confidence without backstabbing each other. "Okay, then, who's for tennis?" She cast an anxious eye at the weather again, hoping it wasn't going to let her down.

❧ 14 ❧

Marisa Paroli was a regular at the Paris collections. She was always placed on one of the gilt chairs at the front where photographers could see her, she was always kissed afterward by Yves or Karl or Marc personally—and she always placed an order at each house. This year she had her young cousin Renata with her and had found herself even more popular, since Renata was coming on like one of the last of the big spenders. Of course, Renata had the money and it was the first time she'd been let loose at the collections—and Marisa was certainly the one to show her how to spend it. It had been fun, even the Mitsoko show, though she despised the shapeless garments that had been paraded like a dirge on severe models in gray and black without so much as a streak of color to lighten the effect. Marisa shuddered at the memory—it was alien to her Italian soul that any woman should choose to hide her shape under formless clothes, and in such harsh, drab colors.

She and Renata were breakfasting in their suite at the Bristol, sipping coffee and scanning the morning papers for photographs of Mitsoko's show the previous day, and the jet-set gossip of people, parties, and places. It was Renata who spotted the item about Paris Haven—just a single paragraph, tucked away at the end of a column.

"But this must be the sister of Fabrizio's India!" she exclaimed.

"What is it?" Marisa took the paper and read the brief obituary of Paris's unattended showing.

It was the last item in the "Daily Diary" of a scandalously vicious gossip columnist:

"Hollywood yesterday tried to outdo the masters of haute couture when Paris Haven—daughter of the lately indiscreet Jenny Haven—showed her collection at the out-of-the-way Hôtel de l'Abbaye, timing it on the same day and at the very same moment as Mitsoko's fabulous show. Poor Paris—her collection, unattended and unapplauded, sank like a stone beneath the Seine. Her Momma should have told her not to take on the giants without first checking her dates . . . and perhaps she should have invested a little more of Momma's movie millions in better champagne and a better hotel. . . ."

The photograph underneath showed Paris glaring haughtily at the cameras from the catwalk.

Renata, though no beauty, was as attractive as her family's money could make her. She had had a cute new nose to replace her long family one when she

266

was thirteen, a severe diet to shed the family tendency to portliness when she was fourteen, and, ever since, the attentions of the best hairdressers and makeup artists, until she was one of the best-groomed, best turned-out young women in Italy. It had been hard work. She stared intently it the picture of Paris. "She's really beautiful," she commented. Renata was also nice, and her tendency to honesty occasionally annoyed Marisa.

"I suppose so." She shrugged. "Better than her sister, anyway."

Why must Marisa be so bitchy? wondered Renata. She was always getting at someone, and no one ever managed to get to her.

"Do you mean India? But she's so attractive, Marisa. I've often wondered how you dared let her be so close with Fabrizio, . . . I mean, don't you ever wonder—just wonder a little bit—if Fabrizio finds her attractive?"

"Fabrizio and *India?* Renata, *cara,* don't be ridiculous. Now, if you'd said Luciana or Graziella . . . Fabrizio knows so many sophisticated attractive women. What on earth would he see in someone like India Haven?"

"She's young—my age, isn't she?" Renata, noticing the frozen expression on Marisa's fare as she caught the implication that she was getting older, added hastily, "I mean, young like American girls are—so energetic and vital. I can't imagine India just lazing around like I do, waiting for something to happen. And you must admit she has a very sexy figure, Marisa—look at her—from a man's point of view, not just from fashion."

"You're talking nonsense, Renata. Fabrizio's not in the least bit interested in her that way. He says she's good at her job, apparently she has a talent for whatever it is she does. Anyway, India was chasing after Aldo Montefiore. I put a stop to that, of course, for your sake! No, I'm quite sure you're wrong about her."

Renata cast a sly look at her older cousin. Marisa was an astute woman, but she was also too wrapped up in herself and her appearance. She tended to be dismissive of people who were outside her social comprehension—but men like her husband were not. And Fabrizio Paroli was an attractive, warm-blooded Neapolitan who'd worked his way up the ladder of success. India Haven was exactly the kind of girl who could topple the Paroli marriage. It was fun to goad Marisa from her self-satisfaction.

"Is Fabrizio totally faithful to you, then, Marisa?" Renata's smile was teasing.

"Of course he is! Why are you asking me now?"

"Oh, just that if so, then he's the only husband I know of who *is* faithful."

"Renata, you know nothing of these things. Once I've got you safely married to Aldo Montefiore you'll know what I'm talking about. A woman knows when her husband is faithful, believe me." Marisa's voice was confident, but she looked away, busying herself again in the newspapers.

Renata sipped her coffee, smiling. Had she succeeded in upsetting Marisa's cool assumption that the world functioned only for her benefit? She didn't know if there was anything between India and Fabrizio but, what the hell, she'd finally got to Marisa. She'd sown the seeds of suspicion very satisfactorily. It would be interesting to see what Marisa would do about it.

Passion had paid for the luxurious offices of Mario Tomasetti, private investigator. *Illicit* passion, that is. Mario preferred his luxury flamboyant—ankle-deep gray carpets, crystal chandeliers, scarlet leather chairs, low and deeply-buttoned, and his own vast swivel-chair of deep green suede. "It's like the traffic lights," he would say to his clients, "—red for stop is you, and green for go for me." Mario's favorite possession was his unusual desk—a thirteenth-century oak tithe-table with a slot at one end where the long-ago serfs had paid their tithe money to the lord of the manor. It amused Mario to have his clients slip their hefty checks—always paid in advance, naturally—into the tithe slot to be collected later by his secretary.

Discretion was the nature of his activities if not his personal style, and the plush surroundings were meant to inform his clients that the services of Mario Tomasetti did not come cheaply. And yet he had more customers than he and his staff of thirty could handle. There was no doubt, he thought as he contemplated Marisa Paroli's tight-lipped face, that passion paid very well—especially when you had a "sideline" like his.

"Here is a photograph." Marisa placed a picture of India carefully on the table. "And here is one of my husband."

Mario allowed his gaze to rest on them for the briefest moment but made no move to pick them up. Marisa looked at him uncertainly. Shouldn't he study them? Ask her questions?

"If you need enlargements," she suggested, "or the names of his favorite restaurants . . ."

Mario held up a small, plump hand decorated with an elaborate seal ring in some inky stone. "Say no more, signora, we have Signor Paroli's office address, and the address of the apartment of Signorina Haven. It is all we need. Ah . . . perhaps there is one more thing. Your maiden name, signora?"

"My maiden name?" asked Marisa, astonished.

"Yes . . . just for the records. It's a formality, signora, that is all."

"Russardi," said Marisa, taking out her checkbook.

"The Russardis of Milan and Turin?" Mario's smile was filled with genuine warmth.

"Yes." Marisa wrote her check and slid it across the table.

"Into the slot please, signora. I never involve myself in the financial transactions personally—this old tithe-table saves me from that. I prefer to consider myself more as a friend who wants to help out in a difficult situation."

A friend, thought Marisa with a shudder as Mario

escorted her to the door, God forbid.

Mario sank into his green suede chair, his elbows resting on the arms, his fingers held in a little steeple in front of him. Russardi, eh? This could be a good one. Mario liked to think of himself as being in the espionage business—the James Bond of marital war games. He even dressed the part—though he was admittedly short. He wore sharp silk suits, burnished Rome shoes, and expensive, custom-made shirts worn with slightly too much immaculate cuff showing. There was no doubt in his mind that he was better dressed than James; only, unlike James, he wasn't averse to playing a double game when he felt it might be mutually profitable. And the Russardi-Paroli marriage should surely be profitable.

Mario had no hesitation at all in picking up the phone to speak with Fabrizio Paroli and stating that he had information in connection with his wife that he thought might interest Fabrizio. And at a meeting later that day he had no compunction at all in parting with the information that Marisa was employing him to investigate Fabrizio's activities in relation to a Miss India Haven—after a certain large sum of money had been deposited in the worn groove of the tithe slot first, of course.

There was nothing as efficient for cooling a man's ardor, thought India, as money. Or rather—*parting* with a lot of money. Not that Fabrizio was stingy— far from it. He paid her a generous salary, bought her expensive gifts—admittedly they were mostly of

271

the intimate lingerie and perfume sort—but there had also been the wonderful carpet that now covered the floor of her apartment, and various chairs and sofas from the showroom, and a case or two of good wine in the kitchen. Perhaps Fabrizio just wasn't practical when it came to presents—and why should a lover be practical? India could find no answer to that, and she sank into a chair, staring moodily into space.

It was time to take stock of her life. Her affair with Fabrizio had been losing its savor even before that disastrous weekend at the country villa. Fabrizio had called the situation right. It had cost him a lot of money to keep the scandal and their names from hitting the papers. He had had to distribute a large amount of money to the police sergeant and the fund for the widows and orphans of the local *carabinieri*. And now there was this creepy private investigator sent to spy on them by Marisa. It was funny in a way, she supposed with a bitter smile, because what the man had said was that he was being paid by Marisa to keep an eye on their activities, and he intended to do exactly that. He would present Marisa with a detailed account of their movements at the end of the week, what he was offering was the opportunity for those movements to be perfectly innocent. After all, he'd added, what man doesn't have a little affair—it doesn't stop him loving his wife and family. The odd thing was that when Fabrizio had repeated his conversation to her, India had known that the private detective was right.

She kicked angrily at the luxurious rug with her bare foot, wondering what to do. It was obvious, she supposed, that things that couldn't go forward came to a halt—and her romance with Fabrizio was at a halt. What Fabrizio had suggested was that they cool it a little, be discreet—just for a while, of course. Damn it! That was the problem with having an affair—it wasn't in her nature to be discreet. When she was in love she wanted to flaunt it, and when a man loved her she expected to be shown off to his friends, to arrive at restaurants on his arm and be greeted at parties as a couple. She just wasn't cut out to be the other woman. Damn it again, though, she just wished it had been she who had said so! God knows, she'd been thinking about it for weeks now. The high-pitched ring of the telephone trilled through the apartment, startling her from her thoughts.

"Hello," she snapped.

"India? Are you all right?"

It was Fabrizio.

"I'm all right—just worried, that's all."

"India," said Fabrizio soothingly, "I don't want you to worry. That's why I'm calling. I've been trying to figure out how to make it easier for us both in the next few weeks and I remembered the Montefiore job. It's a perfect opportunity for you to get out of town for a while."

"Out of town? I'm not going to run away, Fabrizio, just because Marisa—"

"No, no, not *run away*. You don't understand

what I'm saying, *cara*, just listen will you? The Montefiores want to convert part of their palazzo into a hotel. They're aiming for the up-market American tourist. Now, who would know better than you what that sort of traveler would need? The family want to preserve as much of the palazzo in its original state as possible while providing the necessary facilities. Unfortunately for them, in order to pay for this they are going to have to sell off some paintings and antiques. With your knowledge of the art market, India, you are perfect for the job. You can advise them on what they might sell and the possible prices. You can find out what they want to do, inspect the premises, and report back to me. I'll need to know what structural alterations you consider necessary and I'll want technical drawings of what you propose. Now, *cara*, what do you think? Can you handle it?"

"Handle it?" cried India, thrilled. "Fabrizio, you're wonderful! Of course I can handle it, I can't wait."

"Good, *cara*, good. We shall meet in the morning, then, in the office, and I'll brief you on the job. Plan to leave right after that, India. You will stay with the Montefiores at the palazzo. I think you'll like them."

The name sounded familiar, thought India.

"Is that Aldo Montefiore's family?" she asked.

"Why, yes. Do you know them, then?"

India smiled, remembering Aldo's rather battered attractive face. "Oh I met a member of the family once—a while ago."

"Good," said Fabrizio, satisfied that the plan was working out. "I'll see you tomorrow then, *cara*. I must go now. Ciao."

He rang off abruptly, leaving India with the receiver still cradled to her ear. She replaced it with a sigh, guessing that Marisa must have come in. It had happened before—but, she decided, her spirits rising, never again. Fabrizio had just handed her her, freedom; she had a job to look forward to, her first real opportunity to do something on her own. It would be a challenge, and an exciting one. This is it, she told herself, dancing an excited little jig on Paroli's beautiful showroom carpet. From now on I shall concentrate on my career. I shall be India Haven, interior design consultant, in charge of the conversion of the Palazzo Montefiore into a luxury hotel.

She dashed into her bedroom and hauled a suitcase from the closet. How long might she be—a couple of weeks? A month? Maybe even two? There hadn't been time to ask Fabrizio, but she'd bet on at least a month. Would Aldo Montefiore be at the palazzo? she wondered. Wait a minute, though, he was supposed to marry money, wasn't he? Marisa had warned her off him; she was reserving him for her cousin Renata. Well, then, that took care of that. She surely wasn't going to escape from one role as mistress only to jump into another. No, she was going to be a career girl, no more sexy black nighties, and rendezvous for her. Firmly, she packed sensible country clothes, skirts, jeans, sweaters, a couple of good dresses for dinner, a trim, businesslike suit, silk shirts. And as a safety measure in case her resolve should be put to the test, her plainest underwear. After all, she thought with a grin as she closed the lid of the suitcase, how can a girl get herself seduced when she's wearing pants with a Snoopy picture on the front?

❧ 15 ❧

The idyllic coral-stone villa overlooked the powdery pink curve of St. James Beach in the very best part of the island. From her usual early-morning position by its oval pool, Olympe could survey the beach of the smart hotel to the left and the scatter of neighboring villas to the right. Bendor couldn't have chosen better. Apart from the fact that it was the most expensive villa on the island, it was the perfect gossip and meeting place—all you had to do was to take a stroll along the water's edge, or even float gently in the silken blue sea just a little way offshore, and you'd be bound to meet someone you knew, or someone who knew someone else you knew, or at the least someone *very* charming.

A smatter of conversation and the strains of a Gregorian chant on the hi-fi signaled that the rest of the house party was up. Bendor had a passion for Gregorian music and the sound of that monkish singing was driving them all crazy—especially at this time in the morning. Stretching lazily, Olympe flung on the man's white evening shirt she always wore as a beach cover-up, and strolled through the gardens to the terrace. There were a dozen guests, almost equally divided in sexes. The girls were youngish, late twenties, and ranged from very attractive to beautiful. The men were older, well held together, some attractive—and all rich. Bendor had no friends who weren't rich, it was a policy of his. He'd never been poor and considered the poor boring rather than unfortunate.

Pitchers of chilled orange juice and cups of thick strong coffee were being downed rapidly, along with slices of fresh fruits—papaya, mango, melon—the perfect breakfast.

Olympe frowned as she kissed Bendor. He had a can of Banks beer in front of him—his first of the day; he seemed to be addicted to the stuff. She sniffed fastidiously. If Bendor was going to turn out to be a beer drinker it simply wouldn't work. But wasn't beer drinking a German tradition? Maybe this was just a holiday indulgence. She wasn't sure, she wasn't sure about Bendor at all.

Olympe ignored the babble of conversation around her, sipping her juice and staring out to sea at the enormous yacht cruising slowly past on its way to Carlisle Bay. She'd noticed it several times this week; it was magnificent.

"Beny, what yacht is that?"

"It looks like the *Fiesta*—there aren't too many of that size around anymore." Bendor picked up his binoculars, focusing them on the prow. "Yes, it's the *Fiesta*, all right. Fitz McBain usually has her in these waters in the winter."

Olympe's ears pricked up. "Fitz McBain?" Taking Bendor's binoculars she scanned the ship. "Beautiful, beautiful," she murmured, "very, *very* nice. Do you know if he's on board, Beny?"

"I can find out if you like. Why?"

"I thought we might give a little party tonight, invite our neighbors—and the people over at the Sandy Lane and Glitter Bay. We owe them hospitality. Fitz McBain probably has a house party of his own. Let's ask them *all!* We can have a delicious Bajan barbecue by the pool, we'll keep it quite informal. What do you say, everyone—a party tonight?"

Bendor smiled indulgently as his guests cheered the suggestion. She could have anything she wanted when she smiled at him like that.

Fitz was at the controls of his Learjet with Morgan beside him. They were on their final approach, preparing to land, and despite the fact that he was upset with his father, Morgan had to admire the cool expertise with which he brought the plane down onto the runway at Miami's busy airport. Ever since he was a kid he'd felt there was nothing Fitz couldn't do, from scuba diving to flying planes. He had no idea how the hell he'd found the time to acquire all those accomplishments, but that was Fitz—if he'd had just half a day free he had used it to learn something. He'd been hungry for knowledge, above and beyond his business acumen, which

278

was instinctive. "Blame it on my lack of education," he'd told Morgan once, and Morgan could remember being surprised because Fitz had never seemed an uneducated man. Yet it was true, his formal education had been not only brief but sketchy, and Morgan knew it had irked him. Fitz had set his own educational goals, acquiring knowledge through voracious reading—which he still kept up. At the age of thirty he'd disciplined himself to take the time to learn three languages so that he might conduct his foreign business more familiarly and without having to depend on others to translate for him—you can lose the nuances of a deal if you don't understand exactly what is being said, he'd explained to Morgan when he'd balked at the extra German, Spanish, and French tuition Fitz had arranged for him in the school holidays. And, he'd added, those nuances might cost you a lot of money—or even the deal.

Despite his lack of formal education his father was a cultured man and his appetite for the arts was wide and intuitive. Fitz never saw a play merely because it was the fashionable play to be seen at; he saw the performances he was curious about. He liked Mozart's operas, he enjoyed the ballet, and he was passionate about art. It was a fact that he was in the fortunate position of being able to buy what he liked, but he was also known as a generous donor to the American museums, as well as being the anonymous patron of several struggling and talented painters and sculptors.

He was, thought Morgan, unfastening his seat belt, a hard act to follow.

Even on the *Fiesta* Fitz had seemed unable to relax. He'd spent most of today on the phone between New York and various Latin American countries, leaving Raymunda sunbathing sulkily, alone, and Raymunda sulking was not anyone Morgan had wanted to be around! He'd taken himself off to Bridgetown to buy a welcoming present for Venetia, who was expected that evening, and he had arrived back to be informed by his father that instead of next week, he wanted him to leave at once for Rio de Janeiro. Morgan had protested that he'd squeezed a few days out of his busy globe-trotting schedule to spend with Venetia, but though Fitz had been understanding, he had been adamant. He would have gone himself, he said, but he felt that his presence might put too much weight on their side, indicating exactly how eager they were to have this refinery deal. Sending Morgan as his representative toned things down to the next level, a step up from just sending one of their top executives. And he would bring a fresh viewpoint to the stalled negotiations. Morgan had argued that it was a fine point, but he had known his father was right—as usual.

Miami felt humid and sticky, and Morgan thought longingly of the *Fiesta* as they walked together to the airport control. He had just fifteen minutes to make his flight.

"Remember to pick up Venetia this evening," he called as he strode off toward the check-in. "Tell her I'll call."

"Don't worry, I'll take care of her. And, Morgan . . ." Morgan turned inquiringly. "Thanks."

Father and son grinned at each other, friends.

"You're welcome."

Fitz turned away, feeling suddenly tired. The idea of a nice quiet evening on the *Fiesta* with a simple dinner and a little Mozart on the hi-fi was very appealing. He'd get his flight instructions and head right back. He hoped Raymunda wasn't still sulking.

Raymunda hummed a little song as she sorted through the contents of the wall-length wardrobe that contained her newly purchased selection of resort wear, most of which was still unworn. She was humming because she was happy, and the reason she was happy was that tonight she was going to a party and at last would get a chance to show off some of her new finery. Prince Bendor Grünewald's invitation to an informal Bajan barbecue at the Villa Osiris had come as a complete and delightful surprise, and it had been exactly what she needed to cheer her up. She and Fitz had been here on the *Fiesta* for four days and they hadn't left it once—not even to go to dinner at one of the beautiful restaurants, or to any of the good hotels where there were bound to be people they knew and who Raymunda felt sure were having a lot more fun than she was. She knew Fitz was here for a rest, but she was *bored*. "What's the use of a yacht this size if you don't fill it with people?" she'd yelled at him on the third night. "We should be having parties, dinners, cocktails—anything!" What was it Fitz had replied? "Sometimes space is so that you can be alone." Well, she didn't want to be alone, she wanted company.

Shrugging on the marigold silk dress she'd pulled from the crowded wardrobe, Raymunda inspected herself in the mirror. Yes, that was perfect. The dress tied on one shoulder and was slit to the thigh—a bit like a toga. It was island-chic. She knew what these parties were like—"informal" simply meant as smart as possible without being grand.

Now, hair up or down? Down, perhaps. And jewelry? The multistranded freshwater pearl bracelet and the matching earrings? Or should she just wear a flower in her hair? Yes, that was it, no earrings; she'd call Masters, the chief steward, and have him get her an orchid, or perhaps a lily, or maybe a gardenia.

A glance at her watch showed it was nine o'clock. Damn, where was Fitz? They'd been asked for nine. Of course she wouldn't dream of getting to the party before ten-thirty, but still she wished he'd hurry. Brushing her hair, Raymunda imagined herself arriving at the party on Fitz McBain's arm—every woman in the place would be envious of her. And then, she thought with satisfaction, it would be their turn to reciprocate the hospitality—*she* would give a party on the *Fiesta*. She would be made, socially; no one would turn down an invitation like that. Fitz brought the Lear into Grantley Adams and taxied thankfully toward the hangars. He should just be in time for Venetia Haven's flight from London, though Miami control had told him that there might have been some delay because of the fog in Europe. He hoped the delay wasn't going to be a long one; he was anxious to get back to the peace and quiet of the ship. Sometimes, he thought, it was the silence that he enjoyed most on the *Fiesta*—just the sound of the sea at night. He liked being alone then. Occasionally, when he was unable to sleep, he'd prowl the deck barefoot, breathing in the fresh sea smells and listening to the waves.

Barbados's tiny airport was exceptionally busy. Flights were unloading from St. Vincent and Trinidad and the islands to the north, but the flight from London was still posted as "delayed" on the information screen—by at least three hours, confirmed the desk clerk; there were headwinds now.

Oh, well, it looked as though it would be a late night after all. He couldn't send Masters to pick her up—he'd promised Morgan he'd do it himself. Still, he'd probably feel better after dinner.

Raymunda was waiting for him, looking exceptionally glamorous. Fitz felt pleased; she'd obviously emerged from her gloom and sulks and had gone to a lot of trouble to make herself pretty. And she was *very* pretty.

"I like that," he said, kissing her lightly. "It's a nice color—like island sunshine."

Raymunda preened herself for him, pivoting slowly, smoothing her silken skirt over her hips.

"Good?" she asked with an enticing smile.

"Very." Fitz put his arm around her and they walked toward the master stateroom. "I'm sorry I was so busy today," he said, "but something came up that just had to be taken care of right away. God, I'm tired."

Raymunda watched anxiously as he peeled off his shirt and jeans and headed toward the shower.

"You'll feel better after a shower," she said soothingly. "I'll bring you a drink—bourbon and water, just the way you like it, two cubes of ice."

Fitz glanced at her in surprise. What was up with Raymunda? Why had she suddenly changed her tactics?—for tactics they were, he knew her well enough for that. In fact, he thought, soaping himself in the shower, their entire relationship was like a battleground. She marshaled her forces and worked out her tactics against him, and he had his own unassailable defense—work—and his Achilles heel—his liking for feminine companionship and pretty women, not just sex. That was a part of it, of course, but he enjoyed women, he liked being around them. Perhaps their feminine wiles, ruffles, and perfume provided the needed contrast to the stark reality of his business world; he didn't know. What he did know was that no woman could ever come between him and that true reality—he was quite sure of that.

Raymunda handed him the bourbon as he stepped, dripping, from the shower.

"Here, let me," she said, taking the big white towel and drying his back. "There, now you must feel better."

"About fifty percent," admitted Fitz. "All I need now is dinner."

"Dinner? But you are forgetting, Fitz, we have no cook."

"That's right, I had forgotten. Well, a sandwich, then . . . or I'm pretty good at omelettes if you prefer. And there must be smoked salmon and stuff in the refrigerator. We'll do it ourselves until our new cook arrives."

"No need." Raymunda smiled. "Fitz, I've arranged something else . . . we're going to a party."

"Jesus! What party?" Fitz stood naked, the glass of bourbon in his hand, an angry gleam in his eyes.

"We got a call today from Prince Bendor Grünewald—he's at the Villa Osiris. He's giving a Bajan barbecue party tonight. Oh, it's all completely casual, darling," she reassured him, seeing his irritation.

"I can see that," remarked Fitz, eyeing her elegant silk dress. "Damn it, Raymunda, I'm beat. I've just done that round trip to Miami and I was on the phone all day—I need a party and a load of strangers to make conversation with like a hole in the head."

"Damn you, Fitz McBain." Raymunda's temper rose. "I've been stuck on this damn boat for four days now without seeing a soul—I'm bored out of my mind. You're on the phone all the time . . . there's not even any dinner because you have no cook!"

"And it's too much to expect you to slice a little brown bread, take a little salmon out of the fridge, perhaps even prepare a little salad, and open a bottle of wine?" Fitz was tempted to tell her he wouldn't go. He really didn't want to—he'd warned her when they left that he was coming for a rest—a complete rest, the doctor had advised. But she had a point; maybe he had been neglecting her the past few days, though he hadn't noticed it. Perhaps it was just that Raymunda had become a little bit boring with her demands, her tempers and tantrums.

"All right," he said to her sulking back, "I'll go. But no more parties, Raymunda. I'm here for a rest. There is no one here—especially at Prince Bendor Grünewald's party—that I want to see."

"Fitz"—Raymunda turned with a triumphant smile, snaking her, arms around his naked back—"you're so sweet when you want to be. If you weren't so wet I'd show you how very sweet you are." She backed away, brushing imaginary droplets from her skirt.

Fitz drained his glass. She could have taken off the dress. She would have, had he made a move—Raymunda knew how to play her game—but he didn't feel like making the move. Pretty as Raymunda looked in her marigold silk toga with her silky bronze limbs and black hair, at this moment he would have preferred solitude, or maybe just the company of Mozart.

The colonnaded patio of the Villa Osiris was crowded with guests as Olympe threaded her way through, greeting fresh arrivals, checking who was

286

with whom this year, and who was wearing what. The women were taking full advantage of the warm night and their island suntans to wear the skimpiest dresses, exposing bare shoulders, naked backs, and smooth legs—as much of their bodies as they dared. And if any one of them was wearing a bra, then Olympe would have been very surprised; there were more and harder nipples here at the party than on any daytime beach.

But then, thought Olympe, nudity on the beach had nothing to do with sex—and parties did. She'd bet half the women here were looking for it—and not with their husbands, or at least the men they'd arrived with. Holiday romance, shipboard romance—it was all the same: liberate anyone from their everyday surroundings, even if they were glossy and luxurious, and put them in a lazy holiday atmosphere like this—by the time they'd got a little suntan they felt more glamorous, more exciting, and definitely more sexy. She knew she did . . . and it wasn't for Bendor. Ah-ha! Wasn't that Fitz McBain over by the door? And that must be Raymunda Ortiz—the current paramour. Well, she thought, moving toward them, we'll just have to see about that, Raymunda.

When Olympe Avallon smiled at a man he felt drawn into some magic circle, where only he existed, where *he* was the star in her firmament.

Fitz was no exception. He was an expert in flirts, he'd been practiced on by the best, but Olympe was a charmer—there was just a hint of laughter in her eyes, as though she were saying, Look, I know I'm flirting with you, but it's all such fun, isn't it?

"Raymunda!" exclaimed Olympe. "*Mais tu est ravissante, chérie* . . . what a heavenly dress. I simply adore that color. I *must* introduce you to Beny, he particularly wanted to meet you." Taking Raymunda's arm she led her off, turning to smile conspiratorially at Fitz. She'd be back.

A steel band was playing down by the pool and the barbecue fires sent a fragrant drift of woodsmoke and spicy cooking across the crowded patio.

Have I eaten today? wondered Fitz. He didn't think so.

"You look to me like a very hungry man." Olympe appeared at his side. "Either that or a bored one."

Fitz smiled as their eyes met. "A combination of both," he admitted.

Olympe tucked her arm into his. "I'm sure I can take care of one complaint." She smiled, leading him toward the tables scattered around the pool. "The food is excellent. I only hope that I can do something about the second."

Her oblique glance was as inviting as her smile, and in a short black dress that left her shoulders bare, and with her mane of tawny hair, she was dazzling. Fitz was beginning to enjoy himself.

Bendor and Raymunda had lots of friends in common; they had quite a satisfactory chat, she thought, about mutual acquaintances, and he'd invited her—them—to come wind surfing tomorrow and for lunch. She wanted to ask Fitz if they could

288

have Bendor and his friends for dinner tomorrow night on the *Fiesta*, but he'd disappeared. With a pang she remembered Olympe Avallon. Hadn't she been awfully quick to part the two of them? She couldn't see Olympe either. Oh, well—Raymunda shrugged—everyone knew that Bendor was crazy about Olympe and that she expected to be the next princess. Olympe was surely not going to jeopardize that position. No, she was sure there was no need to worry about her.

"Raymunda." Bendor took her arm. "Have you met Salty Majors? Salty's from Newport, you know, he's a sailing fellow. . . ."

Raymunda sparkled on the receiving end of Salty's interested smile; she might as well enjoy herself while she could.

Fitz McBain was exactly the kind of man she had in mind as a long-term investment, thought Olympe, sipping her island cocktail as she sat beside him at a small table by the pool. He was *very* attractive—without a doubt the most attractive man here, in a much less obvious way than, for instance, Salty Majors, who was all suntanned macho muscle, sexist macho talk, and—minimacho brain—if you ever wanted to be close enough to him to discover that he had a brain to go with his old family millions. Fitz had the glamor of his rough pastyou just knew his muscles were earned, not worked at in some gym.

"I hope that we're going to see more of you, now that you've found us?" Her hand rested lightly on his.

Fitz took it, kissing it lightly. "I would have liked that, but I'm here for a rest . . . your party was an exception to my rule."

"You have rules?" Olympe raised her brows in amusement.

Fitz threw back his head and laughed. "I sure do—and one of them is to eat at least one meal a day. Why don't we see what they're serving at your party?"

Raymunda turned her head as she heard Fitz's laugh ring out—she hadn't heard him laugh like that in ages. Peering through the crowd she caught a glimpse of him with Olympe, down by the pool.

"You must be hungry," she told Salty Majors, slipping her arm through his. "Why don't we have a little supper?"

Sitting at a table by the pool with Salty and two other couples who were all houseguests of Bendor, Raymunda cast covert glances to her left where Fitz and Olympe sat, seemingly totally absorbed in each other. They'd been there together for more than half an hour now and Raymunda was just debating what she should do about it without making herself look foolish when the first drops of rain began to fall. A spear of lightning jagged across the sky and hung, purple and fizzling, over the sea. Chairs were pushed back hastily as the guests, laughing, made a dash for the house. Salty put a gentlemanly arm around Raymunda, hurrying her up the steps to the patio. Glancing behind her, Raymunda saw Fitz wrap his jacket around Olympe as she stood, head thrown back, laughing in the downpour. Damn it, this had been a mistake.

"Oh, my God," said Fitz, "it's twelve o'clock!"

"Do we expect your coach to turn into a pumpkin then?" Olympe pushed back her wet hair and smiled at him mischievously.

"Not only that, I'll lose my glass slipper! I've left someone sitting at the airport—her plane must have arrived half an hour ago. I must leave."

Olympe took his hand and pressed it warmly, curling her fingers with his.

"Will you come back?" she whispered.

Fitz hesitated. He had been enjoying himself. It was pleasant flirting with Olympe, she was bright and amusing, but he had to consider Raymunda; after all, he was with her.

"I'm afraid not," he told Olympe, "but thank you for the pleasure of your company."

"It is," whispered Olympe, "a pleasure that could be yours—anytime."

Their eyes met in mutual understanding and Fitz dropped a quick kiss on her cheek.

"I'll remember that," he said.

Salty Majors released Raymunda reluctantly.

"You will come tomorrow, won't you?" He smiled at her, his even white teeth gleaming against his deep tan. He really looked quite a lot like Robert Redford, decided Raymunda.

"If you promise to teach me to wind-surf," she agreed as they said good-bye. She shrugged off

Fitz's hand furiously as he guided her through the crowd and out of the villa, waiting impatiently next to him while the valet fetched the car.

"Why are we leaving so early?" she complained. "The party was just getting going."

"You can stay if you wish."

The valet held open the car door and Fitz slid behind the wheel.

"Well," he asked impatiently, "are you coming or are you not?"

Raymunda flounced into the car.

"I expect you're tired." She sighed. "Maybe Olympe Avallon wore you out."

Fitz glanced sideways at her as he maneuvered the car down the steep driveway. So that was it, now she was jealous. Well, maybe she had a right to be, but she'd seemed content enough with that guy from Newport who looked as though he'd majored in yachting at college. What he was really tired of, he realized suddenly, were all the games between himself and Raymunda. Life was complicated enough without all this.

He took the road away from the coast, heading toward the airport. The rain still lashed down, though the lightning had reduced to a flickering glare and the rumble of thunder came from a distance now, far out to sea.

Raymunda closed her eyes, pondering her next moves. There was lunch tomorrow at the Villa Osiris, with swimming and wind surfing . . . she knew Fitz had been told to rest, but surely he couldn't object to *that!* And then there was to-morrow night. Her eyes flew open as Fitz pulled the car into the airport.

"What are we doing here?"

"I have to pick up someone—a friend of Morgan's. I'll be right back."

Fitz slammed the car door behind him and Raymunda watched his retreating back, smoldering. They'd left the party to come and pick up some friend of Morgan's? Damn it, there was enough staff on that yacht. Surely one of them could have done that?

Venetia stared out of the big plate-glass windows into the pouring night. Rivers of water ran along the gutters, and in the glow of the airport lamps and the flickering lightning she could see the ground steaming as it cooled. She'd left London in the fog and she'd arrived in the rain; maybe it was an omen and the elements were trying to tell her something. Perhaps she shouldn't have come? Morgan seemed to have forgotten her. She glanced again at the big clock. She'd been here for more than in hour and the airport was almost deserted. She'd watched and waited while everyone else was met by laughing friends and swept off to their villas or hotels. What could have happened? Had she arrived on the wrong day? Or maybe they'd got the message wrong.

Fitz strode through the empty hall toward her. She was the only person waiting, but he would have picked her out easily in any crowd. She was taller than Jenny, her hair was a darker blond, and she wore it smooth and straight to her shoulders. She turned at the sound of his footsteps, looking at him with anxious blue eyes, and it was Jenny playing the waif in *Big City Girl*. Dear God, thought Fitz, I hadn't expected the resemblance to be quite this strong.

"You must be Venetia," he said. Her face was London-winter pale and her hand cold in his, but her smile had all the charm of her mother's. "I'm afraid Morgan couldn't come. He sent me instead— I'm Fitz McBain."

She stood, her hand in his, gazing into his dark blue eyes. Of course, she remembered his voice on the phone, deep and with a slight drawl.

"Oh, but I didn't . . ." She stopped, confused.

"Didn't what?"

"Well, oh . . . I didn't expect you to look like this . . . you know, I always imagined you in a city business suit, jetting to important meetings, and . . ."

Fitz grinned. "And what?"

Venetia blushed. "It'll only sound rude if I say it."

"Tell me."

"You're younger than I expected."

Fitz laughed and released her hand. "It's an illusion. I'm forty-four, almost forty-five—pretty old by your standards. What are you? Seventeen?"

"I'm twenty," she said indignantly. "Well, I'll be twenty soon."

"You must be a very tired twenty-year-old. It was

294

a hell of a long journey. Let's get you home to bed." Fitz hefted her one suitcase and looked around in surprise. "Is this all you've got?"

"Oh, yes, I don't need much—just shorts and stuff."

Every other woman he knew traveled with at least six cases filled with clothes for every possible occasion. Venetia Haven was definitely different. Or maybe it was just that she was so young.

Raymunda sat up straight in her seat. Fitz was with a *girl*. Who the hell was she?

"Venetia, this is Raymunda Ortiz," said Fitz, holding the door for her. "Raymunda, this is Venetia Haven, a friend of Morgan's."

"Oh, a little friend of Morgan's." Raymunda's stare lost interest and Venetia felt the smile freeze on her face.

Fitz's jaw set in a grim line as he pulled away from the curb. He hadn't missed Raymunda's "little" gesture. She'd looked at Venetia, simple in her blue cotton trousers, sweatshirt, and espadrilles, assessed her, and dismissed her as someone not worthy of her attention.

"Venetia is to be our new chef," said Fitz, breaking the silence.

Raymunda glanced at him in amazement. They'd left Bendor's party to go and pick up the *help?* My God, she could kill Fitz, really *kill* him, for that!

"Then no doubt," she said icily, "Venetia will be able to take care of our dinner party tomorrow night."

Fitz glared at her. "*Our* dinner party?"

"That's right, Fitz darling. I invited Beny and his house party to dinner tomorrow night. That's *Prince* Bendor Grünewald." She tossed the information over her shoulder to Venetia. "I don't expect you will have cooked for a prince before. I hope your standards are up to it."

"I have a cordon bleu diploma," replied Venetia nervously.

"Raymunda, why wasn't *I* told about this dinner?" Fitz swung the car around the corner angrily.

"I thought you'd be pleased," she said sweetly. "After all, Olympe will be there."

Venetia sat back against the cushions, wondering what was going on between them. Whatever it was, she wished she weren't here.

The rain had stopped by the time they'd parked at the harbor and stepped into the waiting launch that took them out to the *Fiesta*. Venetia stared across the water at the string of lights decorating the enormous yacht. It looked gay and festive, unlike the two silent people next to her.

Masters was waiting for them. Fitz introduced Venetia and asked him to take care of her, as Raymunda disappeared without saying good night.

"I'm sure you'll find your cabin comfortable," said Fitz gently. "Morgan asked me to tell you that he will call. I'm afraid it's my fault he wasn't here to meet you but he should be back next week. You must sleep as long as you can—have a few days' rest and get used to things. Masters will show you everything tomorrow."

"Thank you." Venetia regarded him seriously. "You're a very kind man, Mr. McBain."

"That's not a term that's usually applied to me," said Fitz, feeling oddly pleased. "Now off you go to sleep. Pleasant dreams."

Venetia was so tired she barely noticed the luxurious yacht, or her lovely cabin amidships on the top deck that was close, Masters had told her, to her galley; she'd see it all tomorrow. Casting off her clothes she slid naked into bed. The night was calm now and tropically warm. Her last thought as she drifted into sleep was of Fitz McBain's deep, dark eyes gazing into hers.

Raymunda returned from the Villa Osiris at four and went to find Fitz. He was sitting on the stern deck in shorts and a sleeveless T-shirt, cleaning his fishing gear.

"You don't know what you missed," she said, flopping onto the blue-cushioned seat near him.

"I'm glad you enjoyed yourself." Fitz's tone was polite.

"Everyone's coming tonight," Raymunda informed him, watching for his reaction.

"That's good. I spoke with Masters and he is taking care of everything for you, Raymunda."

"Little Miss Haven's not up to it, then? Why do you have to be so charitable, Fitz? You need a proper chef for this boat. God knows you can afford one."

"Raymunda, I can afford whatever I want. And I

want Venetia Haven as chef. Remember that, will you?"

Their glances met angrily. Raymunda was the first to look away.

"I hope you'll enjoy yourself tonight," she suggested in a meeker tone.

"I daresay I will." Fitz concentrated on the reel he had been waxing, releasing the catch and letting it spin out. "Although, of course, I won't be here. I intend to have a quiet dinner in town. I thought I'd ask 'little Miss Haven' to go with me."

"But you can't!" gasped Raymunda, furiously. "Everyone will expect you to be here."

"Raymunda," said Fitz gently, "no one tells me what to do. Remember that too."

"Olympe will miss you." Raymunda threw the words at his departing back, listening angrily to his laughter as he strode off toward his study. Damn it, damn it, oh, *damn it!*

Rory loved it. He just *loved* it. Barbados had welcomed him and the cast and crew of *Chelsea's Game* that morning with steel bands and official presentations, and were giving them the complete island VIP treatment. Especially Rory. There was no doubt he was a big star—even the British guests at the hotel knew who he was, since the program had been taken up by BBC television in the autumn. Bill had been right, it was exactly what he needed. Sometimes L.A. could lay on the pressure in a lot of sneaky ways that you didn't notice at first, but they caught up with you—you always had to keep your wits about you to make sure nobody was trying to screw you and that your position in the show wasn't being undermined—by your costar, for instance. He'd fancied that lately Shelly was getting more lines than she used to, that her role was becoming almost as strong as his, and he'd had to have Bill do battle with the producers and the writers to make sure that didn't happen. But now all those worries were left behind. You could relax here, in Barbados.

"Hey, Shel," he said, tucking her arm in his as they climbed out of the limousine and headed toward Rockley's Resort Rendezvous, "let's have some fun, you and me. Come on, Dirk, Roger," he yelled at the director and the writer and other members of the crew straggling behind them across the road. "Shel and I are gonna show this island how the L.A. all-stars have *fun!*"

"Christ," muttered Dirk, "I hate to think what that means." Dirk was feeling particularly bitter. It wasn't until after they'd gone through customs and immigration that Rory had told him that the stash was in *his* luggage. Thank God they'd been waved through without any fuss or he might have ended up in the local jail instead of the local disco. He'd make damn sure that there'd be no repeat of that. If Rory Grant had to bring his coke with him, he'd carry it himself.

Rory was an instant hit at the Rendezvous. Everyone in the place recognized Chelsea, and the girls crowded around, demanding autographs and kisses that, in between shots of island rum, he was happy to provide. Yeah, Rory was having himself a good time, playing the star at last. After an hour, though, he got bored.

"Come on, you guys," he called, "on to the next one."

"He's drunk now as well as stoned," commented Dirk as they followed him obediently from the club. Hell, he could go home, he supposed, back to the hotel, and get some sleep, but if he did, he wasn't sure what Rory could get up to. Tomorrow he'd have to put a couple of minders onto him. He didn't give a damn what Rory did when he was on his own, but when he was here and *working*—then Dirk wanted to know. He'd have to keep him in check or they'd never get the show in on time and he'd be the one to blame.

Venetia was wearing what to Fitz looked like a shapeless blue cotton dress with a low neckline, a waist that wasn't because it was too wide, and a full skirt. It looked like a dress meant for someone two sizes bigger, but on her it was charming.

"My sister designed it," Venetia said with a grin. "It's a bit avant garde, but I love it. Of course, she's very influenced by the Japanese since she's gone to work for Mitsoko—all I've got to wear now are kimonos! But she's really terribly good. Mother always said that Paris had the true talent in the family."

They were sitting opposite each other at a candlelit table at the Bagatelle Great House, one of the island's loveliest restaurants, whose thick stone walls dated from colonial times, when it had been a plantation house. The choice had been made on the spur of the moment by Fitz, and it had turned out to be a happy one. Venetia was enchanted by the place and he was intrigued by her enjoyment and her curiosity about her surroundings. She wanted to know everything, from the history of the island and the story of this plantation to the origins of Bajan cooking. Fitz allowed himself to relax in her company; he was beginning to forget even that she was Jenny's daughter, because though the physical resemblance was strong she was a very different person. Now she'd mentioned her mother and it brought back sharply the memory of Venetia's stricken face on the television screen.

"How are your sisters?" he asked.

"They're all right now, I think. Paris tried so hard, you know, with her fashion show—she designed everything herself, practically *made* the clothes, too, from what I can gather, and then just because Mitsoko changed the day of his showing, nobody at all went to Paris's. She'd sunk all her money into it too. Now she's had to take a job as a model. She's incredibly beautiful."

"*All* her money?" Fitz asked idly. "That must have been a considerable sum."

Venetia gazed contemplatively at her glass of wine, a glowing ruby in the candlelight. "Only ten thousand dollars. It was all we had, you see—all that mother left us."

Fitz snapped to attention. "*All* that she left you? But surely, Venetia, your mother was a very rich woman?"

Venetia looked embarrassed; she really shouldn't be telling him this. But it wasn't as though he were a complete stranger—he'd met Jenny, and he'd been the kindest and most helpful person to them.

"Apparently Jenny had been foolish with her money. Her lawyer, Stan Reubin, told us that there was nothing left, she'd made bad investments in property and played the commodity markets. He said it didn't take long to lose a lot of money that way. We didn't want to believe him at first, but Bill—that's Bill Kaufmann, who was her agent and manager for as long as I can remember, before I was born even— anyway, Bill implied that she'd been worried about her career and that she'd had a couple of. . . lovers. . . who had exploited her. So you see in the end there was very little left. It wasn't so much the money that I minded," she added, "though Paris did, terribly— she *needed* it, you see, to launch her career—but it was the sort of slur on her character that they made, and the fact that though they'd been her friends all those years they never did anything to help her. Don't you think they should have noticed what was going on?"

Fitz didn't like to see the sadness that turned her beautiful eyes a grayer shade of blue, and he didn't like the story he'd just heard. In the context of Jenny's sudden death it was open to suspicion. He might have Ronson look into it for him; he had good contacts in Los Angeles, and he'd know what was going on.

"I think they certainly should have known, but it's foolish to pass judgment without understanding all the circumstances. What about your other sister—India, isn't it?"

"India will always come out smiling. She didn't give a damn for the money, only for what had happened to our mother. She was in Rome working for the interior designer Fabrizio Paroli, but when I spoke with her just before I left she was off to the coast near Positano—Fabrizio has put her in charge of a conversion. The Montefiore family want to change their palazzo into a hotel. India seemed very excited at the prospect, but I got the feeling, too, that she was eager to get away from Rome—the paparazzi have been very persistent in their attentions since Jenny died. I think she's probably quite relieved to be away for a while—and from Fabrizio."

"Oh?" Fitz raised an eyebrow and Venetia felt herself blushing.

"Jenny always said I talked too much," she remarked with a laugh, "but quite honestly, I haven't talked—not like this, anyway—about my mother, I mean, not to anyone. Not even to Morgan."

He'd been so absorbed in her, he'd forgotten about Morgan.

"Enough sad talk," he said briskly. "I'm going to order you some dessert and then . . ." He glanced at his watch. Eleven. Raymunda's party would still be going strong. "How'd you like to go dancing?"

Her face lit up. "Dancing? I'd love it."

Why was it, wondered Fitz, that he felt as though he'd just given her something wonderful? She had this endearing ability to make even the smallest kindness or attention seem an act of graciousness. It must be her English good manners. Whatever, he liked it.

The Caribbean Pepperpot was hustling and bustling, getting into its nightly swing, as they arrived. Grabbing Venetia's hand, Fitz led her through the dimly lit room to a corner table. It was silly, he knew, but he didn't want to let go of her hand, it felt small in his—and soft.

The waiter brought drinks and the music changed to something softer as colored lights flickered through the room. Taking her hand he bowed over it, barely brushing it with his lips.

"Will you dance with me, Venetia Haven?" he asked.

It was silly, she knew it, but she didn't want him to let go of her hand—in fact she wanted him to kiss it again. Hand in hand they walked to the tiny dance floor, and as his arms went around her she slid hers around his neck, the way she always did when she danced with Morgan.

This is ridiculous, Fitz told himself, holding her closer. She's just a child—Morgan's girl. He knew that, but then why was his heart beating faster? And why did he have this overwhelming urge to cover the top of her blond head with kisses? He could feel the delicate bones of her back beneath his hands, and glancing down at her face, he noticed the golden-tipped lashes on her closed eyelids. She seemed lost in some kind of dream, her body relaxed against his. It must be this slow sexy music, he told himself, it was too crazy—too crazy that right now all he wanted in the world was to make love to Venetia. Of course it was only the warm tropical night, and the wine and the music—and his memories of Jenny Haven. He was still in love with Jenny.

The music finished and he led her back to their table. She kept hold of his hand and their eyes met. The touch of his fingers sent little electrical thrills up her arm; she was aware of the faint tremor in them as they curled around her hand, and she wanted more, she wanted his arms around her again as they danced, she wanted to be close to him, closer.

They danced some more, slowly, endlessly, just holding on to each other. There was no talk now, nothing, just the two of them in this limbo—and her hair, thought Fitz, smelled of summer meadows.

He shouldn't be thinking of these things! He'd better get her back to the *Fiesta* before he made a fool of himself.

"Time to go," he said gently.

"Ohhh." Her small sigh expressed infinite regret, but Fitz couldn't allow himself to be persuaded. He called the waiter over and paid the bill.

The Caribbean Pepperpot was crowded by the time Rory and his entourage got there. He was up for it, really up. He was just thinking he hadn't had such a good time in ages, and that's when it happened. *He saw Jenny Haven*. And then he freaked.

Dirk watched as Rory's face turned ashen, wondering what the hell was going on. Was the bastard gonna have a heart attack?

Rory grabbed him with a trembling hand. "It's her, Dirk, oh my God, it's *her!* Oh, God, what am I gonna do, what am I gonna do? It's Jenny, Dirk. You see her, don't you . . . or am I the only one? She's a ghost, she's gonna *haunt* me, for Chrissakes."

"Shut up, Rory," snapped Dirk, "you're making an ass of yourself. Jenny's dead. Don't you know who that is? Or were you too busy to go to Jenny's funeral? That's Venetia Haven. Jenny's daughter."

"Her daughter?" Rory laughed, a high false sound that contrasted with the gay music and the happy faces in the crowded entrance. Christ, he hadn't known she looked exactly like Jenny. "Oh, sure, sure it is." He pulled himself together, shrugging on his jacket, running his hand through his hair. Delighted shrieks accompanied the gesture; he had been recognized.

"I'll just say hi," he said nonchalantly to Dirk, "for old times' sake, y'know . . . for Jenny."

"Sure," said Dirk, "sure, Rory, for old times' sake."

Fitz felt Venetia stiffen as the good-looking young man approached them. Was it someone she knew?

"Hi, Venetia," said Rory, holding out his hand. "I'm an old friend of your mother's."

"I know who you are." Venetia ignored his out-stretched hand, and feeling like a fool, Rory shifted it to his head, stroking back his hair, casually.

Fitz glanced at her sharply. Something was wrong; her tone was icy and her voice trembled just a little.

"I just wanted to say, you know . . . like I'm sorry about poor Jenny, it must have been an awful shock to you."

"It was. To all three of us. Good night, Mr. Grant."

Venetia swept past him, leaving him standing there. Shit, thought Rory angrily, tough little bitch—just like her mother.

"Come on, you guys," he called, "let's get this show on the road. Chelsea's gonna take over this place." Grabbing Shelly by the hand he pulled her onto the dance floor to the delighted applause of the watching crowd.

Fitz sat silently in the car next to Venetia, waiting for her to speak. She wasn't crying, she was just sitting there, but he could feel her trembling.

"I'm sorry," she said at last, "but I didn't expect it . . . I mean, to meet Rory Grant like that."

"You know him?" Fitz had had the impression that they were seeing each other for the first time.

"No. I just knew *of* him. He was my mother's lover. Her last lover. Apparently she lavished all her love and attention, and her money, on him. Jenny made him a star. Bill Kaufmann told me that, Fitz. And then he left her."

Fitz thought of what she'd told him earlier, how the other two had abandoned Jenny. And now this one. Something was very wrong with this whole situation, very wrong.

"I can't explain why," whispered Venetia, "but I have the feeling that Rory Grant was more involved in my mother's financial difficulties than Bill Kaufmann would say. He swore that Grant was a nice guy. I've never heard Bill call *anyone* a nice guy before. Oh, it's all wrong. I know it. I just know it."

"Venetia, will you let me look into this for you and your sisters? You are entitled to know what happened to your mother's money."

"But there is no money."

"Wait," he said soothingly. "Let me see, okay? If it's not there I want to know why. Exactly why. Do I have your permission, Venetia?"

She nodded. "Would you?"

He pulled himself back from her tender eyes.

"Consider it done," he said, switching on the ignition.

They were silent on the drive back to the harbor. He was too aware of her, thought Fitz, much too aware of Jenny's daughter, Morgan's girl.

The *Fiesta* wore her full-dress lights, sparkling across the water like diamonds as they sat in the little speedboat, heading toward her. Venetia was looking at him with those tender blue eyes—as he switched off the engine and turned to her. He couldn't help what happened next; for once in his life Fitz McBain lost control. His arms went around

308

her and his mouth came down on hers in a kiss that was far from tender.

Venetia knew she had been right. *This* is what should happen—the surging, trembling, ecstatic sensation—and she knew she never wanted it to end.

Fitz pulled himself away at last. He should never have done it. It was a mistake. Forcing himself to act he turned away.

"Please forgive that," he said. "It shouldn't have happened."

"But . . . Fitz, I . . ."

He held out his hand. "Come on, I'll help you onto the steps."

Doesn't he know how I feel? Venetia wondered. Then how do you tell a man, a man you barely know, that you are in love with him?

She thought Fitz wasn't going to kiss her again, she was sure of it. And then he did, just her fingers, like before—held for a moment in his as he said good-night.

"You're very much like your mother, Venetia," he said as she smiled up at him. "Sleep well—and forget about Rory Grant."

Rory Grant was a million miles away—a visitor from another planet.

Venetia watched as Fitz walked toward the stern deck, where there was still the sound of voices and music. I'm in love, she thought happily. It is love; when it happens, then you *know*. She brushed a hand across her lips, recalling his mouth on hers. She would die just to feel Fitz's arms around her again, his mouth on hers just one more time.

It wasn't a loud ring, just a soft purr, and it was some
time before Venetia realized that it was the telephone.
Forcing herself from a lengthy dream in which she'd
been lying in Fitz's arms on some soft island beach,
shaded by palms and cooled by wafting breezes, she
sat up and reached for the receiver.

"Vennie?"

Morgan's voice jolted her as fully awake as a cold
shower.

"Vennie? Are you there?"

"Morgan—it's you . . . I thought you were in Rio."

"I am, sweetheart, and I'm sorry I wasn't there to
meet you. Did my father explain?"

"Yes . . . yes, he explained. . . ."

"Good. I hope he's looking after you all right?"

"Oh . . . yes . . ."

"Don't let him work you too hard—he's a worka-
holic, you know, and he thinks everybody else is too.
I miss you, Venetia."

"Yes . . ." Venetia wound the cord around her
finger and released it again nervously. "I miss you
too. When are you coming back, Morgan?"

"I'm aiming for next week—and then I'll be able
to spend some time with you. Vennie, I can't tell you
how much I'm looking forward to that."

"Oh, Morgan." Venetia was suddenly only too
aware of the dilemma she was in, and it left her
tongue-tied. What was she to say?

"Are you all right, sweetheart?"

310

"It's just that it's six in the morning—I was asleep."

Morgan laughed. "Okay, then—go back to sleep. I'll call you again later in the week. Take care of yourself, Vennie, and don't let Fitz work you too hard."

"I'm sure he won't do that. Take care of yourself, too, Morgan."

"Speak to you later, then, baby—love you."

"Yes . . . I love you. . . ."

Venetia put down the phone and lay back on her pillows, staring at the ceiling. Oh, my God, what was she to do? Her head was full of Fitz, her body remembered the pressure of his as they danced, her mouth still felt his kiss; she'd been lost in a dream of his lovemaking when Morgan had called. She loved Morgan, she was sure she did—in a certain way. But she was suddenly, completely, and passionately in love with his father. Perhaps tonight, she thought, with a soft smile, perhaps tonight they'd go to some other restaurant to gaze into each other's eyes in the candlelight, and then they'd dance some more. With a shock she remembered Raymunda. Of course! There could be no more candlelight dinners for two. Fitz was with Raymunda. And she was with Morgan.

Downcast, she wandered into the bathroom and turned on the shower. Standing under its gentle pressure, allowing the spray to soak her hair, she wondered what could be done about Raymunda. It wasn't up to her, she decided finally; if Fitz wanted

311

to do something about her, then he would. She'd just have to wait and see.

Bob Ronson was a good man, thought Fitz, putting down the phone. You could rely on him to do what you asked—even if it was something a little out of the ordinary. Ronson's kind of ambition was a good thing only when it was on your side, working for you. Against you, he'd be ruthless and calculating. Ronson would let nothing impede his progress up the ladder of success. And that was exactly the kind of man you needed in a large enterprise—he'd get moved up the ladder, all right, in the McBain Corporation—they could always use a good "hatchet man." Meanwhile, Ronson had promised to be back within the week with whatever information on the Haven situation he could acquire—there had been plenty of gossip, he'd said, and a few who had cast doubtful glances Reubin and Kaufmann's way. He'd find out.

Fair enough, thought Fitz. He'd do what he could to straighten out the situation for Venetia and her sisters, and that was all. Last night had been a big mistake. Venetia was lovely, she was very young, and he'd been tempted. But she was Morgan's girl. He had enough complications with Raymunda, who'd thrown a tantrum last night after her guests had gone, accusing him of being rude to them and of insulting her simply because he'd wished them all good night and gone off to bed. Olympe had been there, watching the interaction between Raymunda

312

and himself with a little smile. He'd had time to notice that she looked very attractive, dressed in red with a mouth that matched, but he'd had Venetia on his mind . . . Venetia. . . .

It seemed as though today was the day for putting the past out of his mind—he would forget about the episode with Venetia, and he had come to the parting of the ways with Raymunda. She was downstairs packing now. He'd never led her to believe that there was a future for them together—it had been an affair of the moment, one that had been fun in the beginning, before she began making demands.

As if on cue Raymunda stalked into his office.

"I might have known I'd find you here," she said scornfully. "The 'rest' doesn't apply when it comes to work, I suppose—only to parties and having fun and paying *me* a little attention."

"Raymunda," said Fitz gently, "I was quite content to spend my time here—alone with you. You could have had all my attention."

Raymunda paced the floor, elegant in high heels and a white linen suit.

"Of course," she said, ignoring his remark, "you needn't worry about me, not that you would have anyway. Salty Majors has been kind enough to say he'll fly back with me to New York—he has a race at Newport on Saturday and I shall be going with him."

She flung the statement at him as a challenge and Fitz smiled—she was still playing her games.

"That's very kind of Salty. Obviously I shall worry about you, Raymunda. I don't want you to be unhappy. And I never wanted to hurt you . . . it just didn't work out, that's all."

Raymunda knew he was right. She'd played her final card—and lost.

Fitz took her arm and escorted her onto the deck. The launch was waiting, piled with her baggage, and a young sailor, smart in white shirt and shorts and peaked cap, stood at the wheel. Raymunda hesitated, turning her face to Fitz.

"Couldn't we try again," she whispered, "one more time?"

Fitz kissed her gently on each cheek.

"It's over, baby," he said, stepping back. "Let's part friends, Raymunda?"

Raymunda shrugged.

"Friends!" she said, stepping into the launch. "We were *never* friends."

She was probably right, thought Fitz, watching the launch speed toward the harbor.

Venetia had spent the morning with Masters in Bridgetown being shown the local shops and exploring the markets, admiring baskets of green- and peach-colored exotic fruits, and dazzling vermilion chili peppers, and the silvery displays of strange fish, fresh from the local waters. She'd encountered friendly, beaming faces at all their stops and had managed to thrust her personal dilemma temporarily to the back of her mind. She was here to do a job, and she wasn't going to let Morgan down—at least not in that way.

The launch from the *Fiesta* was just tying up as

Masters and Venetia arrived at the harbor laden with their purchases. Raymunda stepped out, pausing to throw instructions over her shoulder to the young crewman who was busily unloading her bags. As she stalked toward the car her icy glance swept them just once, and then, with a tilt of her chin, she strode on.

They stared after her in surprise.

"Never did think she was a lady," commented Masters. "It looks as though we're well rid of her."

Rid of her? Venetia followed him to the launch. Raymunda's baggage was piled on the harborside and she watched as it was carried across to the car where Raymunda sat, staring straight in front of her. He'd done it, then! Fitz had done it! He'd finished with Raymunda—sent her away. Because of *her*. She climbed into the launch with shaking knees. He'd be waiting for her now—oh, life was wonderful after all!

Masters piloted the launch back to the *Fiesta*, helped Venetia unload her parcels, and sent the boat back to wait for the other crewman.

In her trim galley Venetia packed away her supplies. The previous chef had left a sheaf of notes and she had planned to read them and to begin to familiarize herself with the equipment, but she was too hot and excited. She would take another shower, put on fresh clothes, and make herself look pretty for Fitz.

Fitz couldn't concentrate. He'd run his eye over the same paragraph three times and he still didn't know what it was about. Angrily, he tossed the book aside. Why didn't he admit to himself that he was waiting to see her, hanging around like some schoolboy with a crush, just to see her smile at him? He was crazy—he'd better do something about it now before it was too late and he became even crazier. Picking up the ship-to-shore phone he placed a call to Pete's Island Sport Fishing. He'd go off for a couple of days with his old friend Pete, go after some marlin or barracuda—that'd keep him busy and out of mischief. Morgan would be with her next week and life would get back to normal.

Fitz had been gone three days, three whole days, and Venetia felt that each one was a loss. She tried to rationalize the shock when she'd discovered he had gone without even seeing her, but ultimately it always came back to the same thing. Perhaps Fitz was upset about Raymunda's departure. Maybe he hadn't told her it was over, maybe she had told him, and maybe he hadn't even thought about Venetia at all. The permutations were endless, and as she sunbathed on deck or busied herself in the galley, practicing her cooking on the crew, the idea gnawed at her that he didn't care about her at all—it had just been a friendly kiss on his part, he'd thought her pretty and young, it was the wine and the dancing. Oh, God, then what was she to do?

He finally returned late in the evening of the third day. It was ten o'clock and the temperature had soared up into the nineties and stayed there all day. Now the air was heavy with humidity, silent and still with the promise of a storm to come.

316

Lying on her bed, Venetia heard the launch. She sat up quickly, pushing back her hair, and ran outside. From her vantage point on the top deck she saw Fitz talking with Masters and then he walked away toward his quarters—without even a glance in the direction of her cabin.

She went back inside and sat on her bed, considering what to do. He *must* care. A man didn't kiss a girl that way unless he cared. He was avoiding her because of Morgan—and he was quite right. Only, she wasn't going to be noble. There *was* something she could do. . . .

Hastily, before she could change her mind, she slipped on a pair of baggy khaki shorts and a loose white tank top, brushed her hair with rapid, impatient strokes, and hurried out on deck. She hesitated for a minute, came back, dabbed a generous amount of Bluebell behind her ears and between her breasts, and made again for the door.

She stopped by the galley to pick up a plate of cold chicken, a basket of French bread, and a bottle of chilled white wine. It would provide a good excuse if anyone saw her going into Fitz's cabin. As she walked down the corridor she could hear music, but the big salon was dark and empty. Knocking lightly on the door of his bedroom, she waited. There was no reply, and she pushed it open cautiously. The lamps were lit and Vivaldi drifted, delicate and melodic, from the speakers. Fitz never turned on the noisy air-conditioning when he listened to music, and he had left his windows open

317

to the sultry night air. Venetia could hear the shower running in the bathroom as she hovered uncertainly, clutching the basket and the chicken and wine. Maybe this was the wrong thing to do. Well-brought-up girls didn't pursue a man like this. She wondered what Jenny would have advised her to do. "Always take your chances on love"— that's what she had said to them once. Well, wasn't that exactly what she was doing now?

The bathroom door opened and Fitz stood there, a white towel tied around his middle, his hair still sleek and wet from the shower. His tan had developed a ruddy glow from his days out at sea, and his body was lean and hard-looking. She noticed the scatter of gray among the dark hair on his chest and the deep scar down one arm from some long-ago accident, and then her gaze met his.

Fitz had felt pleased with himself. He'd thought he'd beaten it. He'd gone fishing with Pete, he'd stayed away three days, drunk enough whiskey each night so that he'd slept like a log, and been up again at the break of dawn ready for the next day's sport. He'd told himself he'd forgotten her, dismissed the episode as nonsense—just something to do with the night and his old romantic dreams of Jenny Haven. And now she was here and it was starting all over again.

"I just thought you might be hungry," stammered Venetia, setting down the food on a table. "After all, I am supposed to be the chef."

"Thank you, Venetia."

"Actually, that's not absolutely true. . . . ." She moved closer to him, standing with her hands in the pockets of her baggy khaki shorts, like a guilty child. Only she wasn't a child. Her nipples stood out against the thin vest she wore. "I came to say something else."

Fitz walked to the table and picked up the bottle of wine.

"Will you have a glass of wine with me, Venetia?"

She took it from him, watching his eyes, searching for a reaction to her presence.

"Would you like something to eat?" he asked politely.

Venetia took a gulp of her wine.

"Fitz," she said, "Fitz . . . oh, God, this is awful." Putting down her glass she ran an agitated hand through her hair and paced toward him. "Fitz, I think I'm in love with you. No. I *am* in love with you. Maybe you think I'm a fool, and that I barely know you . . . but I *do* know you, I feel I know you as I know myself." She took a deep breath. "There, I've said it." Tears pricked at her eyelids and she stared downcast at the golden Persian rug that felt like silk beneath her bare feet.

Fitz had meant to tell her to leave, just to be gentle and polite, but then she had looked at him with Jenny's eyes, and her mouth that was so nearly Jenny's, and she had said she loved him. It was the culmination of all his dreams. His arms went around her and her head bent beneath the passion of his kiss. He was kissing Jenny and he was kissing

319

Venetia, those golden breasts and delicate pink nipples that rose to his touch, her scented blond hair, the satiny flesh under his lips. His boyhood longing for the unattainable woman on the screen was assuaged in the silken, entwined body of her daughter.

Venetia ran her hands down Fitz's back, loving him, loving the feel of his flesh and muscle under her fingers. Her mouth felt bruised from his kisses, her breasts sweetly sore from his caress, and as he entered her she cried out with passion and pleasure, wrapping herself around him, drawing him ever closer, ever closer, until she was climbing to that great height. She heard him cry out, but she was lost in her passion, delirious, confused . . . of course he must have cried Vennie, not Jenny.

Venetia awoke to the sound of thunder rumbling across the water. A flash of lightning illuminated the darkened room and she saw she was alone. Sliding her legs from the bed, she padded across to the bathroom—he wasn't there. She found a white toweling robe and knotting it around her she made her way onto the deck. He was standing in the rain, watching the storm.

She watched him for a moment and then walked up behind him, sliding her arm around his waist.

"It's dangerous to be out in a storm like this," she whispered.

Fitz turned to meet her eyes. He looked strange, she thought, as though he'd been a million miles away.

"Venetia." She lifted her face to him and he kissed

her on the lips, gently and. tenderly. "Thank you."

They stared into each other's eyes for a moment, remembering, and then he took her hand and walked her back indoors.

"You must get some sleep," he said. "It's late."

"Can't I stay with you?"

"We'll see each other tomorrow. Go on, now, off to bed."

He left her at the foot of the companion ladder to the upper deck, kissing her fingers, her hand sliding from his as she trailed slowly up the steps. He stayed there until he heard her door close, and then he went back to his place on the deck, watching the storm, listening to the crackle and hiss of the lightning.

In a glow of warmth and love Venetia snuggled into her bed, reliving their lovemaking. There was just one disturbing thought in the middle of all the beauty and happiness. Why, when he'd said, "Thank you," had it sounded so—so final? Almost like "Good-bye."

Fitz left before dawn broke, taking the little speedboat and then driving himself to Grantley Adams Airport. His plane was the first to leave that morning—en route for New York.

Venetia read his letter in the bright reality of the sunny morning. It was over, it had never been. He wanted her to forget him, she was young and she was lovely and he'd been carried away. He wanted to thank her, to tell her not to be hurt—that she'd been a beautiful and generous lover, more than he deserved. Would she please forgive him and erase the night from her memory—as he would. When they next met it would be as though it had never happened.

But why? Why, when it had all been so *perfect?* Was it because of Morgan? Locking her cabin door Venetia hurled herself on her bed and began to cry. Oh, God, why did life have to get so complicated? Why? And why hadn't she met Fitz first?

Morgan was surprised to hear from the pilot of the McBain Learjet that Fitz was back in New York. He'd expected him still to be on the *Fiesta*, taking it easy. He knew that was what Doc Walden had suggested—and suggested with more than a little firmness. It wasn't that there was anything physically wrong with Fitz, he'd said, but he just didn't see how any man coming up to forty-five could keep up that kind of pace. It was time to take life more slowly, savor it more, quit breaking his neck over the next deal—and the next. In other words, he'd added with a grin, come down to the level and speed of ordinary mortals. As usual, Fitz was playing it his own way. Funny, though, that he hadn't called him in Rio. He was so keen on this Brazilian deal. Well, no matter, he'd call him tonight and tell him that everything was straightened out—the deal would be signed next week when the paperwork was completed.

And now, thought Morgan, I can relax and enjoy being with Venetia.

She wasn't at the airport to meet him, though he'd half expected her to be, and he felt oddly disappointed.

But she was there at the jetty, perched on a stone bollard, looking suntanned and pretty—just as he'd known she would.

"It's so *good* to see you here," he said, hugging her to him. "I can't tell you how lonely I was without you . . . so lonely, I've got you at least half a dozen presents."

"Oh, Morgan . . ."

"Oh, Morgan what? Can't a guy buy a present or two for the girl he loves?"

She stared at him blankly. This was getting worse and worse—and they'd only just begun.

"By the way," he said, tucking her arm in his as they sat side by side in the launch, "Miss Haven, you're off duty for an entire week. Tonight I'm taking you to the nicest, most intimate restaurant on the island. I know how particular you chefs are about food, so I can assure you it will be good—and so will the wine, and the candlelight. The Bagatelle does it properly, you know. And afterward I'm going to take you dancing."

"The Bagatelle . . . dancing . . . Oh, Morgan . . ." She glanced at him helplessly.

"Is that all you can say? 'Oh, Morgan' to a guy who's traveled thousands of miles just to be with you? Oh, Venetia"—he hugged her close again—"aren't you as glad to see me as I am to see you?"

Venetia was thankful he didn't wait for her answer.

"And tomorrow," he went on exuberantly, "I'm gonna beat you at water skiing. *And* have you ever been deepsea fishing? No? Then we'll try our hand at reeling in a barracuda—what do you say to that?"

Despite herself Venetia laughed. "You're incredible, Morgan. Why aren't you exhausted and fed up after such a long journey?"

"Because I'm in love," he said simply.

She had tried to dissuade him from taking her to the Bagatelle, but he had been adamant. It was exactly the kind of place she'd love, he knew it.

Any other time would have been right, but tonight it was unbearable. She must tell him, she just *had* to.

"Morgan." She put down the fork with which she had been pretending to eat the delicate morsels of flying fish on her plate. "Morgan, I must tell you something."

"You don't like the fish," he teased. "Not up to your standards, perhaps."

She couldn't laugh. "No, it's not that. Morgan, it's serious."

He looked at her in surprise. "Okay. What is it, baby, what's troubling you?"

Now was the moment. "I'm leaving the *Fiesta*, Morgan. I'm going back to London."

He was stunned. "But why? Aren't you happy here?"

"It's just that I feel I'm here . . . well, under false pretenses."

Morgan took her hand in his, holding it across the

table. "But why, Vennie? You're as good a chef as anyone—certainly good enough for the *Fiesta*. Has my father been giving you trouble—is that it?"

"No. Oh, no. Not at all." Venetia felt the blush burn her cheeks as she avoided Morgan's eyes. She couldn't do it, she couldn't tell him about Fitz. She'd meant to—but it was too hard, too hurtful. He was so sweet, so very nice. "It's just that there's really no cooking for me to do. No one is there."

"Then just enjoy yourself, sweetheart. Swim, sunbathe, take it easy. It's better than London at this time of the year, isn't it? And besides, it gives me a chance to see you."

"Morgan. That's another thing. I'm not sure that you should be seeing me—I mean, I'm not sure that I'm the right girl for you. I don't want to take up your time, Morgan, when you could be with someone else."

"Hey, wait a minute now. This *is* serious." His grip tightened on her nervous hand. "What's happened? I thought things were pretty good between you and me. Why have a couple of weeks on the *Fiesta* made you feel differently?"

Venetia said nothing, staring at the glass of wine, the same ruby-red wine she'd drunk with Fitz.

"Is it me, sweetheart? Have I made you feel insecure? Unwanted? I didn't mean to . . . I just wanted you to take your time, to get used to me and my globe-trotting life-style. That's what you'd have to put up with if you married me."

Venetia put up her hand to stop him. She knew

325

what he was going to say—and a month ago she would have been thrilled and excited to hear it. A month ago, though, she was just a child.

"Morgan. Don't. Please don't."

Tears rolled down her cheeks and she brushed them away hurriedly.

"Hey, there, Vennie, come on now."

Morgan was so sweet, so kind and thoughtful—and so handsome. Any girl would be lucky to be loved by him. Any girl but *her*.

"Maybe I'm rushing it a bit. I didn't mean to, Vennie, I wanted to give you time, you're so young."

Venetia grabbed desperately at the straw. "Yes, that's one of the reasons. I feel too young for marriage, Morgan. Too young for the responsibility. That's why I should leave the *Fiesta*, leave *you*. I don't want to lead you on. I mean, I may *never* marry . . . you see, Morgan, *never*."

Morgan sat back in his chair. Of all things she might say, he hadn't expected this. She seemed overwrought and confused. Had he pushed too hard, rushed her?

"Take it easy, sweetheart," he said soothingly. "Look, don't run away from me, Vennie. I promise I won't push, I won't bother you. I'll even leave tomorrow, if you like. Let you be alone for a while to think things out. And where better than on the *Fiesta*? Don't leave, Vennie. If you do, then I'll feel I've lost you forever. Please."

She really should go, she knew it.

"Please, Vennie, stay."

"Vennie." She remembered Fitz calling her name in passion. He had loved her that night, she was sure of it, and if she left the *Fiesta* she would never see him again, it would be the end. If she stayed, Fitz would return to the yacht, he couldn't stay away forever, and then he'd be forced to meet her again and there was the slightest chance that he might change his mind.

"All right, Morgan, I'll stay." His face showed his relief. "But . . ."

"I know, I know," he said, "But. I agree to that 'but' for the time being. Deal?"

They shook hands solemnly across the table. "Deal," she said. Judas, she thought.

16

The George V was the best hotel in Paris, as far as Stan was concerned. There were those who preferred the Lancaster, but it was a bit stiff for his taste. The George V was always abustle, things were going on—you felt there was a bit of action, like the Sherry Netherland in New York, his home away from home. In fact, thought Stan, if it weren't for Jessie, he'd be very happy, yes *very* happy, living at the Sherry. Great location, comfort, room service, luxury, familiar L.A. faces passing through the bar every evening, promising a spot of fast action—what more could a guy ask?

"Jessie?" he yelled. "I'm gonna call Paris Haven. You wanna talk?"

327

Jessie was in the bedroom trying on the Dior she'd bought yesterday and which had just been delivered. Good, she could wear it tonight for dinner.

"Paris who?"

"Haven . . . you know, Jenny's kid."

"Oh. That Paris. Sure, I'll say hello . . . wait a minute, Stan, are you proposing to take her out to dinner with us?"

"Well, I kinda promised the kid, you know, when she was in L.A. I said we'd take her out to dinner—she's probably looking forward to it, Jessie."

Jessie glared at him. She didn't want to go to Lasserre with Paris Haven, she was too fancy-French for her liking, and she'd never liked Jenny anyway. Stan had always been too close with her.

"I've asked the Johnsons," she snapped. "They're at the Ritz and I bumped into her today at the Givenchy boutique. I don't want Paris tagging along, she'll be too morbid and want to talk about her mother."

"Bullshit," said Stan, picking up the phone and asking for the number in surprisingly good French.

He lit a cigar and waited while Jessie glared at him. Those damned cigars always smelled up the whole place.

Paris looked beautiful. She was as thin as a rail, passionately pale, with short-cropped hair and wide-angle cheekbones. Thinness became her, but not starvation. She'd faced that fact after the disaster of her show when her ambitions lay in ruins and her bank balance was zero. Not just *her* bank balance; she'd lost her sisters' money too. If it hadn't been for the fact that she felt responsible and had determined to repay them, she might have killed herself that night—especially when Olympe didn't call.

Olympe had been the one bright spark on the scene, the one possible link between failure and success. Olympe knew everyone; people in the fashion world would listen to her, they respected her opinion. When Didi had told her that she had been there, that she'd caught the end of the show and said it was fabulous, Paris had hoped that maybe Olympe would help. Especially after that night. She shuddered as she remembered . . . it was better not to remember. There are things in everyone's life that they're ashamed of, she told herself in those low moments when she reran events in her mind—usually in bed, alone, in the middle of the night when she couldn't sleep.

She climbed the steps to her atelier wearily. It had been a long day at Mitsoko's, where she was working as a model. It had been the only thing left to do, all she was fit for now that she was a proven failure as a designer. The irony was that she had got the job with Mitsoko, when it was because of him that her show had failed—or would it have failed anyway? She slid the key into the lock, still thinking about Mitsoko. That was why her hair was short—all Mitsoko's girls had to cut their hair, it was his look for the spring. Closing the door behind her she flung her big satchel onto her drawing board, stacked now with books and magazines instead of designs. Then she picked up the little white cat—it had been a sort of consolation gift from Didi—that ran across to greet her, hurling urgent meows into the air.

"Of course, love," she murmured into its fur, hugging its warm little presence to her; at least she had someone to come home to.

Her only satisfaction from the whole Mitsoko scene had come when Finola, flaunting her position as a star model, had succumbed to Mitsoko's command to cut off her hair. Without that flowing blond mane she'd looked like a lanky schoolgirl with features about as distinguished as a Barbie doll's—all the drama was gone. Mitsoko *wanted* drama—elegantly chiseled noses, long, long necks, dramatic mouths, flaring cheeks—he wanted *bones,* and suddenly Finola didn't have them. He'd never used her since, and it was taking ages to grow back her hair.

Paris gave the cat a kiss on top of its white head and took the packet of chicken from her bag to the "kitchen," cutting it up small for her hungry friend. "There you go, Alice." She put the dish on the floor and the cat crouched over it eagerly. She didn't know why she called the cat Alice, something to do with a cat in *Alice in Wonderland* perhaps—she remembered Jenny reading it to them and they'd all loved it. She didn't want to think about Jenny tonight, either, no point in rehashing that again. At least, thought Paris, kicking off her shoes and pouring herself a glass of white wine from the fridge, I've learned to face up to the future realistically, instead of crying over the past.

The phone rang. That would be either Didi, checking in as he did every night, just to chat and see that she was okay, or Alain Marcus, a young and talented photographer with whom she had half promised to go to a gallery opening and possibly dinner afterward.

"Paris? How the hell are ya?"

Stan Reubin's voice ran like drops of cold water down her spine. She hadn't expected the past to sneak up on her tonight in the form of Stan Reubin, and for a minute it threw her.

"Stan. I'm fine."

"Great. Listen, Jessie and I are here and I remembered I'd promised you dinner at Lasserre. Well, tonight's your lucky night, Paris. Put on your best dress and get yourself over here—we're at the George Cinq, ready and waiting to buy you the best dinner you've ever tasted." Stan puffed at his cigar happily—he always felt good when he kept his promises.

Paris was silent, struggling with the anger she felt boiling up in her. It was anger against everything that had happened to her, anger at her failure, anger at the reasons behind it, and the bottled-up anger at her and her sisters' treatment at the hands of Bill and Stan. She could hold it back no longer and it focused in on Stan as she let the words pour out in a low, even tone.

"Listen, you thieving old bastard," she began. "If you think you're offering me a big treat taking me out to expensive restaurants and buying me dinner with my mother's money, you're wrong. You made enough money from Jenny to live on comfortably for the rest of your life and then ditched her when things weren't going too good. You didn't give a fuck about her, or about us. You were there to *prevent* what happened from happening—*you*, Stan, the smartest lawyer Beverly Hills possesses, right? So how was it the smart lawyer didn't see his client being fleeced and didn't take care of his client's money properly? You didn't give a damn about us— any of us—did you, Stan? In fact, I doubt if you even gave us a thought—until you had to when Jenny was dead. Quite *conveniently* dead, wasn't she? I mean, what would have happened if she'd stayed alive? There would have had to be some explanations made, wouldn't there? *Public* explanations. You know how Jenny *loved* publicity!"

Stan's jaw had dropped and his cigar smoldered, clamped between rigid fingers. Jessie looked at him in surprise.

What the hell had got into the girl? wondered Stan, as her words assaulted his ear. She was threatening him now, threatening a court case—she was gonna sue on behalf of her sisters! Jesus Christ! Stan swallowed hard. "Now, Paris, I know you're a bit upset . . ." There she went again. She couldn't possibly *know* anything, could she? How? No, no, it wasn't possible.

"Aw, come on, now, Paris, let's have a nice dinner and talk it over. You're still upset."

Paris felt better; for once she had the upper hand, and Stan Reubin was cracking. It was when she'd threatened to sue that he'd suddenly come to life and tried to placate her. Maybe she *should* sue, maybe the bastard really *was* hiding something. "And that goes for Bill Kaufmann too," she said, raising her voice excitedly. "You can expect a lawsuit, *Mr.* Reubin. Oh, and by the way, you can tell Jessie that there's a sale at Chloe tomorrow—she can easily drop a few thousand of Jenny's money there, while you still have it!"

She slammed down the phone and took a swig of the white wine. God, she felt good, better than she'd felt in ages.

Lasserre was everything they'd said it was, everything a good restaurant should be, thought Stan, toying with his pâté de foie gras with white grapes. Then why wasn't he enjoying it as much as he should? Jessie was busy chatting with the Johnsons, a nice enough couple from New York whom Stan met up with now and then on the legal circuit, but Frank Johnson had annoyed Stan by insisting that this was the restaurant where you had to order the duck. "Every duck is numbered," he'd said, "just like good wine. Isn't that fantastic?"

Stan had tried to tell him that it was the Tour d'Argent for duck, but Frank Johnson wasn't having any of it and Stan had given in without a fight. And now they were all stuck with the goddamn duck.

He didn't feel like a fight tonight, he was happy to let Frank and Jessie keep the conversation flowing around him. Jesus, that little Paris Haven had upset him, she'd really upset him; imagine threatening to sue! Of course she wouldn't, she couldn't afford to. He wondered if she was smart enough to take her case to a big lawyer and get him to take it on for a percentage of the damages. She'd have a good case, as a lawyer he knew it, and even if she didn't win, she'd damage his reputation. He'd better call Bill when he got back. Stan took another gulp of the Meursault he'd ordered with the foie gras—that was good wine. Ah, what the hell, he thought, look at him getting all upset over a little nothing like Paris Haven. He could take care of her with his hands tied behind his back. Shit, he should be *enjoying* himself, he'd come all this way to *enjoy!*

The waiter brought the duck and Stan waved it away.

"I don't want that," he commanded, back on form, "I've changed my mind. Bring me the grouse instead."

"But, Stan," objected Jessie, "they've brought it and we're all ready to eat. It'll take ages to get you something else."

"Fifteen minutes, madame," explained the waiter.

"That's all right." Stan leaned back and felt in his pocket for his cigar case. "You go ahead and eat. I'll wait for my grouse. And after that, waiter, I think we'd all enjoy the iced mango mousse." He winked at Mrs. Johnson. "You'll love it," he promised. "It'll cool you down after all that flaming duck."

Stan had finished two glasses of the Leoville Las Cases by the time the grouse arrived. It smelled delicious, and rested neatly on a round of toast and pâté.

"Pâté twice, Stan," noted Jessie reprovingly, inspecting his plate.

"Good," said Stan, digging in, "I'm starving."

They had finished their duck—Jessie privately felt that Stan had been right, they should have ordered something else—and were sitting, drinking wine and watching Stan eat. That's why it came as such a surprise, seeing him turn suddenly purple in the face like that, unable to speak, just gasping as if he couldn't get enough air. He was dead before they knew it.

⋐ 17 ⋑

It hadn't taken as long as Bob Ronson thought it would to infiltrate Rory Grant's entourage; in fact, it didn't take much to crack the scene at all, just the right clothes, the right car, an endless supply of money in your pocket, and the name of a good dealer.

The fact was that Rory was a simple soul, not as well endowed in the smarts department as in the physical, and he was, by nature, friendly. And unquestioning. You claimed you knew so and so, who knew so and so, you showed up at the right places often enough, and he figured he'd known you for years. Even so, thought Bob, tying the laces of his Nikes, ready for a tennis game with Rory, the guy was physically impressive off screen as well as on. He had the body of an athlete and in fact was a good one—he would sure as hell trounce Bob on the court today. Rory moved like an animal whether he was dancing or simply sauntering down the street, and yet he had the clean-cut appearance and wide grin of an engagingly innocent boy. Until he'd had enough coke and paranoia took over. It always hit him like that—old friends became instant enemies, people at the studios were accused of "spying" on him or plotting against him. His wide blue eyes grew narrow and flickered restlessly from side to side, as if he were trying to spot his enemies in the act of bad-mouthing him. And, of course, new friends became his confidants. There was no doubt about it, Rory's bad coke habit would make Bob's task easier.

Bob picked up his Gucci tennis bag and checked its contents. Tucked in with his racket, towel, sun visor, clean shirt, and shorts was a neat little package—gift wrapped. It was time to move in on Rory.

"Good game, Bob," called Rory, jogging up to shake hands.

Bob gave him credit mentally for *not* having leapt the net.

"Beat me hands down." He grinned. "I can't keep up with you, Rory."

"Just need a bit more practice, that's all." Rory

toweled his sweat-soaked hair as they sat on a bench by the court, catching their breath. "How about a swim to cool off?"

"I thought I'd go to the club and steam my aching muscles." Bob slid his racket into the bag and zipped it up. "What y'doing tonight, though?"

"Nothing much—why don't you come around? We'll call a couple of girls, have a party."

"Okay. That reminds me." Bob unzipped his bag again. "Got a little present for you. You can tell me what you think of it tonight." He got up, wrapping his white sweater around his shoulders casually, Rory style, smiling as he headed for the gate.

"Hey," called Rory, examining the pretty beribboned package with a pleased little grin, "hey, that's real nice of you. What is it?"

Bob waved. "Open it," he suggested. "See ya."

Goddamn, thought Rory, nobody ever gave him presents just like that, except for all that Christmas stuff that he didn't even count as presents, just bribes from those who were making money off his back. He ripped open the package and stared at the little jar of white powder. There must be half a goddamn ounce! His mouth pursed in a faint amazed whistle. Goddamn, that Bob was something else—and he'd bet it was good stuff too. The best. Pocketing the coke, he sauntered toward the driveway where his black Ferrari waited. He was a good guy, Bob, a good friend. They'd have some fun tonight, he'd make sure of that. He'd call Margie—he hadn't seen her in ages—and maybe

Joanne . . . yeah, that was it. Grinning happily he slung his bag in the backseat and climbed into the car. What more could a guy need than a black Ferrari, he wondered as he spun down the driveway, and half an ounce of the best stuff?

The four of them sat on cushions around the huge chunk of black-veined marble resting on four stone lions that was Rory's coffee table. The wide picture-windows leading onto a small deck overlooking the Newport Beach marina were closed to keep out the fog that had blown in with a sudden drop in temperature from the day's warm sun and the dimmers were down low, leaving just enough glow from the lamps to illuminate their faces as the four of them sipped white wine from oversize crystal glasses, dipping occasionally into the mound of white powder arranged like caviar in a silver bowl, surrounded by twenty-dollar bills, which Rory always said were the best way to do it. Everyone dipped in except Bob.

Margie was having a ball. She lay back on the cushion, her pretty eighteen-year-old face loose and formless, her eyes gleaming, words spilling from her lips as she chattered endlessly about nothing. She had nice skin and straight blond hair cut in neat bangs, and she wore purple Guess ? jeans and a Ralph Lauren shirt. She was, thought Bob sadly, somebody's daughter, product of some nice middle-class family in Encino who'd given her everything, the credit cards so she could shop at the Galleria on Saturdays, the car on her sixteenth birthday because

all the other kids had cars—how else were you supposed to get to school unless Mom kept on driving
you, and you could forget that! Margie had had her
freedom and she'd blown it.

Joanne refilled the wineglasses and dragged deeply
on her Marlboro. She was a different type, older,
maybe twenty-four? An actress, a serious one, she'd
told him. She was leaving this hick town next week
and heading back for New York to do Shakespeare in
Central Park for the summer season. Playing Juliet's
nurse was better than a dozen "cameos" or "also
starring" on TV credits that went so fast nobody
knew you were there but you, and the movies were
too tough to crack. She was a Broadway chick, and
that's what she wanted—bright lights and applause.
Reality!" Joanne emphasized the word. "No more
of this crap for me, Rory. Oh, it's all right for *you*,
you're different—you look the way you look,
custom-made for the screen. My face doesn't photograph that good, it's too uneven."

"What about you, Bob?" Rory arranged four immaculate lines of coke. "What are you into?"

Bob shrugged. "Nothing much. There's the family
garment business back East—I'm supposed to get
things going here, but it's too easy to get diverted."
He grinned at Rory. "I spend too much time playing
tennis with guys like you, or hanging out at parties.
I'll have to get something going soon, or they'll be
on to me."

"As long as it keeps the money flowing in," said
Rory, passing the stuff to Margie, "you gotta do

that, Bob, you know. Take it from me, I've been poor and it's not where it's at!"

"You gonna do your Rory-when-he-was-poor story?" asked Margie cheekily. She sniffed happily and burst into laughter as Rory glared at her. "You were never poor," she said, leaning around the table to pat his cheek. "There was always some old woman to make sure you didn't starve. Like Jenny."

"Bullshit!" Anger flared in Rory's narrowed eyes. "And shut up about Jenny."

"Why? Feeling guilty?" Margie's peals of laughter rang across the room and Bob watched with interest as Rory's temper rose.

"Come on, you two, stop bickering and pass that stuff over here." Joanne took her line and passed it on to Bob. Bob slid it carefully back across the marble to Rory.

"Hey, Bob, why don't you do this stuff? You buy me the best, and I never see you take any yourself." A thought crossed Rory's mind—and he looked at Bob in alarm. "Hey, listen," he said, bending closer and speaking quietly, "are you into something else . . . you know, hard stuff?"

Bob stared back at him and shrugged.

"Jesus, Bob, that's *bad*, that can *kill* you! Come on, man, you don't need that scene. This is where it's at—it's the only *safe* drug, anything else'll fry your brains and fuck up your body. Look at us, Bob, we're just a bit high, a bit happy, that's all."

"What about free basing?"

"What about it?" laughed Margie, who was now

lying down across the cushions.

"Yeah, well, I don't do that anymore, not since—"

"Since October?" said Margie, dreamily.

"Shut up, Margie, or I'll send you home," threatened Rory.

Margie giggled and shut up.

"I'm starving," said Bob. "What about some food?"

"Sure." Joanne fished around the floor for her bag. "I could eat."

"Let's go to La Scala." Rory reached for the phone without waiting for their response. He liked La Scala; they'd be sure to have a table for him—they treated him right there, and besides, he could put the check on the studio's account. And you never knew who might be there. It was good to be seen around. Not with Margie, though, she looked like stoned jailbait.

"You're staying here," he informed her. "We'll bring you back a pizza."

Margie rolled over on her stomach to turn up the sound on the stereo.

"Sure," she said, "just as long as you leave this here." She dipped a finger into the silver bowl and licked it, laughing.

"Margie's getting to be too much," grumbled Rory as they climbed into the Ferrari. "I'm gonna have to lose her. Send her back to the Valley."

They were laughing as the car sped through the mist toward Santa Monica Boulevard.

341

Margie sat in a booth at Du Par's on Ventura Boulevard eating a stack of buttermilk pancakes swimming in butter and floating in a pool of maple syrup. A double order of bacon on the side and a strawberry milkshake completed her after-midnight snack, and Bob turned his head away, unable to watch as she took a strip of bacon in her fingers and dunked it into the syrup, crunching it cheerfully.

"I didn't realize I was starving," she said contentedly. "That creep Rory should have remembered my pizza."

"He's a busy guy," said Bob. "He can't remember everything."

"Yeah. That's true, I guess." Her laugh rippled through the surprisingly busy room. Du Par's coffee shop was popular with the late-movie crowd and tired singles-bar people, ready for a cup of coffee and a sandwich or their great pancakes. "But I think he just forgets when he wants to," she said, crunching a second strip of bacon and passing one across the table to Bob. "Here, try this, it's good."

Bob laid the bacon on his plate next to the untouched slab of apple pie that he was planning on feeding Margie as dessert. He wanted to keep her here as long as he could. She was just high enough to talk without thinking, and yet not wiped out, as she had been when they'd left her at Rory's place.

"What do you mean, forgets when he wants to?"

Margie pushed back her blond bangs with sticky fingers and concentrated on the pancakes.

"You know—like when it's convenient."

"Like?" suggested Bob.

"Oh, tonight with the pizza—he didn't forget, he just wanted to punish me for talking about Jenny. He's real sensitive about her, you know, especially since . . ." Margie pushed another section of pancake into her mouth, chewing, thinking.

"You mean because he was with her that night?" said Bob, taking a chance on her reaction.

Margie stopped chewing and stared at him in surprise. "Y'mean he told you?"

Bob shrugged. "We're good friends."

Margie remembered the half ounce of coke. "Right, of course. Well, I don't know what went on there, but he came back in a hell of a state. He was sure stoned when he left, but he was straight by the time he got back."

She laughed, remembering.

"What time was that?" asked Bob, pushing the apple pie toward her. "About three-thirty, I guess?"

"Yeah, it must have been . . . I remember she called about twelve-thirty and I was real mad. We'd been having such a great time up until then, and then Rory said he'd have to go and talk to her. Shit." She sucked the strawberry milkshake up through her straw, biting on the end so that it slurped. "Y'know how that made me feel? I mean, we were in *bed*, and then he goes out to meet this old woman! Jesus, Bob, he even took *my* car—said his Ferrari was too conspicuous. I thought that's why he bought it in the first place."

Out of the mouths of babes, thought Bob, calling for the check. He'd got all the wisdom he needed from Margie tonight. Now he knew how to tackle Rory.

"Come on," he said, reaching in his pocket for his car keys, "I'll drive you home. You look as though you could use some rest."

"Home?" Margie gazed at him in dismay from beneath her childish fringe. "But I thought . . ."

"Forget it," said Bob, striding toward the door. "I only go for older women."

"Oh." Margie picked up her bag and followed him quickly. Home! But it was only one-thirty. God, what a dud tonight had turned out to be after all.

❧ 18 ❧

The village of Marina di Montefiore lay in a pocket of Campania's rocky blue coastline, fringed by a curve of clean white sand to the south and a small natural harbor to the north. A thin ribbon of road snaked up the pine- and chestnut-clad hillside behind, linking the village to the main coast road, far away in the distance. Too far for the tourist hordes in their buses and caravans yet to have bothered to discover it. Only those lucky enough to have spotted, in passing, the perfect curve of white beach, the little fishing boats in the harbor, and the faded ochre walls and terra-cotta-tiled roofs of the ancient palazzo perched on its hill overlooking the sea, and who had been curious enough to take the time to inch their way down the treacherous track, had been fortunate enough to discover its charms.

India had fallen in love with Marina di Monte-fiore the moment she saw it. The village had a time-less quality, with its tree-shaded square, gushing fountain, and old whitewashed fishermen's houses. She loved the cool dimness and the pungent smells of the little shops that sold salamis and sausages, wines and cheeses, and freshly baked bread, and she enjoyed poking around the drapery shop, un-changed since the beginning of the century. It sold wonderful hats, ancient straws in biscuit and cream, some of which had been there for sixty years, some perky with floating ribbons, or masculine with a trim band. In the back room there were glass-fronted drawers filled with serviceable underwear, voluminous white and pink knickers with elastic in the legs, demure camisoles of tucked cotton in sizes meant to cover ample bosoms, and shelves of the black nylon stockings that were worn by every woman in the village. Only visitors and children went bare legged, even on the hottest days. Cafés sprawled outward across the pavement beneath cool blue and green awnings, their rickety tables covered in scarlet oilcloth, each topped with its large white Cinzano ashtray, and fishermen and visitors sipped cappuccino and Peroni beer, comfortably soaking up the sunshine and the peace.

That was the trouble, thought India. Love always trapped you. Love of a place as much as love of a person. She parked the Fiat in the shade by the fountain and strolled across to the Café-Bar Ricardi. In the month she had been in Marina di Montefiore

345

she'd taken to dropping in at the café every morning for a cup of espresso and a piece of their crusty bread dipped in local olive oil, grilled on the hot plate, and smothered in fresh anchovy paste. It served as both her breakfast and lunch and was one of the highlights of her day. You could keep all your fancy French restaurants, she thought, digging in enthusiastically. I'll settle for this.

The fishermen at the next table nodded in greeting and she eavesdropped on their conversation of sea conditions and the weather farther north, and the possibilities of lobster that night. India felt perfectly at home, though she knew no one. She was, she realized suddenly, happy here, happier than she could remember having felt for a long time. She had arrived at the palazzo to find that Aldo Montefiore had been called away to Milan—on family business, they said. He had been expected back in a week but so far he hadn't shown up. India had been welcomed by his mother, Paola, the Contessa di Montefiore, a small, frail lady whose deep, booming voice had come as a shock. "Treat this place as yours, my dear," she had said. "Do what you need to do. Aldo suggested that you might start by inspecting the pictures and the furniture. Then, as you familiarize yourself with the palazzo, you'll see what can be done to convert it. I'm afraid I won't be much help to you. It's hard for me to imagine any changes, but I expect we'll need more bathrooms. Maybe it won't cost too much after all?" She had smiled hopefully at India and

India had known it would be painful for the Contessa to part with any of the palazzo's treasures—harder than for her son, because he already had one foot in another world. For the Contessa di Montefiore this place was her life and had been since she was married at seventeen.

The Palazzo di Montefiore was set like a jewel in the crown of a wooded hillside overlooking the sea, and India ached to paint its creamy stone-walled courtyards, its arches and fountains, the crumbling statues and the jasmine and trailing bougainvillaea that surged untamed over every surface. And if the outside of the palazzo was a gem, inside it was packed with treasures. No major ones—those had been sold long ago, and the spaces on the faded silk wall-hangings protested their removal. But there was a pair of large oil paintings in the dining room that, if she wasn't mistaken, were by a minor Italian master, and there was some excellent furniture, particularly in the "French drawing room" in the east wing. The Montefiores, would have to make the sacrifice, but they would be able to raise money.

India ordered another espresso and studied the plans she had spread out across the table. The palazzo was built around a central courtyard and the object was first to convert two of the wings, and then later, if the venture proved successful, a third, retaining the south wing for the family. She could see no structural problems in the conversion; the old building had the high-ceilinged spaciousness of a bygone era that would adapt beautifully. The only difficulty came in preserving the Montefiores' privacy. She pored over the plans, trying to figure out the best place for the new entrance to the family apartments. Whichever way she went, it meant the driveway would have to be extended all the way around to the south side. That would cost a bit, but you couldn't expect them to have to park at the front and then walk all the way around, could you? It would defeat the whole exercise, which was to keep them quite separate from their guests.

Aldo Montefiore spotted India at the table outside Ricardi's as he drove by. Her head was bent over the papers in front of her, but he would have recognized that marvelous hair anywhere. Her pigtail swung across her shoulder and she wore a yellow flower tucked into the spiky curls over her ear. He swung the car around and pulled up beside her Fiat near the fountain.

"Signorina Haven?"

India looked in surprise into Aldo's brown eyes, fringed with curling dark lashes.

"Oh, Aldo . . . Signore . . . Conte . . ." she said, confused by his sudden appearance.

He laughed. "Aldo will do, if I may call you India?"

"It's a deal," she countered, "if you'll let me buy you a drink?"

"Shouldn't I be buying you one?"

Her full mouth curved in the generous smile he remembered.

"Next time," she promised, "it'll be your turn."

Aldo moved his eyes from her mouth and looked down at her plans. "Well, India, are we in business?"

"The Palazzo di Montefiore is so beautiful, I'm in love with it. When I walk through its rooms I imagine romantic young Montefiore counts riding off to conquer a neighboring princess."

Aldo laughed. "You're like my mother, too in love with it to want to take it from the seventeenth century and adapt it to modern life. But I'm afraid if we don't, India, then it will just crumble and there will be nothing at all for this romantic Montefiore to leave his grandchildren."

His grandchildren! India shifted her glance away from him, back to the plans.

"I manage to combine romance with practicality sometimes," she said firmly, "and I think your palazzo will do the same."

The romantic regrets were gone from her eyes and she looked suddenly businesslike and capable, it was a pity, thought Aldo.

"Shall we go through the rooms together later today?" he asked. "You can tell me all your plans."

India leaned forward enthusiastically. "First we must discuss the furniture and the paintings. You know, Aldo, I think we should replace the antiques that must be sold with modern designs from Parolis. Fabrizio's special touch is combining the old with the new. But I warn you, I mean to be drastic; we shall get rid of all those faded wallpapers and frayed old draperies. And the carpets are so worn they've lost all their beauty. We must carpet the upstairs corridors and put Paroli rugs on the bedroom floors. And of course each suite must have its own bathroom."

"Suite?" He'd envisioned just hotel rooms.

"Yes—they must all be suites, some quite small, but still suites. We can partition some of the larger rooms to make a small sitting room, but the larger ones will have their own proper sitting rooms and dining areas."

Aldo listened amazed. He hadn't really believed that India would be able to do the job—she was too young and too pretty. He'd thought she was just a movie star's daughter, playing at working for a fashionable interior decorator, a busy, happy-go-lucky girl who'd left a deep impression on his memory so that he'd snatched at the opportunity of seeing her again when Fabrizio had suggested she come to Montefiore.

"India," he began, "I hadn't—"

"Don't interrupt me yet, let me just tell you first . . ." Her eyes, as glossy and brown and darkly lashed as his, gleamed with excitement, as she continued to expand on her plans for his palazzo, and Aldo listened, enjoying her enthusiasm. After a couple of weeks spent in Marisa and Renata's languid, predictable company she was like a breath of fresh air.

"It was such a *clever* idea, Aldo," she finished. "The palazzo is exactly the kind of unique, out-of-the-way place that would appeal to the discerning tourist. It has the beauty and the charm of its age; all we need to do is add twentieth-century facilities and a little luxury. No, I amend that. A *lot* of luxury. Custom-made mattresses for those ancient four-posters, and we're going to need considerable rewiring for the lighting plans I have in mind—good lighting should contribute to the ambience of the place as well as just allowing you to read the paper. Oh, and excellent linens, and the biggest towels you can find—Americans love those—and we'll keep all those funny old baths with the brass taps, we'll just have to get them refinished. Oh, truly, Aldo, it's a *terrific* idea!"

"I wish I could take credit for it"—Aldo smiled—"but actually it was Marisa Paroli who thought of it."

"Marisa?"

"When she was here with her cousin a couple of months back, she said it was a shame to see the place crumbling and that as the one problem I didn't have was servants, I'd be better off running it as a hotel. You see, the women in the village like to work at the palazzo; some of their families have worked for us for centuries. The idea grew on me as a way to help us all; it would provide employment for the villagers as well as benefiting my family."

"I see," replied India. So then it hadn't been Fabrizio's idea to send her here, it had been Marisa's method of getting her out of the way!

"Well, then." She gathered her papers together briskly. "That's basically what I have in mind. If you have the time, we can go through everything in more detail this afternoon."

351

Aldo wondered what he could have said to turn off her enthusiasm. They walked together toward their parked cars.

"I shall be back around four," he said, "if that's convenient for you."

Damn, thought India, why did his eyes smile so nicely? Aldo wasn't handsome in the way Fabrizio was, but close to her in his shirt-sleeves under the early summer sunshine, she felt the same attraction she had when she had met him at that party. India pulled herself together. She wasn't going to be turned on by Aldo's romantic brown eyes; she'd had enough of romantic Italians! "Fine. I'll see you then."

"Thanks for the drink." He waved as she backed up her car. "I'll see you at four." He grinned as he watched her drive off. India Haven's American energy would turn a few Montefiores in their graves, but this Montefiore was certainly going to enjoy it.

Marisa watched Fabrizio playing with the children. Five-year-old Giorgio, dressed in bright yellow pajamas and his favorite cowboy boots, from which he refused to be parted until after he'd fallen asleep, clambered up the elaborate red tubular frame Fabrizio had designed for him and swung by his hands from the topmost rung. He had Marisa's long slender face and Fabrizio's blue eyes and a devilish sense of humor that made them both laugh. Fabiola at six was a chubby-cheeked feminine replica of Fabrizio, the same curling blond hair and Florentine nose, and a more solemn personality. Fabiola was a cuddler; if there was a lap free she'd climb onto it, if there was an arm doing nothing, she'd snuggle into it. She leaned against Fabrizio now, hugging his knees with her plump little arms. It was the perfect family scene, thought Marisa, and maybe the perfect moment to suggest her next move.

She still couldn't decide whether it had been annoying or satisfying that Mario Tomasetti had found nothing incriminating in the movements of India and Fabrizio. He'd had them both followed for two weeks and had presented her with a typed report detailing their exact movements in every twenty-four-hour period. They had been in the office together but of course nothing could go on there, it was too busy, too many people coming and going. There had been no long intimate lunches together—in fact no lunches together at all, not even a drink or a cup of coffee. India seemed to live a very quiet life; she'd eaten alone most evenings in a trattoria near her apartment and then gone straight home. She hadn't emerged again until the next day. Fabrizio had been out a good deal in the evenings, but that was quite usual—he often attended receptions and dinners without her when it was for business, and these were no exception. Most evenings he'd managed to get home to play with the children before they went to bed—just as he was now.

Marisa sighed in exasperation. She didn't want to believe that her husband was unfaithful to her—especially with India Haven—but since Renata had put the idea in her mind, and despite Tomasetti's innocent report, she had a sneaking suspicion that he was unfaithful. That was why she had decided to suggest—more than suggest, to *state*—that it would be a good idea if Fabrizio offered India the job at the Palazzo di Montefiore. She had been quite surprised, though, when Fabrizio had agreed so readily to her suggestion; in fact, he had seemed almost happy about it. It was all very strange. India had been gone almost two months now. Surely if anything were going on Fabrizio would have made an excuse to visit the Palazzo di Montefiore? Yet, as far as she knew, there had been no contact other than a normal business one. Tomasetti's men had Fabrizio under surveillance, but he still appeared to be the most faithful husband in Italy.

Well, it was time for the acid test. And if, as she suspected, there was anything between them, then it would be a coup de grâce for Miss Haven.

"Fabrizio," she called over the delighted squeals of Fabiola, whom he was swinging high over his head, spinning around, "Fabrizio, she'll be sick. Put her down. Please."

Fabrizio sank to the floor, clutching Fabiola in his arms.

"Ohh," he groaned, "you're so heavy—look what you've done to your poor old papa. Oh, I can't move." He lay back, arms outstretched dramatically, while Fabiola sat on his chest, bouncing up and down, laughing.

"Fabrizio, I think it would be a good idea to take

354

the children away this weekend, get them into the country for some fresh air now that the weather is so beautiful."

"Good idea," he agreed. "You'd like that, Fabiola, wouldn't you?"

"Where?" demanded Fabiola, curling up in his arms. "Where are we going?"

"I thought we might go to the Montefiores'," said Marisa casually. "We could take Renata with us— you know she's in love with Aldo and I'm sure he likes her. It would be a terribly good match for both of them . . . and isn't it time you and India had a little meeting about the palazzo? Surely there must be lots of things to discuss?"

Fabrizio sat up abruptly, clutching Fabiola to him. "There's really no need for me to go. I sent an architect up there three weeks ago. He confirmed that India's ideas were workable and that her technical drawings were faultless. She has itemized all her ideas for the interiors to me and now she's working on sketches to present to the Montefiores. India's doing an excellent job without being bothered by having the boss around."

"But after all, *cara*, the Montefiores are paying for Paroli, not India, aren't they?" She glanced at him slyly. "I mean, there's no reason why India should be upset to see her . . . 'boss,' is there?"

"Of course not!" Fabrizio's voice had a slight edge to it. "It's just that she's doing a good job without me."

"Well, then, that's settled. I'll call Paola now and

make arrangements." Marisa headed purposefully for the phone in her bedroom. She was glad when Aldo answered the phone and said of course, he was more than pleased to have their company. He was sure India would, too. She was working so hard, a break would do her good.

"Oh, Aldo," begged Marisa sweetly, "please don't tell India that we're coming—I'd like it to be a surprise."

"A surprise? Of course, if you wish, Marisa."

"Then we'll see you Friday. Renata will be looking forward to it, Aldo."

"We shall all look forward to it, Marisa," said Aldo.

And that was that, thought Marisa, putting down the phone. She'd put little India to the test this weekend and she'd give the Aldo/Renata situation a little boost—it was time some definitive progress was made there. Two birds with one stone, she thought happily. How clever.

Aldo tore himself away from the muddle of plans, papers, contracts, and bills on the walnut rolltop desk in his room—the same desk used by his great-great-grandfather, who had been one of the more successful Montefiore businessmen, amassing a sizable fortune from a newly industrial era. Unfortunately, his great-great-grandfather had not been as lucky with his children—two willful daughters and a son who had considered the family fortune a bottomless pocket for their wild ways. Enzo Montefiore, the son, whose portrait hung in a deliberately out-of-the-way part of the second-floor corridor, had made his name and reputation—and lost his money—in the cafés and music halls of a fin-de-siècle Paris, competing with British dukes and new American millionaires in the contest for the city's loveliest courtesans. Mind you, thought Aldo, shrugging on a light linen jacket as he prepared for dinner, Enzo, like all the Montefiores, hadn't done things by halves. His women were the most beautiful and fashionable courtesans in Paris and his extravagances had been monumental. Which was one of the reasons now why this hotel idea had to work. The entire remaining resources of the Montefiore family were committed to it. There would be no going back. The old place must pay for itseplf—or it must crumble into dust like its past inhabitants.

India Haven was clever. Her energy and inventiveness were phenomenal. Her ideas had gone from merely the conversion of the palazzo—though God knows she'd done wonders with that—to suggestions for running the place and, most importantly, how to let the world know of the Palazzo di Montefiore's existence. The palazzo was to have a dozen deluxe suites, and a dozen smaller suites on the third floor. The estate manager's house, long unused, since there were no more "estates" to be managed, was to become a special private villa to be rented, fully staffed with maids, cooks, and a butler, at enormous expense, to those who demanded complete privacy. The great hall and the main reception rooms would stay very much as they were structurally, and India was working on the new decorating schemes that would brighten their faded charm and enhance their comfort. There was no doubt she was doing an excellent job, and with the sale of a considerable amount of the Palazzo's furnishings, pictures, and bibelots, he should just about be able to cover the cost.

At India's suggestion he had appointed a good PR company and contacted the Italian Tourist Authority, who were being extremely helpful, as were American Express and Thomas Cook, and most of the major airlines. The palazzo was already being mentioned in travel columns and airline magazines as the new place for the tourist who demanded that little bit extra. Straightening his tie in the mirror, Aldo prayed there were plenty of them. His brown eyes gazed back at him as he paused for a moment, thinking of those past Montefiores. All of them, except for Enzo, who had died in a duel in the Bois de Boulogne in the arms of a delicious blonde, had married for love. The Conti di Montefiore had always been known for their looks and for their charm—and their reputation as lovers. Not a single one had ever married for money. Well, thought Aldo, surveying his flattened nose with a grin, I don't have the looks; I'm not sure about the charm; and as for the rest . . . He turned away from the mirror with a laugh.

The marble stairs were cracked at the edges, but Aldo knew where to avoid the worst bits as he ran down them and across the tiled hall to the small salon.

India was alone, leaning against the long window, gazing out into the garden. It had the dense greenness of twilight, and with the lamp behind her she was like a painting by Renoir, all soft curves and delicate lines. But there was a touch of sadness on her face.

"India," said Aldo gently. She spun around, startled. "You looked as though you were miles away—lost in sad thoughts."

"I was thinking about my mother—missing her," she replied. "I suppose it sounds silly for a grown woman to admit, but I do miss her. She was always there in the background, at the end of a telephone line, when we needed help."

"Then is something the matter?" asked Aldo, concerned. "Perhaps I can help?"

"It's not just me, I guess—it's all three of us." India managed a shaky laugh. "Jenny's daughters don't seem to be making a great success of life so far." She thought of the letters she had had from Venetia, unhappy on a luxury yacht in Barbados, in love with the wrong man. But it was Paris who was worrying her most. "Our family problems seem to have begun with Jenny's death and they get more complex as time goes on. Now Paris thinks she's responsible for someone's death and I just don't know what she's going to do."

This sounds serious, thought Aldo, and she obviously needs to talk. He took her arm firmly.

"Let's take a walk around the garden before dinner," he suggested. "It's so beautiful when the light is like this, and you can tell me all about Paris."

Half hidden by the gathering darkness, India found Aldo easy to talk to. He listened without comment as she spilled their tales of disaster, from Jenny's mysterious and unresolved death and the disappearance of her fortune to Paris's disastrous fashion show, her guilt at losing the last of their money, and now the death of Stan Reubin.

"Paris told Stan that she was planning to take him to court and that she'd get back our mother's money. She practically accused him of stealing it! She said she would never go out to dinner with him at some smart restaurant, paid for with Jenny's money. Stan went out to dinner anyway. And he died, Aldo. Right there in Lasserre. Now Paris thinks that he was so upset by what she'd said that she killed him. She says she was responsible and she'll never be able to sleep again. I don't know what to do about her, Aldo. I'm afraid. Paris is so volatile, so unpredictable, she's capable of . . . of anything. . . ."

Aldo could guess what India meant by "anything"; she was afraid to put into words the possibility that her sister might kill herself.

"Paris shouldn't be alone," he said. "Is she with friends?"

"No. She's at her studio. It's really just a converted loft and she says now it's full of bad memories."

"India, why not invite her here? You know well

360

enough that we've got plenty of rooms."

India's face lit up with pleasure and surprise. "Aldo, could I really do that?"

"Of course, I'd be delighted to have her here, and anyway, India . . ."

"Yes?"

"If she didn't come here, then I know you would feel compelled to go to her. I prefer not to lose you . . . again."

"To lose me?" The scent of jasmine was overwhelming in the dusky garden. Aldo bent closer to look into her dark eyes.

"I lost you once before. I'd only just met you and you ran away from me. I wouldn't want that to happen twice." Her mouth had been tempting him a dozen times and he couldn't resist any longer. Aldo pulled her to him and kissed her, holding her close. India put her arms around his neck, lost in his kiss. She thought that the sweet sound was in her head until she realized it was the bell from the house, summoning them to dinner. She could feel a tremor run through Aldo's body as he held her closer, kissing her again, and she sighed as he released her at last, reluctantly.

"I've been wanting to kiss you since that first night," said Aldo, dropping an extra kiss on the tip of her nose. "Maybe one day you'll tell me why you ran away from me so abruptly?"

His arm was around her shoulders as they walked back to the house. India remembered clearly why she'd run away—because Marisa had made it clear he was to marry for money, a family duty, she'd said, and the Haven girls had no money. And because of Fabrizio. She reminded herself now of her resolve never to become a mistress again. She had no right to be kissing him, no right to be kissing any man who couldn't count her as a part of his life and not merely as an extracurricular activity. Hadn't she made that promise to herself? But no man who was prepared to marry just for money should be as nice as this one and, damn it, as attractive! I must have a gene missing, thought India as she paused on the terrace with Aldo's arms around her again, a commonsense gene . . . but I do like it so much. How can a girl fall out of love with the wrong man and in love again with another so quickly?

India called Paris right after dinner. She was at home alone. She said she'd had a long day at Mitsoko's and she was tired; she hadn't felt like seeing anyone. India could sense her depression, though Paris didn't complain. She protested at first when India suggested that she come to Italy: she couldn't get away from work, she'd be in the way, India didn't need her there hanging about. . . .

"Oh, but, Paris, I do," replied India. "I do need you. Please come."

In the end they didn't know who needed whom most, but she was coming. She'd arrive by train that weekend.

The Contessa di Montefiore was seventy-two years old. She had buried two sons as well as her husband,

and Aldo, her last remaining, and youngest, son was the light of her life. Aldo had always been a charmer, even with that broken nose that he had refused to have fixed, though his brothers had teased him about it. Tommaso, the eldest son, had been the most handsome of her boys; even as a baby he could melt hearts with those wide brown eyes, and later as a young man he'd wreaked havoc among the girls at university. Paolo was a year younger than Tommaso and he had followed in his brother's footsteps. Though not as handsome, he had been attractive. Aldo had been born later in her life, when the other boys were already fifteen and sixteen years old, and he had come as something of a surprise to Paola and her husband. But how glad she had been to have him, a third boy, when the other two died in the car crash on the autostrada near Naples. It was ten years ago now, but she would never forget that day. It was worse even than when her husband died, because she had come to expect that, and though it saddened her, she could accept it as God's will.

All she had left was Aldo, and she was getting older. Paola di Montefiore wanted grandchildren—the sooner the better. It was time Aldo got married. But to whom? Renata had been here quite a lot lately—that is, until India Haven came to stay with them. Paola wondered about that. She'd noticed the way he had looked at India at dinner tonight. It was all quite interesting and she supposed it would sort itself out. All she wanted was for Aldo to be happy. And to give her her grandchildren before she grew too old to appreciate them.

It would be a busy weekend. Renata was coming with that maneuvering wife of Fabrizio's. She couldn't stand Marisa—but then she had never been able to stand Marisa's mother either. The compensation was that Marisa was bringing her children and they would be a delight. And then India's sister Paris would be arriving. Yes, it would be amusing to have the house full again, she must talk to the cook and plan a formal dinner for Saturday, and tell her to get extra help in from the village for the weekend. Now which rooms should she put them all in . . . ?

Fabrizio was at the wheel of the big Chrysler station wagon with the children and the nanny and enough luggage for a family of twelve, while Marisa traveled with Renata in her little Mercedes.

"Let Fabrizio take the children." Marisa laughed. "He always complains about not seeing enough of them. A few hours in a car and he'll be happy to hand them over to their nurse."

"But they're sweet, Marisa, they're really such good children," protested Renata.

"Of course they are, but even the best children can turn into monsters after more than an hour in a car. You'll learn, Renata, when you have children of your own. And that reminds me—try to spend some time with the Contessa this weekend. The old lady wants grandchildren, Renata—she would like nothing better than to have you as a daughter-in-law."

"The question is, though—does Aldo want me

364

as his wife?"

Marisa glared at her in exasperation. "Of course he wants you. It's the perfect marriage, Renata."

"What I mean is, does he want me or does he want my money?"

"What a question! Ask yourself what *you* want—Aldo or his title? Naturally, it's a combination of both. And why not? Marriage is a practical situation and it should be considered that way."

"Really? Then why did you marry Fabrizio? He had no money and no title."

Marisa smiled. "Clever girl. It's quite simple. Fabrizio had what *I* needed, he was very handsome, very amusing, very social. He was an artist and I could help him along in the world. I'm a managing sort of person and he gave me a purpose."

"Tell me the truth, though, Marisa. Were you in love with him, I mean really in love?"

Renata's tone was wistful. Surely the silly girl couldn't be thinking of giving up Aldo when she'd done all this work? This weekend was meant to be the climax. Aldo would ask Renata to marry him. She was certain of it. Marisa had made it plain the last time they met that Renata was his for the asking, and Aldo was a young man who knew where his duty lay. It would never do to admit that when she had married Fabrizio she had been carried away on a wave of passion that had left her helpless. Unfortunately her passion hadn't lasted.

"We all love our husbands, Renata," she said, "and we love our children. There are more important things in life than passion."

Renata glanced sideways at her with a sly smile. "I see. I'll keep that in mind, Marisa, this weekend." She put her foot down on the gas, suddenly anxious to reach Marina di Montefiore.

India dashed down platform six of the big railway terminal in Naples, late as usual. The traffic had been hell in the city, but thank heavens, the train was also late. Paris, slender as a reed, chic in an old cream safari jacket from St. Laurent and with her short Japanese haircut, waited by a mound of baggage, clutching a wicker basket from which piteous meows emerged.

"India, I'm so happy to see you, you don't know how much it means to me."

Tearfully they clung to each other as the little white cat kept up its mournful refrain.

"Oh, by the way, this is Alice." Paris displayed her cat, and India poked a finger into the basket and received a friendly purring rub. "She's very bossy," complained Paris. "She runs my life. I warn you, India, she sleeps on my bed and she eats proper food, none of this canned cat stuff. Alice is a person."

India looked at the little blue-eyed cat and back at her sister.

"A substitute person," she commented, taking the basket and beckoning a porter.

"She's a friend," admitted Paris, "one I was glad of. I've been so lonely, India."

India tucked her arm into her sister's.

"There's no need to be lonely—anymore," she said firmly. "You're here with me now. We can tell each other our problems and cry about them—or maybe laugh, whichever we feel like."

"The trouble is, we're too much like Jenny," said Paris. "She couldn't change our genes just by sending us away to school."

Thinking of Aldo, India knew Paris was right.

The short, sturdy Neapolitan porter hefted Paris's bags and wheeled them toward the exit where India was double-parked—as usual. There was no ticket today, though.

"It's a good omen," she exclaimed. "You see, Paris, the gods are with us at last!" She inspected her sister's too-thin figure worriedly. "Listen, kid," she said finally, "the food's terrific at this place and you're going to eat it *all*—every string of pasta, every sauce, *everything*. A few breakfasts at the Café-Bar Ricardi and I'll soon have you in terrible shape!" They were laughing as India pulled the car out of the traffic of Naples and headed south down the open road toward Marina di Montefiore.

The massive wooden doors of the palazzo stood wide open to the day's sunshine, ready to welcome its guests. Paola di Montefiore, delicate in lavender linen, paused in the hall to adjust the huge vases of flowers that stood on the equally massive hall tables. She patted her hair into place in the mirror and emerged onto the front steps just as the Chrysler with Fabrizio and the children pulled to a stop.

"Hello, hello." She waved. "How lovely to see you. Ah, just look at you children, you've grown so much! Fabrizio"—she kissed him affectionately—"I can't bear it. They become bigger and bigger and it reminds me that I'm getting older."

"You never get older, Paola," said Fabrizio gallantly. His daughter clasped the Contessa's hand, beaming up at her engagingly.

"Can we swim now?" she asked, resting her head against Paola's hand.

"Of course not," Fabrizio replied for her. "You've only just arrived. After lunch and after your rest, that's when you can swim."

Fabiola's eyes widened into tragedy at the idea of waiting.

"Oh, Papa, how cruel you are," she moaned. "That's ages and ages."

Paola laughed. "You're right, Fabiola. Why not go on inside and see our new puppies instead? They're so sweet."

"Puppies!" Fabiola and Giorgio were up the steps in a flash, disappearing down the hall, followed by their nurse, just as Renata's car appeared in the drive.

Marisa was immaculately turned out, as usual. Why was it that she never had the knack of appearing completely casual? wondered Paola. Even in a summery dress and sandals she looked attired for Ascot.

"Ciao, Marisa, Renata. Thank you for bringing

the children. You don't know how much good it does me to have them around. It wakes this old place up."

"I should make the most of the peace and quiet while you can," said Marisa as they walked into the house. "When the conversion is complete and it becomes a hotel, you might find it busier than you'd like."

"But I shall enjoy it," replied Paola. "I'm sure these old palazzi must have been run like hotels when they were first built—otherwise why have so many rooms? Fabrizio, you know that India is doing a splendid job. Aldo says you should be proud of her."

Marisa's ears pricked up, and she glanced sharply at Fabrizio.

"I'm glad to have the chance to see what progress has been made," he replied calmly.

"And where is Aldo?" Marisa settled herself on a chair in the salon, watching critically as the young village girl who was helping out for the weekend carried in a laden coffee tray. Feeling Marisa's eyes on her the girl put down the heavy tray shakily, spilling a drop of coffee onto the immaculate linen napkins. Blushing, she excused herself and departed. "You'll have to get these village girls properly trained, Paola," she remarked, flicking at the stain. "Your guests will expect the best."

"I don't doubt, Marisa, that my *paying* guests will find the local people who work for us charming and friendly as well as very willing. If I remember from my last visit to New York years ago, it will make a nice change for them."

Why, wondered Paola, did Marisa always cause that sense of unease in people? She seemed to have a positive talent for it.

"You didn't tell us where Aldo was," reminded Renata.

"He went into Naples this morning. He should be back in time for lunch. India went too. Wait, I believe I hear a car now."

"Was Aldo in Naples with India, then?" asked Renata jealously.

"India went to pick up another guest, her sister . . ."

India's familiar Americanized Italian accent came from the hall as she spoke to the man who was bringing in the luggage, and Marisa looked toward the door expectantly. Now she would know—India's face when she saw Fabrizio so unexpectedly would tell the truth.

India strode into the salon, her sister behind her, stopping abruptly as she saw them—Renata and Marisa, and Fabrizio.

"Mama, Mama." Giorgio pushed past India, laughing as he struggled to keep a hold on the squirming puppy in his hands. "Look, Mama, look what I've got."

India bent to help Giorgio with the puppy and the moment was lost.

Damn, thought Marisa. Oh, damn it.

"Take the puppy back to the kitchen, Giorgio," she commanded. "It doesn't belong in here."

370

"But, Mama—"

"At once, Giorgio."

"I'll go with you." Fabrizio took the puppy from ins son, smiling hello to India.

"How are you?" He kissed her on the cheek. "Is everything going well?"

"Yes, yes . . . very well. Fabrizio, I'm glad you're here. There are one or two points Aldo made that we should discuss."

"Fine. After lunch, then."

Paris waited, wicker cat basket in her arms, to be introduced. In her simple jacket and skirt that were obviously not new, she had a striking, casual chic that Marisa would have paid dearly to achieve. And with the wild haircut and jutting cheekbones Paris was, thought Marisa, astonishingly beautiful. Now, this she could have considered a rival!

India introduced her sister.

"Contessa, may I present my sister. Marisa, this is Paris." Marisa and she kissed the air at the side of each other's face. "And I remember Renata from your party. What a surprise to find you all here—and the children."

"Yes. Quite a surprise, I should think." Marisa eyed Paris up and down and couldn't fault her. "Then you must be the fashion designer," she said. "I read about your show in the papers. Too bad it was at the same time as Mitsoko's. Was that the reason it didn't succeed?"

India felt herself blushing for Paris. Marisa was such a bitch!

"If one chooses to think so," replied Paris evenly.

"Well, I assure you that whatever you designed, it couldn't be worse than Mitsoko's. God, those dreadful shapeless garments." Marisa shuddered delicately.

"I think that anyone who looks the way Paris does must understand fashion," said Renata kindly. "I'm sure your collection was excellent, and it was just bad luck to show it on Mitsoko's day. I remember he changed it at the last moment, didn't he?"

Marisa glared at Renata in surprise and Renata smiled back calmly. She was tired of Marisa always getting at people.

The Contessa watched the little scene in silence. There were so many undercurrents in this room; it promised to be an entertaining weekend. Yes, very entertaining, she thought with a smile.

India couldn't wait to get Paris alone.

"God, what a shock!" she said, closing the door of her room behind her. "I didn't expect to see Fabrizio and Marisa. And cousin Renata! Well, what do you think?" She sat on the bed and gazed expectantly at Paris. "Of Fabrizio, I mean?"

"He's very attractive, of course, but I haven't had time yet to know what he's really like."

India sighed. "It's over, you know, truly over. My heart didn't give even one little bump when he kissed my cheek."

"That's probably just as well," said Paris, unlocking Alice from her cage. "I thought Marisa was

372

looking very suspicious when he kissed you."

"Do you really think so? I wondered . . ." India frowned. "Well, there's nothing more to be suspicious about. If she's here to check on me and Fabrizio she'll find me entirely innocent. Oh, Paris, I know you've always thought me crazy, but do you think it's possible to fall out of love with one man and directly into love with another? It's Aldo. I mean, I tried to keep it all on a business basis because he has to marry cousin Renata—the family needs the money, you see, they must keep up this old estate . . . for his grandchildren."

Paris stared at her sister in astonishment. "Did *Aldo* tell you that?"

"Well, no, not in so many words. I guess it was Marisa who told me first, and then Aldo said that about his grandchildren. . . ."

"India, I've met a thousand women just like Marisa. They tell you what they want you to hear— not the *truth*. Don't you know that?"

India sighed. It would be nice to believe Paris, and truly, the way Aldo had been behaving this past week he couldn't be in love with Renata. He had gone out of his way to be with *her* as much as possible. They'd jogged together along the beach in the early morning, they'd lunched every day at the Café-Bar Ricardi, he'd been attentive and amusing at dinner each night, and then later, when the Contessa had retired to her rooms, they had walked through the scented gardens and he'd kissed her, and maybe a bit more than just kisses

373

. . . maybe quite a lot more. But she didn't want to be another little "episode" before Aldo Monte-fiore settled down in marriage with Renata. She couldn't stand that.

"Paris, I don't know what to do, really I don't. Perhaps I should just hand this job over to someone else and go away from here."

"Certainly not. You must never jeopardize your career for any man! Your work is important, India, and you are doing well at it. Don't underestimate that."

Oh, God, thought India, here I am, moaning on about my own problems, and it's poor Paris who really needs help.

"I should be worrying about you," she cried, "not myself." She remembered Marisa's unkind remark. "Paris, don't let Marisa upset you about the show. You know she's just being bitchy. Your designs were wonderful and you know it . . . and there will be a second chance, believe me. We'll find a way."

Paris was watching the cat, who was sniffing around, inspecting her new surroundings.

"It's all right," she said. "I'm over that. It's just that, working at Mitsoko, it was impossible to get away from the constant fashion-business hype. It's good to be out of the city and here with you. Alice thinks so too—look." Alice was sprawled across the bed, enjoying the warm rays of sun coming in through the open window.

India laughed. "I know just how she feels. Okay, Paris, you and I'll take on Marisa together."

"And what about Fabrizio? I mean, does he still care about you?"

India pondered the question. "We'll always care about each other," she decided finally, "but it was really finished long ago. I just was too stupid to understand that."

Aldo was late, He sped up the driveway in his little black VW and pulled to a halt in a spurt of gravel. Climbing out of the car he took the steps two at a time, smoothed down his hair, shrugged on his jacket, and presented himself at the salon.

"Please forgive me," he called, smiling. "I got held up at the carpenter's in Naples. India, they'll have the new shutters ready next week." He kissed her, taking her hand in his.

India blushed as all eyes in the room riveted on her.

"I'd like you to meet my sister Paris," she said, pulling back her hand.

Paris was dazzling, thought Aldo, and six feet tall!

"I'm happy to meet you," he said. "I knew India had a beautiful sister, but I didn't realize quite how lovely. Welcome to Montefiore." Paris towered over him as he kissed her hand.

"Marisa, Renata." He kissed them equally—lightly. "And Fabrizio, it's good to see you. I can't tell you what a fantastic job India is doing . . . in fact, I won't tell you, I'll show you. We'll go through the place together this afternoon."

"Surely you're not going to mix business with

pleasure, Fabrizio," snapped Marisa. "I thought you wanted to spend time with the children."

"But, *cara,* you said yourself what a good opportunity it would be to see how things were progressing," said Fabrizio mildly, "and anyway, where are the children?"

"They had an early lunch," Marisa said curtly. "Now they're taking a rest so that they can be with their father later."

At the long refectory table in the vaulted dining room Aldo placed India opposite Fabrizio, seating Renata between Fabrizio and his mother at the end of the table, and Marisa on his left with Paris on his right. Catching Marisa's glare of surprise that she hadn't been seated on the right, he turned to Paris.

"I'm very happy that you could come to us." Aldo smiled warmly at Paris. "It's good sometimes to get away from the city. India tells me you were modeling for Mitsoko. Isn't that a tedious occupation for someone like you?"

Aldo had tuned in perfectly to what was wrong with Paris's life. Without the excitement of her designing and with no other creative outlet, just striding around a salon looking beautiful held no appeal. She found herself chatting easily with him while Marisa ate her melon in stony silence, ignoring India on her left.

Renata was talking to the Contessa and Fabrizio caught India's eye.

"Are you all right?" he asked quietly.

"Fine, just fine . . . sending me here was the best

thing you could have done. It was you, wasn't it, Fabrizio," she added in a lower voice, "not Marisa?"

"A little of both," he admitted. "I had no choice, India."

India was aware of Marisa tuning in to their conversation. "Thank you, Fabrizio, for everything."

"And you."

What a way to end a love affair, at the lunch table with five other people present—one of whom you were already falling in love with. But it had been over long ago, even before he sent her to the palazzo; this was just a formality.

"What are you thanking Fabrizio for, India?" Marisa's voice cut through her thoughts.

"I was thanking him for trusting me with this job, for giving me a free hand, and allowing me the opportunity to be here, at the Palazzo di Montefiore."

"It's we at the palazzo who should be thanking you," said Aldo. "Your work will probably change the fortunes of the Montefiore family."

"Then I suggest you make the most of your stay, India," said Marisa nastily. "You won't be able to afford Aldo's prices once he opens his hotel, and he'll be so busy he won't have time for any of us, especially after he's married."

"Are you planning marriage soon, then, Aldo?" Fabrizio's voice was innocent.

Aldo beamed happily at them.

"Yes," he said positively, "yes, I hope to get married very soon."

The silence in the room was total as all eyes suddenly focused on him.

"Well, Aldo," said Fabrizio, breaking the spell, "let us know who the lucky lady is when you get around to it, won't you?" He smiled at Renata opposite him. "I don't suppose we need to look too far for her, though."

"Not too far," agreed Aldo.

Paris caught Marisa's triumphant smile and turned quickly to look at India, who was pretending to eat her food. What was all that supposed to mean?

After lunch India toured the palazzo with Fabrizio and Aldo; they checked each room, detailing the changes that would be made. They inspected the brand-new hole in the grounds where the swimming pool was to be and went over the plans for the poolside patio/bar. All was in order.

"It will take time, of course," commented Fabrizio as they returned to the house, "—at least six months before it's complete. India will have to be here for quite a while longer."

Aldo grinned at India. "That's fine with me."

India managed a polite smile. "If we're finished," she said, "I think I'll go and find Paris."

She found her playing on the lawn with the children, kicking a rubber ball around and laughing at their delighted faces. At least Paris seemed cheerful; she had been so afraid for her when she'd received that letter.

"Stan's death was the final straw," explained Paris as they strolled barefoot along the beach, "coming on top of everything else . . . I mean—well, there are some things I can't tell you, India, but it just seemed as though everything I did was jinxed. Nothing has gone right since Jenny died." Paris trailed her toe in the tip of a tiny wave. "If it weren't for Didi, I don't know what I would have done. And Alice. India, I don't think I can ever be truly happy unless I achieve success. It's more than just a creative urge— I *need* that other thing, the excitement of winning, of being *someone*. It's what Jenny had. I understand her now more than I ever did before. *I have to make it,* India, I just have to."

"Then if you need it that much, you will. Nothing will stop you, Paris. What happened was only a setback. One day you'll do it. Stay here for a while, get your spirit back and your energy—and you'll be ready for another try."

Paris linked her arm through her sister's. "What about you? I like your Aldo, he's sensitive and aware—and he doesn't take any nonsense from that silly woman Marisa."

"I guess Aldo's going to marry Renata." India shrugged, doing her best to keep it casual. "You saw what happened at lunch."

"Then if he is, it won't be for her money. He's not the type, India. Why would he sell the family treasures to finance his hotel scheme? Surely he could have waited and used her money?"

It was true, he could have done the whole thing on Renata's money. He needn't have sold possessions that obviously meant such a lot to his mother.

"I noticed it was you he greeted first," said Paris, "your hand he held onto, and he treated Renata and Marisa exactly the same, friendly but not intimate."

"Perhaps he's saving that until after they are married."

"India, for God's sake! The man said he was planning marriage and Marisa obviously thought it was to Renata. *I* think it's *you*. Aldo is too much of a man to be manipulated by the Marisas of this world, and he seems to me a man of his own opinions and actions. Are you going to disappear into the background and leave him to a Renata? Whatever happened to the old fighting India Haven spirit?"

"But what should I do? I mean, I can't just ask him, can I?"

"Tell me the truth. Are you in love with Aldo? If he asked you to marry him, would you?"

India was silenced by her sister's logic. Would she marry him? Yes, like a shot. She knew it. But wouldn't she have married Fabrizio in the beginning too—if he had been free? Yes, she would, but it hadn't worked out and life had moved on. Her affair with him had nothing to do with her feelings now for Aldo.

"Yes," she said at last. "Yes, I'd marry him. But he hasn't asked me."

"I bet he hasn't asked Renata either. You know what Jenny would say, don't you, India? There's only one way to find out."

"Ask him," breathed India.

"Damn right. Jenny wouldn't have waited around

380

for any man. Get on with it or get rid of it, she would have said. If he's not interested in marrying you, then call it a day—forget him. And if he is? India, you've got nothing to lose."

India hitched up her skirt and dashed into the waves, laughing as she jumped them.

"I do love you, Paris," she called. "You've made it all seem so simple."

Paris decided that India should look sophisticated at dinner and nothing India had brought with her would do.

"Do you realize your competition down there?" asked Paris, shifting a complaining Alice from the top of her open suitcase and rummaging through it. "Now, how about this?"

India inspected the little pale gray lace dress. "It's way too long and, anyway, I look awful in gray."

"Not when I've finished with you." Paris spread the dress across the bed, checking the seams. "I made this for Naomi to wear, so it's bigger than my usual things; it's a more traditional dress, the kind that always sells."

"You mean to persons like me who aren't born models?"

Paris laughed. "Exactly. If I unpick this here and cut the neck lower and then chop about six inches from the hem—maybe more, it should be quite short, just touching the knee to get the proportions right . . . hand me the scissors."

Paris's sure hands swathed through the lace.

"You'll never get it done in time," India protested.

Paris grinned confidently. "This is nothing," she said. "I'll have it ready in one hour. Go take a shower—and don't bother with your makeup. I'm doing it for you."

Paris was as good as her word. In forty-five minutes she had expanded the bodice with panels of lace taken from the hem, shortened the skirt by cutting around the scalloped pattern of the lace, and hastily tacked up the silk taffeta underskirt.

She sat India down in front of the dressing table, took out her makeup box, and went to work. In ten minutes she had transformed India from a pretty girl into an exotic one. And when Paris eased the dress over India's head and zipped her up, tying the gray taffeta sash in a bow at the back, India realized just how clever her sister had been. The dress fitted closely, emphasizing her tiny waist and full breasts, the neckline was low, and the sleeves just a tiny ruffle of lace—it was the perfect dress for the formal dinner planned for that night. And for asking a man if he wanted to marry you!

India was suddenly aware of the passing of time. "Paris, you've only got twenty minutes."

"I'll be ready in fifteen," called Paris, heading for the shower.

The Contessa and Aldo were waiting in the grand salon for their guests when they came downstairs. Paris noticed the way Aldo's face lit up when he saw India, and thought that at least one of the dresses from her collection had been worthwhile.

Marisa, sweeping into the room behind them, eyed them in astonishment. Paris, in a severe white satin dinner jacket and black skirt, was superb— Marisa felt overdressed in the Valentino blue organza with the full skirt, and she'd thought it so charmingly feminine when she'd bought it. Damn. And just look at India! Damn, thought Marisa, damn. She wasn't used to being upstaged.

The son of Ricardi from the bar in the village, who was being trained as head waiter for the hotel, handed around glasses of champagne. Marisa watched carefully as Fabrizio talked with Paris and India . . . no, she had been quite wrong, there was nothing going on. His smile was easy, and hers was innocent. It was more of a relief than she had thought.

The children appeared in their nightclothes with their nurse and were pampered with a tiny taste of champagne and a chocolate before being carried off to bed by Aldo and Fabrizio.

Conversation at dinner was light and easy, with none of the odd pauses of lunchtime. Even Marisa seemed to be behaving, and Aldo, seated between India and Renata this time, was being equally attentive to both.

Afterward they had coffee in the salon. The night was warm and still, and the long windows stood open to catch some air. They wandered out onto the lawns, admiring the full moon that spread itself over the calm sea. Renata, sliding her arm through Aldo's waited for him to say something. Surely if he wanted to marry her, this was the perfect night to ask.

"Where are you planning to be this summer?" he asked instead. "Sardinia or the south of France?"

"I don't really know." Renata was startled; it wasn't quite what she'd expected him to say. "The de Bohans have asked me to stay at their villa in Antibes, but I haven't decided yet."

"You should go, Renata, you'd enjoy it."

"Yes. Well, perhaps I may." Renata was subdued. "What about you, Aldo?"

"I? I'm afraid I won't be taking holidays for a long time, not until I get this place on its feet. Hopefully I'll be helping other people enjoy their holidays instead. Look, India and Paris are going down to the beach. Shall we join them?"

"No," said Renata abruptly. "I'm feeling rather tired. I think I'll go to bed."

"Good night, then, Renata. Sleep well." Aldo kissed her gently, watching as she joined Marisa and his mother on the terrace.

He caught up with Paris and India by the steps that led down to the beach.

"I've come to gaze at the moon with you," he called. "Renata's gone to bed, she felt tired."

Paris yawned extravagantly. "I'm afraid it's been a long day for me. If you don't mind I think I'll turn in too."

Aldo took India's hand and helped her down the stone steps.

"It seems you and I are the only true romantics

who long to see the moon's path on the water," he said.

"It seems so."

He put his arm around India's shoulders as they walked along the firm sand by the water. "India, I haven't seen you alone all day. I've missed you."

"Have you?"

"Haven't you missed me?"

India didn't answer, and he looked at her in surprise. "No, or yes?"

India took a deep breath and said it. "Aldo, are you going to marry Renata?"

"Why are you asking me such a question?" Aldo stared at her dumbfounded.

"I want you to tell me the truth. Are you?"

In the moonlight Aldo's eyes were dark. It was impossible to read what he was thinking. "Has Renata suggested that we might be going to marry?"

"Well, no . . ."

"Then it's Marisa! India, why would I be here with you? Why would I have spent these past weeks with you if I were in love with Renata?"

"Marisa didn't say you were in *love* exactly. I mean, well, Renata has a lot of money and you need it for the estate."

"Jesus Christ, India," said Aldo furiously, "what sort of man do you think I am? Do you really think that I'd marry Renata, marry *any* woman, for her money? Why did you listen to that damned stupid woman, Marisa?" He shook India furiously. "You *believed* her!"

His anger was impressive and India stared back at him in dismay. "I didn't know what to think . . . perhaps you might just have been flirting . . . maybe I was just a little 'affaire' for you."

Aldo was shocked. "How could you think that? Let me tell you something, India. *No* Montefiore has *ever* married for money. We are a family of lovers, not financiers."

India listened, awed, as Aldo's anger gathered momentum. "I had not thought, India, that you could be so stupid as to believe a woman like Marisa Paroli."

"I didn't want to believe it. I really wanted to believe that you were falling in love with me."

Aldo grabbed her again by the shoulders. "Of course I was falling in love with you. I've been falling in love with you ever since you spilled champagne on my jacket, but you've been keeping me at arm's length. Come here." He pulled her closer, tightening his arms around her. "You crazy girl," he murmured between kisses, "of course I'm in love with you."

India felt all her good resolutions melting along with his kisses. She ran her hands through his shaggy hair, holding him closer.

"Oh, Aldo. I love you, too, but I can't be your mistress."

"Mistress? Good God, India, I'm not asking you to be my mistress, I'm asking you to marry me."

They stared at each other in the moonlight.

"Marry you?" asked India in astonishment. "But why?"

"Why? A thousand reasons. Which one do you want to hear? That I can't run this hotel without you? You bossy American woman!"

India threw back her head and laughed. "That's a sensible reason. I'm not sure Jenny would approve of it, but it's sensible."

"Then I'm sure she'd approve of the other reasons. I can't live without you, India Haven. You bring joy to my life. I want to love you forever, to have children with you, to grow old with you. Please say you'll marry me."

It was as romantic as one of Jenny Haven's movies, thought India; the lighting man had got the angle of the moon just right, the sound man had provided the soft, rhythmic background of the waves on the shore, and she knew her lines perfectly.

"Yes. Oh, yes, Aldo," she said, "I want to marry you too."

As her lips met his she knew Jenny would have approved the ending . . . *fade out over lovers, camera pans onto moonlit sea and the surging waves*. Only, this was better than Hollywood.

19

New York was not the smartest place to be seen in June, but Olympe thought it would be worth the sacrifice. She swept from the air-conditioned comfort of her limousine into the climate-controlled foyer of the Helmsley Palace Hotel on Madison, glancing around her in appreciation. At least the hotel was a good one; you could always tell by the flowers and the type of people you encountered in the foyer. She checked in quickly and was wafted to her suite on the tenth floor. Flowers and fruit awaited her, the gift of a respectful management. Picking up the phone she called room service and ordered a large, very cold bottle of Perrier water and a club sandwich. Olympe never ate or drank on planes, even on the Concorde; it only dehydrated one and contributed to the jet lag. Consequently she was starving. Kicking off her shoes, she sank onto the bed, dialed the operator, and asked for an outside line. Holding her address book open at M, she dialed and waited for Fitz McBain. The number was his private line that only he ever answered, and it purred gently, but without response.

Damn. Could he be out of town? Surely not. He'd mentioned to her that he had to be in New York most of June on business and that he planned to be in Europe later in the summer. Olympe hoped she hadn't gambled wrongly—this was costing her a fortune. She'd take a shower and try again.

Thirty minutes later, fortified by the sandwich and cooled by her shower, she dialed his number again. Fitz answered immediately. If he was surprised to hear from her he didn't show it, and when she put down the phone five minutes later Olympe had a dinner date with Fitz at Le Cirque for eight-thirty that night.

Fitz sat opposite Olympe at a discreet corner table

while waiters did a complicated ballet around them, flourishing bottles for his approval, lighting her cigarettes, and brandishing menus. Olympe beamed her approval at him.

"I called it right, then," he said. "I thought this would be the perfect place for you."

"I adore it, Fitz. It's charming, the service is good, and it's . . . intimate."

Fitz sipped his Scotch on the rocks. He didn't usually like to drink whiskey before wine, but Olympe had ordered a Campari, so he had to have something.

"I've never thought of it as intimate, Olympe."

"Of course it's intimate—for certain people. Look at them." Olympe gestured with her cigarette to the tablehoppers greeting those they knew, or hoped to know better. "They make it intimate for people like us who are here to have dinner—alone together. They scarcely even know we're here."

Fitz laughed at her backhanded logic. "I guess you're right, though I had supposed that you were one of that sort of people yourself."

Olympe gave him her most demure smile. "Only when circumstances force me, Fitz. Certainly not otherwise. I can't think of anything I enjoy more than dinner alone with someone nice, someone I like. Except maybe . . ." She laughed, gesturing happily with the cigarette that she was using for effect rather than smoking. "Ah, my dear Fitz, I don't know whether you are used to the direct ways of us Frenchwomen."

389

"Certainly not before the appetizer," murmured Fitz as the waiter appeared with her asparagus and his smoked salmon. He felt good for the first time in weeks, and it reminded him of the other time he'd been with Olympe at Bendor's party in Barbados. He'd enjoyed himself with her then too; she had the happy knack of making it all so easy for a man to be relaxed; her flirting was straightforward without the games Raymunda played. But she wasn't Venetia, he remembered with a pang. And it was a good thing she wasn't! Placing a sliver of salmon on some brown bread, he offered it to Olympe. Instead of taking it in her fingers she leaned forward and took it in her mouth, pressing her pink tongue gently against his fingers.

"Delicious," she said. "I have to confess, Fitz McBain, that I adore good food. It's one of my weaknesses."

Fitz didn't ask what the others were. "How's Beny?" he asked instead.

Olympe finished her final asparagus spear before she replied. She wiped her extravagantly red mouth delicately with her napkin. "Beny is well. He's also in Australia, not a place I've ever fancied particularly. All those sheep farmers, darling, drinking all that *beer*. Poor Beny, I'm afraid he's addicted to beer, you know." She shuddered delightfully. "I hope you don't drink beer, Fitz?"

Fitz grinned. "It has been known," he admitted. "Don't forget I grew up in the backlands of Texas. You're talking to a rough old wildcatter here."

"Am I really?"

How did she manage to say so much with her eyes? Fitz was fascinated. If Olympe had meant to enchant him with her flirting, she was succeeding.

"What brings you to New York?" he asked as the waiter removed their plates.

"Oh, shopping. And . . . curiosity."

"What can a Frenchwoman possibly buy in New York that she can't find in Paris?"

"Well, maybe just curiosity, then."

Fitz leaned forward, smiling. "And exactly what are you curious about?"

"Among other things, what the apartment of a rough Texan wildcatter looks like. . . ."

Olympe was as beautiful naked as she was dressed—a rare event in fashionable women, as Fitz knew. She stood before him with a body that looked as though it were sprung by Rolls-Royce, dazzling him with her nakedness and her wicked, amused eyes. It was those eyes that made him like her so much; they acknowledged that she was being wicked, but wasn't it fun? And why shouldn't they be wicked together? And they were, oh, they were. Olympe seduced him as beautifully and efficiently as any woman could, taunting him and then receding, leaving him trembling on the brink until he could bear it no longer and he grabbed her, thrusting himself into her well-tuned body as she murmured her pleasure to him, matching him in passion. And afterward she lay, propped up on the pillows, smoking a lazy cigarette, smiling at him with that mischievous little-cat smile. She looked elegant, in control, and ready for whatever he might suggest, though how she managed to convey all that, Fitz wasn't quite sure. But there was no doubt that she was his kind of woman.

"How do you like the Mediterranean at this time of year?" he asked.

The warm, blue-black nights were driving Venetia crazy. They were even worse than the hot sunny days with the warm, soft breezes that tantalized her naked body as she lay sunbathing on the afterdeck of the *Fiesta*. Alone. She should be back in England, she knew she should. Back home she wouldn't feel so . . . so physical! With a sigh Vennie sat up in bed. It was not good for her, being here all by herself— she didn't even have Kate to talk to, and her letters, long though they were, weren't the same as a good heart-to-heart. And she should have told Morgan that she definitely wasn't going to marry him, though honestly she had tried. It was just that he refused to accept her refusal. He came to see her every week or so, when he was able. And once he had even come with Fitz.

They'd arrived unexpectedly, but she had known Fitz was on board by the way the crew reacted— there was an energy, a pace to things, when Fitz was around. Morgan had popped his head into her galley to say hello and ask her to have dinner with them, but she had said that as their chef she welcomed the opportunity of working for her salary.

She couldn't face meeting Fitz again with Morgan there. She had stayed away from the salon, and later, after dinner, she'd seen father and son pacing the deck together, discussing the meeting they were en route to Caracas for. She knew that they were to leave early the next morning and she'd been up at dawn, hoping that Fitz might come to see her, that he still felt as she did.

She had taken a mug of coffee onto the deck and was standing there, watching the sun rise, when Fitz appeared. He was formally dressed in an immaculate beige suit. His thick, dark hair was firmly brushed, still wet from the shower, and he had left the top button of his blue shirt open with the tie loosely knotted. She could smell his aftershave—fresh and citrusy. He hadn't smiled, just looked at her, a deep look at first, and then he'd turned away and gazed at the shore. "It's a lovely morning, Venetia," he'd said noncommittally. She had clutched her mug of coffee, unable to speak. And then he'd turned back to her and said, "How are you, Vennie?" It was the look in his eyes that puzzled her, even now. She'd thought about it endlessly. He had stared at her as though he were seeing her for the first time, checking her against some memory of his own, as if she were some new person. And then she'd blurted it out, letting him see how she felt. "I've missed you, Fitz." His expression had changed; it was as though a mask had come over his face, a polite, smiling, formal mask. "You're too lonely here," he'd said, "but I plan on keeping you busy for the next few weeks. I have some friends coming to stay on the *Fiesta*. There'll be about a dozen or so of them. You'll be better being occupied—and having some young people around. Morgan will be here some of the time too. I guess that'll make life a lot happier for you both." He'd glanced at his watch. "Five-thirty," he'd said with a frown, "—we must be off. I'm sure Morgan'll be out to say good-bye to you." She'd faced him helplessly, still holding her coffee. "Oh, Venetia, one more thing. I haven't forgotten . . ." Her heart had stopped, he was going to tell her he hadn't forgotten that night, he hadn't forgotten her after all. "I haven't forgotten my promise to look into Jenny's financial affairs. I'll let you know as soon as I have any definite information."

She'd thanked him, managing to keep her voice from shaking, and then Morgan had appeared on deck, cheerful and matter of fact, and the moment alone had gone.

That was the only time in two months that she had seen Fitz, and yet she was trapped here on the *Fiesta*, like the fly on the end of the slender thread that held her to him.

It had been a little easier when the lovely boat had been filled with people and she had found herself busier than she could have imagined. She'd enjoyed that, and Fitz's friends had been young and jolly with that American quality of open friendliness that had counted her in as one of them as often as she wished. But now the moment of truth had come. Yesterday the captain had told her that the *Fiesta* was to leave for the Mediterranean for the summer months. There was a message for her from Mr. McBain. He would be delighted if she would remain with the *Fiesta* in her new summer quarters, but of course would understand if she preferred a change. A flight would be arranged for her either to London or to Nice, depending on her decision.

Sitting up in bed, with her arms clasped around her knees, Vennie stared into the soft darkness. Of course she should leave; he'd meant it when he'd said good-bye, that he would forget all about that night, and so must she. But would she?

Slipping out of bed she pulled on a robe and went out on deck. The air was a little cooler now, in the darkest hour of the night. Vennie hesitated just for a moment and then she glided softly along the deck and down the companionway. Everyone except the nightwatch on the bridge was asleep, and she reached the master stateroom without notice. Closing the door behind her she padded across to the bathroom, and taking the bottle of Fitz's after-shave, she dabbed a little on her throat and between her breasts—and then a little more lower down, on her belly and thighs. Returning to the bedroom she dropped her robe on the floor and slid between the cool sheets of Fitz's bed, cradling his pillow close to her, wrapped in the smell of his cologne, pretending he was with her. It wasn't the first time she'd done it; it made her feel closer to him somehow. . . .

The bright sunlight of the following morning forced the reality on Venetia that she would have to make a decision, and she knew what it must be. She couldn't bear to go on living in limbo any longer. Fitz obviously wanted nothing more to do with her. She would go home. But first she must clear things between herself and Morgan, tell him the truth— that there could never be anything between them. It wasn't fair not to—and neither was it fair of Morgan to refuse to accept that. They must both be free. She couldn't wait until she saw him—she would write to him instead.

It was India's letter that brought reprieve—or rather the excuse for a reprieve. The fact that India was to be married—to a wonderful Italian count whose name was Aldo—and that she would live happily ever after in a palazzo overlooking the Mediterranean, brought the first taste of pure happiness Vennie had known in ages. At least *one* of Jenny's girls was getting it together, she thought, reading again India's looped, American scrawl. She and Paris were to be bridesmaids. It was all to take place in the village church at Marina di Montefiore.

It was too easy to tell herself that as Marina di Montefiore was in the Mediterranean and she was going to be there anyway, she might as well stay with the *Fiesta* for the summer. After all, why not give it one more chance . . .

❧ 20 ❧

Marina di Montefiore had pulled out all the stops for their young count's wedding. The village was *en fête,* decorated with bunting and streamers, with colored lights strung in the trees and trestle tables set up in the square for the celebration dinner—a gift from Count Aldo and his bride—that would take place that night. Afterward there would be fireworks up at the palazzo and then some serious drinking for the older fishermen and dancing in the square for the younger ones. The local band had put in some hasty practice and were there to serenade the young couple as they left the tiny whitewashed church in a carriage—lavishly decorated with ribbons and flowers, drawn by two matching white donkeys—and made their way back to the palazzo for the reception.

India was a glorious bride, small and slender in creamy silk taffeta designed and made by Paris, with an orange blossom in her hair and happiness in her eyes. Hand in hand with Aldo in her pretty donkey-carriage, she smiled and waved to the crowds that lined the square, tossing flowers to the young girls and laughing as the donkeys stopped for a quick nibble at the juicy grasses growing by the fountain.

It was a true country wedding, simple, informal, and full of the vigorous, warmth of the Italian people, and India was enjoying every minute of it. There had been a pang of sadness and regret as she had left for the church on the arm of the Contessa's brother—it wasn't that she had no father of her own to escort her down the aisle, she was used to not having a father, but that her mother wasn't there to see her married. Jenny would have enjoyed a wedding like this—she would have drunk champagne with the guests and danced tarantellas with the fishermen, and she would have been thrilled by her daughter's happiness.

The palazzo was crowded with Montefiore relatives. Aldo seemed to be related to half of Italy and most of them had decided to come to his wedding. All the grand, interconnecting reception rooms milled with people greeting each other in a flurry of kisses and loud exclamations of surprise and delight. Champagne flowed, as neatly dressed girls in white aprons threaded their way through the throng with trays of hors d'oeuvres, and photographers busied themselves arranging and rearranging family groups until Aldo and India laughingly called enough.

Venetia and Paris found themselves the center of attraction for the younger male guests, complimented and caressed verbally, with proper Italian appreciation for their charms. They, too, had cast away their cares for the day and were wholly enjoying India's wedding.

"She's getting an enormous ready-made family," commented Paris as India and Aldo cut their wedding cake. "I always thought India was the one who missed not having a family most. You had the Lancasters and I—well, I've always been a loner."

Isolated for a moment in the middle of the crowd, the sisters remembered their mother.

"Poor Jenny," sighed Venetia. "How she would have loved all this."

"She should have been here to see India married." Paris's face tightened with remembered anger. "I still believe that something was wrong about it all, you know."

"It's odd you should say that. I told Fitz McBain what had happened and he felt the same way, just that it wasn't right. He even said that he would look into it for us. He had people in Los Angeles who could find out things. I'm not sure what he intended to do, or what he expected to find, but . . ." Vennie shrugged away the memory quickly. "Anyway, this isn't the place to be talking about such things. We should be enjoying India's day. Oh, look out, here come some more cousins bearing champagne. . . ."

India and Aldo were to spend their honeymoon at the palazzo, the first people to use the grand yellow suite that had been hastily finished for them. The Contessa, tactfully, was to spend some time with her relatives in Florence, leaving the young couple alone to enjoy their privacy.

"I should have hated to go away and miss all the fun," confided India as Paris helped her out of her bridal gown later. Vennie had slipped off her shoes and was sprawled on India's bed, listening. "There are the fireworks and then there'll be dancing in the village square. Oh, it's all so perfect—I just wish you two could be as happy as I am." She turned to Venetia. "Vennie, what's all this about Fitz McBain?"

Venetia sat up, blushing, "Oh, that's all over—at least I suppose it is."

"Oh, really?" India's tone expressed disbelief "Then why're you going back to the *Fiesta*?"

"I was here anyway, in the Mediterranean, and it was easy somehow."

"Yeah?" India sat beside Vennie on the bed. "How about some advice from an old married woman? Just think what Jenny would have done in the same situation. It's the advice Paris gave me. Remember, Paris? And it worked! Vennie, don't hang around in limbo wondering whether the guy loves you. Think what Jenny would have done—and do it."

"It's all so complicated, though."

"Why? Because of Morgan? Come on, Vennie, think things through—if it weren't for Morgan, would there be any obstacle between you and Fitz?"

"He's already told me to forget him, but I'm not sure if it's only because of Morgan."

"Well? Why not find out?" India glanced at her watch. "I must get changed. Aldo will be waiting for me."

Swept back once more into the circle of India's happy enthusiasm, Vennie had no time to think about what had been said until the next morning as she waited with Paris for her flight to Nice.

"I'm not like Jenny," she confessed. "I can't just go up to a man and ask him if he loves me. What if he said no? And he might. I might have been just a passing fancy, a pretty girl on a warm tropical night."

"It's up to you, Vennie. It's your life."

Paris was very quiet this morning. She was returning to her lonely life in her studio, thought Venetia, and here I am, selfishly worrying only about my own problems.

"What will you do now?" she asked.

Paris shrugged. "I can't bear to go back to modeling. Anyway, after all those good Italian meals I'd be no use to Mitsoko—he wants his girls to be all bone. I have a few ideas for resort wear. I thought I might make some things and try to sell them to the boutiques in St. Tropez and Monte Carlo. You know, quick, fun, sporty things. It's a long way from couture, but I've changed, Vennie. I'm willing to start at the bottom now. Anything, just to get a foot through the fashion door."

"Don't think of it as the bottom—think of it as a beginning," said Vennie comfortingly. "Anyway, good luck, Paris. Keep in touch with me—call me if you're coming south, I'd love to see you."

Venetia's flight was called first and Paris was left alone in a crowded Naples air terminal. She was going to miss India's company and the gentle days at the palazzo, but work beckoned like a challenge. And Jenny would have expected her to accept the challenge—and win. Paris squared her shoulders. She walked toward the gate where her flight was boarding. Okay. She'd give it another try.

❧ 21 ❧

It had been a long day. The set of *Chelsea's Game* had been crowded with visitors, and that always bothered him. It was tough enough to get through the day, remembering everything, looking good and doing your best, thought Rory irritably, without a bunch of visiting bankers or accountants, or whoever they were, getting the VIP treatment with him thrown in as the cabaret.

"You tired?" asked Bob, sitting with him in the back of the limo, driving back from the studio to Rory's place.

"Beat." Rory closed his eyes.

He looked it. Without the makeup his face looked puffy and slack. Bob had spent the day on the set with Rory and had been amazed by how much time was spent waiting around. There was always something that needed adjusting, or a new setup to be arranged, and then they just shot the disjointed bits and pieces of scenes, or did close-ups, repeating the lines they'd just said in the long shot . . . and yet each week they churned out another episode of *Chelsea's Game*! It was not, decided Bob, a business that would suit him. And he was getting very restless playing at being Rory Grant's "hanger-on". He hoped Fitz McBain would understand what he was going through and be suitably rewarding afterward, and not just— with money. He wanted a leg up to the next level in the corporation.

"Okay, Rory, we're here."

The driver leapt out to open the door. "G'night Mr. Grant. See you tomorrow."

"G'night."

Rory fiddled with his keys, found the right one, and let them in. The house was hot from the day's scorching sun.

"Aw, shit!" he grumbled, switching on the air-conditioning.

"You should have a housekeeper," said Bob, going to the refrigerator and getting out a bottle of Mondavi Chablis. "Here, have a glass of this."

Rory looked at it in disgust. "I'd rather have a beer. . . . I know, I know, it's a million calories and I shouldn't. Fuck you, Jenny Haven," he called to the empty house. "You got me on this calorie kick and I can't goddamn stop." He looked at Bob. "If I have a beer," he complained, "I'll gain two pounds and tomorrow those goddamn tight jeans won't fit and my belly'll hang over the top."

"You're exaggerating, Rory," soothed Bob. "Have the beer—one won't do you any harm."

Rory pushed his hands into his pockets and slouched moodily to the window, staring at the glossy cruisers and speedboats bobbing at their moorings.

Bob watched him silently. He'd never seen him down like this before; he was nervous and tense as well as tired.

Rory turned from the window and headed for the stairs.

"What's happening?" called Bob. "We gonna eat, or what?"

"Wait there," called Rory. "I'll be with you in a bit. I'll just take a shower."

403

Bob waited. He flipped through the pages of *Esquire*, and then *Playboy*. He poured himself another glass of the Chablis. He stared out over the darkening sea. What was going on? He'd been an hour.

"Hey, Rory, you all right?" he called from the bottom of the stairs.

"Sure." Rory appeared on the landing. "Why shouldn't I be?" His grin was wide and his step jaunty as he ran down the stairs. He was more "up" than Bob had ever seen him. "I see you're admiring the Playmate of the Month. Tell you what, Bob, we'll go around to the Mansion—there's always something going on there. We can shoot some pool, dance a little—those pictures don't lie, you know, they really look like that."

"I thought you were wiped out."

"I was. But I'm not anymore." Rory laughed. "Just a little extra boost, man, no sweat. I'm okay. Come on, then, let's go."

"What about work? You have to be up at five-thirty."

"I'll be okay." Rory grabbed his car keys and headed for the door. Bob followed, slamming the door behind him. He had the feeling it was going to be a long night.

It was four-thirty when they got back home. They were sitting on Rory's sofa. Bob was into his second wind and Rory had crashed, plummeted from some lofty peak to white-faced misery. He sat, head in hands, staring at the pattern on the marble table.

"Something's really bugging you, Rory," said

Bob, rolling a joint. "I mean, I can tell. It's like you've got something bottled up inside you, something that really worries you."

Rory lifted his head and stared at Bob.

"You're right," he said.

"It's no good, you know," Bob went on, dragging at the joint, "keeping things locked away inside you like that. You'll end up doing ten years on a psychiatrist's couch . . . cost you a fortune, and at the end what have you got? Nothing you couldn't get talking to a friend."

Rory put his head back in his hands, staring at the table again, wishing he didn't feel so down. He had everything going for him, he was the hottest success in a town where only this year's success counted. He was coining money—more than he'd ever dreamed of making. He didn't need Jenny's money now. There she was again! Always at the back of his mind, ready to sneak up on him when he was feeling low. Always there, her blue eyes wide and accusing. And frightened. The way they had looked that night. . . .

"You're right," he said slowly. "Bob, I need someone to talk to, and you're my closest friend. But it's not all the way it sounds. I mean, I was a young guy trying to get on in a tough world. You understand what I mean, don't you, Bob?"

Bob switched on the micro-tape recorder in the pocket of his Ralph Lauren denim jacket.

"Sure," he agreed, "I understand."

The *Fiesta* was the gayest, most social yacht on the Mediterranean that season, cruising lazily along the coast, from Monte Carlo to St. Tropez, and across to Porto Cervo in Sardinia, anchoring occasionally at tiny Calvi in Corsica, or, for a change of pace, drifting westward to Puerto Banus at Marbella. With a constant flow of guests spilling from every cabin, Venetia found herself thrown in suddenly at the deep end. In a way it was good; it left her little time to brood, and even with the help of the two girls whom she had found it necessary to recruit from London to help her she was usually too tired at night to crave anything but sleep.

In the first month Fitz McBain had been aboard twice—each time for one night only, bringing with him a party of guests who were to enjoy his hospitality, though not his presence, for the next couple of weeks. Venetia had not seen him alone; in fact, she had seen him only once to speak to, and that was at the dinner table when the guests, merry on champagne, had called for their chef to compliment her on her dinner. Venetia had had to stand there, blushing, dressed in old shorts and her huge striped apron, feeling hot and illkempt compared with the elegant, leisured guests in their summery, floating silks. Fitz had smiled at her as their glances met, but she had only wanted to escape. Afterward she'd watched from her position outside her galley on the upper deck, feeling like a pantomime Cinderella left behind when the others went to the Prince's ball, as they trooped laughingly ashore, heading for some party at the Hotel Cervo.

Often the guests would choose to eat in a harborside café in Calvi or a smart restaurant in St. Tropez and then they'd dance the night away at a party or some wild disco. It would all have been such fun if only she'd been sensible enough to fall in love with Morgan—but how could any daughter of Jenny's be expected to behave sensibly? There was no doubt that Morgan was hurt, but his bitterness was against her, not his father. "I might have guessed," he'd said cryptically, when she'd told him about her feelings for Fitz, "but I would have thought it would be the other way around—he's always loved you."

She'd gazed at him, puzzled, wondering if he'd misunderstood her, but she'd forgotten his remark in her relief that he had finally accepted that she could only be a friend to him. "The biggest cliché of all," he'd said wryly. "I surely never thought anyone would say it to *me!*"

"It may be cliché," she'd replied gently, "but I mean it. We've been good friends from the beginning, Morgan—it would be nice if we could keep it that way."

Still, she was relieved that he came rarely to the yacht, feeling oddly shy with him in her new role.

The message that Mr. McBain would be joining the *Fiesta* for a few weeks ran through the crew in minutes. The gleaming yacht was given an extra spit and

407

polish for its master until its brasswork glittered in the sun and the crew, dressed in their crispest white shorts and shirts, caps gleaming with gold braid, awaited his arrival. The boat was quiet—the week's complement of new guests was due to arrive late that afternoon, and Venetia, her heart pounding, pondered over what to wear. Showered and cool, with her blond hair freshly washed and left to dry in the sun, she chose a short, white cotton skirt and a big white shirt that she left unbuttoned, just clasping it, at the waist with a wide leather belt. With her winter suntan topped up from her weeks in the Mediterranean and her hair brushed in a new shaggy style, she looked like a healthy young animal. It was time, she decided firmly, gazing at herself in the mirror, it was time for a bit of Jenny's "action."

The hours ticked by interminably on the strangely quiet boat. He was late, thought Venetia anxiously; perhaps he wasn't coming after all. Oh, please God, let him come, please . . . she couldn't bear it any longer, she *must* see him.

It was six-thirty when they finally arrived. Venetia heard his familiar deep voice and the sound of feminine laughter. Hurrying from her cabin she ran along the deck, almost colliding with them as she turned the corner. A beautiful tawny-blond woman stood with Fitz and a half-dozen other laughing guests who were still straggling on board.

"Venetia." Leaving Olympe, Fitz took her hand in his. "How are you?" His dark eyes were concerned. "Not too overworked, I hope?"

Venetia felt herself blushing again. Oh, God, would she never outgrow that childish habit? Her hand trembled in his and she pulled it back hastily. "No, no, of course not. It's what I'm here for."

"Morgan told me he thought you were doing too much and should have more free time," said Fitz, "and I agree with him. Let's discuss it later, shall we? Meanwhile, we shall be dining out tonight, so there's no need to consider us."

Venetia's heart sank. He was going out, with that gorgeous woman, she supposed.

"Very well," she said in a small voice.

Olympe watched with interest the quiet exchange between Fitz and the lovely blonde with the fantastic legs. If there was a rival for Fitz's attentions, then she'd like to know it. Olympe could sense a liaison almost before it happened, and there was something between these two, she was sure of it.

"Aren't you going to introduce your friend, Fitz?" she called.

Anger sparked in Venetia. She wasn't going to take a backseat just because this woman was here, she was going to fight for what she wanted, just as India had—and Jenny.

"I'm the chef on the *Fiesta*," she announced loudly, "at your service." She gave a mocking little bow and received a spontaneous round of applause from the guests crowding the deck. "If you wish anything special cooked, I'm the one to ask. My name is Venetia. Venetia Haven."

"Haven?" Olympe stared at her with renewed interest. "Any relation to Jenny Haven?"

"Jenny was my mother."

"Of course, there's a very strong resemblance, isn't there, Fitz?" And of course, too, she thought, this must be Paris Haven's sister . . . ah, well. Olympe strolled off in search of her cabin, leaving Fitz on deck with Venetia. She couldn't see this one being much of a rival. Venetia was young and very pretty, but she didn't know how to play the game. Now, if it were Paris, the beautiful Paris . . .

"Right, Venetia," said Fitz briskly, "then we'll talk tomorrow. By the way, Morgan asked me to tell you that he'll be here at the weekend."

With a casual wave of his hand he was gone. Venetia turned angrily, leaping up the stairs two at a time, slamming the door of her cabin.

"Damn him." She stomped the few feet of floor space impatiently. "Damn him and damn that woman. Who the hell is she? Oh, damn, why did she have to come here?"

She lay unmoving on her bed, hearing their voices drifting from the afterdeck where they had gathered for drinks, and later she heard them leave. Lying there on the narrow bed in her hot little cabin she had plenty of time to think. It was time for action. Flinging off her clothes she turned the shower on cold, flinching as the water struck her warm body. But it left her cool and refreshed as she sat before her mirror carefully applying her makeup. She brushed her hair forward, catching it in her hand and pulling it on top, allowing just a few tendrils to

fall around her face. There, that was more sophisticated. A hint of the Bluebell perfume, and she was
ready. There'd be no little-girl-lost look tonight, she
decided, sliding her arms into the short, blue satin
robe that had belonged to Jenny. A glance in the
mirror showed that she looked just right for what
she wanted—slightly tumbled hair, eyes shadowy
and mysterious, long, smooth brown legs, and a
glimpse of her nakedness in the casually tied robe. A
portrait in seduction, she thought, remembering the
last time she'd gone to find Fitz in his cabin, in her
baggy old shorts and T-shirt. If it had worked then,
then this should surely do the trick. She felt better
already. India was right—you didn't just grin and
bear it, you did something about it. Now, all she had
to do was wait—again!

They came back earlier than she had expected,
tired no doubt from the day's traveling. Venetia
heard them saying good-night and the sound of
doors closing, and then the boat was quiet. She allowed fifteen endless minutes to tick by, then
opened her door and peered cautiously along the
decks. They gleamed emptily in the moonlight. On
bare, silent feet she made her way to the master
stateroom. She had made the same journey often
before, to spend lonely nights in Fitz's bed, but this
time she would be with Fitz. Venetia hesitated for a
moment outside his door, listening, but all seemed
quiet. She pushed it open gently and peered into the
darkness of the outer room that Fitz used as his
study. A glow of light came from beneath the bed-

411

room door, and with her heart beating faster Venetia tiptoed across.

If it hadn't been that the door had developed a faint squeak due to the salt air, they wouldn't have noticed her. As it was, Olympe, splendid in black lace French knickers and nothing else, turned her head inquiringly. With Fitz's arms still around her, she smiled at Venetia.

"Well," she said in an amused voice, "did you intend joining us, or is this merely to discuss what we would like for breakfast?"

Venetia stood rooted to the spot, her eyes on Olympe's nakedness, the beautiful breasts that Fitz had been kissing. Oh, God, she wanted to die, just die. . . .

"Shut up, Olympe." Fitz pushed her aside roughly, making for the door just as Venetia turned and ran. "Venetia, Vennie, come here!" He grabbed her by the arm as she turned into the corridor. "Come here, you bloody little fool. Whatever possessed you to do such a thing? My God, Vennie, you're crazy. . . ."

Vennie raised her arm and hit him, putting all the force of her slender body behind it.

"You're right," she yelled, "I am a bloody little fool. My mother didn't bring me up to know any better, that's why I did it. I hate you, Fitz McBain, I hate you. . . ." Wrenching her arm from his she escaped from his grasp and turned to run, tripping over the slippery satin belt of the seductress's blue robe—the sort of robe that was meant to swing open, as it did now, allowing Olympe Avallon's amused eyes a glimpse of her nakedness as she took off once more.

"Well, darling," said Olympe, "do we continue where we left off, or should I have a headache?" Olympe could see that at this point withdrawal was the better move. Whatever was going on, Fitz was definitely upset. Could there be more to this situation than had met her experienced eye? How very boring.

"Unless, of course, you want to talk about it?"

Fitz's voice had a harsh edge to it. "You shouldn't have said that, Olympe."

"Oh? Do I have to make excuses to little Miss Haven for being with you?"

"Olympe, I'm sorry. She's just a kid . . . I would have given anything for that not to have happened."

She may be young, thought Olympe, but Venetia certainly hadn't shown up at Fitz McBain's cabin, dressed—or rather undressed—like that to play any childish games. Shrugging her negligée over her shoulders she walked to the door.

"You should remember, Fitz, that young girls like that can be dangerous," she warned. "They take things so seriously. They don't understand your sort of games—my sort of games. One of you could end up getting hurt." The door closed softly behind her. Olympe never slammed doors.

The phone rang suddenly and Fitz picked it up impatiently. Who the hell was calling at this time of night?

"Sorry to disturb you, sir," said the duty officer, "but it's a Mr. Ronson calling from Los Angeles. He said it was urgent."

"Very well, put him on."

Bob Ronson's voice came on the line. "Good evening, Mr. McBain. I apologize for the late hour, but I thought it was important that you knew right away. It's about the special matter you asked me to look into."

Fitz was all attention. "Right. How's it going?"

"Pretty good, sir, if you can call it 'good.' I have the information you needed, it's all here. I have it on tape, Mr. McBain. I don't want to go into details on the phone, but I think it would be worthwhile your hearing this as soon as possible, sir. I could take an evening flight out, if you wish."

"No," he replied quickly, "don't bother, Ronson, I'll come there. We might have some interesting meetings coming up. Thanks, Bob. You've done a good job."

"You're welcome, Mr. McBain." Ronson's normally businesslike voice sounded pleased; he hadn't missed that switch from "Ronson" to "Bob." "Then we'll expect you tomorrow, sir?"

"Right. I'll let you know later what time. Goodnight, Bob, and thanks again."

Fitz sat at his desk wondering what it was Ronson had on the tape. Then he placed a call and left a message for his pilot to have the plane ready for a flight to Los Angeles at eight in the morning.

❦ 23 ❧

Bill fiddled with the knot of his sober blue tie, nervously rebuttoning the jacket of his gray flannel suit as he waited in the hallway of Fitz McBain's Bel-Air house, wondering why he was here. The phone call had come out of the blue—not McBain himself, but some assistant or secretary: "Mr. McBain will be in Los Angeles on Thursday and would like to meet Mr. Kaufmann to discuss a business matter."

Perhaps McBain was thinking of getting into the movie business, or more likely cable TV or satellite, but if so, why ask him? There were other, more impressive, names who would have welcomed Fitz McBain's interest. That was what was making Bill so uneasy. He had the sneaking feeling something was wrong. But, if so, what?

He peered at the tiny painting propped on a gilt easel next to a tape deck, on a table by the sofa. He'd bet his boots that it was a Matisse. . . .

Fitz stood by the door, watching him, watching Jenny's ex-agent, ex-friend. Her Judas. Or one of them; one was already dead.

"It's a Matisse," he said. Bill jumped back awkwardly. "It was one of my first purchases when I started making money. *Real* money, that is."

Ignoring Bill's outstretched hand, he waved him to a chair. "Sit down, Kaufmann. What I have to say will not take long . . . I'm sure you are a busy man."

"I can't think how I can help you, Mr. McBain," replied Bill, "but just let me know what I can do. . . ."

"I'll certainly do that."

Bill shifted uneasily in the deeply cushioned chair. Why had McBain not shaken hands? What the hell was all this about?

"I'm here to discuss Jenny Haven," said Fitz, "and the interests of her three daughters."

Jenny! Jesus Christ, so that was it, those girls had put him up to something.

"A very sad situation," agreed Bill. "We all felt badly about it, and I'm sure the girls told you that Stan and I—that's Stan Reubin, the lawyer who died so tragically a couple of months back—well, Stan and I told the girls we would always do whatever we could for them. If they're in trouble now, I'm sure Stan's law firm would be glad to honor that promise without any charge."

"I'm glad to hear that, Kaufmann," Fitz replied smoothly, "and I hope you, too, will honor your promise."

Bill felt relief surge through him. So that was it. The girls needed a spot of help, probably got themselves into difficulties already, though if Fitz McBain was helping them, surely it couldn't be *financial* trouble?

"Damn right I will," he said heartily. "You know I looked after Jenny's business for twenty-five years. I'll be happy to do the same for those poor girls."

"That's just it, Kaufmann—those girls *are poor!* And the reason they're poor is because when Miss Haven began to be somewhat less of a 'star' and therefore became someone who needed more time,

416

more work, and more effort on your part, and also someone considerably less lucrative than she had been to you and Mr. Reubin over the years—*twenty-five years*, I think you said? Well, then, Mr. Kaufmann, you dropped her. You left her to struggle by herself, a woman who'd been looked after, in the business sense, all her working life. You left her to the vultures, Mr. Kaufmann—and they were there, ready and waiting. Ultimately, they included yourself. And Mr. Reubin." Fitz's penetrating dark eyes met Bill's apprehensive brown ones. "As well as Rory Grant."

Bill's mouth felt as though all his spittle had dried up, leaving his throat a hoarse desert. His voice rasped like metal on sandpaper as he forced out the word. "Rory?"

Fitz smiled again.

"Rory," he said pleasantly. "I happened to meet him in Barbados a while ago. A very good-looking young man: such a pleasant, open face, a good smile—perfect for television. And I hear that his role in *Chelsea's Game* is only the first step up the ladder. Young Rory is on the high road to success, with you hanging on to his coat-tails!"

Why the hell was he so interested in Rory? worried Bill. Had the bastard been complaining to Fitz McBain that he was being exploited?

"Now, just wait a minute"—anger lent power to his dry throat—"Rory is a client of mine. Everything's quite legitimate there. Every actor needs an agent, y'know, *and* a lawyer. Why, without us they'd be in a hell of a mess. Believe me, Mr. McBain, we *earn* our money!"

"I'm not interested in how you earn your money from Rory Grant—nor in how much. My concern is with Jenny Haven's money, the money that was stolen from her by your client, Mr. Grant." Fitz watched as the expression on Kaufmann's face dissolved from anger into shock.

"What do y'mean? Rory never stole a cent in his life—"

"And then, of course, we should discuss the considerable sum that would come to the Haven estate from the lawsuit I plan to bring on behalf of the daughters."

Good God, what was he saying? What had Rory told him? Bill gripped the carved wooden arms of his chair, feeling his heavy signet ring bite into his flesh as it pressed against the wood.

"What lawsuit?" he spluttered. "You're crazy! Those girls have put you up to something. . . ."

Fitz walked across to the small tape deck waiting on the table near the Matisse. "Before we go any farther, I think you should hear this." Pressing the "play" button he stepped back, watching Bill's reaction as Rory's distinctive drawl came over the speakers.

"Y'know, Bob, it's hard for a young guy to make it alone . . . you've never had it bad like me, your family have money. I liked Jenny, y'know, I *really* liked her at first, but she was so tight with the goddamn money. There I was, dressed in Rodeo Drive's best, without a cent in my pocket. Jesus, I even had to sign *her* name at the goddamn hairdresser's. I tell you, Bob, that kind of thing can be humiliating to a man. . . . Anyway she was having business problems, the guy who was her agent and manager had chucked her—she wasn't earning enough to make it worthwhile for him to jump through the hoop, I guess, and her lawyer was avoiding her calls. She'd begun to manage her own affairs and she hadn't a clue. I tell you, man, it was too easy . . . *I* needed the money and *she* had it. What was so wrong with that? I could have spent as much as I liked on clothes anyway. I know *legally* it was wrong, Bob, but shit! I had to have *some* cash—coke isn't cheap, you know, and besides, I was seeing a couple of girls from the studios . . . you know how it is. . . ."

Bill sat with his head in his hands listening as Rory described how he had taken Jenny's money. It was unbelievable that he could have been such a goddamn fool. And who the hell was he talking to? Obviously someone he considered a good friend— he kept on repeating that, saying how good it was to have a *friend* he could really talk to, how the whole thing had been on his mind, sometimes he even had dreams about it. . . .

Fitz pressed the pause button to stop the tape. "I think you should listen to this part carefully," he suggested, clicking the machine on again.

"I've got to tell someone, Bob, and I know I can trust you. . . ." Rory's voice was emotional, as though he were on the verge of tears, and Bill felt his

419

stomach tighten in sudden fear. "After I left, Jenny did some checking up. She called me on the set that day, threatened to go to the police. She made me promise to meet her, to talk things over. I meant to go, but we worked late that night. I was messing up my lines because she had me worried, and we were running behind schedule. When I got home it was nine-thirty and Margie was here. She'd picked up some coke for me and she had it all set up . . . it got a little wild, I was really high, higher than I've ever been—but I felt good, y'know, like nothing could get to me now, and Margie was cute. I just kinda forgot Jenny. And then she called—said I'd better get my ass over there, or else! Christ, I wish you could have heard her, Bob, talking to *me*, Rory Grant, like I was some *dumb kid* or something! I told her I wasn't about to drive all the way to Beverly Hills for no one, so she said okay, the beach house—and *now!* I decided I was gonna tell her where she got off, no old-time movie actress was gonna teach me my manners. . . . I took Margie's Seville because my black Ferrari would have been goddamn conspicuous parked outside her beach house. She was there, waiting for me. . . . I guess it must have been about three o'clock then, and she could see I was high and it got her mad, really mad. She said she was going to open the windows to get fresh air into my lungs so I could talk straight and I told her not to be such a goddamn *mother* to me—I already had one mother and that was *enough!* She hit me, Bob! Scraped her long goddamn nails all down my cheek—and I had *close-ups* the next day! Jesus, she got me *mad*. I just let her have it—oh, not physically, I didn't hit her; even stoned I'm not the kinda guy who beats up his women. But I wounded her *verbally*, Bob. I got to her in the way I knew mattered to her most. And ever since, I've wondered whether it was because of me she ended up at the bottom of Malibu Canyon. . . ."

Rory's voice grew thick with emotion, strangling on a sob as he poured out his fear. "I swear to God I didn't mean anything by it—they were just words, easy clichés hurled at her in the heat of the moment. . . . I told her that of course I'd taken the money—why else would I have stayed with her? She was just an old has-been movie star no one wanted anymore. I told her to take a good look in the mirror in daylight—without the backlighting and the makeup. Her body was sagging and her jawline had gone and she still thought she could play the young leading lady . . . even her agent had left her. *Nobody* wanted to know. She was lucky I'd stayed as long as I did, considering the tight rein she tried to keep me on . . . of course I'd taken the money. What the hell else did she expect me to do?" There was another long pause and then Rory's voice came back, quieter this time.

"She just stood there gazing at me with those big blue eyes and I could see the fear in them—fear that I was right, fear for the future . . . oh, I don't know. She'd gotten all dressed up to meet me. . . . I felt suddenly like I was the older one and she was just a kid, all pretty in her sparkly evening dress, a girl at her first prom. She could still look like that, you know, it was nothing to do with age—it was that she always looked sort of pure and innocent despite that sexy body and the reputation . . . and she was—innocent, I mean. That's how I was able to take the money from her, she just believed in everybody. There was no badness in Jenny. I'll bet even now that if I'd told her I'd done it and I was sorry she would've forgiven me. But I'd pushed her too far. She didn't cry, she didn't threaten or try to get back at me. 'That's that, then,' she said. She walked to the door and then she turned . . . she looked as though she'd had a knife twisted in her heart." Rory's voice sank to a whisper. "I can't tell you what she said next, Bob, I just can't . . . but I'll tell you this, it haunts me, it fucking haunts me. . . . I hadn't realized what I'd done, what it *meant* to her! She turned and left the house. I heard her start the car. . . . I could have gone after her, told her I was sorry, that I hadn't meant it to be like that, that things had just sort of got out of hand. . . ." There was another pause and then a sigh. "You know what happened next."

"Are you saying she committed suicide, Rory—because of what you did?"

"I don't know! Don't you understand, Bob? *I don't know!* That's what keeps me awake at night, and what I dream about when I finally get to sleep— Jenny in her pretty blue dress and the fear in her lovely blue eyes . . . I feel like some goddamn murderer. The verdict was open, so I'll never know for sure. Y'know what I'm saying, Bob? I'll never know if it was because of me. And the stupid thing is that I didn't think she was a washed-up has-been actress, she was a nice woman—and she was still beautiful. Goddamn, I don't just screw around with any old woman—Jenny was really something. And she was nice, too good for a shit like me. . . ."

Rory was choking on his own tears. One of his better performances, thought Bill sourly.

"I never told anybody I'd been at the Malibu house," said Rory, pulling himself together. "Nobody knew except Margie, and she was too dumb and too stoned to count. I couldn't go to the police and say *I* was the one she'd been to meet and that we'd had a row—they might have wanted to look into things further . . . you know how one thing leads to another. I just couldn't afford that kind of scandal at this point in my career. You can imagine how they would have reacted at the studio—*Chelsea's Game* would have been finished. What advertiser stays with a show where the star is involved in such a scandal? I could imagine the headlines—'Sex, Drugs, Money—Suicide?' Maybe they'd even think I did it—killed her, I mean. People speculated on whether she'd done it on purpose, whether it was really an accident. Anyhow," he added wearily, "it seemed to blow over . . . last week's scandal, y'know. And then Stan Reubin called. . . ."

Bill Kaufmann stiffened, feeling McBain's eyes on him.

423

"Jenny had spilled it all to Stan and Bill Kaufmann the week before, the whole story about the money. She'd asked them, as friends, to help her, but apparently they told her there wasn't anything they could do. She'd called Stan again that night just before she left, to tell him she was meeting me at the beach house to have it out with me. I guess Stan wasn't too thrilled at being woken by an ex-client at one in the morning, but he advised Jenny to tell me that if I gave back all the money I'd stolen—*stolen*, Bob; goddamn, I *earned* it—then she wouldn't prosecute, and she'd forget about the money lost on the bad investments.

"They came to see me, Bob, the pair of them. They caught me at the end of work when I was real tired and the day's coke high had worn off. Bill was all smiles, said he understood my position as an up-and-coming actor and that Jenny was a difficult woman. Stan was smooth and legal, 'protecting my interests,' he said . . . all I had to do was tell him everything that'd happened and he'd know how to protect me. So I told him. And then the scene changed. . . . Jesus, Bob, those two bastards *threatened* me! Stan said I could be indicted for fraud and grand theft." Rory choked on the words. "Even if I got off it would ruin my career. *If* they went to the police. Then they changed their attitude, said they'd be willing to forget they'd ever heard anything if we could come to some satisfactory agreement. And that's why Stan Reubin became my lawyer and Bill Kaufmann my agent—at higher percentages than any others in the business. And I do what they say—Rory Grant jumps when they say jump!"

Fitz switched off the machine and slid the ejected tape into his pocket.

Bill's frightened eyes met Fitz's calm blue ones.

"What're you going to do about it?" he demanded hoarsely. "You can't prove anything. Anyway, I didn't do anything wrong. Rory was just over-wrought, he was disturbed about Jenny's death. Stan and I just took him in hand to protect him from himself . . . he's a cokehead, y'know, nobody'll believe him."

"*I* believe him." Fitz controlled the contempt and anger he felt as he watched Kaufmann squirm. "I believe that you and Reubin contributed to Jenny Haven's death drive down Malibu Canyon just as Rory Grant did. And what you did to Rory was as close to blackmail as you can get."

For once in his life Bill was speechless. He stared it Fitz in silence.

"However," said Fitz briskly, "I'm not here to save Rory Grant from blackmail, nor to salve his con-science—or yours. I'm here on behalf of Jenny Haven's daughters. There's a considerable sum of money owing to them—both the amount stolen by Grant and further monies that they might win in a loss-and-damages claim for negligence by you and Reubin. My own lawyers tell me this would come to a very considerable sum." Fitz paused, assessing Kaufmann's reaction. He was obviously very fright-ened; his eyes blinked rapidly and his hands gripped

425

the arms of the lovely Charles II chair so tightly his ring would probably leave scratches in the wood.

"It is the wish of the Haven daughters," Fitz continued, "that their mother's name should not be dragged unnecessarily through the courts. They will not tolerate any further scandal in connection with her name. Therefore, Kaufmann—and *only* for that reason—I am prepared to talk terms."

Terms? Did he mean he wanted to make a *deal?* Bill perked up a little.

"Terms?"

"The girls are prepared to let you off far more lightly than either I, or any court, would. And both you and I know that the actual sums involved are far more than they are asking."

"How much?" croaked Bill.

"One and a half million."

Bill restrained himself just in time from asking, "Each?" His senses were beginning to clear, his brain was ticking over again. There might be a way out after all.

"One and a half million dollars," repeated Fitz, "not a great deal to ask. And I say again, Kaufmann, it's *far less* than a court would award them." He could tell from the agent's face that he'd judged the sum nicely; a million and a half was accessible money, he'd get his hands on it somehow.

"I don't have that kind of money, McBain." Bill released his grip on the chair arms. "A million and a half cash is hard to come by."

"Look at it this way," said Fitz. "It's five hundred

thousand from Rory, five hundred thousand from Stan Reubin's estate, and five hundred thousand from you personally. You're getting off lightly, Kaufmann, much too lightly!"

Five hundred thousand each, thought Bill, juggling facts and figures busily. He knew Rory was good for it, he'd just have to cancel the purchase of the house on Benedict and get an advance from the studios . . . and then there was Stan's estate; Jessie would be sure to cut up rough . . . maybe he'd have to talk to Stan's partners . . . yeah, that was it, he'd talk to them, they surely wouldn't want to have the name of their firm involved in any scandal, it could ruin them just as it could ruin him. They'd pay up. Maybe they'd even go for a mil—they didn't know the exact sum asked for, and they'd pay whatever was needed. Bill almost smiled in his relief. He could see a way off the hook; not only that, he might even *make* a bit. . . .

"I'll see what I can do, Mr. McBain," he promised.

"Just one more thing," said Fitz, walking over to the door. "My name is not to be mentioned to anyone. Is that understood?"

He pulled open the door and Bill stared in surprise at the tough, unsmiling young man standing in the hall.

"If it is," said Fitz, "I shall know."

Bill had no doubt he would; he'd known about Rory, hadn't he? "Right." He hurried through the door, pausing in the hallway. "What about the

427

tape?" he asked. "I get that when I hand over the money, right?"

"Wrong. There are several copies of that tape, all of which will remain in various safe deposits of mine scattered around the world. They belong to me."

"But then, I'll never know . . ." Bill knew he was trapped.

"Exactly. You'll just have to take my word for it." Fitz was enjoying himself. "The option would always be open to me to go to the police."

Bill walked across the hall toward the door. The young man didn't move to open it for him, and as Bill's hand rested on the knob, Fitz's voice rang again in his ears.

"One more thing."

Bill turned, beaten.

"You have exactly a week. You will be expected here at noon next Thursday. I shall not be here myself, but Mr. Ronson here will take care of you."

Bill's eyes met Ronson's. They were as cold and gray as flint, and he shuddered.

"I'll be here," he promised, stepping hurriedly outside and closing the door behind him.

❦ 24 ❦

Paris flung the last of her six suitcases into the back of the rented station wagon and slammed the door shut. She might just as well throw them in the sea for all the good they were. She'd driven from Monaco to Antibes, calling at every smart boutique, and hadn't made a single sale that was worth a damn. Everyone had admired the clothes, but it had been the same story at every shop—if only she'd been there in February or March, but now they were fully stocked. It was just too late in the season. One or two had bought a couple of outfits where there had been a gap in their stock, and that might just cover her expenses, but she would have to face up to the fact that once again she was almost broke. Not only that, her belief in herself and her talent had taken a second beating. It wasn't enough just to be a talented designer and a hard worker as well as your own model, you had to be a good businesswoman and you had to have the right contacts; you had to be *luckier* than she was, that was for sure! She hadn't understood the workings of the retail fashion business, her sights had always been set higher—she was to have been the next Chanel, wasn't she? So much for that dream; the closest she could expect to get to Chanel would be as a house model in the salon.

Paris pushed her way through the throngs of holiday makers toward the shade of a terrace café and ordered a *citron pressé*. It was still early in the morning and casually dressed tourists, wearing shorts and shirts, relaxed over their morning coffee, reading newspapers and gossiping idly. Paris felt very alone, isolated by her problems from the lazy holiday world of the resort. She debated for a moment whether she should call Vennie, as she had intended, or whether she should turn the car around now and head back for the city. It was deserted this month, restaurants and shops would be closed, everyone in France was on holiday. No, she couldn't bear to be alone there; she'd call Vennie on the *Fiesta*.

Paris bought some tokens for the phone from the man behind the bar and dialed the operator, waiting impatiently while the phone clicked and hummed, and at last she was through to the *Fiesta*. It took only seconds for them to get Vennie.

"Hello," called Paris, "Vennie, I'm in Antibes. I thought I'd come to see you."

"Paris, oh, Paris, you don't know how glad I am to hear your voice. Can you come and stay? We're in St. Tropez. Please come, Paris, I need you."

Venetia sounded on the point of tears, and Paris frowned. "Is anything wrong? You sound so odd."

"No. Yes. Oh, everything's wrong, Paris. I'll tell you when I see you. How soon can you be here?"

"I'll be there as soon as possible, Vennie—whatever it is, it'll be all right. Don't worry, I'll be there soon."

Paris banged down the phone and hurried back toward the car. What could have happened to upset Vennie so much? And what else could go wrong, for God's sake? Thrusting the car into gear, she threaded her way back through the town and took the coast road west for St. Tropez.

By nature Olympe was adaptable and easygoing. In her view changes were a part of life. Some were good, some bad, and somehow she always managed to shrug off the bad ones. That's why Fitz's absence from the *Fiesta* was irritating rather than disturbing. Meanwhile, though he'd flown to L.A. supposedly on "urgent business," she suspected that Jenny Haven's youngest daughter was the true cause. It was most annoying, she thought, turning over on her sun-lounger to toast her back. Fitz was too old for that child anyway . . . and he was just right for her. They *understood* each other.

The *Fiesta* was unusually quiet. Most of the others had taken a picnic and gone off for the day in the little fleet of Hobie Cats, tacking around the coast in search of new, unpopulated beaches. Olympe had declined to go with them. She knew they'd probably come back scarred from the lethally sharp sea urchins that clung to the rocks, or burned from too much sun, and she was much too careful of her appearance to risk that. Another five minutes and she'd move into the shade, having achieved her daily permitted quota of fifteen minutes direct sunlight on each side. It was all very restful—and quite boring with no one to tease, no games to play. Olympe closed her eyes and concentrated on the delicious heat of the sun on her back.

Venetia hovered on deck waiting for Paris, but thinking of Fitz. She had read the short letter he'd left for her a hundred times and it still said the same thing, no matter how hard she tried to read between the lines. He was sorry to have upset her, and he

431

apologized too for his anger. He hoped she would try to understand that it had been a difficult situation for all of them. He had been called away on business and didn't expect to be back to the *Fiesta* this season. He hoped she would feel able to continue her job there and that she would enjoy the rest of the summer. How could she without him?

There was nothing that implied that he cared for her, no tender regrets, no confessions of secret longings. She remembered laughing ages ago with Kate Lancaster about being the object of a "secret passion"; it had been Morgan they were talking about then, though. How far away it all seemed, and how uncomplicated, when she'd just been playing at being in love. Nobody told you that the real thing hurt! She'd finally made up her mind to return to London in a few weeks and take a job there. She wasn't cut out for this sort of life; she wanted to immerse herself in hard work, and one day she planned to open her own restaurant.

She wished Paris would get here soon; she needed to talk to someone. If she didn't she'd go crazy. Venetia paced the deck impatiently, wondering how long it would take to drive from Antibes in the summer traffic. Probably forever. She ran an agitated hand through her shaggy, sun-bleached hair. She must do *something,* she couldn't just hang about here, *thinking.* Because every time she did, the image of Olympe, beautiful and naked in Fitz's arms, sneaked its way back into her mind, no matter how hard she tried to forget it. *And* the memory of her own humiliation. She couldn't blame Fitz for that, it was her own stupid, naive fault. She'd acted like a child, believing he'd be there all alone waiting for her like the last time. Well, she'd never be that foolish again, she was quite sure of that. If only Olympe Avallon would leave, but she had stayed on. In fact she didn't seem to be the least bit upset by Fitz's absence; she was having a wonderful time going to all the parties on the other yachts and villas. And she was so bloody beautiful!

Venetia kept well away from the guests' quarters and the afterdeck where everybody gathered to sun-bathe or for cocktails. She hoped she'd never have to meet Olympe again.

Damn it, she really must keep busy. She wasn't going to think it through all over again. She'd go and write another letter to Kate while she waited for Paris.

Paris was hot and dusty and tired. The coast road had been one endless traffic jam and the drive gru-eling. She stood under the shower in the well-equipped bathroom that adjoined the cabin Venetia had arranged for her, enjoying the cooling spray of water and wondering what the hell she was going to do about her sister. Of course Vennie had made a fool of herself, but then, she would hate to re-member how many times *she* had made a similar fool of herself. . . . The shudder that ran through her body was not because of the chill of the water. It seemed that neither of them was destined to have

433

much luck.

Toweling herself dry she slipped on a pair of shorts and a brief bandeau top. Venetia was busy in her galley. Perhaps she'd take a look around this wonderful yacht. Paris hadn't realized that the *Fiesta* would be so impressive. She explored the spacious interconnecting rooms, the big salon with its deep, comfortable sofas and a Cézanne on the wall, the dining room with a table big enough to seat at least two dozen. Everything had a solid feel of comfort, yet was simple and unostentatious, unless you considered a Cézanne ostentatious, she thought with a grin. The decks were spotless and a young crewman was polishing brasswork that surely could gleam no brighter. Paris was staggered by the realization of exactly how rich you had to be to afford a yacht like this . . . rich enough not to care how much anything cost. Strolling the *Fiesta*'s decks only brought home exactly how broke she was.

The sun was still burning down and she made for the shade of the blue awning on the afterdeck. Someone was there before her . . . a sleek brown body drowsing in the afternoon heat . . . a body she knew!

"Olympe!"

Olympe's eyes flew open. "Paris! How wonderful to see you—and what a surprise. I didn't know you knew Fitz McBain. Ah—wait a minute, I expect you've come to see your sister—the mysterious Venetia."

"Venetia? Mysterious?" Paris couldn't think of

anything less likely.

"Well maybe I'll tell you that story later." Olympe's smile was mischievous as her opaque gray eyes checked Paris out from head to toe. "You look wonderful, Paris, but then—you always do. Come and sit by me." She patted the chair next to hers and leaned back, stretching her arms above her head lazily.

Paris settled on the cushions, averting her eyes from Olympe's lavish display of smooth, suntanned flesh. A different kind of heat from that of the sun burned her as she remembered the night with Olympe and Hugo . . . she pushed away that memory hurriedly.

"I owe you an apology," said Olympe. "I was going to call you after your show, Paris, I promise I was, but I was called away suddenly that same night—swept off my feet you might say—by Beny." She laughed. "Well, not quite—*you know* Beny. But I am sorry, Paris," she added seriously, "that it didn't work out. It was bad luck."

Paris shrugged. She wasn't so sure about that anymore. "I'm beginning to doubt that I had enough talent in the first place."

"But how can you say that? I wish I had half your talent." Olympe seemed genuinely shocked by her statement, and Paris looked at her in surprise. Did Olympe believe in her, then? If so, she was the only one.

Venetia appeared carrying a tray of iced coffee. She stopped as she saw Olympe sitting with Paris.

435

"Oh, I didn't realize there was anyone else. I thought you'd all gone on a picnic."

"I loathe picnics," said Olympe, "and I'm really glad I didn't go because now I've met Paris again. We know each other quite well," she added wickedly, "don't we, Paris?"

Venetia avoided looking at Olympe. "I've rather a lot to do . . . you know where to find me, Paris, if you want me." She hurried away and Paris stared after her in surprise. What was the matter with Vennie?

"Are all the Haven women beautiful, then?" asked Olympe lazily. "There is another one, isn't there?"

"India. She got married a few weeks ago."

"Lucky her. I hope he's successful—and can keep her in her old age." Olympe sighed exaggeratedly. "It's beginning to worry me, you know, this marriage business. I don't know if I *could* marry Beny— even though I *should*. But perhaps he won't ask me after my little flutter with Fitz McBain."

Paris stared at her. "*Your* flutter with Fitz?" She remembered Venetia's story of the woman in his cabin . . . Olympe . . .

"A very nice flutter. I'd hoped for more, but I'm afraid your little sister may have beaten me to it. In fact young Venetia has hit the jackpot—two McBains! Morgan was here the other week bearing gifts and with a gleam in his eye. He left a couple of days later looking brooding and chastened. I had the feeling that little Venetia had turned him down because she had something more interesting going with his father."

436

"I think that's Vennie's business," said Paris coldly.

Olympe laughed. "Of course it is. You mustn't be upset, darling, I adore this sort of guessing game . . . who is doing what with whom. Come on, Paris, don't be angry with me. We are the same, you and I, you know we are." Her soft, long-nailed hand stroked Paris's bare shoulder. "You mustn't blush," she murmured. "That night was one of those delicious moments. . . . I haven't forgotten you."

"It was a mistake. I shouldn't have done it."

"Whyever not? Sharing a man—and each other— is fun, now and again. You shouldn't deny that to yourself. Sex is so simple, really, it's just a question of what you enjoy, and it shouldn't be taken seriously." Olympe laughed. "It's all so ridiculous when you think about it."

It was true, thought Paris, and she had enjoyed that night. She had made love to them both because she had wanted to—was that any more shameful than making love with Amadeo Vitrazzi so that she could get him to back her financially? She thought not.

"Well, then," said Olympe. "Tell me about yourself. Are you planning a new collection?"

She was so easy, so companionable; Paris felt suddenly that Olympe would understand. "I can't afford another collection," she admitted, "and besides, who would come to a show of mine after the last fiasco? I've had to change my approach. This 'great couturier' has been trying to sell her designs

437

to the boutiques of the Côte d'Azur—with her usual resounding lack of success."

Olympe sat up, wrapping her arms around her knees, listening interestedly. "But of course the boutiques wouldn't buy them," she said. "They all buy in December for the summer. Didn't you know that?"

"I didn't think of it," admitted Paris glumly. "I've no head for practical details. I just assumed that if you had something pretty and exciting people would buy it anyway."

Olympe considered what Paris had said. "In a way you're right. There is always a market for something fun and new here on the Riviera. Most women I know would kill to be different! It's just that your timing was off. Perhaps you should have opened a shop here instead of trying the couture line. It would have been a hell of a lot easier way to begin. You'll probably hate me forever for saying this, Paris, but your fashion show was doomed before it even got on the runway—no matter how great the clothes. It's a harsh world, my friend, and if you're going to succeed, you're going to have to become a little more street wise. The first rule is publicity. No one can make it without the right publicity—no matter how good the designs are. And to get that you need to be on first-name terms with every fashion editor from *Vogue* and *Women's Wear Daily* to every newspaper. And—on top of that—you need an international public relations company to make sure that your name is there every time a woman picks up a magazine in the hairdresser's or on a plane."

"But I couldn't afford a public relations company—I barely had enough to cover the cost of the clothes. As it was, I had to model for Mitsoko for three months before I had enough to pay off the bills for the show—the rent of the salon, the chairs, the speaker systems, and all the other 'little details' that seem to have added up to a fortune. The clothes I'd hoped to sell to the boutiques were put together on a shoestring, and even so, I'm broke."

Broke? How could she be? Perhaps Jenny's money was all tied up in trust, or something. "Forgive me asking, but what about the money Jenny left?"

"There is no money." Paris stood up abruptly and began to pace the deck. "It's a long story."

Olympe's eyes rounded in surprise. In Olympe's terms you were broke when you were down to your last diamonds and only one fur. If Jenny Haven had left her daughter no money, for whatever mysterious reason, then the situation was serious. My God, Paris had meant it—she was broke!

"Tell you what." Olympe stretched lazily. "Let's go and take a look at these clothes. Maybe we'll come up with some ideas." What the hell, she thought, taking Paris's arm, she could use a few new things herself—and maybe she could persuade a few friends to take some. It sounded as though every little bit would help.

Paris flung open the six suitcases and spread garment after garment across the bed, brief little dresses meant for evenings spent in lazy cafés and summer discos, soft flowing gossamer gowns for romantic nights, baggy shorts to be worn rolled high on the thigh, cropped pants, wide at the waist and cinched with a chunky belt, enormous masculine shirts for the beach—they were innovative, witty, and different, and, on Olympe, who was trying them on as fast as she could, they looked terrific.

"Fantastic! Great! Oh, I *must* have these, Paris," cried Olympe, squirreling aside a hoard of favorites. "I adore them—I wish I could buy them all!"

Olympe was being kind, but Paris didn't want her charity. "Take anything you want." She shrugged. "I can't sell them anyway. They are a gift from me."

"Paris!" sighed Olympe, exasperated, "you're just *too nice!* Of course I won't take them as a gift—why should I? I'm *buying* them from you. I'm a customer, damn it—don't you recognize one when you see one?"

Despite herself Paris laughed. "I'm just not used to it," she said. "You're the first, Olympe—and you may be the last."

"However," said Olympe craftily, "if you really don't mind giving some away, I have an idea. I know several top models who are down here on holiday—they would go wild for these clothes. What if we gave some to them, Paris? I can guarantee they'd be worn in all the smartest places and to all the very best parties—and I'll make sure they tell everyone *whose* designs they are. It would be a start—your name would be getting around."

"Really, Olympe?" Paris sounded hopeful. "Will anyone really care whose designs they are?"

"These women live and breathe fashion—the newest, the latest, the most innovative, interesting, avant garde—crazy even—and with a name like Haven to add spice . . ."

"Haven?" said Paris, surprised. She'd always made a point of *not* using Jenny's name. "I thought about the name 'Chanel,'" she added with a grin, "but it's been done. And Jenny didn't do me any favors, you know, calling me Paris."

"But we'll need a name for the boutique."

"What boutique?"

"Why, *our* boutique—the one we must open next season. I'm not going to let your talent escape me—and with my contacts, and of course a little hard work—how can we miss? Now, how do you feel about having me as a partner?" Olympe held up her hand. "No, before you answer, let me tell you a secret. Behind this pretty face and model's body lies the soul of a true bourgeoise. My mother—a very *wise* woman—has run the Bistro Corsaire in Marseilles for more than forty years—as my grandmother did before her. She rules that place from her high stool behind the cash register like Napoleon at Moscow, only more successfully. My mother has probably made more money than she's ever let me know about—and, Paris, there's nothing more exhilarating than making money. You know, she never approved of my being a model—she always told me that if a woman wanted to get on in the world she

441

should use her brains—and her contacts! If she knew I was serious about becoming a businesswoman, she'd produce the money in an instant! So what do you say, Paris? Are we partners?"

"Could we really do it?" wondered Paris. "I mean, would you really want to be partners with me? I can design great clothes, I know I can—despite my failures. But I have no contacts to offer, and no money."

"Ah, the money! This advice may be a little late, as you've already learned your lesson. Never, but *never*, invest *your own money* in a speculative venture, even one as good as this. You are investing your *talent*. What we need to do next is to take our idea and make it a reality. First we find the premises. At the end of the season there are sure to be shops that have had a bad season and are going out of business. I know all the best locations. We'll snap up something while the price is low, we'll have your designs—and then we'll get our backer. I guarantee it. Oh, Paris, how exciting!"

Olympe looked like an exotic bird of paradise as she pranced up and down the tiny cabin in one of Paris's hot-pink silk chemises, with the brief ruffled skirt. Who would have guessed the bourgeois background? Paris could almost see their boutique now, in St. Tropez or Antibes, a bright white façade, its window displaying her latest sensual temptations. Inside, the shop would be cool and arched, cavelike after the hot sun outdoors, hung with her summery garments and spiced with gorgeous fake jewels. Oh, Jenny would have *loved* it! But Jenny would never see the boutique, never wear a dress designed by her, never share her pleasure—and hopefully, her success. Yet it was always Jenny who had encouraged her to believe in her own talent, who had sent her out alone—to win. Perhaps she had sought a little bit of immortality through her daughter's success, a continuation of the Haven name? But Paris had steadfastly denied her that privilege, refusing to use her mother's name, wanting to "make it on her own." Poor Jenny, thought Paris, poor, darling Jenny.

"How would this look in the magazines?" she asked Olympe with a grin. "Paris Haven, daughter of the fabulous and lovely star, Jenny Haven, designer of delicious clothes for the innovative Haven Boutique in St. Tropez—owned with her beautiful partner, supermodel Olympe Avallon—frequent visitors to the McBain yacht. The beautiful partners are already planning the opening of their second shop next season in Porto Cervo, on the Aga Kahn's Costa Smerelda. . . ."

Olympe shrieked with delight as Paris collapsed on the bed, laughing.

"You're learning," laughed Olympe, "you're learning fast, Paris Haven."

"Jenny was clever enough to send me out into the world to find my own opportunities," said Paris, more soberly, "and I stupidly thought that meant I must do it all alone. *Now,* I see what she meant! Find your opportunities—and seize them, she said.

I was just too selfish to realize that one of my assets was my name—her name."

"It's a name to be proud of," said Olympe.

"Then can it be the Haven Boutique?"

"Correction"—Olympe grinned—"the Haven *Boutiques*—after all, we are opening one in Sardinia, too, aren't we? Wait here," she called, disappearing through the door. "I'm going to find some champagne to celebrate."

The smile lingered on Paris's face as she contemplated her turn in fortune. Olympe was exactly the catalyst she needed. It was stupid—impossible—to try to do everything alone. Two heads were better than one—and when one of those was Olympe's, it was better than four! They'd make it, she knew they would. She was already thinking of new colors, fabrics, designs . . . she could just see that pretty boutique with its tempting windows and, across the top, the Haven name in lights once more. How pleased Jenny would have been.

❦ 25 ❦

It had been a while since Margie had been to Rory's place. She let herself in with the key she'd stolen from him months ago, wondering if he was home and, if so, whether he'd be glad to see her. They hadn't exactly parted the best of friends; in fact, held told her to get lost. Still, knowing Rory, he'd probably forgotten that by now, and if he hadn't, well, she could just remind him that she was a *true* friend! Anyway, she wasn't here for his company.

Closing the door softly behind her, Margie glided across the hall into the galleried living area.

"Hello?" she called tentatively.

No response. Crossing to the staircase that spiraled up from one corner to the gallery, she called again, louder this time. Still no response.

No one at home. Good. Margie ran up the curving stairs, laughing out loud as she reached the top, shaking her shaggy blond head to relieve the dizziness—there must be something left from last night's high after all. Now, where did Rory keep his stuff? Was it still the bathroom cabinet, or had he moved it? She didn't have to look too far. An old crystal bowl, once used for the sort of face powder that came with a swansdown puff to flick across some pretty twenties face, waited on the bedside table. The white powder it now contained needed no swansdown, and Margie sniffed at it deeply. Trust Rory—whenever she ran out of money to buy it herself, or out of friends who had some, Rory always had plenty. And he wasn't stingy with it either. God knows who had paid for it; it must have cost a fortune. He served it the way other people offered drinks. Margie pulled off the red suede French boots she'd bought at Joseph Magnin's last week, and lay back comfortably on the bed to wait for Rory. Sure, he'd be glad to see her, why not?

The black Ferrari ate up the miles as Rory covered

445

the distance between Palm Springs and L.A. in a record two hours. It would have taken him less if the patrol car hadn't stopped him outside Bakersfield doing 130 miles per hour—that'd be a couple of hundred dollars' speeding ticket. A couple of hundred! Jesus, that was *nothing!* Three quarters of a million was the amount he had on his mind! Three quarters of a million dollars! Shit!

Rory slowed down as he entered the city's stream of traffic, weaving in and out of lanes impatiently, oblivious to the anger of those drivers he cut in front of, intent on his own problems. He hadn't believed it when Bill had told him. As a matter of fact, he wasn't sure he believed him now. How did he know that Bill wasn't conning him, just telling him that "someone" knew—and that "someone" was going to the police unless he handed over three quarters of a million dollars? Bill was supposed to pay the same, of course, or so he said, and Stan too. That would make a total of two million and a quarter.

It was blackmail, he'd protested. "Sure," Bill had said, "and what's your alternative? Ya want them to go to the police? I'll tell you, kid, you don't mess around with these guys."

A prickle of fear ran along Rory's spine; *"these guys"* . . . who had Bill meant? Jenny had been friends with all sorts of people, and Bill had let it fall that the money was for those daughters of hers. He'd said that they were "protected."

Rory was trapped and he knew it. Not only trapped, he was in hock. The studio would have to come up with a good part of the money as an advance on his salary, which meant he'd be in their power and unable to demand the raises he'd had in mind. Worse, he would have to cancel the purchase of the house on Benedict; in fact, Bill had already done it. Rory had been forced to sit there while Bill got on the phone and told the real estate woman that he'd changed his mind. He'd talked her into returning the deposit, saying that Rory had decided he wanted something bigger, maybe in Bel-Air. Bel-Air! My God, he'd be lucky if he ended up with a condo in North Hollywood!

Who, he wondered, slamming through the gears at the lights and heading toward Newport Beach, who *were* "they"? And how did "they" know? He still wasn't sure that Bill wasn't conning him, that he wasn't just taking the money and pocketing it, now that Stan wasn't there to double-check every detail. There was just one thing, though—Bill had mentioned a tape. Rory swung the car through the courtyard and into his garage, turned off the engine, and stared blankly through the windshield. There were only three people who knew: Margie, because she'd been around that night, but even she didn't know everything, he'd never told her what happened; Bill, who could be inventing the tape as the evidence for his own blackmail; and Bob Ronson, the friend to whom he'd confessed all.

No, it couldn't be Bob, he was a *good* friend; look how he'd helped him. Then that left Bill Kaufmann as the blackmailer, or Margie, but surely she was too dumb and too coked out even to try?

Slamming the car door, Rory walked wearily across to the house. He hated this place now. Funny, he'd liked it so much at first, he'd thought it so smart, exactly the right sort of place for an up-and-coming actor, a chic wood-and-glass duplex condominium on Newport Marina. But now he was a star, now he needed a place where he could entertain, a fancy drawing room and a screening room of his own, a pool and a court . . . *goddamn Bill Kaufmann!*

Margie heard him come in and sat up, cross-legged on the bed, waiting.

"What the fuck are you doing here?" Rory stared at her angrily. She looked terrible, she was so thin she was scrawny! Her face was puffy and her eyes nervous as she smiled at him. Well, at least she was a friendly face! Or was she?

"I let myself in," said Margie sweetly. "I thought you might be pleased to see me."

"You came to see me?" Rory pointed to the crystal bowl, its lid off. "Or you came for that?"

"Both," admitted Margie. "It's been a while, Rory. Haven't you missed me?"

"No," said Rory, pulling off his shirt and throwing it on a chair. "I can't say that I have." Tugging off his loafers he stepped out of his jeans. He kicked them out of his path as he headed toward the shower.

He looked good, thought Margie, admiring the broad-shouldered, sleekly muscled body of the nation's number-one television star, he really was terrific.

448

"Wait a minute." Rory turned and retraced his steps. "I've got a few questions for you."

He stood by the side of the bed, staring angrily at her. Margie put out a tentative hand to stroke his thigh. He surely was mad at her. What had she done that was so bad? All she'd taken was a little coke.

"Who've you been talking to about me?" demanded Rory. "About me and Jenny?"

"Jenny?" Margie stared at him, puzzled. "I haven't talked to anyone. What is there to say? Oh," she remembered, "that is, no one except Bob, and he already knew you were with her that night—"

"Bob!" Rory felt his knees go weak as he sank into the bed next to her. "You told Bob?"

"*I* didn't tell him," she corrected, "*you* did. He told me so, and then I asked him how he knew—"

"When?" demanded Rory. "Tell me *when*, you dumb bitch!"

Margie shrank back from the violence in his voice. "It was that night you all went to La Scala and wouldn't take me. You forgot to bring me back a pizza and I was hungry, so Bob took me to Du Par's on the way home. But he *knew*, Rory, I swear he knew."

Rory's hand itched to slap her stupid burned-out little face, and with an effort he drew back; he was in enough trouble without being accused of beating up teenage girls. Shaking, he made his way back to the bathroom. So it *was* Bob. The bastard had tricked Margie into telling him, and then he'd tricked *him* into confessing. "It's no good keeping things locked away inside you, you should talk to a friend"—wasn't that what he'd said? Then was it Bob who was blackmailing him? The money was for the Haven girls. So who was Bob working for?

Rory turned the shower to cold, and stepped under the stinging jets that spouted from all four sides as well as the top, gasping as they hit. He didn't want to think anymore about who Bob was working for. Goddamn, he was a fool, a stupid fucking fool.

Margie had pulled on her red suede boots and was sitting nervously on the side of the bed. She hadn't even dared to touch the coke in case he got mad at her.

Rory ignored her as he opened and shut drawers, slamming around finding clean shorts, a black track-suit, sneakers. He wanted to get out of here, he couldn't stand this place any longer. Goddamn everybody. That house in Benedict was *his*, he had *earned* it.

He stared into the mirror, suddenly transfixed. He could hear Jenny's voice as clearly as if she were in the room . . . saying it, saying those words that haunted him every night: "I *earned* that money," she'd screamed. "I got up at five-thirty every morning for twenty-five years. I sweated under those lights, I had my legs waxed, my hair bleached—I stayed *thin* for that money. *And I gave up my kids to stay here and earn it.* Goddamn you, Rory Grant!"

A sigh shuddered through Rory's tense body. Okay, okay, then, he'd give it back. He knew what she meant now, she'd played the Hollywood game and almost won. So he'd pay his dues, but he'd make sure *he* came out a winner. He'd pay Bill the money, but he'd get a guarantee that every cent of it went to the Haven girls. It was going to cost him the Bel-Air house, but what the hell—maybe he'd be able to sleep nights again. And then Bill Kaufmann would have nothing on him anymore. In fact, Bill Kaufmann was in it just as deep as he was.

Snatching up his car keys Rory strode toward the door.

"Where are you going?" Margie's plaintive voice followed him as he headed down the curving staircase.

Rory paused at the foot. Looking up he grinned at her.

"I'm gonna fire Bill Kaufmann," he said.

✽ 26 ✽

The first mistral of autumn blew across the Côte d'Azur, scudding heavy, gray clouds before it in a thin spatter of rain as Venetia, shrouded in a serviceable Guernsey sweater and blue jeans, hurried through the quiet streets of St. Tropez. The last of the summer visitors had gone—departing that weekend like migratory birds for warmer winter quarters, leaving the resort a ghost town. Tired summer awnings flapped in the wind outside empty terrace cafés and SALE signs hung hopefully in the windows of silent boutiques.

Venetia shivered, clutching her parcels closer as the wind tugged at her. Summer was dead and London and the prospect of a lonely winter lay ahead. The only good thing she could see on the horizon was the reunion with Kate and the Lancasters. She'd been out buying presents for them all, spending a good deal of her accumulated salary on extravagances she knew they would love, and all that remained now was to pack her things in readiness for an early departure in the morning. The crew had asked her to dine with them that night as their guest of honor and she had made an enormous iced cake, inscribed with their names and a little boat—and "Farewell *Fiesta*." On an impulse Venetia stopped at the store that sold wines and picked up a magnum of champagne as her contribution to the festivities— maybe it would help to cheer her up tonight. Laden with her parcels she staggered back to the *Fiesta* to find it in a state of surprising activity.

"It's Mr. McBain," said Masters, meeting her at the top of the stairs. "He's back unexpectedly—and he's been asking for you."

Fitz was here! Her heart was jumping as she followed Masters along the deck. Why? Why had he come back? It must be to check on his beautiful boat before she sailed tomorrow for Rotterdam and her annual overhaul—of course, it could only be that.

"You'd better go along there, miss," said Masters, relieving her of her parcels. "I expect he wants to give you your bonus—we all get one at the end of the season."

So that was it. Venetia sought around desperately for an excuse not to go, but found none. She was still a member of his crew, and if the captain summoned, you went. She smoothed her hair futilely with her hands as the wind snatched at it again—she hadn't even put on any makeup this morning, she must look about fifteen and just as silly in this old blue jersey. Stop it! she told herself angrily, there's no use pretending you're the most sophisticated woman on the Riviera—you are what you are! Squaring her shoulders she marched off to his study.

Fitz, in jeans and a windbreaker, was at his desk reading some papers, and he glanced up as she came in. He looked just as she remembered—his eyes were just as deep and dark a blue and they met hers in that familiar penetrating way, as though he could read her thoughts, and his hand had that remembered rough firmness as it held hers.

"Venetia. How are you?" He held on to her hand for a moment longer.

"I'm fine." Her voice sounded small, even to her own ears, and she coughed. "Just fine," she repeated, louder.

Fitz sat back in his chair, his eyes on her, saying nothing, and Venetia glanced away uncomfortably. . . . She couldn't bear this. She had thought she'd got over the worst—why did he have to come back and remind her all over again?

"Vennie, do you remember that I made you a

453

promise," asked Fitz, "that night we had dinner together in Barbados?"

She remembered every word they'd said that night. "About Jenny, you mean?"

"Yes. About Jenny. I didn't forget that promise, and one of the reasons I'm here is to tell you what I've been able to find out."

She waited, her eyes fastened on him, forgetting herself in the unexpected announcement that he had news about her mother.

"It's both bad news and good," said Fitz. "I had someone look into her business affairs and I'm afraid they uncovered some very strange facts." He hesitated—there was no way he was going to tell her about Rory Grant, no way—ever. Death had cloaked Jenny in dignity, and she would keep that. "It's better, Venetia, if I don't go into great detail; let it be enough to know that your sisters' suspicions were correct. Money belonging to Jenny found its way into the wrong pockets."

Venetia remembered that day at the Malibu beach house, Stan and Bill explaining so very reasonably just how Jenny had managed to lose her fortune. "Bill Kaufmann?" she whispered.

He nodded. "And Reubin—among others. I'm sorry, Vennie."

"I've known them since I was a little girl," she said, bewildered. "Why would they do that to us, Fitz?"

He shrugged. "Who can say why? Hollywood is a strange town. Values become distorted, friendships are different—not for everyone, of course, but there are always the weak and the unscrupulous, and when there's that much money around, it becomes a temptation. Don't try to understand it, Vennie, just feel glad that your mother had the sense not to get you involved."

Fitz thrust his hands into the pockets of his jeans and began to pace the floor restlessly. "Anyway, I've managed to recover some of the money for you. Again, it would be better if you didn't ask me how. Just believe me when I say it was a better way than dragging your names—and Jenny's—through the courts."

"Yes," said Venetia, believing him.

"There's a million and a half dollars waiting for you and your sisters in the First National and City Bank in Los Angeles."

"A million and a half," repeated Venetia, stunned.

"It's not nearly as much as you were entitled to, but believe me, it was the better way to go. If you like, I can have cashier's checks drawn up for you tomorrow."

All that money, thought Venetia. Paris would be able to open her Haven Boutiques; India and Aldo would have enough to pay back their bank loans and run their hotel—maybe they'd even have their babies now, sooner than they had planned, but not, she knew, too soon for India. And me? What shall I do?

Fitz was leaning against the desk, hands in his pockets, watching her.

"You don't know what this will mean to my sisters," she said.

"And you?"

"And me," she replied quietly. "Thank you."

"What will you do now, Vennie?"

Venetia lowered her gaze. She couldn't say she was hoping that he might tell her what she was going to do, and that it would be with him. She gripped her hands together tightly, entwining her fingers, trying to concentrate on what he was saying.

"You talked of opening a restaurant," he said. "Maybe this would be a good time—you've got the money behind you and the flair. My London office can help you, with the legal end, leases and such."

"Thank you."

Fitz sighed. "You're not making it easy for me, Vennie."

"I had thought there was more between us than just business." Their eyes met in the silence.

"It was a warm tropical night," he said finally. "There was a big lazy moon over the water, a gleaming white yacht—and an older man who took advantage of a situation he'd dreamed about for years."

Venetia gazed at him, puzzled. Odd, thought Fitz, how she no longer reminded him of Jenny; even that wide, blue-gray gaze was her own now. She was just Venetia. And he loved her. He steeled himself to carry on. He had to be fair, he had to tell her, give her a chance.

"Vennie, I don't know if you're going to understand this, but there's something you should know."

Venetia watched him uncertainly. She tucked her suddenly cold hands into the sleeves of her navy sweater, waiting. Whatever it was, she had the feeling he would rather not have to say it. A sudden thought struck her. Oh, God, please let it not be about Olympe. Was he planning to marry *her?*

Fitz began to pace the cabin. "When Morgan called me from London to tell me that Jenny Haven was dead and that he was with her daughter, I was stunned. I had met your mother, just once—years ago. But more than that, Vennie, I felt I'd known her forever. I'd fancied myself in love with her since I was thirteen years old when I saw her in *Love Among Friends.* I can still remember every detail of that movie—all her movies. I saw them a hundred times. You can't possibly know what Jenny meant to a poor boy growing up in the grim little town I called home . . . she was silk and satin to a boy used to patched denim. Women like that didn't exist in real life—not my sort of reality, anyhow. When you're a woman, poverty means more than just not enough to eat—it means never being pretty or feminine, it means romance buried in the demands of a hungry brood of kids and a husband who drinks too much—to forget that he can't afford it. Even the young girls I knew were toughened, old before their time. Venetia, Jenny was a young boy's dream, she helped me through many a bleak and lonely night. I never forgot her. When I heard she was dead it was as though I had lost someone very close to me—a woman I loved."

Fitz stopped his pacing and looked at Venetia. How could this child of an affluent world, of good schools and solid English traditions, ever be able to fathom what he was talking about?

"Fitz, I didn't realize . . ."

"Listen to me," commanded Fitz. "When I met you, I was shocked. Venetia, do you have any idea how much you resemble your mother?"

"But I'm not the same," she protested. "I was never *like* her." Suddenly she didn't want to hear what he was going to say.

"Don't you understand? I never knew what Jenny was *really like*—only what she *looked like!* She was a dream, Vennie—*I was in love with a dream.* That night when we danced and I held you in my arms . . . you could have been Jenny."

Worse, thought Venetia, getting up from her chair, it was worse than that. He'd made love to her. "I have to know," she said. "Tell me the truth. When you made love to me, was it because you wanted *me* . . . or . . ." She couldn't finish the question.

"I wasn't sure," said Fitz softly. "I couldn't tell if you were Vennie or Jenny. You were my fantasy, my dream girl come true. I knew the way your mouth would feel under mine . . . I knew you, Vennie. I had loved you forever."

Venetia remembered that final moment of passion when he'd called out her name. She had wondered then . . . oh, God, she must know! "Then was it my name you called," she asked in a voice so low he could barely catch it, "or was it . . . ?"

458

Gazing into her blue-gray eyes Fitz wasn't sure which it had been—but he couldn't hurt her again. "It was Vennie," he said. "Of course it was you."

Tears spilled from her eyes. Was it pain, or maybe relief? Fitz loved her, he had just said so. Hadn't he? He put his arms around her and she leaned against him, her tears staining his shirt.

"It's odd," he murmured, "but I don't notice the resemblance anymore. When I look at you now I just see you—Vennie. My beautiful young Vennie."

She caught the implication. "You're afraid I'm too young for you." She sighed. "That's it, isn't it?"

"That I'm too old for you," he corrected. "Think about it, Vennie. You've got your whole life in front of you. I've already lived a dozen lives. You can do anything—open your restaurant, build a business, marry someone your own age, make a life together, have babies . . ."

"And a cottage with roses round the door," she added, smiling at the dream images he had conjured up of herself. "But I love you, Fitz McBain."

"You should be with someone Morgan's age."

"It was never Morgan," she murmured. "We were friends, it was fun . . ."

"That's what I mean, Vennie. You are so young, you should be having fun, finding out about life, what you want from it. I love you, Vennie, but I must give you a chance."

"A chance?"

"To meet other people."

"Other men, you mean?"

459

"Yes. Other men." They fell silent.

"It's the only way, you see," he said, letting go of her, "the only way for you to be sure. I'm afraid that in a couple of years you might regret being Mrs. Fitz McBain, that you might feel that you'd lost your youth, missed the freedom to be with people your own age, that you might say to me one day, 'I had potential, I was young, I could have been something too—not just the wife of a rich man. An older man.' "

"But I wouldn't. I mean . . . I love you, Fitz."

"And I love you; that's why I'm saying this. Vennie, I couldn't bear it if you married me and subsequently realized you'd made a mistake. Don't you understand? I'd rather not have you, than have you and lose you. Go away, Vennie, just for a while. Try life on your own terms, experiment with your restaurant, make friends, do all the things people your age do."

Vennie longed . to hurl herself back into his arms, to lock herself into his life now, to be loved by him forever. But she could see his mind was made up. His face was stern and she wanted to smooth away the frown between his brows, to stroke the small, fine lines that radiated from the corners of his eyes, to reassure him that her youth was a liability to her, not an asset. But it would do no good. He was sending her out into her own world. But for how long?

"How long," she whispered, "would it take to prove to you that it's you I love, you I'll always love?"

Fitz sighed. He knew he could tell her to forget it, that he was being a fool, that he needed her, couldn't live without her, that he loved her because she was so young and sweet and lovely. But he wouldn't. There were probably dozens of young men out there who would tell her the same thing. It was a chance he must take.

"Try life on your own for a year, Vennie," he said. "Twelve months isn't very long, after all. And at the end of it, if you still want me, I'll be here—waiting."

Venetia gazed at him uncertainly. Surely if he loved her, he couldn't send her away. She recalled a line from one of Jenny's movies, one she'd watched her mother rehearsing, pacing endlessly up and down some hotel suite clad in a creamy satin robe. Jenny had flung her arms wide, declaiming to the open window and some invisible lover. "True love is not selfish," she'd cried. "True love never demands. It gives." Fitz was giving her her freedom to choose. Her mother would have understood that, and approved.

"A year, then." Vennie ran her hands through her untidy hair. "Just a year, then, Fitz McBain." She managed a grin. "It's a business deal."

Fitz laughed. "If that's the way you want it," he said.

"It is," she replied fiercely. "That way you can't back out."

"I'll never do that, Vennie."

"You're sure it can't be any other way?" Even as she said it she knew his reply—and despite herself

461

she knew he was right. "Okay, okay," she added hastily, "I know when I'm beaten. Maybe I'll make a businesswoman yet!"

Their eyes met and she read the love in his. It would be all right. He would be here, waiting for her. Meanwhile, there was a year to be lived, a whole year without him. She could almost hear Jenny saying it, just the way she had when she'd left her at school in England that first time: "Look at it this way," she said. "It's time to achieve, time to grow." And Jenny had always been right.